About the Author

T. D. Duff is a Minnesota based semi-retired investment executive. His writings appear in many online publishing sites and national newspapers. *The Find* is his debut novel, and he is currently working on additional novels, *The Surf* and *The River of Iniquity*.

The Find

Tim Duff

The Find

Olympia Publishers
London

www.olympiapublishers.com
OLYMPIA PAPERBACK EDITION

Copyright © Tim Duff 2024

The right of Tim Duff to be identified as author of
this work has been asserted in accordance with sections 77 and 78 of the
Copyright, Designs and Patents Act 1988.

All Rights Reserved

No reproduction, copy or transmission of this publication
may be made without written permission.
No paragraph of this publication may be reproduced,
copied or transmitted save with the written permission of the publisher, or in
accordance with the provisions
of the Copyright Act 1956 (as amended).

Any person who commits any unauthorised act in relation to
this publication may be liable to criminal
prosecution and civil claims for damage.

A CIP catalogue record for this title is
available from the British Library.

ISBN: 978-1-80074-905-4

This is a work of fiction.
Names, characters, places and incidents originate from the writer's imagination.
Any resemblance to actual persons, living or dead, is purely coincidental.

First Published in 2024

Olympia Publishers
Tallis House
2 Tallis Street
London
EC4Y 0AB

Printed in Great Britain

Dedication

For Annie-the highest of the good.

Acknowledgements

A special thank you to all that provided timely assistance as I was writing THE FIND. Tracy at the Excelsior, Minnesota library was a great help in compiling chapters and printing the chapters of THE FIND. A special thanks to dear Annie who helped me interpret my dream that November morning and helped me format the characters in THE FIND.

Oh, Oh, Dear St. Annie…Higher than the Moon!

Prologue

Hopefully in some way my memory can act as an organizing principle that will, I trust, determine the structure of my narrative, the actuality of events, real and fictitious being remembered, and more importantly the authentic presence of doing the remembering.

The novelist, as I find myself becoming to become, must engage with world, because it is this intervention that makes experience, and it is adaptive experience, in my opinion, the makes for wisdom. For in the end it is the wisdom or at least the path towards it that counts, as we travel together, on a voyage of discovery.

The writer must be possessed of an insight that organizes the writing, while bringing about an organic wholeness of being that the reader can experience as reliable. An experience, we can trust that will take us on a journey, make the narrative present and bring us into a mental clearing, where the sense of things becomes larger than it previously was. I have come to understand that many writers, including yours truly, might not "know" themselves having no more self-knowledge than anyone else, but in each respective case they "know" who they are at the moment of putting pen to paper.

In each instance the writer is discovering the mysterious in the familiar, looking hard at experiences, on which everyone has an opinion. The story I have come to see is an experience in the meaning and value of watching a writer attempt to conquer his own sense of threat and confusion, and to deliver himself of wisdom. Only slowly as in life itself, my making of the tale as a reflective mirror of all our anxieties and embarrassments, can it lead us to a deeper insight.

Today, the chaotic urgency of our linear lives seems to attach itself to the notion of a story taken directly from life, rather than one fashioned by the imagination taken out of life. Modernism seems to have run its course and left us stripped of the pleasures of the narrative. It seems for many years now our novels have been all voice, a voice that speaks to us from inside its own emotional space, anchored neither in plot nor in circumstance of life. This voice has spoken the history of our time, of lives underground, trapped in inferiority, well enough to impose some sort of meaning and create literature, but driving the story telling impulse into oblivion.

The impulse to tell the story, rich in context, alive to situation and impacted throughout with event and perspective, is as strong in human beings as the need to eat and breathe. This impulse can be temporarily suppressed, but it can never be eliminated.

As the 20th century wore on, the sound of voice alone grew less compelling, the insights repetitive, the wisdom wearisome, and the longing for narrative came again, asserting the oldest claim of the reading heart, the measure of whose deprivation is to be taken in the literalism of the newly returned "tale." What after all, could be more literal than the story of my life, now being told it seems, by every woman and every man?

At the same time that the power of voice alone has been dwindling, the age of mass culture, paradoxically much influenced by modernism, has emerged on a scale unparalleled in history, and today millions of people consider themselves possessed of the right to assert a serious life.

Our age it seems is characterized by a need to testify to a life one reflects on, trying to make sense of and bear grim witness to. Throughout the world, people are rising up to tell their stories, out of the new commonly held belief that one's own life has significance. All around our cultural rights movements and the therapeutic social environment at large have been key influences in facilitating this belief. In this country alone, the politics of liberation and personal effrontery and aggrievement have produced an outpouring of personal testament from all walks of life that is astonishing.

In the wake of political interpretation since 9-11 and the closed loop of understanding that followed, the echoing response of people's lives seemed to become a self-centered pedestrian chaos, the effects of alcohol, domestic violence, sexual disorder and death. They have a story to tell, but it is a mere testament or fable, a banal analytic transcription, and not a work of sustained narrative prose, controlled by an idea of the self, under obligation to raise from the raw material that life provides, a tale that will shape experience, transform events and deliver wisdom.

Truth is achieved, not through a recital of actual happenings, but rather when the reader comes to believe that the writer is endeavoring judiciously to involve and enlarge with experience at hand. What is integral, is the larger sense of what the writer is able to make of what has occurred.

The ideal of self, the one thing that controls the narrative can be an immense exercise of vanity, I rapidly learned, is however best served through a single piece of awareness that clarifies only slowly in the writer, gaining strength and definition as the story moves forward. That awareness becomes the organizing principle, the thing that lends shape and texture to the writing, driving the story forward, providing direction and unity of purpose.

The question clearly asked is, "who am I," and who exactly is the "I" upon whom turns the significance of the story drama, taken directly from life. It is on that question that the writer hopes to deliver, not with an answer necessarily but with rich depths of inquiry.

"I have nothing but myself to write about and this self that I have, I hardly know what it consists of." These were Rousseau's words and he is saying to the reader, "I will go in search in your presence. I will set down on the page a tale of experience just as I have imagined it may have occurred and together we will see what it exemplifies, both of us discovering as I write, this inviolable self that we are all in search of." It posits that the shaped presentation of one's own life is of value to the disinterested reader only if it dramatizes and reflects sufficiently on the experience of becoming, and undertakes to trace the internal movement away from the sludge of being told who you are by accident of circumstance, toward the clarity and understanding that identifies accurately the impulses of our inviolable selves.

It is with this as prelude, and the finding epiphany of a tale in my dream as I slept that November night, that I hope to pull from my own boring, agitated self, the truth speaker in the personal narrative, that will tell the story that needs to be told.

Yet with a Gandhian faith in the power of truth, mankind continued to hope.

"Every slightest effort at opening up new areas of thought, every attempt to perceive new aspects of truth, or just a little truth, is of inestimable value in preparing the way for the light we cannot see."

-Thomas Merton

Chapter 1

Though our futures are unwritten, they are inspired by our past.

Long afterward, he would remember this day, for while it meant nothing to most, and something to a few, to him it was the beginning and always would be the beginning, the break between two periods in his life and two periods in the life of mankind, the time when he would discover who he was, what stuff he was really made of.

For as long as Ryan Davies could remember he had always been concerned about himself and his own cloistered life, and little else, until today. He knew of nothing of knowing who you are, and having the courage to share the reasons for the catastrophe of your character with the world.

Telling the truth was a hard thing, and in a young man's attempt with the distortions of his vanity, ego, hot passions, and lacerated pride, it was almost impossible. Ryan was indeed marred by all these imperfections, there was truth in that.

He watched the black sedan with government plates pull away from his childhood home, and cruise toward the end of the block, while a vague memory seemed to stir in his head.

His thoughts however returned to the luncheon investment seminar he had just conducted at the Radisson Hotel. It was Friday, the end of another week, and he felt smug, alight with the flame of second-hand distinction and the optimism he had received amidst the frantic scribble of unexamined ambition; in what in his circles passed for "happy". The seminar had gone well with eighty-five people in attendance and the brokers sponsoring the event seemed happy with the potential results. They had not been distracted this day by the usual post-lecture crowd of exegists and second guessers.

The applause meter was always a key indicator of these public events; if it was strong and hearty as you finished the discourse you were mostly assured of success. This particular luncheon had looked productive from the start, with a room full of high net worth, well-coiffed men and women eager to take advantage of the latest tax nuances and the Federal Reserve omens foretelling declining interest rates.

Ryan Davies had exhorted his audience, spinning out investment metaphors congenial to their spirits, urging them to "do it now", and guarantee their financial future. The audience had been shown, he thought, the metaphorical investment hat and rabbit. He knew by training that you never reach into rabbit-less hats, and his prestidigitations had tremendously appealed to the audience and the cast of self-regarded brokerage supernumeraries and apprentices who had not quite yet mastered the potions and spells.

He had orchestrated privately, at the luncheon sponsored by yet another demanding broker dealer, an exercise in the sheer eroticism of riches and power, making them mellifluous and as treasurable as honey to the investing public, all the while pillowing them in self-satisfaction. It was the same overfed, over-pleased crowd that generally attended these affairs. They were all there for the same opportunistic delight at the offer, although perhaps not quite so immoderate to be found elsewhere.

All the brokers and high finance grunts looked spiffy in their mental dress whites and ties, which were in accordance with the politics of the simplicity of supply side and trickle down economics of the day. They all seemed ready to be much better friends to him than he would be in return. He smiled at the thought of how he had paused before making his closing statement, enjoying the satisfaction for a few more moments, before bringing in the fish he had hooked. He chuckled inwardly, as he recalled the old adage: "Put in enough of a commission for the goat and you'd be surprised at how easy it is to sell the goat's milk as cream."

All he was doing was just a way of making something essentially simple seem complex, which is how the investment business works. To prop up its enormously important self-esteem, so called financial wizards had built up a contraption that resonated with expertise, complexity, reconditeness and significance, creating a semantic monumental mystery that hid the real work; the process of buying and selling pieces of paper.

To exploit Wall Street, Ryan had quickly grasped, you had to find what the market maker wanted to exploit. Feed the audience with the right euphemisms in equilibrium that would spike their vanity. The market relished euphemisms like lollipops, because they helped to build the specious artifice of analysts who could provide the necessary psychic rate of return. Wall Street dealt in fantasies and they traded those fantasies as promises.

In the short duration of his career he had witnessed first-hand how financial products were evolving, a devolution really, contributing to the debasement of the investment business, which was now becoming merely an exercise in sound marketing. The big brokerage firms could create nice fission patterns throughout the markets for any new investment product, making it the hottest deal going, capable of "retrieving Lazarus from the dead," as long as it had enough spread and marketing vig, it would be immensely profitable.

Ryan was on a fishing expedition, using just the right baits, greed, pride and opportunism to lure his fish to the surface. The fish fed on his words and each other.

How long could the balloon stay afloat? He wondered, with all these types nibbling at the edges with their sharp teeth of self-indulgence? He knew he was being used, but in the shadings of his young life this present day, this was the way of life. He was young, one to whom the catastrophes and imbecilities of mankind were still more or less novel. It was the way it worked.

Maybe he often thought he never had a choice and would have been an uncertain performer at whatever he did, but his decision to aim for the stars had been a conscious one, and this was the way it was, this America, the land of, "do it or shut up". Ah well, he thought, it's the way of the world; we are all just rungs of someone else's ladder.

As the memory and circumspection of his meetings and his business were left behind, his thought focused, and he flogged his neurons to produce a confirming memory of the ebony sedan and the mysterious, yet familiar, government plates. He often had the feeling that there was something disagreeable that his family wanted to forget, something only he insisted on remembering, something requiring only his nod, a go-ahead to be forgotten.

Here was that feeling again. Was it a warning sign? Had he seen that car before or not? Some voice out of his childhood whispered, but he could not catch what it said. He had the vague sense, rising from the depth of time, and of himself, of being a child, of entering a room where adults were, of knowing that they had just stopped talking, because he had come into the room and was not supposed to know what they were talking about. Had he overheard what they had been talking about?

He listened as he drove into the driveway, for the voice whispering out of his childhood, but the spectral voice was far away, and could not provide the answer. If there was something to find, he would not find it all at once, he thought. It was probably something buried under the sad detritus of time, where it no doubt belonged.

But something was familiar about them; he was near certain, as he entered the home of his youth, his only baggage was his white sudden smile that he had carried with him from boyhood to manhood. The delicious aroma of baking bread and caramel rolls, instantly floated over him creating its oedipal tug. Their smell and taste were unmatched anywhere and could lift the hardest heart into intoxication conveyed to a renewed exotic pleasantry.

His mother looked healthy and effervescent again, having regained, thank God, the rosy-cheeked luminescence that was the true index of her character. Mary had been a homemaker all her married life and thanks to her his boyhood home had been made painstakingly easy and well. They had lived a charmed life, Ryan and his older sister Colleen. His mother had always been like the food he needed to live and thrive. Every day she endeavored to cleanse the diction of her children, smooth out their manners, whiten their morals, and brighten their attitudes.

She had made it possible for Ryan and his sister to believe that their world would be effortlessly cared for, because she had seemingly effortlessly cared for it. He remembered how her kind hazel eyes had often lost their shine, during her illness, sagged, as if they had seen one lifetime pass into another. Then she would take a deep breath and marshal her strength and her eyes would light up again like lanterns. She smiled at him, and he felt as if the light would last forever. He stepped forward and gave her a loving hug.

"Smells delicious," Ryan said. "Say, who was that driving away from the house?"

Mary ran a slightly quivering hand through her thick black hair, and fought down the taste of panic forming in her throat. "Oh, oh that was just Doctor Mason from the clinic. He's one of those old time docs who still likes to make house calls," she nervously explained, looking at him with wounded sympathy, drawing in the edge of her lower lip and setting her teeth to it. She looked as if a distasteful memory had passed through her mind, like a quick cloud had just crossed over the sun, as her brown eyes fixed on Ryan with a mixture of appeal and affirmation.

Ryan looked at her steadily and she was silent, missing nothing of her speechless anguish and misery. His mother looked, for a moment, as though her face had lost its usual pose of patient resignation, as if a mask had suddenly been stripped from it. Hopefully, Ryan thought, whatever he sensed was orbiting his mother's mind would not give way to a desperate lonely vulnerability, an expression made almost unbearably poignant by the feeling that he was being asked to share in her despair, as if she was reaching out to him, for him.

Ryan was proud of his mother's lifelong refusal to give in to the pathetic narcissism of depression or remorse. Each moment bore only on the next one and if you were going to be successful in this life, this was the level on which you had to live. If you started going down on your knees to the past, demanding something from it that it hadn't given you the first go around, you were a goner. She had asked nothing from it and willed herself forward. That was the level on which the Davies family operated.

Ryan cleared his throat. "Caramel rolls in the oven?"

"Oh yes. I need to put the icing on them now, so why don't you take Gabby out to the lake? She's been downstairs eying the geese all afternoon."

"All right," Ryan said, happy to change the mental scenery, shoving his faintly building anxiety back to the furthest reaches of his mind.

Ryan thundered down the stairs past watercolor portraits and photos of Colleen and him at various ages of adolescence, the myriads of family birthdays and Christmases and a more recent collection of grandkids and in-laws. Portraits of his youth, those early amorphous years when memory had only just begun, when life was full of beginnings and had no ends, and everything was forever. He was still in excellent shape at thirty-five, not from going to the gym every day, but from still being young enough that his body was still imprinted with the sports he played in high school and college. He chuckled as he saw the family's black and white springer spaniel glaring menacingly at the geese floating leisurely on the backyard ponds cold and clear late April waters, outside the rec room window.

"Go get 'em girl," he urged as he opened the back door. In a whirlwind of floppy ears and stubby legs, she was at last free to throw herself upon her evil long-necked tormentors. It was a routine that started in the spring and occurred at least three times a day, through the spring, until the fall arrived. The geese would mercifully fly south in their instinctive annual migration, and the salt and pepper spaniel would at last get the satisfaction of ridding her estate of the foul predators. Ryan howled as Gabby flew headlong into the air landing with a splat, belly-first, into the pond. The geese easily flew away, glaring back down at their eternal predator, with beaded, black-eyed disdain, as they began their arrowed flight to another body of water.

Ryan saw his mother looking through the oval windows of the kitchen, shaking her head in constant amazement at the dog's primal instincts. He walked to the far end of the pond nearest the lake, the earth moist and giving under his feet from the recent spring thaw, wondering why a physician would drive a car with government plates. Had he seen that car before or not, or was he dredging up withered memories? He was proud of his memory, "prehensile," his mother once called it, and the vague feeling he had now troubled him. He allowed the matter to fade from his thoughts.

He dropped the black polyethylene into the pond and waited for the water from the main lake to flow back into the waters of the pond that had served as the neighborhood skating and hockey rink, during all the winters of his childhood. Just then the wind picked up and he saw the waters of the lake ripple toward the Davies' home. He clapped for Gabby and started for the house.

Mary's hands trembled as she looked down at the document she had hurriedly stashed in a drawer when Ryan had arrived. She thought all this past was over. It had been so long ago, long enough that she and Wally had longed for it to be forever behind them.

With the untimely death of Dorothy, along the shores of White Iron Lake in 1963, they had mistakenly, as was now evident, been pursuing their own folly of false hope. She heard the back door open and Gabby's nails skittering on the hardwood floor and she slid the document back into the drawer and covered it with cook books.

"Got to go, Mom," Ryan pleaded as he rounded the corner coming into the kitchen. "Say hi to Dad."

"Say hi to Nan and the boys," Mary responded, putting a Tupperware container full of caramel rolls into her son's hands. Mary made herself smile. Whence came the smile and how she had mustered it she had no right idea, but it pleased her to smile at him.

"Well until later then," he said, as he went down the front steps, the door closing behind him, leaving the image of his uncertain smile to remain, beholden in his mother's eyes.

Mary watched as Ryan backed down the driveway, lowering her head into her own raised hands, fingers splayed now from forehead to chin, and let out a long nervous sigh hoping to find some level of composure. She hadn't yet been ready to face this, feeling the lesions beginning to grow in her mind. Until now her visitor today had been more of a presence than a person, but now with this emergence, she felt a shiver to her bones approaching. She had remembered him surprisingly well from their first uninvited meeting back in 1963.

Still quite tall, he had the same angry gray eyes of a war bird that she recalled and a nose that would have done honor to the Capitoline. His skin, Mary repulsed inwardly, was now psoriatic and acne pitted and oddly pulpy as if the flesh beneath it had worked itself loose from the bone. They had chatted briefly for no more than five minutes just inside the front door, neither giving or getting, like money changers of old just swapping coins. She had faced life up to this point and had fought it at least to no worse than a draw, she thought. She and her husband had always believed deep in their subconscious that this potential enemy was lurking out there biding his vengeful hour, waiting patiently like wolves stalking deer, to bring Mary's family and its deserved heritage down and punish all, for having been smarter than their predator had thought.

The trick was to see life as it was, she reminded herself, as an unending series of impending cases, one after the next, to be fled from if possible, and if not to be punished by each punishment, to be shriven, to gain an extra dollop of toughness to seal up another pore of vulnerability. Over the course of time she hoped the tears would be fewer and fewer to come and eventually a state of grace would be attained and life would finally let you alone.

Mary thought now of how she had looked at him as beseechingly as she could, "I don't know what you are talking about," imploring to her visitor, with mild scorn tinged with faint incredulity, looking intentionally inscrutable, innocent and unknowing.

He had stared back at her over his huge nose as if on a high lectern, an altar so that he looked imperially on her as from a great height, his eyes narrowing to pinpoints of baleful yellow light, while trying to be as amiable and off hand as possible. She took another deep sigh, walking away from the window as Ryan's car faded into the distance.

Carrying the ruthlessness of the power of everyday anxiety with her, she walked briskly to her bathroom and splashed water on her face, blessing the mirror in front of her for telling her she didn't look as tired and as old as she now suddenly felt. Hoping she had enough reserve of resolve, she slowly padded her way back to the kitchen. She knew what had to be done.

CHAPTER 2

He heard the phone ring at the check in desk of the pool at the club, as he finished his fifty-sixth lap, doing a flip turn that would have made Mark Spitz proud. This was not one of those clubs based purely on snobbism and he appreciated that. He had started swimming more than ten years ago, ever since the day he had seen an image in the full length mirror that had repulsed him. Doing at least a mile a day, sometimes much more, had trimmed him down to the weight at his Army physical in 1943, getting free of that middle-aged belt line bulge. As he swam down the lane in the pool dedicated to his swimming marathons, he could see Karl, the club's nearly blind elderly masseur, wave at him, phone in hand.

"Your wife is on the hook, here Mr. Davies," his old Slavic voice gurgled hoarsely.

Walter finished his crawl stroke with a strong final two bursts and hopped up on the deck, Karl handing him a towel. "Hi, Mary, is everything okay?"

"He was just here."

"Who, Mary, are you all right?"

"Our intruder from the lake, in the sixties."

There was silence on the line as both seemed frozen in trepidation of time past.

"Wally, Walter…"

"Yah, I'm here, dear, I guess I was just hoping we would never…"

"Yes, me as well," she quickly added.

Walter heard the nervousness in her delivery.

"I'll take a quick shower, Mary, and be home in thirty minutes. Stay calm, Mary."

Borgen, Walter Davies mouthed silently to himself as he cradled the phone with exaggerated care and walked to the shower.

The patriarch of the Davies' family scolded himself mentally as he pulled out of the club parking space, thinking foolishly that this old annoyance could have been trivialized by time, and simply go away, never reappearing to haunt the family. As CEO of a prominent food manufacturing and distribution company, he chastised himself for not having better judgment. He made key corporate and financial decisions daily and yet he had dealt with this matter as if it would just disappear into the foggy mist of the distant past.

A man tried to live a placid, well-ordered, and useful life, meeting each problem with prudence and detachment. He liked calmness and sense, despising hysteria and emotionalism. He had proved to himself that this was the only intelligent way to live, and he had discovered that by living pragmatically, he remained master of most all circumstances, and nothing had disturbed him overmuch.

Then a day, or days, would arrive and everything was in disorder. Some center in his life, or life about him, disintegrated and flew apart. He suddenly realized that he was not only not a master of himself, but also not a master of circumstance. So Walter thought on his way home.

A thousand times he had foreseen this thing. A thousand times he had foreseen, as a man will foresee, the coming of the enemy; and he had always pictured him in a definite form and guise. He had come before with insolence and power, badged with the open menace of the jeering world, the sneering tongue, and the brandished fist. He had come to strike terror to the heart with naked and open brag, to try to break the courage of another man, to win his menacing domination of another's life, by violence and brutality of force. The enemy had come, not armed in might and from the front, but subtle, soft and infinitely cunning, and from a place and in a way that Walter had always foreseen.

"Damn it," he said aloud as he merged onto the freeway heading west toward the setting sun, recalling now from his philosophy studies in college the aphorism, that, "Nothing was as easy as self-deceit, for what we wish, we soon also come to believe to be true.'

"Damn it," he cursed again, squinting at the golden setting sun, annoyed with inner rancor boiling inside him, hoping the blazing rays penetrating his blue eyes, would give him a new occasion for catharsis.

Another ten minutes and I'll be home, he reminded himself, and he squared his mental shoulders and tried to think through this latest news from Mary. He blamed himself, accepting his consciousness of error. How often we let things go until the iron seemed to get humiliatingly cold.

Perhaps destiny had finally presented itself and it just might be time to seize it, even though doing so could involve breaking through the confining crust of career, family responsibility, and all the questions that go with the potential of throwing off all the burdens of caring for extended families, dependents and dependencies and his own contractual obligations he must continue to meet with the company he ran and the people he employed.

He looked out at the rush of traffic moving in every direction, the cars that all look the same, like bombs, sleek tapered weapons. It wasn't the open road any more, it's all a mad man-made track, an eight lane freeway, which wasn't free in any way, all bound up and tangled in a mass of clover-leafs and off-ramps, going in all directions, no direction that you could see, traveling in mindless projectiles, with everything flashing by so fast, so diabolically fast. Where did time go, all those years with the demands of the job, the mounting needs of his wife and family?

He thought momentarily of the war, and the men he'd fought with, some like him home and safe, others left behind out beyond the Atlantic. He felt a twinge of real loss. He remembered his father speaking of the hole war made in man's soul; even if a man came out of it intact, it was as if some part of him had been amputated or left behind on the battlefield.

He was civilized and had been born with the right passport, a very decent man who wore laces in his shoes and bought his clothes at JCPenney throughout the blabby, hairy, self-expressive decades that followed the Eisenhower years. Whatever vestigial inclination he might have had toward "me-first-ism" was mantled over with ideologies of morality and ethics, so out of date they appeared ridiculous to the noisy blatant post-adolescent world of sixties and seventies Wall Street. The old ways of talking about politics were falling away. Candidates for national offices were now serving up rhetoric that tingled with strains of utopianism, intercut with equal and opposite strains of apocalypticism. They gave forth stories of hope of a society that could surpass any the world had ever known. But they also told stories that spoke to the dark looming fear that the world bequeathed us by science, technology and the Pax-Americana that would not make us more secure but might instead unleash the devil.

The feelings of community and interdependence engendered by the war were fading away, moving in a selfish direction. A new generational fault line seemed to run through the middle of the country, with what was once considered revelatory now becoming old hat. They were being replaced by the march of narcissism, solipsism, paranoia and self-indulgence, a certain stealthy pandering to grosser tastes.

He could sense the strange new spirit even as early as the Korean War. It might be, he thought, that America, the birthplace of an "all or nothing" attitude, was now simply too vast a nation to deal with the small wars of moral conviction. Public opinion was turning in the direction of "every man for himself". Patriotism was all well and good but it seemed to be reserved now for the other fellow. To die for ones principles and country was hardly the best way to put a second car in the garage. The country was awash in goods and the near maniacal love of them, the ravening appetite stimulated to climax by television, which pushed the possibility of material luxury into the humblest most hopeless shacks.

He had learned that the world, as he mentally scolded himself, was like an enormous spider web and if you touch it, however lightly, at any point, the vibration ripples to the remotest perimeter and the spider feels the tingle and is drowsy no more but springs out to fling the gossamer coils about you who have touched the web and then inject the black, numbing poison under your skin. It matters not whether you meant to brush the web of things. Your strong stepping foot or your free wheeling wing may have brushed it ever so lightly, but what happens always happens and there is the spider, bearded black, and with his great faceted eyes glittering like mirrors in the sun, or like the Devil's eye, with fangs dripping.

He thought of the maxim he had learned in English lit courses, that your character was your fate, that your rewards and failures were the result of your faults and virtues. In Lord Jim, a book he must have read at least three times since he was a boy, the hero is killed eventually because of a flaw in himself that permitted him to leave a shipload of poor beggars to die. He paid for his cowardice in the end by being killed himself. He had always thought it just, fair and inevitable.

He began to realize as he wound up his internal soliloquy that he indeed may have to shed whatever fogginess, real or imagined, he had developed, like a snake sheds its skin, and join the fight once again. He and Mary had both found their ways of hiding from the facts, one with solipsism and the other with his seductions. Anxiety would have to be shoved back into the farthest most nearly invisible reaches of his mind, Walter instinctively knew. As he turned onto Cedar Lake Road, in deep reflection on the past and what steps they may be required to take, something suddenly came into his sight that piqued his interest.

A white van that appeared to be unmarked was stationed just two houses away from his own. The war had trained him as a Pathfinder in Normandy and France, to be acutely aware of changes in scenery and landscape. This was a private residential neighborhood where service vehicles parked in the driveways of their clients, not out on the street. He passed his house and circled around the block passing the van once more. No windows in the rear, no one sitting in the driver's or passenger seat. It was likely nothing, but his war bred instincts were now on full red alert.

Walter began his deliberate measured response as he walked through the door and greeted Mary, canvassing her face for a quick reading, making a gesture across his neck and bringing an index finger to his lips, clearly realizing that the urgency of the conversation needed to be deflected. He could clearly see that her face had lost its usual look, of patient resignation, as if a mask had been stripped from it. She put an urgent hug around him, a hug of desperate lonely vulnerability, an expression made unbearably poignant, as Walter had been invited to share in the despair.

"It's so nice out; let's take Gabby for a run at the geese, before the sun gets too low."

He motioned her to speak and she confusingly took the lead saying, "Okay, that sounds great. Maybe we can take the paddle boat out on the lake."

"Come on, Gabby," Walter hollered as they walked out the back door toward the pond and Cedar Lake, which sat adjacent to it.

"What's going on, Wally?" Mary whispered.

"No geese, Mary? Did someone we know already dispense with them?"

"Ryan was here earlier and took her out, so they haven't dared to make a return."

Gabby looked out at the glistening water, feeling forlorn, and dove into the chilly water regardless. Walter helped Mary on the paddle boat, untethered it from the dock, and nearly fell headlong into the cold winter lake thaw, as the springer ran between his legs and sat perfunctorily next to Mary as if it were her royal queenly throne.

"So what's happening?" Mary asked as they drifted out on the shimmering azure water.

"It may be nothing. I'm just trying to be cautious. Tell me what went on, Mary."

"It was the same man who visited us at the lake back in the early sixties. He's much older, obviously, but it was him."

"Arthur Borgen," he whispered just loud enough for Mary to hear. "God, I really had myself convinced this was behind us," Mary moaned.

"I know, I know, I feel the same way. Tell me everything that occurred, from the moment he arrived until he left. Remember everything, Mary. You know how important this is!"

She went through every detail of her conversation with Borgen, which had lasted no more than five minutes, with a faint glow of dread appearing on her face as she spoke. "How far into the house did he get?"

"He stood only at the marble entrance, just inside the door. What did you think; I was gonna feed him lunch?"

"Did he ever get out of your sight?"

"No, only when I ran into the kitchen, to turn off the oven timer." The caramel rolls, he thought, a serene smile creasing his face as he put his arm around his wife's shoulders, the dog applying a slobbery loving lick as he did.

"He may have planted a bug." Walter said, explaining to Mary about the mysterious white van parked two doors down.

They sat in quiet contemplation, the companionable silence of the long-married, as they paddled down the North Shore of Cedar Lake. By summer's end the lake would be a storehouse for a mess of newly developed weeds called Eurasian Milfoil, transported to many of the state's lakes, by boats that had taken port on Lake Superior. The sun was beginning to make its last appearance over the stately white pines as they sat together holding hands, drifting along, watching the hens and mallards scramble for shore as they sensed the perched predator making her way toward them.

Walter was beginning to come up with a plan. "We can't let on, right, Mary? Do you still agree with me after all these years?"

"I guess so, Wally, but I'm scared. He would not have come back if he didn't have a good reason."

She was right, he thought, but instead he heard himself say how he wasn't so sure and that he felt they should play this out a little longer. He stopped paddling and looked at her angelic pale skinned face, her still rich, lustrous, peppered black hair and deep into her piercing brown eyes. It was after all, her decision, her family's heritage at stake.

They had been married for nearly forty years now, and they had laughed when they remembered the phases of their marriage when it was still a mirror, reflecting back on both of their carefully constructed, easily shattered conceits. Mary had many times recalled the first Valentine's Day after they were married, when Wally had given her red bath towels. She cried when she unfolded them.

The towels were a metaphor, she came to see, that momentarily blotted out the sun, shrieked across the reassuring hum of a gradually gathering darkness of her newly married life. It was a romantic high noon to her, an emotional and historic accounting in which her husband had been found sadly wanting. She would say to herself then that they were not really married, still in the teen romance mode, of he loves me; he loves me not, still riveted by the high drama and pitched emotion of courtship and passion, in which a passing glance can detonate a sudden emotional danger. She couldn't remember any more why she was so angry, but she reasoned that it must have been that she had staked everything on this man and he was not the way she thought. She had defined herself in terms of this man she came to realize, and he was a man who gave towels.

They both smile now when they recall this story and now Walter gives her red bath towels and pink and red roses every Valentine's Day. It has become part of their mythology and the laughter now is its own edgy commentary on how things have changed, how they have changed each other, and how the two people, who now smile at this are indelibly stained with each other's expectations and disappointments, how who we are is a composite of who we might have been refracted through the lens of whom we married, the shared laughter becoming a counterpane covering the lumps they've dealt each other, the scars left from various surgeries they've performed on each other, and the enthusiasms dampened so a that a couple could emerge.

Walter and Mary were the living testimony that all marriages are like mended garments. In marriage, you don't always make it all better, you just get over it. Through marriage they had both come to realize you have willfully introduced a witness into your life and can no longer close the mind's eye on uncomely passages, but must stand up straight and put a name upon your actions, because if you don't, your partner will. Marriage, as it had worked for Mary and Walt, was a mystery, made up of such a complicated ebb and flow of affection, admiration, ritual and gradually unfolding understanding that with the right person, it's not a bad life to live.

Their marriage was now steeped in the music they share and enjoy, in their family, in the way they both have changed and the things they have come to know, in exasperation and elegance, in the poetry of darkness and in the solace of each other's company. They see each other in the manner in which Walter has saved Mary and the ways Mary has saved Walter, providing each other with a modest continuity of care, rather than seeking some miraculous cure, listening to one another and caring for their welfare in such a way that had become such a comfortable experience, that the magic aureole of love had descended upon them when no one was looking.

"Okay, what's the plan?" Mary finally softly whispered.

It was a brilliant plan first put together by her father back in the late 1930s before the war and Walter had a huge role in bringing it forward, but it was the patriarch of the Chisholm family on the Iron Range, her father David, who had originally staked it out. He always felt that Mary wanted to bring it to fruition, but he also knew that fear would eventually play its fateful hand. A year ago Mary would have most likely backed away from the current urgency, but now with her cancer defeated, she was feeling her old strength and stamina one more.

"When we go back to house, Mary, we must act as you did with Borgen, expressing our mutual dismay that he thinks we know something about the matter. I'll look for a bug near the front door and take Gabby for a walk and see if the van is still there." Mary nodded in solemn agreement.

"Let's unyoke the oxen for now, Mary; after all, it is the cocktail hour," Wally said as he slipped the boat up to the dock and escorted Mary arm in arm, back to the house, spaniel afoot.

Chapter 3

It was late April and spring had come early, as if to atone for the winter's savagery. It was almost warm and the sky was tinseled with early stars, and the new moon was barely a crescent stitched into the darkening sky. Ryan and Nan walked leisurely down Lakeside Drive to the Duncan's soiree. Their two boys, Tommy and Adam, ran ahead of them to explore the lakeshore and the boat docks on St. Louis Bay of Lake Manoa.

The leavings of the winter had recently melted away, giving way to the blue bird weather of spring. This evening was sweet enough to make even the most downcast heart sing out in joy. The ground had thawed and stretched and turned into a bright green shade. Branches of the elm and century old oak trees were starting to bend under the burden of their fresh leaves that were feathering out like little ferns. Willows' greening boughs met above the avenue and dripped stalactites of moss rendering a mysterious drape of loveliness, beside the lakeshore. The clear and fresh twilight of the evening sky was purpling above them, and the scent of lilacs drifting down from their neighbors' backyards, were like a series of little benedictions, amidst the enchanted arboreality surrounding the lakeside homes. There was the smell of dogwood and laurel in the cool slow passage of the world.

The Davies couple took a moment before walking up the drive, to the Duncan home, as two mourning doves cooed softly, like an easy conscience.

The couple watched their two boys interact with the two older Duncan boys, who were tending four boat slips of guests arriving by water. Dave and Jenny Duncan's boys, in the adaptive niche of the family ecosystem, were bluff charming boys, well-poised for their age, quick and strong with mature sporty personalities, perfect grandchildren, eager to scramble up on laps when younger, unafraid of bitter vegetables, unexcited by television and computer games, and skilled at cheerfully answering questions like, "are you loving school?" It was easy to love these children as they lived outside the realm of cynicism and irony. They were the sort of boys in whom every older man likes to think he sees his own young self, and yet they were still young enough to harbor life's better illusions. The Davies' kids seemed to idolize their older role models.

Ryan and Nan entered the Duncan's home through the double doors along the white marbled floor to a babble of noise that greeted them. They enjoyed their friends at the Duncan's affairs greatly because for the most part, the attendees were not trying to earn oodles of money to buy a toehold on some vacuous social ladder. These were not dinner parties where no one teased, flirted or argued. They were not one of those awful garish parties hosted by awful garish sacks of money masquerading as human beings.

True to form, the hugs of Dave's huge hospitality were in active mode, their long friendship being no excuse for abridging the appropriate formalities. Upon entering the Duncan living room, Dave had already drawn them two crystals of the driest martinis this side of the Sahara. It was some new Eastern European Vodka, he boasted, that would have poleaxed a Russian poet. Nan sniffed the toxic brew, and smiled knowingly, giving the host a warm hug, and kiss, and made a deft departure away from the greeting masses, to Jenny's side in the pine beamed silver appliance kitchen, to assist her in incorporating the customary splendors, making her famous baste for the salmon, the two of them performing, their usual forms of culinary sorcery.

There, in Jenny's expansive gourmet kitchen, the pans hung high over the stove and grill in regimented order, at instant readiness, shined like mirrors, scrubbed and polished into gleaming disks, the battered cleanliness of well used copper, seasoned iron and heavy steel. Jen's pantry shelves were crowded to the ceiling with the growing treasures of lavish victualing; an astounding variety and abundance of delicious foods, enough it seemed to supply an Arctic expedition, the likes of which had never been seen, or dreamed of in a country house, let alone a suburban kitchen.

The Duncan's parties were always great fun, because for one, Jenny was always at the vanguard of discovery when it came to chic eating, preparing good viands and wines, special delights for delectation. She did not like to confound her own cooking viewpoints with the opinions of experts. Rather, she carried divine laws down from the mountaintops of connoisseurship that were written in her own hand. "A good time to be alive," she said as Nan approached, toasting, her glass of burgundy, its richness catching the light and shimmering like ancient rubies.

With every soft ringing of the door-bell, with every opening and closing of the door, there came new voices and new laughter, a babble of new greetings, new gayety, and new welcomes.

Ryan and Dave chatted and sipped their cocktails for a moment as the party host waved other guests up the circular drive. Dave Duncan was the owner of the City's most up and coming, fastest growing advertising firms and these social enclaves were part of his clout importance, that would help insure better doors to be opened. Ryan watched him and grinned, as Dave was currently involved in memorizing the social geometry that was now ever increasing. It was a task his talents could so easily conquer, though it could have perplexed Euclid.

Dave's guests were helpless before the stream of pleasantries that he could pour from the pitcher of his effusive personality. He was walking, talking, hugging, drinking and noshing with his grin as wide and sweeping as a searchlight. By turns he was jovial, lordly, reassuring, confidential, personally philosophical and worldly or he could mantle himself in dignified rectitude, as he sampled the viands. He was perspiring, as if it was a day of the vaporous heat of summer, not the cool warmth of an early spring. The big figure mopped vigorously at his brow with a large mauve handkerchief as sweat ran down his mottled cheeks. He had a big buff-colored face, bright golden eyes full of laughter and friendliness, a blunt and amiable nose, a big gay mouth with excellent flashing teeth. His hair once quite blonde was now becoming a silvery mass of thick shining waves, though he was only in his mid-forties.

All this, combined with a certain splendor and warmth and solidity, made him the ideal pitch man, trusted by many, disliked by few, even his enemies, and admired by almost everyone. With all these admirable assets, a certain hearty bluffness and a rollicking affectionate voice, Ryan noticed the increased webbing of his scarlet cheeks, below his full shock of hair, were slowly graduating into a virtual symposium of capillary breakdown. He lived a full dawn to dusk calendar, going head to head, glassful to glassful, with the big new rich who clamored for the wow life, people whose millions were as trembling, fresh and fragile as spring buds. His was about a high rate of living, taking in all life packed layer by layer like a bulging tub of ice cream. Ryan and Nan worried privately that if he kept up his current pace, it would cause him to beach like a whale, on the sands of his fifth decade, just a few years away.

Sipping his cocktail and gingerly balancing a cracker spread with caviar, Ryan chatted with a neighborhood guest as he noticed one of Dave's newer clients who had just arrived rather late to the party with his platinum plated third wife at his side. They entered the partying throng with their tardy hands fluttering like light-becalmed moths, excusing their extended arrival.

Dave rolled his eyes clandestinely, his habit of stylizing certain glances, and gave an arched eyebrow for Ryan's edification at their arrival. Ryan tilted his glass toward him in a little mock salute which was both commendation and appeal. Punctuality was, after all, the buyer's prerogative Ryan supposed.

Dave and Jenny greeted them warmly with Dave's genial voice betraying no special feeling about the new clients. He had once been the number one coiffeur in New York City but, after his fall from grace in Manhattan, he had returned to his mid-western roots, in order to franchise a fleet of chic ultra-high end salons. He was a fragrant looking man, elegantly turned out, just short of slickness, and it was being noised about that he was now the trichologist who tended the locks of the current governor, dyeing his hair and also his wife's mustache. He apparently had just the right equipment his third wife was looking for in a partner; sallow, slick good looks not quite greasy enough to give offense, but yet the classic stereotyped homosexual talent, necessary for making up older women. He had no personal convictions on any subject apart from clothes and dinner.

Dave had confided to Ryan that his new client had said he had graduated from Princeton, yet when Dave asked him how he liked Thackeray he said he had never tasted any. His wife was bedecked with gold jewelry at her neck, wrists and ears that must have weighed three pounds, and had a specially designed Dolly Parton bosom that was draped with a multi-strand gold neckpiece that could have drawn gasps of envy from a pharaoh. Her hair was the biggest anyone had ever seen on a Caucasian, a frizzy henna-rimmed Watusi "do" half halo, half mop, that must have been two feet across. She greeted everyone with "darling" and a damp fusillade of kisses. Ryan could easily discern that her face was well past the prime that her bosom still enjoyed. The both of them conducted their conversations with an overdone aggressive superficiality and gesture that seemed designed to let the rest of the party know what a keen time they were having talking to one another, as though they had some kind of craven Copernican wish to be the sun, around which all things revolved.

They were both so prodigiously self-important, Ryan intuited, that Dave was easily able to attract their business and guide them, with the reins of their own conceit and vanity, ambition being a powerful pair of blinders.

Dave glanced over his new clients' shoulders giving Ryan a look of incredulity as he chuckled back at him, turning toward the kitchen to talk with Nan and Jen and make himself another drink, while the party bravely moved on.

The din of the Saturday evening party was growing and the sun was making its way to the bottom of its orbital arc, its magical light beams making the bay glisten a deep azure blue, as Ryan made his way out to the expansive deck, overlooking the bay.

The salmon had been prepared with Nan's miracle baste and was thirty minutes away from being devoured, by what was becoming the traditional rollicking well lubricated throng of friends and neighbors.

Now, came a commotion along the Lake Shore from the Duncan and Davies boys as Billy Jenkins the local police chief who lived down the shoreline arrived to oohs and aahs, as he slipped his beautiful mahogany '41 Barrel Back Chris Craft gurgling into one of the boat slips, to the boys' delight.

Billy had been a friend of Ryan and Dave since junior high school and all he ever wanted to be was a cop. With a Master's degree in criminal justice from the State University he had joined the local sheriff's department and was now the police chief at one of the largest sub-stations in the tri-county area. Tragically, his wife was killed in an icy winter road accident eight years ago. He had not remarried, choosing to spend more and more time as a dutiful public protector. Yet all knew that he needed the society of his friends, to avoid giving way to intense melancholy.

He lived in a little three-bedroom cottage nestled along the lake purchased only three months before Nancy's car slid off black ice into a massive oak along Grays Bay road. His home was now, as attested by all those that had ventured inside, decorated in the style of Early American. Early American, Ryan thought, enjoying a private chuckle, as in Early American, Ma and Pa Kettle. All that was missing was a pot-belly stove in the kitchen and a goat tethered to a pole in the ground in the backyard. The new love of his life was the classic boat now being slipped and tied off safely, on the dock, for all to admire.

Ryan watched as Billy made his way up the freshly mowed lawn as the boys gleefully secured the gorgeous wooden craft, proudly polished to a reflective sheen.

Billy had Falstaff's capacity for drink, talk and revelry and Ryan chuckled as he watched him have a slight stumble as he started up the stairs of the deck, indicating that he may have done some private pre-partying. He noticed his torso had shifted a few latitudes to the south since the last time he had seen him. As only a concession to public expectation, he was wearing khaki pants with at least thirty-year old topsiders, a tattered white button down shirt, and the usual ragged navy blue blazer that he proudly proclaimed to have not seen the kiss of an iron, since the Eisenhower administration. He was also said to be the town's premier atheist, and had left orders that his ashes were to be disposed of by throwing them into any convenient ashcan.

As he reached the top of the stairs, to the heckles of his friends, Ryan noticed how his cheeks and nose were bright pink, with broken capillaries and spider veins, the marks of dissipation perhaps, but on Billy it was subtly charming, almost intentional, like a touch of powder and rouge on a handsome Hollywood actor's face. His big cherubic countenance was so rosy, so engaging and candid it almost glowed, like a full moon. His little round eyes twinkled, taking on the appearance of sparkling agates, pale gray shot with streaks of brown and yellow, his thick tufts of sandy eyebrows raised themselves with certain quizzical fondness.

He was decent, reliable and dependable, usefully obtuse and intellectually absolutely unthreatening, an honest meat and potatoes sort. If Billy was a politician, Nan had always said he'd be the best kind of politician, because he never ran for anything and asked for nothing. He would go out of his way to shake your hand to see how you were doing and give you the shirt off his back, if that's what you needed. But he wasn't running for anything and never had, so he was the best kind of politician and all the community along the shores of Lake Manoa loved him.

"Anybody got a Heineken around here?" he bellowed, a smile widening his face as he topped the stairs bringing forth a burst of laughter from all gathered on the deck, as Dave promptly placed the beckoned brew in his chubby fist.

"You've fixed her up beautifully," said Dave as he threw his arm around him and walked him into the neighborhood throng of his friends. Jenny and Nan quickly joined the group giving Billy motherly kisses on his cheek, while Dave popped another beer into his hand as he visited with his friends.

In the scheme of things for Billy, time had only two dimensions, today and tomorrow. Ryan watched, as Billy had deftly broken away from conversations, now circling the wet bar, emitting small orgasmic exclamations like a cormorant searching for food. He had finished his second Heineken and Dave made him a Stoli which he politely snatched like a seal taking a mackerel from its keeper, gulping it down, like it was the last ounce of vodka on earth.

It was his gluttonous epicureanism that really set him apart, for Billy could eat enough to feed three longshoremen. He was now feasting like Belshazzar, munching down the caviar stuffed blinis, as if there were no more sturgeon left in the Caspian Sea. He gave a nod toward Ryan, as if it were the cultured accolade of the connoisseur. He ate with such unusual vigor that you could have stuffed a porpoise into his gaping mouth. As he chewed his face was mired in exudations.

He finished his tray, looking around expectantly, as if a genie might be arriving with more fresh victuals. His Buddha-like omniscience was so pervasive that more than one guest, Ryan was certain, overtaken by their inebriated condition would try to rub his stomach for good luck.

Though loved by all, physically he was a mess. Nerves of the job had created a dependency that took the form of an addiction to soda pop. It was reputed that he drank a case a day, and it apparently didn't matter what the flavor was. He was carbonatically omnivorous to them all, and it looked recently as if a six-inch layer of blubber had been glued to his corpus, the several thousand calories a day of the newly manufactured high fructose corn syrup, adding suet to the coming of his middle age. His face was slowly becoming grainy, veined and coarse.

It seemed as if all the party watched as Billy's on again off again attempts at temperance, appeared to be off once more. As he waded into his second martini his capillaries began to glow like neon. More and more he was taking on a drinker's face with a florid nose and cheeks that were becoming a pasty thicket of busted capillaries, the features slowly becoming puffed and roughened by decades of hard duty with the cocktail shaker. His brown sandy gray hair was oddly pale at the temples as if it had been dipped in the nicotine that stained his fingers.

You could make his type rather easily, Ryan's saddened muse informed him. Billy was what many a mother thought the men their daughters would marry would turn into, barking for their gins and vodkas at local watering holes. People of an order of being, at whose shores liquor lapped like the sea. It was a particular social order, in which alcohol had passed from being an accessory, to being an absolute value.

The bell timer in the kitchen rang as Billy made his second pass at the trays of hors d'oeuvres, as if scripted, with perfect timing, signifying that the main course was done. Everyone moved to make fresh drinks and pour goblets of wine and prepare to enjoy the salmon delight, with fresh asparagus and Jenny's to die for spinach salad that was the current in style roughage of the time, with her special vinaigrette. It was just then that Dave bellowed to everyone, from the front double doors, that, "Our future Senator is here."

Local neighbors William and Winnie McWilliams stood under the archway of the flowered front porch. They were a very well landed couple, from family heritages of lumber and grain, and were very well liked. Money and property were to both of them too evanescent to be little more than trifling. They lived modestly, had no discernible airs about them, their egos well checked in egalitarian order.

Winnie and Will waved to Nan and Ryan with an amiable countenance, from across the partying mass that was making their way toward them. Winnie held a purposeful glint in her eye, her face implicit with grace and a protean quality, as she smiled at them. She had high cheekbones that gave a faintly Oriental cast to her face; her chestnut hair fell away from it in an easy sweep to her shoulders. She was dressed plainly in khaki slacks and a sleeveless orange silk jersey, a thin gold chain at her throat. There was a kind of elegance in the way she stood there greeting friends, her weight on one leg, one hand to her chin, the fine flowing line of a Brancusi figure.

This group of friends was part of their sticky protective social web, out of the constant public scrutiny. Friendships needed discretion to flourish, and now especially with Winnie running for State Senator in Washington, good friends were all the more important, keeping each other's confidences while not wielding their personal value systems against each other like sabers. Very rich people practically never gave a good party because they only understood what they could buy and that was never the right people, because they were not for sale. That's why Winnie and her husband, who took refuge not in who they knew but rather what they knew, loved these parties and their attendant friends.

They were a delightful couple constantly involved in community and state activities. Will was an investment counselor and operated an investment advisory firm downtown, and Winnie last year announced her candidacy for Senate. They were now, very actively, involved in the campaign. A skiing accident she had at the age of eighteen on the back bowls of Vail had denied the couple of children, but they had adopted two beautiful Korean twin girls twelve years ago, one of whom was currently babysitting the Davies boys.

Dave uncorked a new rich French merlot and delivered the stemmed bowls to the McWilliams as he gracefully swirled the red, showing off its rich legs.

"For two glorious days of hearth and home," Dave toasted, knowing that Will and Winnie were taking the weekend off from the labors of campaigning. Everyone now seemed to gather round the wet bar to toast the two campaign warriors.

"To the next senator from our great state," Dave continued. Winnie sipped graciously, and laughed once, two low notes half an octave apart, as she languidly pushed her auburn hair back behind her right ear.

"Hear, hear." The gathered group of friends clinked and drank in unison.

Ryan stood next to Nan at the wet bar, across from the Duncans, treating themselves to the epicurean delights as Winnie and Will made their way onto the deck with their plates and wine.

"Delicious as usual," Winnie commented, directing her accolade to Jen and Nan, just as a large fish leapt out of the slowly darkening waters in front of the docks, in its spawning madness.

They were standing among a small group of friends and neighbors who were listening with the impassive expressions of those who have tried hard to learn the forbearance necessary to be around people who talk too much.

They listened more indulgently, than intently, as a neighbor from up the street, Arlene Goldstein, sipped her wine, made a denture plate smile and tattered on about her beagles and her police radio updates for the week, to mostly unhearing ears. She was one of those chronically unsatisfied types, loving nothing better than to nurse along some scandal, substantiated or otherwise. She paused intently for a moment, while studying the table cloth upon which her wine sat, as if truth was somehow somewhere woven into the linen. She returned her gaze then with frowning contemplation to her wine glass, while others stood restlessly, staring into the Ruby depths of their own claret, peering for auguries.

Fate had deprived her of a pretext for becoming vain. She was a blousy woman and was the wife of Marvin Goldstein, the head of forensic medicine at the University Hospital, who rarely made appearances at these events.

A peculiar fate seems to overtake homely women, Ryan mused, at the end of parties. Their curls and their ribbons come undone, particles of food stick to their teeth, their glasses steam and the wide smile they planned to charm the world with lapsed into a look of habitual discontent and bitterness. They did everything imaginable to make up for the irremediable absence of men. They remained lonely women with a natural proneness for gossip. She was not ugly, her face was simply permeated with the implacable dullness of the Midwesterner. Her rice terraced hair was a bit absurd, Nan mused, and it seemed to her that many women her age with a lot of hair had a reputation for glottal virtuosity and seemed to feel that a lot of hair baroquely arrayed, might compensate for failings of personality.

The bouffant hair framed a head with bony features which seemed almost too large and dramatic for her facial planes like a smile in a funhouse grimace. She was a big woman with a comforting unchallenging plainness who possessed fashion instincts unexpected in a woman of that stereotype. It was her gift of sorts and so she was accorded the slightly condescending sympathy which provincial female society reserves for those sisters unlucky enough to lose their money, or misguided enough not to have made it, or found it. She was the local gossip, Nan quickly discovered soon after they had moved to the neighborhood, and for all the satisfaction and excitement to be had in life, there was only one small consolation for such people, who reserved their greatest relish for the disappointment of others.

Nan had come to understand her as one of many who had a depressive personality type, and she had apparently been analyzed within an inch of her id. Its seemingly perverse persistence in the human gene pool was that depression was a successful adaptation to ceaseless pain and hardship. Pessimism, feelings of worthlessness and lack of entitlement, inability to derive satisfaction from pleasure, a tormenting awareness of the world's general lousiness, was what Arlene's Jewish parental forebears, who'd been driven from shtetl to shtetl by implacable anti-Semites, had bequeathed her.

Depressives, in grim situations, oftentimes handed down their genes, however despairingly. Feeling bad all the time and expecting the worst had been natural ways of equilibrating themselves with the crappiness of their circumstances. Few things gratified depressives, Nan came to understand, more than really bad news. This obviously wasn't an optimal way to live, but it had its evolutionary advantages.

Ryan secretly taped Nan on her thigh as he edged his way down the deck to overhear a story Billy had now started telling a couple of their buddies from school about a woman that had been taken into custody that week, with the biggest "hogans" he had ever seen.

This was an indication to Ryan that his efforts to rinse his vocabulary had lapsed now, after his ongoing retinue of cocktails. Profanity for Billy was less a matter of expression, than his native rhythm when he was away from his working hours. The epithets corresponded to the ticks of the metronome of his inner workings. Sadly, Billy had become a mandatory ornament at the Duncan and Davies parties, and though everyone loved him, if all held true to form, as he proceeded to get majestically drunk, before the end of the night he would be speaking in the fashion of the moment, which would devolve into English undistinguishable.

Ryan watched him with sadness. Oh, how the thoughts of loss could be cauterized with drink. The alcohol and the amounts he began consuming after his wife's tragic death was a regular part of his metabolism now. When he was half drunk, he seemed almost at peace. When the conversation and the chuckling between them had finally run thin, Ryan put his arm around Billy and motioned them toward the interior of the party, the cool post sunset winds now attracting the party goers inside, to surround the wet bar in search of more conversational prey.

Ryan poured himself a glass of the rich merlot and then winking at Nan refilled her crystal as well. A lively dialogue was ensuing with a small group of self-proclaimed politicos around the wet bar, as Winnie seemed to be the center of attention.

"Everything has been fundamentally flipped on its head," she continued her profound erudition. "We have an actor, and a bad actor at that, in office, and if that wasn't bad enough the men around him, Stockman and the whole crowd, have this starve the beast, government is evil mentality. This trickle down supply side stuff is a joke. It's an economic theory, where the fraud of it is not so obvious but the scholarship behind it is so damn self-serving that it verges on fraud. Never, in the history of economics, since the first economy was created by Gilgamesh, more than two thousand years ago, has an inverted tax system, taxing the wealthy less than middle and lower class proved successful. Never! Adam Smith, the author of the great treatise of 1776, *An Inquiry into the Nature and Causes of the Wealth of Nations*, that brought forth his system of natural liberty, is rolling in his Virginia grave as we speak."

She is really quite brilliant, Ryan thought, putting his arm around Nan, standing at his side as Winnie continued her exposition. Educated at Stanford and Yale with a degree in philosophy and a PHD in economics and finance she knew her subject matter cold. Will winked at them, as Winnie continued her learned dissertation.

"Keynes said it all correctly," the candidate continued, "it's pure economics 101. Demand creates its own supply. Prosperity has always started from the ground up, not from the top down, like the current head of the Federal Reserve suggests. The government economist's assigned task today is one of mystification." Winnie leaned over the wet bar and reached for a ladle that was laying in the sink winking at Jenny, with a smile that asked for permission, holding it up for all to see.

"This," she continued, "was once just a piece of wood." She twirled it in her hand as she sipped her wine. Winnie's face filled with that familiar high excitement she always carried, a sea surge toward life's boundless possibilities. "It has no value whatsoever until labor was applied and made it into this useful kitchen utensil. Labor," she stated emphatically, "labor created the value here, and that is the essence of an economy and trade. Demand is created by labor and thus labor is superior to capital because capital cannot create value, it can only help to finance the production of the item driven by the demand that labor has created. The entire supply side charade is cloaked in a masquerade of public benefit. The entire tax system is becoming increasingly regressive."

"Yeah, but if I have to pay less tax for my corporation, I will put money back into my company to make it more profitable and gain market share," intoned Stewart Closway, owner of a small manufacturing firm.

"I'm sure you would, Stew," Winnie acknowledged, "but what happens to your employees' purchasing power if their taxes go up as they are now proposing while yours become less? What does that do to the demand curve, Stew?"

"Think of it this way," she opined, handing the ladle back to Jenny.

"Tell me which of these two business situations you would prefer." As she gave a professorial pose toward her husband standing next to Ryan and Nan.

"You can build two buildings each employing ten laborers or one building employing twenty laborers. Where are you creating more demand, creating more purchasing power and expanding the ever important middle class?"

There was a mumbling moment of silence.

"You see the supply side acolytes have predicted that sharply lower corporate taxes will increase national supply much more than demand, so that inflation and unemployment would fall quickly and the budget deficit would vanish by the time of the next election. And what have we seen so far?" Winnie asked, turning her palms to the sky. "The public has paid the price of this dogma, this thought virus, forced on us by the supply siders. Both the deficit, this President creating more debt than any other President in the history of our nation, and unemployment rates are rising rapidly. It's all been an intellectual fraud promulgated upon the hard working American middle class.

"Hey I thought we were taking a couple days off, Will," Winnie said chuckling as she took a healthy draw on her merlot.

"Anyway that's why I am running, good friends. Cheers, I hope you're with me," she toasted, holding up her wine, as friends and neighbors applauded her sincere exhortations.

Winnie and Will were making their amiable way among the party throng, chatting with friends and neighbors as the aroma of Jen's baking apple crisp began to float through the air, portending the coming of manna from heaven. Their social assent was nothing needed or anything they sought after. Their conversations were wide ranging, as they were both blessed with an ease of manner, which made them accessible to their contemporaries without seeming overly familiar or condescending.

Planed smooth by martinis and now sipping a second stem of merlot, Ryan found himself again listening to the fickle bustlings of a conversation Arlene was having with Billy, when something he thought she had asked him piqued his interest. "What was that you just asked Billy," Ryan pleaded, leaning back on the wet bar for support, as a sudden flash of intuition, an instant flood of recognition and horror went through him like a knife.

"I asked him why all the local squad cars are parked outside the station, when they are usually inside the police garage," Arlene repeated.

"What's up with that, Billy," Ryan asked, feeling suddenly unsteady on his feet, hoping that Billy's liquid analysis of his question would be sufficiently English understandable. Billy made some tentative preparatory shapes with his mouth, tipping his head from one side then the other, like a flower too heavy for its thick stalk, as if to shift memories around and make them retrievable. He was now righteously and irredeemably drunk.

"Oh yah," he said mercifully, in rather clear discourse. "Some of da FEDS are in town from Washington running about and they want their pomp, pompous black sedans out of harm's way I guess." As he slurped at his newly filled glass of red. "It's all kind of hush-hush, nobody's quite fu, flippin' sure what dere up to, but they're outta here on Tuesday, not a minute too soon." Burp.

"Did you hear any good stuff on your scanner Arlene?" Billy blurted wryly. "They have three of their sedans in our garage and four at the station in midtown."

"Who are they, Billy," Ryan asked, feeling a dizzying faint overtake his psyche.

"I think they are part of an agency in DC, called the Office of ass, ass, Asset Control or some fin like that," Billy wheezed, as he puckered his lips savoring another surge of merlot over his palate. "Oh, and of course they all must have those elitist VIP issued government friggin' license plates."

Ryan leaned back hard against the wet bar and closed his eyes while Billy's words penetrated his merlot haze as the crystal of wine left the trembling grip of his fingers smashing to the floor, in a display that looked like the blood-letting of wine and glass... For nothing is lost, nothing is ever lost. There is always the clue, the canceled check, the smear of lipstick, the footprint in the sand, the condom under the mattress, the still visible blush of an old wound, the baby shoes dipped in bronze, the taint in the blood...

It was one of those funny moments in your life he would later recall, that the stained little mirror you normally looked at turned into a truly magic glass, giving the world a lens through which to view with consummate clarity the whole contradictory muddle of the past, sister, parents and strangers...

Colleen refused to move from the pleasing rays of the afternoon sun and tilted her head back in the perpetual hope of a sun shot transformation, that a certain young man who summered on the nearby shoreline might notice the tan and sun streaked hair and the slimming effects of her daily swims. It was mid-week and the town had settled into that quiet unpolished lull it always acquired in the time between Sunday night and Thursday afternoon, when the city weekenders began to make their appearance once again.

"Did you get the new slalom ski from the garage?" he asked his sister. "No," was her indifferent response. "Take me skiing first then we can go back and get it."

"Jeez, Colleen," he shouted looking back at her as she put cocoa oil all over her bikini body, that was beginning to glow a deep bronze, under the warm summer sun, as the wake of the Well-Craft widened behind them.

"We can go back for it when I'm done skiing," she said evenly. That won't take long, Ryan thought ruefully.

"Ryan, Ryan, you okay honey?" Nan asked, holding his trembling hand. Ryan opened his eyes, now back from his misty recollection, that had wavered up slowly in his mind's eye, like a chunk of water-logged wood stirred loose from the depths, and stared at Billy, in a minor state of shock. He shook his head a few times trying to gain some focus.

"You okay, buddy?" asked Dave as he snappily grabbed a dust broom and a bar towel to quickly tend to the spill.

"So sorry, Dave," Ryan apologized as he took the towel from him gazing out past Billy, toward the deck and the dark waters of the bay beyond, his faded brown pupils now numb, expressionless as a brace of gray oysters on the half shell.

As they walked up Lakeside Drive to their house, Ryan began to tell Nan what he almost had forgotten what happened at his parent's home the day before.

"Why don't you ask Billy if you can take a look at the cars in the garage? Do you think you would recognize them as the same?"

"Good idea, I'll drop by in the morning and then if warranted talk with Dad on Monday."

"It's probably nothing, Ryan," Nan hoped as they walked arm in arm up their driveway and into the mudroom of their five bedroom colonial.

The kids were asleep in their beds and Ryan and Nan were feeling swirly amorous. Ryan kissed her as they made their way upstairs into the master bedroom. Kissing her for Ryan, was still like being drawn into the interior of some wild rich flower and enclosed in its blossom. The world was being shut out and there were noiseless hints of damp secrets being exchanged as they entered the bedroom. There was to be no practiced sequence, no commonplace ritual of ascending sexual procedure.

Movement slid liquidescently into movement, as under her skirt Ryan drew her panties down and rose to stroke her sex, the intricacies of the female pudenda, bedded in hair like silk, a moist sweet purse.

"Please, ah yes please," she whispered as she shifted on the bed to give him access. She was always as juicy as new fruit and as passionate as a milkmaid.

Somehow Ryan's clothes were off now and he entered her as surely and smoothly as if all life had been practice and prelude for this moment. As he rose and sank above, her breath became louder, faster, becoming a moaning and then something rougher, although hers or Ryan's could no longer be distinguished, as every infinite capacity of sensation was gathering in them at a single microscopic point of tickling pain. He heard her muttering voice rising to an octave shy of a shriek, a rattle in her throat of pain and delight and pure sensation, but now Ryan was wound down to a point just short of being turned inside out, and he told her so, and Nan responded.

"Please, one more time." There was no more possible restraint and he felt the spasms opening into a long sweet spreading flow and he heard her groan and roar and say something and felt her twitch and then it was his turn to tumble un-tethered and breathless, through the half blank length of the universe.

Later, both blinking in the soft light of the bedroom, she rose and stepped out of her dress. All she had on was her black brassiere. Her blond hair had shaken loose and flowed to her shoulders seeming to sweep years away, looking now thirty, even younger. Nan let Ryan look at her for a moment in the silence of the late night, to admire her legs and the startling patch of nightshade at her crotch, the dark sweet sensuous mystery, at the heart of all being.

She let him watch her slide off her bra. Her breasts showed few giveaway puckering and blemishes as Ryan reached, Nan came down to him and he commenced again. She brought her head up to kiss his mouth and her hand slid low and got busy, until she shifted over him, taking him in once more. This time was more for her, better for her, longer and deeper, as ecstasy came earlier to her and continued until Ryan was once again strung out, reduced like mercury, balanced on a needle. He couldn't hold it a second longer, feeling in the last fractional instant, as if he held within himself the entire moment of all creation.

Ryan looked down at Nan sleeping, barely stirring the covers with the rise and fall of her breathing, the soft in and out rhythmic seashore sounds, of her respiration. How forceful emotions are, he thought. It took a rocket, months, even years to reach the planets, but in seconds one could traverse the entire universe of feeling. Why did love have to make every moment together so indispensably precious, so that tomorrow ceased to exist for fear of its not coming and every moment lost, seemed a lifetime.

We had been placed on earth to love, to transform each other magically into far more than either partner felt they could be alone; and the purest joy in all the world was the naked generosity of lovers that shared all disparate burdens as one, that solaced and sustained…

Ever so quietly, he put himself under the downy bed covers aside his love, pillowed by the thought of non-stop happiness and not the potential danger that lay ahead.

Chapter 4

It was Monday morning, an exigent, toneless, colorless Monday, the day of renewed monotony for so many.

Driving down University Avenue toward his father's office, Ryan listened to a tape by the classic value investor Harry Markowitz, happy to avoid the dread of the vast array of sports talk shows that had recently taken over the radio waves and the cultural tribalism, of my team is better than your team, that they insidiously promoted in the unconscious psyche of the majority of low information society.

He thought how nothing seemed safe from the intrusive fingers from the realtors' rapacity and the wrecking ball of neighborhood gentrification. Each year it seemed the architectural visual masochism became more obtrusive as he viewed the extrusions forced from the ground, the new architecture of the city. The high sides of half-built buildings rose far above, their mountainous weight perilously balanced by spider web scaffolding. Huge cranes bowed their heads over each building, like the adoring Magi surrounding a giant manger.

The streets were swarming with the dense web of the morning; the sensuous complications of life and traffic, the vast honeycomb of business and desire. The ganglia of concrete streets, freeways and overpasses were jammed with a snarl of motors and horns, and the throbbing menace of machinery.

He could smell the odor of the city at that hour of the morning, the scorched beginning of another expiring day. All around him was the treeless brick and steel jungle of business. Ryan stopped at a downtown crosswalk as a soft eternity of feet thronged past him, the daily pageant of life that was forever before him on the street, the daily monotony, the rootless and desolation of these young pavement lives, caught up in the great and tragic rush and spell of time.

America's main street didn't last very long, he mused. Nothing in America did. If a product or enterprise didn't constantly reinvent itself, it would be superseded, cast aside, abandoned without sentiment in favor of something bigger, newer and nearly always uglier.

Sports, politics and religion were the three passions of the badly educated, Ryan mused as he drove along. They were the Midwest's and America's open wounds. They were ugly to see and a source of constant discontent that ate up the body's strength. Absurd and appalling sums of money, time and energy were wasted on them. The American pedestrian mind was narrow, passionate and brutish on these spectacles of divide and conquer. They had made men vote squarely against their interests for centuries. Their surly, dogmatic and fatalistic Christian views had prevented them from moving forward in an Enlightened progressive manner, dumbly blinded in mental straight jackets to buy into war making. They backed their country like they back their local publicly paid for team. They have an infantile, and fanatical desire to win. Screaming and hollering is their forte, and if things go badly and winning wanes, they sack the coach, not the governing body.

Here the real business was up close and upon him; gas stations, Kmarts, Sears, Dunkin' Donuts, Blockbuster Videos, a ceaseless unfolding pageant of monopoly commercial hideousness. He drove through the university past the houses that depressed him, those dreary two-storey gray-and-brown clapboard student housing affairs wedged between two others nearly identically cut up now into what avaricious landlords liked to call studio apartments.

The early spring seemed to be making an impression of the sticky nadir of August, as the heat was already scorching at ten a.m. He felt like a hyper-allergic child, suitably suited, sealed in a bubble, being able to survive only in a permanently air conditioned rolling microclimate environment abandoned just for the few seconds it took to run across the infernal un-climatized spaces that separated the chilled chambers of his existence, home, vehicle, office and meeting place, as if across the embers of hell. Even in the strange fetid blaze of early May, he dressed, sheathed for life in the operative of around sixty-five degrees Fahrenheit.

The morning following the Duncan dinner party, he had called Billy at the police station offering the rather feeble excuse for dropping by in order to pay a three month old parking ticket. Billy had looked up the ticket on his internal system while slurping down a diet Dr. Pepper, and promptly deleted it from existence, the petty tyranny of parking tickets, marking it paid in full. When Ryan objected he quickly waved him off. It was good to have friends in high places.

As he left the station he slyly peeked into the windows of the parking garage and sure enough there sat four black sedans with those special VIP plates just like the one he saw driving away from his childhood home and all those years ago at the lake.

He had to run all this by his dad, he told Nan, hoping it would amount to nothing but misplaced paranoia, though the seeds of doubt were beginning to plant themselves in his head, as he pulled in next to Walter Davies' assigned parking slot.

"Good morning, Terry," Ryan obliged to his father's executive assistant.

"Good to see you again, Ryan, your dad is on the phone, go on in," she said as she motioned with her left hand toward the large center office directly in front of her.

Walter's daily routine was one of being on the telephone constantly with clients, distributors, jobbers and salesmen, growing the business as best he could while putting out what seemed like the constant fires of pricing sales campaigns and discounting issues. Ryan knew his father would have to hand over the reins someday but as he sat across from his father now in front of his great walnut desk, he could see how much he was enjoying himself, his pale blue eyes had an inscrutable gleam in their depths. There was a charm, in that smile, nothing fatuous in it, nothing facile or calculated, reflecting his tolerant amusement, yet there was a fixity about them like a cat's unwinking gaze. It was an offering of life, of immensely human warmth. Under his slightly receding thinning gray hair his high forehead creased now and again as he dispensed his learned instructions to one of his sales managers.

He had the Davies short broad nose, strong and harsh in contour, with wide nostrils and the square shaped Davies chin. His mouth, though firm and sharp of outline, was kind and gentle. A father's a good thing Ryan mused, especially when he can tell you who he is and how he got that way, and who his father was and what's good and what's bad about where he came from, what's worth keeping and what you can flush. You can be successful and still be a country boy, and Walter Davies personified exactly that.

He had begun working for the food manufacturing and distribution company directly out of college and when he returned from war as a highly decorated hero, he continued with the firm, quickly moving up the sales and management ranks with an earnest dedicated work ethic and a war hewn resolve, a prodigy of resolve and everyday endurance, always aware that ambition was a good servant but could become a destructive master.

For the last fifteen years he functioned as the President and CEO, but still operated as the same gutter rat street smart "get the business" guy that he had always been and the ranks that he managed loved him for his never forgotten blue collar ethics. He was like Xerxes, the ancient King in 485 BC, who listened first to the humblest workers and only second to his ministers. For the ministers were loyal for his favor but the lowly worker had nothing to lose by telling the truth. He represented a dying breed, the heartland WASP particiate, something that set him apart from many of his colleagues. There was something in his bearing, the way he dressed and spoke, and the way he wore his life, the most truly pulse sensitive man Ryan had ever known.

He came from a long line of prudent and concerned men, decent, humane and worshipful men, perhaps not saints but not animals either; bankers, farmers, lawyers and doctors, men who saw no contest between principle and principal. The man of character took the former ten times out ten often. Seven generations of Davies stretched back to the cold waters and shoreline of the Massachusetts Bay Colony, the part of the ancestry of the generations who had heard Jon Winthrop orate, who had fought the King and the confederacy and Kaiser and Hitler, believing themselves to be fighting God's good fight for God's idea of freedom.

Davies was brought up to believe that God had ordained capitalism as the way, his way, which was why communism hated the name of God as fiercely as it hated the name of any American oligarch. Davies believed that capitalism could be fair, generous, productive and good natured, as the Christian credo instructed. In Walter Davies' view, a man was entitled to at the very least a chance to a rung at the ladder, to a hand up to whatever the goods his talents and abilities and efforts could generate, and not to walk all over the human rights and livelihoods of others.

Walter had planned, he recalled his father telling Mary, all those years ago now, that he hoped to make a fair and decent company in competition with thieves and exploiters in other businesses. "I'll make a sample of what American business can be; honest, fair and honorable. Perhaps I won't make much money competing with the new generation of robber barons. You see—" Ryan reflected as he watched his father talking on the phone to one of his distributors, "—there is something called destructive, which solves nothing, but only hinders the harborer, and there is a kind of pure and constructive hatred that seeks out to right wrongs, to oust injustices, to liberate and cleanse. I think that good men through all the ages had that hatred; from Jesus to Lincoln, from Luther to Washington, to the Kennedys and Martin Luther King."

The hater had no virulence, Ryan had come to understand, so as to see the virulence in others. He hated, and that hatred, it seemed to Ryan, was the most piteous of all. The hater was the most helpless of men, the most injured and the most tormented and those who made him hate were truly the wicked ones.

Walter had known all too well that an honest man in a den of thieves was, more often than not, stripped to his eyebrows and that an honest man was considered within this den to be a fool, and that in their minds the wages of sin and injustice were a rich old age, and the wages of honesty only led to the workhouse. These sociopath oligarchs of the late twentieth century, especially with the recent policy of disregard for antitrust regulation, had become convinced by experience that honesty was a virtue no one but the dying and dead could afford. The whole idea of honest engineering was mere novelty.

His office was modest and moderate, not covered with artifacts of self-esteem, self-validation and self-promotion, badges of eminence, usually found in the offices of men enthralled with their self-importance. It was a spare and elegant workspace for the humble likes of himself, strictly below the salt, on the far side of the velvet rope, in sharp contrast to the modern kitschy ostentation of the day.

He was a cool eyed scion, and had thankfully, not fallen prey to the moral basis of an American executive culture that dealt with the evolution and degeneration of basic emotions, in the face of aggrandizement by values based on expediency and competitiveness for its own sake, all the while dripping undisguised upper class-ridden social contempt.

He was one of a handful of men that had an undying capacity for enduring loyalty. He always tried to be realistic about his role in things. In business, he instinctively knew realism was usually equated with modesty, and modesty was much highly esteemed by men who had the really big business to give out. He was a man who wore laces in his shoes and still carried his own father's pocket watch, maintaining his ethical identity throughout the blabby, hairy self-expressive decades that followed the Eisenhower years. Whatever vestigial inclination he might have had toward me-firstism was mantled over with ideologies so good and right, yet by today's measure so out of date by society, they appeared to be ridiculous to the noisy recognizably post-adolescent world of the sixties and seventies Wall Street and Madison Avenue, where everything was subjugated to a drive for short term results, dosed with managerial egotism.

Ryan knew that his father had thought long and hard about the shape and dynamics of American history. The more he looked at it, the more he became convinced that the boom and bust cycles characterized by the national financial chronicles, derived from the uneasy dynamic between industrial America on one hand and financial America on the other, between Main Street and Wall Street. They functioned in the nation's business life almost as two hemispheres of the brain operated in the life of the mind, dividing up activity while each striving for ascendancy.

Main Street was the world of work of factories and labor shops, the making and selling of everything from bread to bonnets. But Main Street was now becoming lined with giant entities like Standard Oil and AT&T, with Wall Street corporate owned franchised corner restaurants, gas stations and dry goods stores. Wall Street was all about pieces of paper and was psychologically remote from the factory floor and the hand soiling realities of labor and of the production and marketing, which the pieces of paper represented.

He was civilized and born with the right passport, a man with a mind to improve, a heart to cultivate and a character to form, a man who shouldered responsibility with deceptive ease, whose eyes would well up with tears, elicited by the grace of ordinary people. A decent honorable intelligent man, he knew through his experience that sometimes these qualities were rather despised and could potentially leave him vulnerable in a world ruled and governed by expediency.

There had been through the decades after the war a pathological mutation of capitalism. The politics of the fifties was looked upon now as a listless interlude, glorifications of stalwart, lone individuals who chose authenticity and autonomy and risk over conformity prosperity and ease, who seemed to be the cultural personification of Robert Penn Warren's Pulitzer Prize winning novel, *All The King's Men* in 1946; the story of a restless man bound by a limited moral horizon, who heals his alienation by filling himself with devotion for a charismatic strong man, but who then frees himself as the story progresses from his own existential horror.

Then after the Strontium 90 fallout scare of 1959 America had witnessed a jeremiad from Ike, as his farewell address voice darkened with a gravity that recognized the Icarus, a tower of Babel, a fallible nation angrier than it realized, an America that needed to avoid becoming a community of dreadful fear and hate.

The conservative demagogues had produced a Leviathan, a vast national authority out of touch with its people and out of control. The sixties and seventies would give way to the incremental powers of the market that began to diffuse corporate ownership, so that no responsible owner would exist, bringing about the moral corruption of capitalism, replacing the ownership society with the new agency society, via financial intermediaries that would effectively control American business.

Imperial condescension would make its way into the culture with workers and laborers now becoming mere units of indifference, while bestirred republicans long buried the folklore memories of John D. Rockefeller buying up every refinery in his path through fair and mostly foul methods, neatly folding individual enterprises built up through the sweat of generations, into the juggernaut Standard Oil, rendering once independent men into mere nodes within a great and impersonal bureaucracy.

It hadn't been easy for Walter Davies, on his return from war just before Christmas in 1945. The war had upended America, by inserting a wedge between men and women, as it had sent millions of men overseas to murder, bomb, strafe, and witness death, have sex with local girls who had thrown themselves into the arms of their rescuers, for nothing but gratitude, or who had been sought out by the exasperated, frightened, morally exhausted heroes in a strange land, while their wives, fiancées and girl friends back home pined away with brave cheerfulness, nursed their belief in the goodness of their country's plight, and shouldered the intellectual load of the burden of being clueless to what was happening, all the while hoping that honesty and open dialogue of the horrors their men saw, could repair any broken bond between the psyches of the war-torn couples, and bring healing to an aging society.

Many of the soldiers returning from war were confused and unhappy, not realizing the war had created a nihilist mentality and a certain moral anarchy. The war had exposed a terrible truth about human nature and even the most sanguine were forced to admit that education and cultural sophistication were no guarantee against barbarity.

Not since the religious wars of the sixteenth century had combatants indulged in depravities like those perpetrated by the "civilized" Axis powers. Confronted by the probability of their own deaths, many of these percipient men of that generation killed off those parts of themselves that were most vulnerable to pain, and thus lost forever a delicacy of feeling upon which intimacy depends. To a less tragic extent the women also had to harden themselves and stood to lose with them, the vulnerability that is one of the guardians of the human spirit. The taciturnity of many post war men became a silence held for so long that it could become a material thing, its weight increasing until finally it could not be borne.

The spirit of the fifties was one of uneasy conformity, for many veterans of war, a flight from conflict, a political quietism, the cult of the nuclear family, the embrace of class privilege.

Ryan recalled, as if yesterday, he about to begin his freshman year at Cornell and Colleen a junior at Northwestern, how Walter, holding Mary's hand as the four of them took saunas that summer at the lake, told his two children in the most delicate manner he could construct, of the war horrors he had faced. "Yes, I came home as a war hero I guess," he confessed, "but the unbroken terror of the dreams that soon followed, the faces of the dead, both friend and enemy, were beginning to destroy me and affect my daily life. Two years of this personal hell was enough for me, to finally tell your mother all. The people I killed, the slaughters I had witnessed and taken part in, and the infidelities from the grateful women we had freed, that I had fallen from grace from in war-torn France. I have since come to realize that war was just the finished product of universal ignorance, avarice and brutality."

"After a few days of confusion," Ryan remembered his mother saying, "the grips of jealousy and distrust on my mental health fell dead away, and I told your father, that at this moment, I have never loved you more, once again bathed in that dense abiding affection." In the end, Ryan understood, it had ultimately been all about trust, love's most powerful aphrodisiac. The demonic dreams soon stopped or subsided to such a rarity, that the couple could now live in peace and commitment to love one another. The year was 1950 when Walter had confided to his bride, Ryan mused as he watched his father begin to wind down his phone conversation, and after all it was the fifties that gave the sixties of him and his sister, the idealism, and the search for justice and moral integrity.

Yet Walter Davies continued to perform on the flaming pyre of the values he'd been raised to live and love. Ryan's father had a kind face that bespoke inner qualities, a kind of epiphanic knightliness, which once fastened on an objective would see the struggle to completion, a problem to him being just another opportunity in work clothes.

We are sons of our fathers, Ryan mused, whose life like ours was lived in solitude and the wilderness. We were the sons of our fathers, to whom only we can speak out of the strange dark burden of our heart and spirit. We were the sons of our fathers, and we will follow the foot of his print forever.

"Okay, Chuck we'll set up the drop ship for Wednesday afternoon, good work," Walt said as he cradled the phone and smiled at his second born. "Let's get a cup of coffee in the lunchroom," he suggested, moving around his desk to give his son a hug.

Any opportunity Ryan's father had to get away from his office, he happily took advantage of, for it was an occasion for him to walk about the company and mingle with the route drivers as they filtered in and out from the loading docks. His dad's managerial instincts did not adhere necessarily to a management certainty, the certainty that held a no time to despair mentality over the past, in remembrance of other human beings whose life had overrun. His bottom line had not been ethically and morally neutered, because he cared deeply about values and issues. War had helped to develop his management into a style that tried to encompass all of the human condition. He tried to remain intellectually clear of the worn out idea that every human frustration requires another human being to blame that frustration on. He did not wear his nerve endings on his sleeve and he didn't fear solitude, and a blank page, and an unallocated hour in his appointment book didn't terrify him.

He seemed to know all of his employees' names, even the lowest on the pecking order. To Walter it was truly an expression of an honest form of "noblesse oblige". Others of his peers might practice the art of knowing their employees as pretentious, gross social condescension but that was not his style. The time he spent with labor, kept him in touch with the lifeblood that coursed through the firm helping him to intuitively understand its vital importance. It was certainly Dantesque, Walter always thought that all of who were relegated to the truck and short and long haul seemed to forget the prospect of higher advancement, as he bade goodbye to one of his drivers headed out for deliveries.

"I'm not surprised you called, Ryan, you sensed something awry. Your mom was definitely agitated on Friday," assaying Ryan against some background, some purpose. It excited Ryan even while he worried about it.

"No, Dad, it's not about Mom, it's what I saw driving down the street away from the house as I arrived. It was that license plate that I knew from somewhere, that I had seen before on that black sedan, and then Saturday at the Duncans' party, I discovered that a fleet of those black vehicles, with the VIP plates, were being parked in our local police station's garage."

As he listened to Ryan, and what he had heard from his friend Billy the station chief at the Lake Manoa police headquarters, he knew what the next step in dealing with this long festering issue must logically be. Walter's worst fears were beginning to be confirmed, but again he knew this day would inevitably come, he regretfully reminded himself, but now it had to be dealt with, a plan had to be devised. He and Mary had talked about it and he had turned it over in his head now for nearly four decades.

"Dad," Ryan gently implored, "who was that I heard you and mom talking to all those years ago at the lake?" he asked, replaying the flashback he had at the Duncan party in his head. "I had swum back to the cabin to get the slalom ski when I saw the black car and those plates, identical to the ones I saw on Friday, I'd almost forgotten about it," he bemoaned, pouring out his mind ache.

"What gives, Dad? I want to help if I can in any manner possible." Walter grinned bested, and spread his palms to the sky as he leaned against the loading dock and the sturdy character of the scar-faced loading dock doors, wishing the answer to his plea was as simple as the question.

"Your mother and I knew this day would come, Ryan." Looking at him gravely impregnating the moment with inescapable significance. "And maybe we should have had the fortitude to deal with it earlier, but let me give you a smidgen of the background story."

Ryan watched his father build a mask of quiet concentration behind which, he was certain, his mind was feverishly working, as he now, leaning against a six foot stack of pallets, began a brief synopsis of the historical saga known only to himself and Mary and her mother and father, both long deceased.

"He was the same man, Ryan, that had visited us that summer at the lake in 1963. His agency had a different name then but with the same intents and objectives as today. Your mom was understandably unnerved when he showed up unexpectedly after all these years." Walter began to slowly unfold the tale of Ryan's maternal grandfather and what he had so craftily devised. "It was your mother, Ryan, as the youngest child, that would most likely still be living, that he entrusted with the secret plan, in hopes of ultimately carrying it through."

He stopped his translation of the true life tale abruptly and looked imploringly into Ryan's brown eyes, a noble gesture it seemed, an emblem of moral amplitude, and as agreed to with Mary, asked Ryan to visit his sister Colleen in Evanston for all of the details.

"When your mom was diagnosed, she felt the entire story needed to be finally documented and she sent it to your sister for safekeeping."

"Why can't you give me all the details now?" Ryan impatiently implored.

"I promise you, Ryan," his voice becoming muted by the engine of a sixteen wheeler heading out for warehouse deliveries, "you'll learn the entirety of this matter when all of you together read the transcripts of this family secret with your sister."

As Ryan gazed up at the mid-morning spring sun making its noon time ascent, his father gave him a nudge and walked him away from the loading docks toward Ryan's car. "Oh and by the way, Ryan," his father said to him as he removed an invisible topper from his head, tipping it to him as Ryan opened the door of his Audi 4000.

"Yah, Dad," he responded reflexively.

"Get the business," Walter commanded with a wide friendly grin. Ryan chuckled and gave his father a civilian salute and tumbled into his car. Some things never change, he thought as he backed out of the parking space, looking up briefly, catching a last glimpse of him in the rear view mirror.

His father raised a hand to signal goodbye, just as a cloud passed over the sun, his father's face changed suddenly, now careworn, a gesture that seemed somehow now more tentative and forlorn than Ryan could ever seem to recall him make before. Then Ryan was around the corner and the image of his father was gone, now thinking to himself that maybe there comes a point in life, like a dare line drawn in the dust by a bully, and when we cross it everything becomes at risk. Was his father telling him he was at that point?

Ryan hoped not, as he drove off with an entirely new perspective on what may be looming on life's horizon.

Chapter 5

The gorgeous naked woman in her mid-thirties, who would become a heroine to the Davie's family, stared at herself in the full-length bathroom mirror of the upscale hotel, a block away from the Eiffel Tower. She spun around and examined her backside, looking over her shoulder and then gave the reflection she saw, the reflected image of her compromised virtue, the middle finger.

"Damn it, Bridget."

She was realizing regretfully, that her life had once again seemed to be moving from one vaginal Armageddon to the next. I'm not going to make my body in the service of my ambition, she promised herself fiercely. Never again would she take refuge from the evil troubles of the world, and put her body in service to the prey of exigent men. She thought about that whole argument between evolution and creation. All you had to do, she remembered thinking as a young girl, was to smell in order to understand that Darwin was right; we come from animals. At least men did.

Maybe both sides were half-right after all: men evolved in the sludge and women were created out of the cosmic. The night before, she had left yet another man, foolishly asleep, in the wreckage of his bed clothes. It was a simple exchange: They could enjoy their bodies for this brief time without emotional complications. They were of good temporal use to each other, she thought, feeling the rising tide of good girl guilt cresting inside of her. Neither of them were destined to be the other's answers to the great puzzles of life.

They had exchanged one or two minor, universal, carnal truths. Pleasure was so often more exhausting than the hardest work or a life of dissipation that could sometimes give to a face the look of giant suffering spirituality that a life of asceticism was supposed to give, but quite often did not.

Ah, the penis, it was such a ridiculous petitioner. It was so unreliable, though everything depended on it. The world was balanced on it like a ball on a seal's nose. It was so easily teased, insulted, betrayed, abandoned, yet it pretended to be invulnerable. It was a weapon which conferred magical powers on its possessor. This muscle less inchworm and the Freudian disturbed arrogance of its owner consequently tried continually to bluster its way through life, controlling and thieving everything in its way, stealing mankind's sovereignty.

She was out of bed like a wraith in the darkness and quickly out the door, leaving the man talking to the vague hum of the air conditioning.

Her life now seemed to consist of nothing but some days, measured in articles, opinion pieces, telephone calls and plane tickets. She was disgusted with the way opinion was formulated and merchanted in the world. She was currently covering a series of stories on predatory finance that seemed as antediluvian as a fight between two brontosauri.

Her self-disgust would have puzzled most onlookers however, as it appeared she was endowed with just the right stuff. She was really a paragon of loveliness.

Sophie Nichols was an absolute knockout, full down covered lips, cheekbones to waltz on and dark blonde splendid eyebrows framing dazzling blue eyes, under beautiful blonde hair, that today she decided to wear in a tight disciplined page boy in hopes of concealing some of the drama of her features and good looks. Even as an adolescent, Sophie was physically stunning to behold, a blonde nymph from an ethereal dimension, strong and beautifully proportioned, at once athletic and graceful, yet uncompromisingly feminine. The problem with men, she had learned, was that they were just men, mostly adolescent grown boys. She knew she was handsome enough, with fabulous legs suitors insisted she be proud of.

But she didn't want, and never did wish to be the persona and the voice of a seductress, the figure that drew ogles, so that men, their private parts plump, would fawn and favor her and inadvertently in their minds make possible a fuller and freer realization of her talents and her dreams. She would not ever allow her smooth untroubled face become a passport to tyranny, Hollywood inspired by craven idol worshipers. She didn't want or need their money, and even if she did, she knew you often had to marry them to take the next step up, to enjoy the new found security of their money, and the station they could confer, or enjoy acceptance society gave to such arrangements, except that when trod upon, these "life partners" grew taciturn and unruly, wanting the pleasures of her body, without giving any psychic pleasure in exchange, so that when refused, their passions grew petulant, their entreaties tiresome, their presence wearying.

Beauty did not make her proud or vain, instead it gave her emotional and intellectual energy. No ism, or ist or ology, could tempt her educated mind. No fashionable jargon could lead her into obfuscation, or fad of thinking, seduce her Pulitzer Prize winning intelligence.

"Bridget", was the name given to her by her uncle Henry when she was a young blossoming girl, who claimed her looks and blonde locks were identical to those of Bridget Bardot, the huge international starlet at the time. "Soph", as she was sometimes called, was short for Sophie as in Sophia Theresa Turnbull Borgen. Turnbull was of the corporate dynasty of Turnbull Steel, Turnbull Bridge and Iron, Turnbull Chemical, First Pennsylvania Bank and Trust and other commercial interests founded by her maternal great grandfather.

She got an undergraduate degree in philosophy from Vassar and went to earn her doctorate in history, philosophy and political science from Columbia. It was at Columbia University that she had found the furtive pleasure in her book-weltered cubicle deep in the stacks of Butler library, bound in inaccessibility, in silence; a miner oblivious to the deafening crush of the world, picking at the stubborn rock, picking at the truth, the dense obdurate essence of things.

Sophie's mother was the journalist Ruth Nichols who also had attended Vassar and Columbia, before becoming a journalist in New York. Shortly after college, Sophie took a job working as an assistant metropolitan editor and later the metropolitan editor for the New York Times. She urged her reporters to cover the homeless, the poor and the victims of real estate developers like the Trump family.

The commercial press, no longer shamed into good journalism by the Vietnam War, had less and less incentive to challenge the power elite. Most in the establishment press viewed Sophie's concerns as relics of a dead era. After two years she was removed from her position as metropolitan editor and given a column about New York. She used the column to again decry the abuse of the powerful, especially real estate developers against the poor. The editor of the paper began to refer acidly to her as the resident "Commie."

The city that Sophie continued to profile in her column did not look like the glossy ads in the *Times* fashion section or the Sunday magazine. Sophie's city was one in which thousands of homeless people were sleeping on the streets, and where there were long lines at soup kitchens. It was a city where the mentally ill were tossed on the sidewalks or locked up in jails. She wrote of people who were unable to afford housing and New Yorkers who were being displaced by the greed of overzealous developers. She profiled landlords who charged exorbitant rent that drove out the working and middle class. She had become a pariah.

After her expose of wealthy patrons of the Metropolitan Museum of Art, illegally using their status to obtain custom clearances provided to the museum to import personal items including jewelry which was going to the museum, she was relieved of her column.

She then wrote mostly for left-wing publications. An ardent, self-styled feminist who wrote for the masses, at the *New Republic* and the *Nation*, she eventually started her own bi-monthly paper, the *Progressive*. She came from a family of courageous liberal thinkers. Her paternal great grandfather reportedly lost his life in an underground railway after freeing slaves.

The Maryland and DC political cynicism she had seen in her youth had been her mainstay and the prop of her peculiar brand of defiance, spreading that old, inflammatory – but oh so just – doctrine of land, to those who till it. She, like her mother Ruth, ran on the philosophy and worldview and the utilitarian vision of John Stuart Mill, who defined social good as "the greatest happiness for the greatest number of people". Upon her graduation from Columbia, Sophie had legally changed her name to Sophie Theresa Nichols, that of her deceased mother, after years of argument and discord with her autocrat father.

Her objection to her looks was that it called attention to her, when as a journalist she just wanted to slide into the background. She hated the constant sexual pursuit and being reduced constantly to a cultural stereotype. Even though the lamps in her life seemed to be going out one by one with a diminishing circle of friends, she would not fall prey, she pledged silently, to herself and learn like many of her fallen sisters before her, that the glittering world she yearned to crack was not worth cracking.

Sophie's small office in Paris was located in a suite of offices overlooking the Place Vendome and for about two weeks she had been staying in a small hotel high up on the Ile St. Louis. She was a journalist and the co-owner of the inside the beltway National political bi-monthly known as the *Progressive*, whose ability to create ulcers and torment for the rich and powerful was as notable as was the desperate state of the magazine's financial condition. Her magazine was not at all a puff organ for the plutocracy, as her publications never took on tycoonish submissions from men or women who'd made a pile of money and seemed to think that their wealth licensed them to prescribe for the problems of the rest of the country.

It would be difficult to justify, she often told her staff, printing nostrums written by the very people whose piggishness and conceit had gotten us into the current state of affairs. Sophie's publication was cordially hated and feared in all corners of influence, on the Hill, on Wall Street, The Beltway and the New York law, lobbying and public relation firms, and by the suck up talk show media and anyone else whose hatred was worth earning.

It seemed as though anywhere she went, tyranny surrounded her, taking many forms, like the tyranny of her own routines, her own habits that rose around her like the sides of her own grave. There was the tyranny of the cultural castle where the girl with the golden hair was kept, a beauty set in stone that becomes only a diamond, subservient to the cries of the crows, the customs of society and the demands of decorum and confining conventions, frightening people from their freedoms, beating the soles of their feet till they mince their step in time to the tyrant's goose-wide stride, making men line up as though they were made of tin or lead, tipping over for this week's war. Their lead headed patriotism was petty and bred from hatred, because after all, though war may topple their cows, the tyrant can in any case melt them, these tin-lead men and mold them anew and make their britches fancy, the martial ideology lying over them like a smog that stings any eye that dares to stay open.

She was doing what she wanted to do more than anything else in the world. She was dealing with good versus evil, the ubiquitous dualities. She was delving into why and how to make things right. She was peeling back the leaves of that grand old artichoke, human existence, endeavoring to push for the right actions taken. Justice for the benefit of the most people, not for the few. Sometimes the hunger to seize the heart of it, to know it, would clutch her so she would sit up till the wee hours of the morning studying her current subject. It was like penetrating the darkest continent ever.

The intrepid truth seeker she was, the brave truth announcer, the dauntless Portia striking deadly blows at the malefactors of great wealth.

She always had something deep inside of her that gave her the power to look at the world and know, to see justice and injustice, and feel in her own soul the whip that had been laid on the backs of millions. She was a skeptic in the tradition of Swift and Voltaire, naively thinking maybe we will make a difference, that what we expose to the world will change the world.

She was almost thirty now, and what hadn't been broken inside of her had been forged into a hard core of steely determination. It was her determination, like Thomas Paine's, to create a people's government for the people, a government to see that no man starved and no man wanted, to see that hate and misery and crime disappeared through education and enlightenment, to see the iron grip of organized religion loosened, replaced by a tender deistic creed wherein the brotherhood of man turned its face to the singleness and goodness of God, a creed without hate or rancor or superstition. There would be an end of war, an end of despots. Christ would come to earth in the simple goodness of all men, a goodness she believed in so fervently, all men turning their faces to God, and would never lose sight of the vision.

Sophie knew that was Paine's dream, his conception, one so awful and terrible and wonderful in its implications that he had hardly dared speak of it fully, even to himself. At that time, it depended on too much, the course of revolution in France, and his power to sway men with the written word, the course of the post-revolutionary world in America, and finally, the revolution in England.

Something had soured and tainted so many aspects of American life, an American life that she remembered from her childhood in Maryland as having been fresh and sweet and innocent and altogether wonderful.

American life now was pervaded with a meanness, avarice and incivility. It was hard to put your finger on it, but it seemed like a base brutishness, long appeased by our beautiful nature and comforting geography, had finally shown its ugly greed driven face. Maybe this, that was occurring, is that we were just reverting to base, after a thirty-year post war free ride. We were a country now that seemed uncomprehendingly angry that something had gone wrong for us, and our collective voice sought now to place the blame elsewhere. What sort of country were we?

Sophie mused as she looked out her hotel window at the bustle of dusk traffic along the avenue below, to look for leadership from someone who had emceed a television show, performed ads for multinational companies and shared star billing in a movie with a monkey. Perhaps it wasn't leadership at all that we wanted. It would seem in a nation of two hundred and fifty million people, logic would suggest, sincere in their desire for certified leaders, that we would have produced a few. Maybe we had declined to the point where we gave ourselves what the culture truly wanted, the cottony delusions of the Hollywood actor who now occupied the White House. She could easily see that the rich and upper middle classes were now seething with resentment over protecting their position and were demanding an enforceable mono-ethic which was gradually turning the country into a fascist Disneyland.

As Sophie began dressing, she did a rapid mental stocktaking of the business ahead, strategizing about the upcoming dinner party that William Duggan, the senior director of the IMF and The World Bank, was throwing, when the pink bedside phone chimed with its distinct Parisian tone.

She bore no regret, as she denied receiving the call coming in from Washington DC Better for now, she thought, to keep him mildly conflicted for the game was barely afoot. He had become an aggravating fixation, which was now beyond any sort of therapeutic postponement. I'll take on Borgen and his agents of darkness, she pledged to herself as she viewed her mirrored reflection.

She would not seek the veneration of a bunch of people whose respect she didn't particularly covet anyway, and she would not pursue the perpetual collection of stuff, that especially the young seemed to be doing with grim avariciousness. She would not give him the posterity he craved, but rather at the very least, she would deliver him the kind of cruel permanence of memory he and his agency deserved. She knew her father was always trying to force her back into orbits where she was painfully uncomfortable, as she watched the pink cradled phone finally fall silent. She had come to be nearly dependent on his animosity, as it seemed to define her in a way, and gave her an edge, just as the artist who cuts out ones silhouette from a sheet of black paper.

There would be, Sophie reasoned, small hints of trouble, then a crescendo of small facts and large innuendos, the rumors gathering centripetal force, fusing like blown glass with a core of actuality so that the facts themselves would seem to grow in size and terror. She promised herself to call him back the following day, deciding that if she was to become a sacrifice to his ego she would become a living reproach to him, escalating her resentment into a Jihad, pitting his influence against an existential set of facts. She would swat the patriarchal gnat and be the heroic crusader pitted against massive malign forces, declaring for the one side, the one of just fairness, in the coming internecine fight.

She moved away from the bathroom and carried her worries to the window and looked out at the glistening clockwise flow of traffic lights that circled the Eiffel Tower and the Louvre, shrunken in the heavy grip of her thoughts. All across this city tonight, she thought, women, slaves to their wombs, would sleep in peaceful ignorance of their men's falling from grace and infidelity. She spun through her head how some women were fixated on intimacy as an essential constituent of their unexamined lives, and how men were always slaves to sex, like money, being so numinous, and to that thing between their legs, that twist of flesh and cartilage with its funny nicknames, that boy's toy, that gun, that armed itself and demanded to be shot, and would not abate until it was.

Sophie's meetings with the executives of the World Bank and IMF had proceeded in a predictable manner, with polite give and take between the journalist and the inoculating intonations, the willful denial and ignorance of the international banking cartelists, where successful defiance was not to be tolerated.

She was not at all surprised at the responses she received from some of her questions about the predatory lending practices, the dominion of the few, over the many, that were these trump organizations, acting as world creditors of last resort. She knew she had to suffer fools, in order to harvest material against the day when she would blow them all away to a journalistic kingdom come and tip over their golden rock. Their current practice of lending policies that promoted free and fair trade was being railed against throughout the world, especially in the underdeveloped countries.

They held a craven binary world view of us versus them, a global caliphate, an enslaver of an unseen world, an intimidator culture, an abuser controller class, feeding the visceral needs for imperial expansion, that may have taken on a more cryptic, subtle form today, but it operated ever more diabolically now because of its increasing opacity, operating a control grid driven by a Cartesian worldview that the world has replacement parts, by an ever co-opted and compromised political capital elitist class promoting a command and control system over a market grid of sovereign nations.

It was unconscionable to Sophie, that these men and institutions still remained un-chastened by their continuing misdeeds. These lenders looked upon other countries as England and The Virginia Club of London, looked at the Americas in the sixteenth century: as a corporation first before that of a country. Today Sophie knew well that the weapons were not muskets and cannon fire but the cryptic complexities of tender control of what should be sovereign nations, written into the technical annexes of the credit and financing agreements, a moral syntax that had the effect of slyly dividing, diverging and inoculating motive from action.

The older version of colonialism was fueled by envy and avarice, and it imposed its grim logic: What was ravishing would be ravished, what was captivating would be made captive. The west brought bloodshed and it took root, spreading across the landscape, like a toxic weed, nourished on injustice.

This was merely the new iteration of the age old game being played, where triumph on one side and misery on the other were the only events being played out, nine hundred years since the Norman conquest and the establishment of what was called the crown. Pains, punishments, torture and death were made the business of mankind, until compassion, the fairest associate of the heart, was driven from its place, and the eye, accustomed to continual cruelty, could behold it without offense.

It was a new form of anarchy as old as that driven by the monarchies and kings ever since the Norman invasion, that first begat tyranny and hatred. It was just another centuries old band of robbers parceling out the world and dividing it into dominions, governed like animals, for the pleasure of their riders. It all began when what was first obtained by violence was considered by others as lawful to be taken, and a second plunderer succeeded the first. They alternately invaded the dominions which each had assigned to themselves.

The brutality with which they treated each other explained the original character of monarchy. Then, as it was today, with the new ruffians, being the bands of neoliberal bankers and economists, the new cultural conquerors, who considered the conquered not prisoner, but their property. They were merely the newest reflection of the dysfunctional cultural Calvinistic and Darwinian belief, that wealth is proof of goodness and that goodness then justifies the taking of more wealth.

It was their vision of the truth, offered up to us, as a stuffed bird, not the real world that Sophie knew was given to us in all honesty, given with good intention, given as tradition claims it gives everything, with keen and absolute accuracy and the serene assurance of knowing the truth.

It will not be our world, she opined silently, until it is allowed to live freely, to issue from our mouths, even if uttered poorly, inadequately said, open to the risk of misstatement, or misstep, or error or chance of mind, because we have a right to be wrong and to be mistaken. We have the right to travel the road less taken, the low potholed road of doubt and skepticism, instead of the cultural induced high road of constant assurity and conceit. We have the right to drift and dawdle when called, to dance, instead of marching.

Yet it is our tyrants that are always in need of excuses, inflicting upon us enemies that are always spying, undermining, plotting and arming, in order to seize new ground, inventing new horrors, who, deep beneath robes and undergarments, hold a gun, a knife, a bomb or a book full of dreadful ideas, so as to then develop more sophisticated weapons in their never ending heresy hunt.

It does not matter, Sophie surmised in her soliloquy, what the party motto is, what flags fly, what history pretends to teach, what rewards will be ours, what ill feelings will follow. We need to be free to select our own errors, our own timeless myths, to furnish our soul, as one deems most fit. The World Bank and the IMF worked in concert as unabridged savage capitalists with the multinational American corporations, extensions of the United States Treasury and the CIA, to deepen the dependence of low income countries on the global system and then to open their countries to corporate colonization, feeding the visceral needs for imperial expansion.

It was a model of deliberate economic sabotage, neoliberalism they called it, conducted by the CIA, the IMF and the World Bank. In the early 1980s the politics of the fraud of supply side economics had ridded the IMF, World Bank and other financial organizations of Keynesian economists that had successfully created healthy economies through demand-side policies since 1930. The first step was to coerce a country to sign a plan for economic development, which may include the construction of a dam, airport, factory or other infrastructure. The plan would be deliberately oversized in such a way that there was no hope the country could ever repay the loan.

The country then would be deliberately misled, by overly optimistic forecasts of success and the need for such projects. A few corrupt local politicians and rich families would receive some funds to grease the way for the projects. Once the economic forecasts began to fall short, the country would slide into default on the loan. The World Bank would then force the country to accept austerity measures, which required the government to privatize property at fire sale prices, or grant other economic concessions to American corporations.

Sophie was in Paris to attempt to begin to change a system that now seemed to be beyond control of even those who had created it, and whom it richly rewarded for serving its ends.

She looked again, at her reflection in the full length mirror and all seemed to be as it should be, thighs and butt in proportion and firm, the hair at her crotch shiny and thick, veins tight, upper arms firm with no sign of flab advancing upon her as she aged, all in all giving every indication of making forty, in fighting trim, at least physically anyway. Whether her mind and soul could see her through to the horrors of forty, was another matter.

Dressed now, she took another last look at her mirrored reflection. She had bought her outfit at Kenzo's, a shop across the square from the little office the *Progressive* had rented. She looked charming, in a loose tweed suit and a plain blue blouse, high at the throat and her dark blonde hair pulled back and tied with a blue ribbon in girlish fashion. She hoped it made her look as if she was a sophisticated French woman. She went to great lengths not to look like the pert, mannishly dressed, ladies from New York, Chicago or London who trooped through investment firms peddling stocks, bonds and syndications.

Am I un-American for not wanting to appear American? she asked herself as the elevator rattled its way down. She thought not, especially in Paris. She wanted to be liked and not be too despotic in her intellectual and moral intensity, her endless efforts of cutting edge leather-jacketed righteousness. Yet, she knew she had to join the peerage, in order to destroy it.

Chapter 6

At the kiosk on the corner, she bought the evening edition of the *Paris Match* and the international *Herald Tribune*. She walked briskly that early evening, across the Louis-Phillippe Bridge, the Seine taking on its early spring coloring, more bluer now than brown under the city lights that shimmered above her like dimly lit candles. She cut behind the Louvre, dashed across the Rue De Rivoli, and took the passage through the Rue Des Petit-Champs, where stood the palatial like residence of William Duggan.

As she walked up terraced steps lined on both sides with spring lilies and plants, the thick double doors of the residence in central Paris opened as if on cue and she was greeted with the purchased deference, of one the director's man servants. She was led to a room off the main entryway that was openly intentionally ambassadorial, quickly discerning that the only thing of substance at the party would be the house silver on the dining tables. An enormous crystal chandelier, like a series of icicles, hung from the plaster scrolled and gilt ceiling. The furniture and other objects emitted an odor, a fine lemony whiff of the great European houses with Ducar pedigrees.

Famous pieces of furniture were everywhere, much of it reproduced, museum quality stuff, solid noble English furniture: handsomely tapestried wing chairs and settees, richly adorned fat sofas, finely polished secretaries and sideboards and tables, stately pieces suitable for public moments and private satisfactions of these supposed great people. These were pieces which seemed to speak to each other, like gentlemen in fine clubs in deep secure voices, expressing a considerable pleasure in finding themselves in each other's esteemed company. The works on the dark paneled walls bespoke the pretensions that furnished their Eden. There were reproductions of *Starry Night*, *Café Terrace at Night*, and *Branches of an Almond Tree in Bloom*, by van Gogh; *Garden Path at Giverny*, and *Poppy Field at Argenteull*, by Monet. The adjacent walls were ostentatiously adorned with the art works of Picasso, *The Dream*, and *The Old Guitarist*, and *The Kiss*, by Klimt; *Farbstudie Quadrate*, by Kandinsky and

Persistence of Memory, by Salvador Dali. A hideous fomentation of good taste, Sophie grimly deducted, from a group of evil institutions forcing their debt peonage upon the world.

William Duggan greeted Sophie with debonair style, offering her a crystal of a rich looking burgundy, quickly flitting off, easily moving among his guests, dispensing his presence in precisely calculated dollops of familiarity and bonhomie. After being handed off from here to there, making agreeable noises, where every international dreck seemed to be represented, and to all the World Bank and IMF potentates in their resplendent double-breasted dinner jackets with lapels the width of a promenade deck and their evening female companions, she had already seen enough and began to slyly seek her stealthy exit. She continued to stand around, wincing a little as the drinks began to take effect on the rising curve of conversation, a glass tactfully in her hand at all times, smiling bravely, like a small girl at dancing school.

They were hostages to their own self-indulgence and had a pathological need to enslave. This was the central fact of the divine scheme of things for those with the IMF and World Bank and perhaps her father's agency as well, a modern day colonialism now fueled by avarice and envy. It was a checkerboard earth under which they operated, resources to be taken from others, marginalizing the identities of people from other impoverished countries who once owned it. Grown men, who were programmed never to grow up beyond prep school, who showed off their type. The bravado of basically adolescent boys was about as far as they progressed in the way of personal development.

They were all brains without substance, noise without sound, shapes without forms. They were permitted by their privilege, to act out fantasies with the money of others, corporate shoot-outs, with dollars instead of bullets. Their souls were the color of their money and that was a terrible stain.

Sophie glanced over at an antique chair in which an over-bred cretin from the Bank now sat, his eyes going immediately to her crotch, that thatch of blonde hair that he thought was the banner of her dominion over him. She never regarded that russet between her legs to be her ultimate weapon and she hated having a private personal moment spread out for the delectation of a room full of strangers.

He beamed at her with a knowing urbane salaciousness, licking her naked with his eyes that made her ankles quiver. He was one of those Frenchmen who made you want to firebomb Paris, her mind retching in the thought. She knew he never had fewer than three on the hook and led a fully carnal existence. He was a tomcat she knew reputedly able to produce a dance floor erection on demand. He and the other men like him assigned executive duty with the IMF and World Bank were men who could manipulate a world that believed what it read in the newspapers, and saw on the television screen.

Yet she obliged herself to be as cordial as possible, as there may be a major benefaction in the offing. There was no more energy left for sex in her metabolism and no blank spaces in her appointment books. She certainly was not going to become just another tramp who whether clothed in Paris silk or Odessa cotton housed a merry insatiable brush fire between her thighs in need of asbestos drawers continuously on the make of a parvenu with multi-millions, nor did she want to become the awkward, unsexed woman spayed by hatred.

The circle here, a libidinous wolf pack on the prowl with a testosterone count, the estrogenic equivalent of a Geiger counter, she noticed seemed to increasingly include emotionally late blooming multimillionaires and their young extravagant consorts.

She found them to be tiresome men, all preoccupied with the discovery of sex at sixty plus, grateful to their shopworn child brides, who breathed new fire into their musty loins as they suffered the spending of their millions, by their consorts at a clip and vulgarity that were frightening, with uncomprehending grins, "chicly cadaverous" women who had succumbed to a life of wanting of nothing, looking like retards at an outing. They were all a bunch of crumbs held together by dough. She was introduced to people by various executives of the World Bank and IMF with a faintly discernible pride of possession, as if she was to be admired as a trophy.

She was suddenly presented in front of a young World Bank economist she knew to have been educated at the conservative school of economics at the University of Chicago, who produced the statistical larva who believed themselves to be accumulating an important mass of data from which monetarist truth must emerge.

They were smart enough men, the lot of them, complacently certain, but they held not a lick on Keynes whose economic policies stretched into both Whitehall and the Whitehouse. She was getting the expurgated version now of his life, as he slobbered down his brandy, that she could have cared less about. She reluctantly acquiesced to his demands and followed him to a moist tangle of humanity banging elbows on the dance floor.

As they danced apart from one another, the brandy from his crystal decanter that he brandished at her began to disappear and so too did his hold on logic, pawing at Sophie's bosom when he came in close contact, his lubriciousness so nauseating that any more time near him, she knew, would be like a bath in sludge. Easily able to morph into the role of the ferocious she wolf, she pleaded a plane to catch and quietly but firmly made her discreet exit, turning her drained cheeks to solemn kisses and the press of damp hands, gratefully sighing and heaving and bidding them goodbye, finally, mercifully, taking her leave.

As she washed up readying for bed, the events of the night came back to her in small paroxysms, each jab of memory occasioning her a minor convulsion. This night, she was against anyone with a purpose to declare less important than hers, against any less lonely and beaten than her. The blank soulless world she had confronted after her mother had died in that accident so long ago lay again before her like the limitless unmoving sea. She would have to reconcile herself to it again, finally against her evil unwanton father, to find meaning in it and self-transcendence, to make the leap of faith she knew to be true once more, again.

One way or another, it always seemed possible to her that the world would be ordered to suit her scruples and moral code and become inhabited with satisfaction. In the name of the God of Humanity or some larger idea, a new order of ages would come about, with a true north and south and sides demarking east and west, proper consequences following proper right actions.

A fantastic view of the world she had deduced in college and honed hard in graduate school. If it prevailed, she thought, it would produce its own art forms, its own architecture, its own diet, a new age of enlightenment, she dreamed, as had her mother, the worthy revolutionary against the enemies, that were putting her entire fatuous country to sleep, where everything that occurred in the world seemed to be the predicate to the absolute evil that her father personified, that then disappeared in the way steps do to the front door of a comfortable home. It seemed her only friend was her objective, unceasingly struggling, self.

She could not sleep, her twilit imagination projecting a Dickensian procession on the screen of her mind, coming forward to take a last bow. It seemed somehow, a replay of the jagged jigsaw puzzle dream of her mother standing by her car smiling, all-knowing, then her visage turning into a downcast expression of doom and dread. It was all very well to sit here, swaddled in her fine feelings and calibrated aggrievements and delusions, bathing her exquisite wounds, feelings and sulks with little morsels of Weltschmerz, in her own way perhaps every bit as phony and presumptuous as her step mother, her father's third wife, queening over at her cocktail party dinner table.

She supposed it was really time now that she get her nose jammed up right against the rough wall of reality, like a burglar being frisked, before she could in the end, see the whole picture and understand how insubstantial her frustration and sadness was, that it was more pique and anger than grieving. She realized she needed something created, grown, planted, nurtured and harvested, to right this hereditary wrong, vowing never to obey the powers that be, with the reward of only being obeyed.

Only then, could her moral absolutism shine through and she could feel like a sure small beam of light, in a dark boundaryless world of vaguely defined sovereignties, in which orders were hinted at or whispered from the shadows, where activities and actions were rumored, where nothing appeared what it should be and where everything was quite something else, all involved, being murkily tarnished by other prior acts of complicity and compromise hidden behind a great citadel of prevarication. She finally fell asleep, to an onrush of monstrous dreams peopled with demons, in the swirl of her unconsciousness. Dying men, in the interest of fierce justice, were depicted as noble kamikazes, willing to yield the remnants of their lives, in grand apocalyptic apotheosizing gestures.

Chapter 7

Seven thousand miles west, and four time zones across the Atlantic, Nan gazed out the window of the 747, as it climbed after takeoff, at the beautiful pines and lakes that dotted the countryside, quickly disappearing under the thick gray storm clouds, as she and Ryan and the boys made their fifty minute trip to Chicago O'Hare. It was another run of days, with intermittent gray clouds but now over the western chain of lakes thunderheads were massing, slate and silver. A large storm was moving in from the west and by nightfall, it would be over the entire corn and soybean belly of the Midwest.

Now as the plane banked left and turned to the east the skies had cleared, and the checkerboard mosaic of the fecundity of farmlands appeared from margin to margin of the horizon. Once more, the pendulum of the seasons had swung its mighty ark from harvest and death back to abundance, with the seeds of life, recently planted in the farm fields. The earth, long empty since fall, would soon be teeming with green life, rising again in a life unconquerable.

The Midwest, the consonance of towns, a dissonance of parts and people, and politics. In time the citizens and the cities, even the streets would divide, loyalties, friendships and certainties would be undermined. The cities would be shaken by strife, Ryan mused at thirty thousand feet. Hard rain would fall from formerly friendly places and by people compromised by earthen manna. The impending aggrieved would become ubiquitous, their grief unforsaken forever.

Acres upon acres, miles upon miles, of productive farmland, neatly portioned into fields of corn, oats and soybean farms, cozy and comfortable, homelike, where the farmers loved their land, caressing it, nourishing it as though it were a thing almost conscious. This was the food of the people, Ryan mused, this elemental force, this basic energy, there languishing under the sun, in all its unconscious nakedness, like a sprawling primordial Titan. Then, suddenly the great green blanket of the Midwest became covered by gray clouds.

For most of the trip Ryan and Nan had remained closeted within themselves as they tended to the boys' needs, excitement reigning upon them, in a constant need to always be looking out the window at some hoped for object of childhood angst. Ryan fiddled with a paperback book of Emerson's essays, trying to study it with what seemed like the intensity of a country priest at his breviary. He closed the book on his thumb.

Outside the window, the clouds carved of solid silver seemed to be slowly darkening. The boys watched excitedly between the clouds as they flew over the countryside, as imperceptibly the occasional town became an increasing suburban sprawl, and the sprawl became the city. Moments later the plane dipped below the clouds and sudden swathes of earth and city seemed to press up toward the sky.

They had a Hertz sedan waiting at the airport, and piled their black wheeled bags of polyester plunder in the trunk, and Nan gathered up her ubiquitous black travel bag, slash purse, a shapeless wishing well, from which she managed to wrest whatever item of familial need, medicinal or otherwise, necessary to keep her two urchins in a state of oblivious peace and comfort.

Rain was softly falling, and in the distance a streak of lightning flashed through the sky, followed by a thunder beyond that, that grumbled at being left behind, as Ryan strapped the boys in safely for the twenty-minute drive and the five p.m. dinner at Hackney's in Wilmette, with Colleen and her husband Dan and their two boys Jeff and Tony. It meant for a rambunctious weekend to be sure. Dan and Colleen Kephardt lived in north Evanston, both professors at Northwestern, in sociology and behavioral psychology respectfully. They had a good marriage, stably founded on childrearing, teaching, reading, eating and sex.

The deep fried burgers that the restaurant specialized in were delicious decadence and if Nan partook, it would be a venture away from her vegetarian diet that both she and Ryan had sworn to after their eleven years of marriage, with Ryan only deviating on rare occasions. Nan could just not bear to think of devouring anything that was a living breathing ruminating fellow life creature and over the years the base moral goodness and health aspects of the vegetarian regimen, not to mention the environmental impact, had made a positive impact on Ryan as well. Ryan had spoken with Colleen and Dan earlier in the week and was looking forward to a meal of burgers, fries and the best onion rings in the loop, knowing full well what it might do to his mortality tables.

Between the horrors of bovine methane, the lakes of watershed-devastating excrement generated by pig and chicken farms, the catastrophic overfishing of the oceans, the ecological nightmare of farmed shrimp and salmon, the antibiotic orgy of dairy-cow factories, and the fuel squandered by the globalization of produce, there was little Ryan could ever order in good conscience besides potatoes, beans, and freshwater-farmed tilapia.

You eat a hamburger from a restaurant, and it might have come from a steer that grazed on pastureland cut out from a Central American rainforest. The felled trees mean less forest cover and a loss of species that live in the forest canopy. Fewer trees also mean fewer forests available to serve as sinks to absorb industrial CO_2 in the atmosphere from the burning of coal in centralized power plants.

The resulting rise in the Earth's temperature from too much CO_2 in the atmosphere affects the hydrological cycle, leading to more floods and droughts around the world, a diminution in crop yields and a drop in income for poor farmers and their families. A loss in income means greater hunger and malnutrition for at-risk populations, all of which is traceable to the burger in the bun. So went Nan's refrain.

True to form, both Nan and Colleen watched in amusement, yet with looks of self-reproach on their faces, as Ryan, Dan and the four boys reveled in their lowly victuals, washing them down with cokes, and Old Styles. The girls munched on their salads secure in the knowledge of their culinary integrity, eating nothing of the higher vertebrates.

Colleen and Dan lived in a stately three-storey red brick Tudor, a half block west of Lake Shore Avenue with a nice view of the Western shores of Lake Michigan. Dan was working on his tenured professorship at Northwestern in Sociology and Colleen now lectured just twice a week in the clinical psychology department continuing to work on her PHD. "I'll take the kids up and get them ready for bed," Colleen said as Ryan and Nan grabbed the roll-on suitcases out of the rental and traversed their way up the winding walkway to the heavy oak double front doors.

Ryan prowled about the den and the kitchen while Nan had gone upstairs to help Colleen with the kids, noticing as he looked down at the large rustic pine kitchen table that Colleen had been busy correcting compositions, her papers she liked to call them, taking over possession of them, from the writing class she held at Northwestern, attempting to decipher the spinning synthetic emotions her students brought forth, out of the silky yarn of their intelligence.

"Don't get grease on my papers," she admonished as he was about to take a review of her students' work. These were her papers after all, the only tangible form of her teaching, except for the finished product of the student, but even that is ephemeral he recalled her saying. Colleen held up one of the papers. "You watch your students work in class and you know what they're working on is beginning to take hold, but there is really nothing to show for it, other than this." Ryan looked at the paper covered in red ink. "Bad example but you understand what I mean. You look at the papers and you see what has resonance and what doesn't. It's one visible manifestation of how well you're doing what you do. Occasionally, I'll get a letter from one of them that lets me know I did a good job."

"I wish I could be in one of your classes," Ryan offered, smirking at his sister with an insolent grin. She had always wanted to be a teacher he remembered now. She was still quite striking at the age of forty. Her soft brown eyes were warm and empathetic and her streaked auburn hair that fell to her shoulders was complimented by a face that formed a graceful image, with tight cheek-bones and slightly arching eyebrows that seemed to be perpetually at the ready to pose some deep purposeful question of life.

"I would flunk you for certain." Giving him a stern look that only a teacher could give to a wayward student, waving her index finger in his direction, as her look turned to a smile.

For a while they talked of nothing in particular, their conversational wheels needing greasing, old imprinted triangulations needing replanting. She talked about some of the books she was reading, updating Ryan on some of her friends from college and high school and the general way of her world. Ryan listened as his sister began explaining how researchers in the botany department at Northwestern had recently found that simply going vegetarian would reduce the average American's carbon footprint by more than one and a half tons of carbon per year. This was equivalent to half again more than doubling the gas mileage of ones car by moving from a big sedan to a small hybrid.

She explained that she was currently teaching her class in social psychology, on theories put forward that were now explaining the how and why the warrior mentality came about. It was suggested that with the beginning of animal husbandry, herding and pastoralism, when we started to domesticate large animals that share the limbic or emotional brain with mankind, something birds or reptiles don't have, we developed emotional ties to them. In some cases these ties became so strong that the people were known to die in order to protect their animals.

Building these emotional bonds with cows, goats, sheep, pigs and camels, and then killing those same animals for food, Colleen proffered from the study's findings, required a certain type of disconnected thinking, a break of the bond between emotion and intellect, between seeing another living thing as a fellow-feeling being and objectifying it as an "it", seeing it as just an animal. This learned ability to disconnect, she explained, oneself from the product of mammal-to-mammal killing was, that the emotional psychological disconnect that then led people to more easily objectify and then kill one another, starting around seven thousand years ago with the early forms of pastoralism. This and the development years ago of abstract alphabets and the literacy based on them fundamentally rewired our brains as children, so as to disconnect from the right hemisphere of our brains, where the non-verbal part of the brain exists that process music, relationship based behaviors, and what we would call ones creative efforts.

Ryan chuckled to himself, enjoying the new knowledge that Colleen had bestowed upon him, as his sister padded back up the stairs to assist Nan in dealing with the bedroom parcheesi that would be taking place with the arrival of new house guests making bed time negotiations for the boys.

Looking now at the family pictures displayed along the walls, he focused on his sister's proud face, frowning approvingly at the world beyond the portraitist's camera. He made his way down the hallway off the kitchen looking at the framed family pictures neatly displayed along the walls into the study where Dan sat in front of a flickering computer, plying the web for some deeply nested bit of information, waving him in. As Ryan walked about the study, the sight of the titles of the books that stood at attention spines out on the pine bookshelves it seemed as if their titles flew off their covers and hung in the air like hummingbirds turning the unpretentious room into an enchanted aviary alive with the past.

The shelves were lined with books for reading, not perusal. No bookseller's furniture, no resplendently bound unopened sets of Scott and Conrad and the Victorian poets that usually rest supine, no histories of Northumberland, runs of the *Edinburgh Review*, illustrated memories of long journeys to the deserts of Arabia. These were vessels of the imagination so often rescuing us from daily disappointments, giving us pages of insight, which never settled, to sift our unconsciousness still.

There was a Nonesuch Dickens about half a Trollope in a motley of editions, a few Russians, some Waugh, A.J, of Anthony Powell and Faulkner, more of Hemingway and Fitzgerald, Proust, huge volumes of history, Detoçqueville, the *Federalist*, a clutch of volumes of the Civil War, Macaulay, biographies that ranged from Lincoln to Gordon Liddy. There were shelves of books on current events, mostly of the "what has gone wrong", variety; two shelves of adventure stories, "boys books", with a pine shelf of Henty: With *Gordat Khartoum, Win by the Sword, By Pike and Dyke* and a score more on the shelf beneath them, Conan Doyle, Buchanan, Dornford Yates, Beau Geste, the Sussex Kipling, Penrod and a complete compilation of Owen Johnson: *Stover at Yale, The Tennessee Shad* and all the rest.

There were thrillers and atlases, and reference books, a great deal of everything, it seemed, a good library for voyaging, rich in memories and resounding with potentialities. How delightful it was to be a student, he thought. Men should never cease from studying, from returning to those springs which so intoxicated their youth. For in books there is much wisdom, and there is no end to what a man can acquire in knowledge. All becomes stale and jaded that is of the body, but that which is of the mind and spirit is never satisfied, never satiated, never exhausted. It is as if one possesses eternal youth, for one is always discovering and is always thrilled at some new treasure revealed to him. Every path is a pristine one; it has been touched by no foot before. Every portal opens on a new vista, never gazed on before by another man, bringing to him a unique mind and novel soul.

Ryan looked at the marble statue of Athena, standing quietly majestic, between rows of books on the top shelf. It was given to Colleen, by Walter and Mary, when she graduated from High School. Athena, the Goddess of wisdom, wisdom based on knowledge. But, knowledge is not always wisdom. There was intuitive knowledge, the source of wisdom, and there was objective knowledge, which was a collection of irrelevant facts. The man of wisdom was slow to give opinion, for he must sort out the intangibles. The man who only had knowledge was very rapid in his judgments, for he did not recognize and did not see the vast imponderable forces, which operate in the world. He was dangerous.

Ryan ran his finger along the fading spines of writers and thinkers he studied in college, Aeschylus, Sophocles, Herodotus, Plato, Aristotle, Thucydides, Virgil, Dante, Shakespeare, Milton, Aquinas, Goethe,

Wordsworth, Augustine, Machiavelli, Hobbes, Locke, Rousseau and Tocqueville. Then he saw the two epic poems, the *Iliad* and the *Odyssey*, and he remembered what his professor had said with compelling gravitas about these two classics. They were the seedlings, he had said, from which the great oak of Western literature had grown, and continued to grow, extending branches to each new generation. Though written nearly three thousand years' ago, each poem remained as fresh and relevant as a story in the morning's New York Times. Each grappled with that timeless theme – the longing for home, and the tinfoil armor of manhood.

A number of books sprouted slips of paper. Ryan took one down idly as Dan continued at his computer, plying cyber-space for answers. The book was *The Hart-Davis-Lyttleton Letters, Volume 1*, a book he didn't know of. At the first marker a fine line had been drawn under a comment quoted from Justice Oliver Wendell Holmes, apparently about Virginia Woolf. "It was like watching someone organize her own immortality." On the other page was underscored: "It is not what old men forget that shadows Their senescence but what they remember." Ryan replaced the book as Dan stood up, having apparently ended his cyber-search, suggesting now that they move to the den and decant some rich merlot.

Dan poured a rich looking merlot into the stemmed rounded crystal as Ryan continued to admire the Davies family framed memories that Colleen had artfully positioned around the Martha Stewart styled kitchen laden with stainless steel appliances adjacent to the rustic pine paneled family room. "Here you go, Ryan," Dan said, pushing the glass toward him. "This should help us wash away the Old Styles from dinner." He chuckled, pulling up a chair along the wet bar in the kitchen.

The fire that Dan had terraced with oak in their stone hearth, that was big enough to roast a Volkswagen, began to catch a healthy spark, the flames rose without smoke, sparks flaring up the stubby chimney and into the velvet night waiting to the east. Colleen and Nan escorted the boys down to their dads to say good night.

After hugs and wishes for sweet dreams from their dads, Ryan and Dan watched through the white bones of the bannisters up the stairway at Nan and Colleen as they led the boys upstairs to bed, disappearing heads, torsos, knees and feet as though they were ascending into heaven. The fire in the stone lodge styled hearth was beginning to glow a fiery orange-yellow flame as the girls quietly tip-toed their way down the oak slatted steps, hopefully having read sufficiently to the boys to have induced them into four gold stars of good behavior and an eight hour state of unconsciousness.

Dan poured wine for them while the girls took simultaneous sighs of parent child relief, as they settled next to their husbands on the rich twin leather sofas strewn with woolen pillows woven in reds, oranges, yellows and greens that sat in front of the fireplace, with a large square antique pine low table fronting them. Armchairs and ottomans in rich fabric flanked the sofas, with crocheted afghans lying about. Candles flickered on the pine table and the fire blazed as they folded their bodies into comfortable positions.

"How much of this family secret have you read Colleen," Ryan asked softly, spreading a throw over Nan's blue jeaned legs and his khakis.

"Not a word," Colleen returned, her voice hushed, her soft brown eyes widening, pleading her case. "Mom and Dad said two years ago when they brought it to us shortly after she was diagnosed that it would be best to read it when we were all together. I totally respected that, but don't think I wasn't tempted."

"It's a minor miracle," Ryan said, drinking, widening his eyes, grinning at his sister with adolescent mischief, nudging Nan with his elbow. "You were always the biggest tattletale in the neighborhood," he implored, turning both his palms to the sky.

"Shut up Ryan," Colleen snapped with a big grin, and they all shared a hearty laugh.

As the fire began to crescendo toward warming conflagration, Colleen went to the study, her hands just barely trembling as she dialed the numbers on their secure lead lined safe, low on the bookshelf behind a row of hard backed college texts.

Dan refilled everyone's crystal as the group comforted themselves around the crackling fire. History was now being removed from its sealed envelope, as Colleen slipped on her cheaters and looked into Ryan and Nan's attentive gaze. As she began to read the narrative, the firelight leaping from the hearth vivid and scarlet, profiled her face, hardy with resolution, and Ryan was reminded how she had always been a spunky forthright child and now at this moment very much her family's protector and advocate.

"You look so professorial, sis," Ryan chirped before she started. "Shut up," she barked again back at him, as was her patterned style, ever since childhood, flashing her charming smile, her eyes abeam. That night, she sat nearest the fire, her still young face a sparkle of reflected flame.

And so it began... *To my loving family, this is a true story that Walter and I knew would someday be required to tell.* Colleen held up the first page, written in Mary's perfect cursive form of grammar school black board penmanship.

The first thing I remember hearing as a child was the chilling shrill of the all alert siren at Oliver Mining, warning of yet another mine cave in and the possibility of the deaths of family, friends and neighbors. I can still hear it clearly in my mind today, she wrote, as Colleen began reading page one of the thirty-two eight by eleven pages. *There was never a day that went by, or a minute that passed, when the residents of Everest and the surrounding towns were without fear and dread of the ominous sound of disaster. Over the years, I have absorbed it all inside and out, the lore, the legend, the fact and the apocrypha.*

As his sister paused for a moment the firelight and the candles Nan had lit on the table in front of them seemed to dance together, they sipped their wines and Ryan transported himself back in time to the late nineteenth century and the early 1900s and the history of the Slavic and Nordic European mining cultures. This was the age of the McGuffey Reader type of education, which worked by teaching such subjects as civics, the humanities and Latin and algebra, that taught children to think rationally and logically about problems. This was a time of expanding railroads, widening frontiers, wealth and growth in gold and industry. The age of a new world stretching its young arms and speaking coarsely without much refinement, but at the very least speaking cogently. Into this age came second generation Prussians and Irish, and Czechs and Bohemians and Finns, whose fathers were damn happy to come over here in cattle boats and work fourteen hours a day in mills and factories and mines for more to eat than they ever had before in their lives. They lived lives of unending hard work, the men winning the iron underground, the women raising the next generation. They had strong and smart minds and all on their own had created a culture that made life worth living. They gained hope from nonconformist Christianity and left-wing politics and they were bound together by generosity in good times and solidarity in bad.

Impudent rabble, their employers condescended, feed a dog and he thinks he is a wolf. They were starving in their own countries, and utterly hopeless. But bring them over here, their employers worried, put them to work, put a shambled roof over their heads, pay them all they are worth, and once the edge was off their hunger and they had cleared their mouths of their food, they would begin to yelp for more, just as Oliver Twist had asked for more, full of thunder and indignation.

These men of power, Ryan had come to learn, had either not known of the piteous human desire to be of significance to the world, and to improve it by work and volunteer effort, or they had not cared about it. It was nothing to them that this desire has the profoundest promise of good for the world, a promise of universal harmony and greatness and kindness, and that it had the power to cure much of the sickness and ruin of mankind. The desire may be conscious or subconscious, but it is there, demanding that he believe that he and his efforts are necessary to his fellow men and their welfare. Some, like the captains and the kings of industry, think it very silly, not realizing that it is the only noble thing in man.

How can modern automated industry allow a man, for a single moment, to believe he is of importance and that he and he alone gives some peculiar touch to his work that no other could? Machines had removed the personal joy from handcraft, from individual workmanship and creation. What joy was there in mining or making castings or strips of metal identically the same, at an identical machine, by an identical human robot? When modern industry removed the personal element from its giant shops and plants and factories, it began to destroy man's will to live, which is based on his individual sense of worth. And so, it had laid the groundwork for devastating wars. It was why fascism inevitably led to war. It was the last convulsion of a despairing people. War, in the end, became delightful to people, because war was now the only thing which allowed a man to believe in his own individual importance, and that something depended on him personally.

Mary's narrative began with some historical background of labor struggle in order to better understand those turgid years on the Iron Range. *World War I had been good for American corporations' bottom lines; many reaped fat profits and leaders of corporate America were spoiling for a fight. Prices were frozen during the war and the government seized many corporations for trading with the enemy because of their illegal trade restricting cartel agreements with IG Farben of Germany. Moreover, before the war, corporations had suffered under the great trustbuster, Teddy Roosevelt. Businesses were eager to raise prices once the government lifted the wartime controls. The leaders of corporate America saw themselves as victims of the political atmosphere of the previous twenty years.*

The muckrakers largely fueled the liberal and progressive movements that ushered in the new century. The press had exposed the robber barons and their practices for all to see. The attack on organized capital and the rich elite, such as the Rockefellers, the Morgans and the Mellons was fully justified. Their policies were universally detested by the public.

Corporate America naturally resented the attacks and sought to resume its old methods. Business as usual meant recreating the huge trusts and reestablishing their monopolies. Inking new cartel agreements was merely reinstituting their imagined right to rule the world. The likeness of the cartel agreements to the behavior of the robber barons could not be underestimated.

At the end of World War I, the leaders of corporate America saw two threats to their dreams of grandeur looming on the horizon: organized labor and the Bolshevik Revolution. Out of these threats, the right wing launched one of the most shameful periods of political repression, the infamous Red Scare of 1919. Having experienced first-hand the power of the press, corporate America employed the media in a full scale assault to regain its stature. It used the three most successful propaganda methods ever devised: the dialectical moral relativism of patriotism, religion and anti-communism.

Everyone took sips of wine, as the fire enriched itself as the logs settled in on one another.

It all began with a discovery made by the Merritt brothers of Duluth, Colleen continued, *near what is now Mountain Iron, Minnesota. It was an incredible find, as it lay just under the surface of boggy pines whose roots they noticed were mysteriously red in color. It was sixty-five percent pure iron ore and all one had to do to "mine" was scoop it up with a shovel. It was then and remains today the most staggering largest discovery ever made. It was here that myriads of money making men were scheming, bartering, buying and selling, thinking of new uses for new products to be forged from iron ore. It was the harbinger of death, made into an armor plate for battleships, into the sinister, cylindrical walls of howitzers. Iron was soon flowing in preparation for the doom that was to come for ten million men in World War I.*

Having lived and worked under economic and social oppression for so long and now with certainty of forced conscription of an upcoming war they detected was brewing, thousands upon thousands fled their countries legally, most illegally to a country they heard of that treated its people fairly and paid them a living wage. Many of these men and women found their resting place near the rich geological deposits that had developed over millions of years along the northern tier of states surrounding Lake Superior providing a natural draw to these hard working cultures.

As you know, Colleen read on, your grandfather David Chisholm was the manager at the Oliver Mining operations, from 1918 to 1945. Oliver Mining was owned by Henry W. Oliver the plow and shovel magnate from Pittsburgh. In 1892 Oliver leased the Mesabi basin from the Merritt boys paying them $75,000 in cash. Oliver guaranteed to mine a minimum of four hundred thousand tons of iron per year. With a corking royalty of sixty-five cents for every ton, the Merritt brothers were sure of earning better than a quarter of a million a year, as well as the rest of the stockholders, such as Andrew Carnegie, who ran U.S. Steel, a boyhood friend of Henry Oliver.

David Chisholm had been witness to many mine beam breaks, disastrous explosions of toxic gases and cave-ins burying his friends and co-workers many times with a final hopeless and desperate cry of help. Your grandfather, Colleen and Ryan, lived a hard life as did all during those days of intense iron ore mining extraction. U.S. Steel makes sure they get the most for their money, my father used to say to your grandmother wearily many nights after he arrived home, and believe me my children they did. Your grandfather was a very wise man, and well read. One of his favorite writers and philosophers was Thomas Paine, and I remember his favorite quote that he would often speak to us. "The world is my country, all mankind are my brethren, and to do good, is my religion." Little prickling sensations of enlightenment like dancing points of fiery flame were felt by all, as tears began to form behind the eyelids of Colleen.

"How am I doing so far," Colleen asked, pinching away an oncoming tear throwing her blue jean legs over Dan's. Nan snuggled closer to Ryan as the fire in the stone hearth began to reach the crescendo of an oncoming roar.

In March of 1933, Colleen continued, *your grand-father's dear friend and the on-site mine inspector for Oliver, Henry Theno, came upon something while fortressing beams and closing off an adit along the northeast quadrant nearly a mile deep in the mine that took his breath away. He had taken enough metallurgy classes in junior college to know what he had seen. He had been in this section of the mine before but never down this precariously boarded up spur. He saw veins of precious metals, gold, platinum, copper, and even strains of lithium embedded in the hard rock. It had to be, he told my father, although he still could not believe his eyes. The day of Henry's discovery was March 23, 1933 and on the following day he led your grandfather into the mine to show him the drift and exactly what he had discovered. That was the day David Chisholm and Henry Theno began to devise their ingenious plan.*

With that block of the mine now completely boarded up, not ready for stoping, the blasting and extraction being done on the far southwest quadrant of Oliver their plan was safe for now, from being exposed, with the annual inspection coming as it did every year the week after the 4th of July by the agents from the Bureau of Mines. They understood the action that was necessary nearly a mile below ground.

For the next two months, your grandfather and Henry assiduously went through the land plats of the mining operation and the contiguous land it covered. Mineral rights were separated from surface property rights on much of the private and public land in that region of the state in the 1800s. The state required property owners to file claims for their mineral rights every five years and also imposed a tax on the potential value of those minerals. When the claims weren't filed or the taxes weren't paid the mineral rights could return to the state. U.S. Steel had a seventy-five year leasehold and ownership rights on the property and upon realizing that they had not applied for an extension of their leasehold, the two of them quietly scraped together three thousand dollars and secretly purchased the lease and the rights to future ownership. They registered the purchase documents and lease and ownership conveyances with the State auditor's office using an attorney in Duluth and by June 21 had all the documents registered and safely stored in a safety deposit box at American Exchange National Bank in Duluth.

A glow of new-found energy emitted a calming warmth across the den as Colleen continued, taking a sip of her wine.

This is also a story, Mary's narration continued, *of a multinational company and corporate colonialism with hundreds of millions of dollars at its disposal in the 1920s and thirties, debauching its own workers and their neighbors so that it may make more millions and then purchase the honor of the men they had already reduced to nearly slave labor. Using the weaknesses of human nature, the hard pressure of disease and debt and worth and ambition, The Steel Trust as they were referred to back then, rotted the character of strong and good men until they were degraded into becoming spies at their own workplaces.*

It was in the summer of 1925, he told me, that he first sensed and learned for certain that spies were amidst the Oliver Mines that he managed. The man who directed the operation was named Chauncey A. Peterson, a member of the legislature from Duluth, who had been expelled from the Farmer-Labor party which had elected him, because of disloyalty. Your grandfather further learned through some independent query that he had been "bought" with an office provided for him by the power company.

On June 11, 1925, after serving about a month's "apprenticeship" at fifty dollars a month, he went on the payroll of the Oliver Mining Company at one hundred dollars a month, with the additional job of spying on the Electrical Workers Union No. 31, and the general labor movement while at the same time representing the Steel Trust in the legislature. He later came to learn through his loyal friends working the mine shafts that there were a handful of spies at Oliver corresponding with U.S. Trust agents.

This is the story of some of these men, their co-workers, their families and neighbors and the economic constraint that they lived under. It is the story, dear family, of how all this impacted my family over the years and now has come to possibly impact all of our lives. I want to dedicate the telling of this story to the group of men and women who, despite the deceit that surrounded them in their ranks, the reactionary and dishonest leadership and all the vile power of wealth, were slowly and honestly trying to build a better day, who are known in the organized labor movement as the rank and file.

The United States Steel Corporation America's first billion dollar trust had a far-reaching spy system which was reminiscent of the British secret service stories and the old work of the OSS and CIA. Its tentacles reached into the trade unions back then and got the names of new members long before it was known at union headquarters. It reached into radical organizations and picked the most revolutionary to do its evil work. It manipulated its poorly paid employees with the lure of easy money and if that was not successful, they would find a more potent lure, the forgotten slip of younger days perhaps.

The entire narrative as told to me by your grandfather, Colleen and

Ryan, was so astonishing to me I found it hard to believe and to this day I still have moments of disbelief. But, you have to remember, that this was a time of severe economic hardship on the range all under the control of a company that would not allow labor unionization even after the worst mining disaster in Minnesota took place in 1924 on the Cuyuna Range where forty-one miners drowned in the Milford mine when nearby Lake Foley broke through the underground mine. It should be noted here that this is not a matter of a labor spy detective agency; these were men who lived many years in the communities and who in some cases had grown up with the men they were reporting on. In the eyes of the Steel Trust, there is no radical or conservative, there are only workers who want to unionize and their friends who are U.S. Steel's arch enemies.

The Mesaba Iron Range at the time of my youth produced nearly three-quarters of the iron ore used in America's Steel Industry and Duluth its port was held in the deadly grip of a great fear. Comparable only to the rule of the Czars in old Russia, with their secret police, was the rule of the United States Steel Trust with its network of spies in the conservative trade unions in the IWW the communist party and even the hotels and barber shops. They set brother against brother, neighbor against neighbor, creating distrust and suspicion and hatred and even more an all pervading fear, so that it seemed no miner could call his soul his own.

The Steel Trust as it operated within the Oliver Mines furnished their spies with self-addressed envelopes so that the communication they sent to Duluth could not be identified by the clerks in the small post offices of the Iron Range. The Oliver spy system used three boxes for the spy reports at the Duluth post office where they were collected by a person with the name of Mike Mitchell and then taken to the Trust headquarters at the 507 Lyceum building in downtown Duluth. As soon as the letters reached headquarters, they were turned over to a Finnish man named Gustave Lahti, my father described to me. It was his job to translate those written in Finnish while Mr. Mitchell translated any reports written in Austrian. The reports were then taken to a man by the name of Charles P. Pray in the Wovin building, who was the lead spy in the Oliver operation. Pray would then review them carefully and issue any orders that may be necessary, such as having a superintendent instructed to discharge a man who had been reported as joining a union. The reports were then brought back to Mr. Lahti at the Lyceum building with instructions from Mr. Pray who passed the reports on to the stenographers. They would copy any information about individuals on a comprehensive card index. They would copy activities of labor organizations on a weekly summary which would show everything real or supposed done by individuals and organizations of the Iron Range. Five copies of these reports were then made, going to W.L. Fubershaw, Illinois Steel Company, Chicago; C.W. Tuttle, Carnegie Steel Company, Pittsburgh; Pentecost Mitchell, vice president, Oliver Mining Company and the others would be filed away.

"I'll be damned," Dan declared, all entranced now by the breadth of the story.

"I need a drink," Colleen affirmed as she took a gulp of her merlot, continuing:

The Oliver and the Steel trust knew what kind of men they were dealing with and they did not take any chances by trusting any of them. These men would go about their normal lives little realizing the details that were being collected and charged up against them by the spies in steel. They joined the unions, they went to meetings, participated in parades, were on committees, took part in labor plays, gave gifts to aid other workers who were on strike or to help their own newspapers. These were all innocent acts my father had described, but every one of these blemishes was recorded by the Oliver spy network in Duluth.

When the Steel trust created this department for the production of disloyalty, it did accomplish its end. But, there was one thing my father had told me it cannot do. It could not set a limit on the productive power of that department. Men close to the heart of the spy system who did its work most clearly, who dealt daily in disloyalty came to revolt at their task via the cryptic prodding of your grandfather. Your grandfather once said, "He that taketh by the sword shall perish by it."

The spy system, Colleen continued, of the Steel Trust had reached out for the weak spots of the workers movement but the spy system had weak spots of its own as little known and as carefully hidden as those of the workers. In spite of all attempts to keep them covered there would be an inevitable future. The spies were generally getting a hundred and fifty dollars a month for their work, usually less than four reports per week. The irony of life, which my father tried to secretly point out, for the spies was that if they did their reporting too well and blocked organization and any life of unionizing their value decreased until the time came when their one hundred and fifty dollar salary was decidedly cut or ended all together.

In certain cases men became so prosperous from the fruits of their espionage that they had lost their contact with the workers and had been taken from the payroll for that reason. In other cases it was because they had become known and so lost their value or had shown their friendship for the Oliver spy operation so plainly that they lost the confidence of the workers. When their services were no longer valuable they were off the payroll. That was how much the Steel Trust appreciated its spies underground.

In 1926 the Mesaba Range produced thirty-eight million, two hundred and forty-nine thousand, seven hundred and ninety-three tons in one mine, the Hull Rust, a mine that had been dug in the ground nearly two miles long, a mile wide and seven hundred and twenty-five feet deep. In the summer there were from thirty to forty locomotives and from fifteen to twenty steam shovels operating, handing over ten thousand five hundred tons of ore a day. Hibbing, the largest town on the Iron Range, had to be moved to escape the maw of these giant shovels. One gained the impression, my father had said, that eventually the Range will be one vast hole in the ground.

The Steel Trust was hauling away very rapidly an amazingly valuable natural resource that could never be replaced and which did not renew itself in any way and the people, and the community were continuously being ruthlessly exploited as was the earth itself. To be sure, the most powerful effect of the spy system on the workers was the fear and suspicion it engendered. No one dared to trust his closest friend or his nearest neighbor. The only way to overcome this effect seemed a determination to go ahead with normal activity despite all the spies the Oliver Company may hire.

It was by your grandfather's counter force that he stressed for the workers not to allow themselves to be crushed by the fear of the vicious power of the Steel Trust. It would be only then that all of the Trust's efforts to inspire fear would be to no avail. He stressed quietly to all his workers and friends that the best weapon against the spy system was publicity. Colleen paused with timely dramatic effect at the gathered family now seeming to be in a trance of the tale being woven and continued.

The entire glue of the system will come undone my father had said when the victims know who is doing the spying, where he reports and who his clients are and what he is likely to do and say. When even a part of the system is exposed the rest will become ineffective at least for a time until the rest of the network is exposed!

With that as background let me return to the discovery made by Hank Theno. All had gone according to plan until that fateful day on the 4th of July when the small detonation your grandfather and Theno planned in order to seal off discovery from the mine inspectors, due on site the following week, during the din of the and music of the high school marching band during the 4th of July parade somehow occurred prematurely taking the life of my father's dear friend the beloved Henry Ernest Theno. Henry had gone down into the mine one last time to position the small explosive and set the timer for one p.m., the peak of the holiday parade that Saturday and return to your father's side to watch us all march in the parade. He was a consummate professional with explosives and detonations, there is no way he could have made a mistake such as that, my father would tell me over and over.

To this day as you are reading this, dear family, Wally and I remain unsure as to what really happened that fateful summer day. I must tell you that rumor slowly drifted about town that summer and as my father eventually disclosed to me shortly before he died in 1948, some seemed to affix him as the likely belligerent. Your grandfather entrusted this secret to me only, he said as I was the youngest of his five daughters and one son, the child most likely to live past the period of the leasehold. With my recent clean bill of health over my recent malady however, I am now, we are now, confident of that fortuitous possibility.

The land here, my father had told me often, had betrayed itself, its gnarly topography and wealth of extractable resources had discouraged the egalitarianism of Jefferson's yeoman farmers and miners, fostering instead the concentration of surface and deep mineral rights in the hands of the out of state wealthy, and consigning the poor natives and imported workers to the margins: to logging, to working in the mines, to scraping out pre, and then later, post-industrial existences.

We must now decide as a family our next course of action. With all our enduring love: Mary and Walter.

There was a shared quiet; a silence that seemed to deepen around them, each of them in their own gnawing thoughts, as Colleen finished the last page of the Chisholm family secret, their eyes glittering now with un-spilled tears. They all stared expectantly into the dying embers of the fire that snapped and creaked as if a genie might rise from the low flames bringing them providence and a divine course of action. As the fire slowly drifted into its last crackle and amber glow, they finished the last of their wine. They sat in a common world of wordless silence and reflective repose, hard silence that followed hard truths. The antique grandfather clock of Mary's youth, given to Colleen and Dan as a wedding present, stroked it's even measured rhythm, driving time. As if calling them to sudden attention, it offered three sonorous, individual pellet tones of time.

Colleen and Nan quietly made their way up the steps to check on the boys, four tangled webs in deep sleep, tucking them snug into their twin beds, four beating hearts. They would soon pillow their own heads, beginning the restless dreams of what may lie ahead, sleep sealing their eyes and lips from the contents of their minds, so that they shall not know for a spell what they already knew. Outside, the steady night rain continued, like a lonely drummer practicing his beat long after the rest of the band had gone to bed.

The family succumbed to sleep, wishing as Athena had done when she showered sleep upon Homer's eyes, that it would wash away their family weariness, restoring and reinvigorating, bringing to their troubled minds, what showers do to the thirsty earth.

Chapter 8

He tossed and turned this night and as he slept the dream he had was truly American, so mellow and still confident in this misguided and arriviste nation. It was one of those familiar dreams he had much less now but they never really disappeared from the faded memories of his unconscious. War always took precedence; it seemed nothing captivated in real life or in the dreams of our past like military adventure. For some unknown reason this cosmic vision of the past was different in a vague way that could not be interpreted as he turned again now onto his right side.

They sat in a booth at Emma's saloon southwest of London near the shores of the English Channel two miles from Witham Air Force base. They had recently discovered the pub and immediately fell for its walnut paneled walls and the sturdy eighty foot long bar. The order of four more shots of rye and pints of ale arrived with a generous basket of fish and chips placed in the middle of the foursquare table giving each of 101st Pathfinder groups equal access.

The general had not yet provided any indication of a call to action, as the weather up and down the sea coast and across the channel remained a wet dense and foggy late spring misty chill. They watched the curt cockney waitress with thick upswept auburn hair with a complexion of Celtic ruddiness sway her hips as she padded away from the high backed booth. The young soldiers threw back their English ryes together nervously pondering their upcoming fate.

"Nothing until the weather clears," the oldest of the group at twenty six said to his compatriots. While the others argued over the current baseball season back in the states and the worth of their respective home teams, the elder Pathfinder Walter Joseph Davies strained to listen to the conversation of some officers in the booth behind him. It was pure but fortuitous coincidence but something he had thought he heard one of them say piqued his interest. It was something called the Devisenschutzkommando or DSK, a Nazi network of informers and torturers that were to track down private gold holdings in occupied territories. The stated purpose of the handpicked

SS soldiers was to control the currency traffic across the Third Reich. Its actual purpose, he overheard, was the acquisition of gold by any means, including deceit and brutality. In Paris alone the DSK employed eighty informers, from the lowest levels of society to the highest circles. Victims were lured with supposed sales of property or land. They were then arrested, beaten, and tortured to reveal how they would pay for such an expensive purchase. The illegally recovered gold was then deposited in the account of the German Reichsbank at the Bank of International Settlements in Basel Switzerland.

He continued to attempt to decipher the dialogue as he pushed himself up higher in the booth hoping to catch a better audible drift. He listened carefully hearing a high-pitched rather effeminate toned voice that seemed to dominate the others. The officer lowered his voice now in exaggerated gentility but he could clearly hear now his hushed conversation regarding the acquisitive nature of the war time agency they worked for and how plans had already been devised to advance it to the United States after the end of war.

The war was out there, most certainly, in France and Italy and there in London, but it seemed to these men the war was not the all-engulfing cataclysm it was to the lesser breeds. The talk here was not over whether the gas and ammunition ought to go to Montgomery or Patton or if there should be a diversionary landing in the Balkans, but the gleaming post war world that would emerge after the echoes of the final gunshots had died away. These were the people, his dream was whispering, who would remake the world after Armageddon, not the Churchills or the Roosevelts. They wrote the reports and recommendations that those harried giants would read too fast and act upon. The musty smoke-webbed air of Emma's saloon was heavy with power.

"It's priceless," Walter heard the man with the high-pitched voice say. "It is the first time in recorded history that a military strategy has become the perfect instrument of sound political theory. Our carpet bombing will transform Bismarck's industrial Moloch into a wasteland, which is precisely what should be done, a buffer zone, no longer a menace to Europe or the world. The vast majority of our bombs are falling on the poor. We are wiping out the proletariat at a faster rate, more effectively, than the runaway inflation of the twenties ever did."

Walter turned on his side, but his disturbing dream continued. Maybe they were right after all, somebody was telling him that human history wasn't any more than a reptilian grapple for power, the imposing of will, the inflicting of pain, on the weak and vulnerable. Maybe that's all it was… but he would never believe it.

This sort of operation was not his line of country but his dream seemed to hint that these were confidence men for whom the hyper-activities and energies of World War II would make post war America a little slow and guarded but for whom the sixties when they zapped upon the scene seemed to have been specially designed for.

They, the cold blooded ambitious cherubs with a thirst for empire, would be on the make in a post war world which in time would become ready to be made. There would be no cautioning for these agency men his dream was foretelling during the euphoric days following the VJ Day celebrations, as they set their feet along a path dusted with primrose blossoms and the promise of the financial riches of king cattle and Panhandle West Texas oil and gas.

As Walter began to slowly awaken from his bestirring dreams, he remembered that in pain sometimes we are more alive than in complacency.

All war ever taught was that war was just as unfair as life. Our calling today he could still hear from the echoes of his unconsciousness was like a call of God to Moses: arising from the world's pain it is a call to alleviate that pain by sharing it, and with not so much time in the bud the moment was ripe. "How the mighty have fallen," he said aloud, shaken from his dream.

Walter jolted upright in the king sized bed, a bead of perspiration trickling down his forehead. He swung his feet over the edge of the bed, the stiffness in his lower back reminding him that he was sixty-three and that perhaps all his accomplishments had already been counted and weighed no matter how youthful the song in his heart. He got out of bed now and made his way into the master bathroom. This was all ancient history now, he thought, rubbing the mist of deep sleep from his eyes feeling as remote as the Ziggurats of Babylon, but there was something in that dream he knew he had to decipher from the jagged jigsaw puzzle of unconscious resolve.

In his dream he flew higher on the metaphorical wings of exuberance than any aircraft could ever have taken him. He sighed deeply as he sat on the edge of the bed as if communing with inner truths of unimaginable depth and portent.

It was that voice, why now did it seem so eerily familiar, where had he heard it before? It was resonating with a familiar echo in his head, but where, who, when or maybe it was just escaped him. He nodded prayerfully to the sky as he rose again to splash some water on his face. This may be our last act and as good cobblers we will stick to it, he thought, looking at his reflection in the mirror hoping manfully to convince himself.

When he came back to bed he jotted down some words to remind him of his new war time recollection and proceeded to write down the name of someone who came to him in the dream. It could not be or could it? he spun in his head as he drifted off returning to the muse. But now something was different: the familiar faces from the dream had been sucked back into his unconsciousness; they were lodged in his awareness now and he came to know them.

It seemed in his dream that a mountain was being pushed up and growing beneath him, thrusting and expanding volcanically, bearing him heavenward to questions he didn't know existed with no particular effort or direction from him.

The replaying of the internal soliloquy of his dream portended a Hercules and Hydra confrontation, a Hercules he wanted to presume during this night of restless sleep that still had some significant meaning for a culture that got most of its mythology from gossip magazines. His lips creased into a confident smile as he drifted away into a deep REM state knowing it must be a total obliterating victory and that the nobility of the cause would excuse any duplicity.

Chapter 9

Sophie's estranged and hated fathers had just spoken with his agents via the conference call and the reports back to him and his low profile staff at Ft. Dietrich Maryland were positive on the whole with one troubling exception. There had been nothing whatsoever to report on the Cedar Lake case. Surprised, he licked his lips and ran a hand down his belly. He was jowly, of German descent, with matted gray hair and earlobes that could have held an entire thumbprint. "Where did you put the device," his agent covering the case had asked him.

"Quiet, agent Fisher," the head of the agency snapped back at him vehemently, his voice blasting through the phone line. "Report back to this office in two days on the other cases and drop this case immediately," he firmly demanded with a quick military cadence, slamming the phone into its black cradle.

He slowly and methodically pressed five numbers on the interoffice secure phone network as his hand rose to his breast pocket, instinctively rearranging his bright paisley handkerchief as he spoke. "Yes sir, Mr. Borgen, I'll be right there."

Arthur Borgen, the former OSS officer stationed in London during the war, had been part of a group formed nearly fifty years earlier at the Air Force's RAND Corporation, a think tank in Santa Monica, California. With a graduate degree in economics from the University of Chicago in 1949, he joined a group of future-war strategists whose job was, in the words of RAND nuclear specialist Herman Kahn, to "think the unthinkable," playing nuclear war game strategies and imagining horrifying scenarios.

It was Borgen who was part of a team that helped Wild Bill Donovan start the 0SS and helped Allen Dulles reorganize the CIA after the war into an organization that would match the efficiency of a totalitarian enemy, as U.S. military leaders urged legislation that would mobilize the nation to a state of constant readiness for war. Thus it was the National Security Act of 1947 that laid the foundations of a national security state: the National Security Council, the National Security Resources Board, the Munitions

Board, the Research and Development Board, the Office of Secretary of Defense, the Joint Chiefs of Staff, and the Central Intelligence Agency. Shortly before the act was passed, Secretary of State George Marshall had warned President Truman that the legislation granted the new intelligence agency in particular powers that were "almost unlimited". On June 18, 1948, Truman's National Security Council took a further step into a CIA quicksand and approved NSC 10/2, which sanctioned U.S. intelligence to carry out a broad range of covert operations. The CIA was now empowered to be a paramilitary organization.

Since NSC 10/2 authorized violations of international law, it also established official lying as their indispensable cover. All such activities had to be "so planned and executed that any U.S. government responsibility for them is not evident to unauthorized persons, and that if uncovered the U.S. government can plausibly deny any responsibility for them. The national security doctrine of "plausible deniability" combined lying with hypocrisy. It marked the creation of a Frankenstein monster.

So it was Borgen that had been part of a group of strategists who accompanied FDR to Yalta, Truman to Potsdam and Ike at Pyongyang. It was Borgen while at RAND in the late 1950s who worked with not only Herman Kahn, the model for Stanley Kubrick's Dr. Strangelove, but also with Albert Wohlstetter, one of the early guiding lights of the early neoconservative movement.

While at RAND, Borgen and several colleagues played an important if hidden role in the 1960 presidential election when they served as advisers to John F. Kennedy and devised the bogus "missile gap" which JFK used to help defeat Richard Nixon. Later examination of Presidential archives and other materials confirmed that Kennedy had genuinely been convinced of reports coming out of the Pentagon, particularly the Air Force which was close to the RAND people, that the Soviets would have an overwhelming intercontinental ballistic missile capability over the United States by the early 1960s.

Borgen was also part of the operation run by Dulles and Colonel L. Fletcher Prouty, a career Army and Air Force officer since World War II, to set up the Pentagon's "Focal Point Office for the CIA." This was a network of subordinate focal point offices initially in the armed services and then throughout the entire U.S. government. Each office that he helped Prouty set up was put under a "cleared" CIA employee. Such "breeding" resulted in a web of covert CIA representatives accountable to no one but the CIA, in the State Department, in the FAA, in the Customs Service, in the Treasury, in the FBI and all around through the government, even into the White House. It was these CIA "focal points," as Dulles liked to call them, that constituted a powerful, unseen government within the government, whose Dulles-appointed members would act quickly, with total obedience, when called on by the CIA to assist its covert operations.

When President Kennedy realized he had been deceived, it clearly fostered his deep distrust of the Pentagon and CIA, and he proceeded to cut back the Pentagon's agencies, "scattering the CIA into one thousand pieces," putting Dulles, Prouty and relative minions like Borgen out of a job.

That asterisk on his record burned in Borgen's mind like a brand that fed his hatred, even after he begged his way into a job as an agent for Office of Foreign Asset Control back in 1963 where he had now served as the agency director for more than twenty years, continually being passed over for important jobs in every presidential administration that followed.

The only child of a mid-western minister from Springfield Illinois, he had worked hard to get where he had but in time his hatred had grown to include the entire American business polity where he had been consistently snubbed. Time seemed only to uncover new layers and forms of animosity to provide the basis on an entire geology of ill will. He was better at figures than men, at strategies and concepts rather than souls. His mind operated with a remarkable reductive clarity, but it was a clarity that penetrated institutional structures better than personalities. It could summon up the great determining forces that underlay economies and markets, but it blurred when it came to understanding another man.

He hated anyone who had the luck of good looks and fate had given him plenty of opportunity to practice the emotion. He hated those that could be easily persuasive and had the power of grace and charm. All these could be put down to envy, but there were other more transcendent objects of his dislike, the many of his former colleagues now sleuthing at the Office of Net Assessment, the secretive internal Pentagon think tank that would never return his call and wanted nothing to do with him. It was a protracted act of vengeance on a world that had sold him out that he had acted out now for over twenty years.

He was careful however never to put his feelings on public display, keeping it tucked up in his carapace of ambition and certitude, remaining churchly, upright, square jawed and thin lipped personifying a buttoned up rectitude and optimism that the lesser and the wavering, whether American or heathen, lacked. A healthy uplifting dose of Yankee pride and courage, all the while attempting to remain a cynosure of that world where big decisions and big money were made.

Borgen's desk was a huge mahogany piece, something directly purchased from one of the estates at Mount Vernon or Monticello, and its big surface was polished with such a glean that Matthew Winslett, Borgen's son-in-law, and one of his agents could see the reflected image of his boss's bulbous nose as he stood in stiff still attention above him, the prolonged silence rubbed raw with the sound of the agency director's raspy breathing. Matthew Morgan Winslett had married Arthur and his third wife Audrey's daughter, Meagan, and after finishing up his MBA in three very challenging years at a second tier institution of higher learning, and upon matriculation, joined Borgen's agency as a field agent. Meagan their only child had spent her adolescence as part of the country club sailing set of Bethesda Maryland and had advanced with sublime insouciance to life inscribed by sorority and now lived a junior league existence with two young children she felt somewhat burdened she now had to raise. Matt, a fraternity blind date in college, seemed as equally intellectually challenged as she, as Borgen began to address him, concerned once more about the intelligence dynamics of his controlled asset.

"Sit down, Matt," Borgen barked at him as he pointed at one of his two prized Elizabethan high backed chairs from the sixteenth century positioned in front of his desk. He looked at Matt without exasperation but with an obvious effort at patience like a teacher obliged to take a pupil through an equation over and over unsure whether the student is obtuse or stubborn. Matt sensed his expression and found it maddening wishing he could punch him right in the middle of his smugness. "I have an assignment for you, Matt and you may be away for perhaps a week or more, everything okay on the home front?" he asked with feigned interest. Matt nodded a message that all was fine.

"How can I help, sir?"

"It's one of the asset reclamation cases we've been working on for years, it's an old case that we have resurrected recently and if you can help tracking down some vital information regarding it, you will be richly compensated. I'll give you the brief of the case that you can read on the plane. You're booked on the eight thirty p.m. flight to Minneapolis out of Dulles. You'll be taking a morning flight to Duluth, Minnesota, check into your hotel there and await further instructions."

"Yes, sir," Matt retorted quickly, like one of the overly obsequious labor class, rising quickly with a cadet-like regimen, trying to hide his excitement as he was handed the brief enclosed in a manila folder.

"Have a safe trip," Borgen said, trying to sound sincere as he watched his son-in-law leave the office, shutting the door silently behind him, the meeting now suddenly leaving a bad taste in his mouth that did not easily translate into a rooted interest for his employer.

Borgen then, as if urged by an uncontrollable instinct, put through another international call to Sophie in Paris. No loose ends, he thought, as the hotel operator patched his call through to her room. Keep everyone and everything at the tip of your spear, was what they drilled into him during OSS training in 1940, he reflected, as the call continued with no answer coming from the other end.

As he cradled the phone deciding not to leave a message he felt the all too familiar pangs of uneasiness as it related to his very successful Pulitzer Prize winning first born daughter. She was an entrepreneur, just the like the family dynasty of her maternal grandfather, although the magazine of which she was co-owner was one which her grandfather Turnbull would have shouted down from beyond the grave, with such vehemence, nearly equal to that expressed by Sophie's stepmother, Borgen's second wife, currently in her fourth marital incarnation, from the steps of her great Newport mansion.

CHAPTER 10

Matt's mood was gloomy as he arrived at the Duluth Holiday Inn, so blindly he tried the old remedies of the jogging platform in extenso. Duluth, Minnesota had been called the Emerald City, the Zenith City, the Gem of the Freshwater Sea. It is the world's largest inland port, at one time surpassing even New York City in the oceangoing tonnage it handled. It was built on the hills that rise steeply out of the vast, frigid water of Lake Superior, a beautiful city in a beautiful setting.

This whole business was beginning to make him mentally exhausted and concussed, the orbit of his mind was intimating, as he entered his room, the "knock" of the deadbolt sliding shut making him feel that it was he that was being locked up in a cell for the rest of his life. He had that groping confusion about him, of a man who had been brutally slugged in the base of his brain, and was not yet certain what was happening to him.

He hoped that the forward stretch of unused days would be easing and unburdened by Borgen. He would now seek to disport for a few hours and find some small oasis of warmth and friendliness and familiar things, in the hope of finding desperate relief from all the alien and hostile loneliness of a life which he had entered. For it was a tradition that a troubled man, greatly put upon, and ill-treated, headed for a house of assignation or at least a bar, put his foot on the rail, ordered five straight whiskies in a row, downed them one after another while he stared with uncompromising eyes at the white tortured face in the mirror opposite him, and then engaged the bartender in sardonic conversation about life.

The bar at the Admiralty up the street from the hotel was cool and dark and it gleamed in sundry places like a jewel and it caught the light along its polished surfaces, in its forty-foot brass rail, in the mirror that ran its length, and in the various glasses and bottles that lined the stately counter across its back.

The air seemed to be the color of beer, and smelled of beer, and as he drew a breath it tasted like beer-malted, foamy and thick. Sifting through the beer aroma was an odor of disruption and decay. It was not an unpleasant smell, it was rather like an old forest in which rotting leaves and pine needles and mold refresh your faith in life's endless cycle. There were also faint hints of perfumes and colognes, hair tonics and shoe polish, lemons and limes, steaks and cigars and newspapers, and an undertone of iron ore mist drifting off Duluth harbor. Matt took a seat along the rail smiling a promising smile at the bartender who threw a rag over his shoulder and turned toward him the red candle globe in front of him making amber shadows across his face.

He ordered a double Dewar's on the rocks taking a large initial helping after the barkeep pushed it toward him. He sniffed over it disdainfully, the bottom of his face, mouth and chin blocked out from the mirror by the wall of bottles of Absolut, Stoli and Bushmills and Dewar's and Courvoisier and other darker bottles of Wild Turkey and Canadian Club. "How is it?" asked the barkeep.

"Fantastic," he told him. The barkeep smiled, a sommelier approving his palate, then glided away to serve three men in suits who had just walked through the front door.

Matt sat there and listened to the working men gathered about before the college crew bombarded the place. He could hear the voices of men raised in argument, protest, agreement, denial, affirmation, belief and disbelief, and of skepticism, evoking a ghastly travesty of all man's living moments of faith, doubt and passion.

The landscape at the bar was not gutted with placards and slogans with movements of the way to live now, just beer and bottles of booze stacked along the mirrored backdrop. The forty foot long mirror over the bar was edged with college pennants, UMD hanging in with Minnesota, Michigan, Iowa, Stanford, Nebraska and all the others Matt thought of in an attempt to show how important this little state school really was.

He ran his hand along the solid oak bar top. Three inches thick. It had been given several dozen fresh coats of varnish and it showed. The surface was a tawny orange-yellow, like the skin of a lion. He petted it tentatively and admired the tongue and groove floors, buffed smooth by a million footsteps. Matt found himself talking to himself in the mirror as the bartender who had introduced himself as Carl moved to the other end of the bar to deal with two kids who had produced atrociously ill-forged fake lDs.

The barkeep at the Admiralty looked like the classic Irish bartender, Matt noticed. He was a large burly man just the far side of sixty, he supposed. He had square blunt features under thinning light brown hair fast becoming gray neatly parted high on the temple. His eyes were knowing and attentive with a slight twinkle, not the reptilian glitter one might expect. He had a good firm mouth with a hearty smile not the down turn of a snapping turtle that lips tend to turn into after years and decades of bitter sadness. He seemed strangely to have some sort of mystical manner, the accredited shaman in chief potentate, to be the noblest of men, wise attentive honestly cultivated yet possessed with a compelling measure of theatricality, a bar baron whose role was not one of pasteled mindless affability, imparting the normal sort of Johnny Walker wisdom that usually ran high and vapid.

It was here, Matt reasoned, behind the bar, the only place for a temperate man to be, that the barkeep anticipated spending his yellow leafed years as a Magus, an oracle, a unique combination of Socrates and Nero Wolfe, dispensing miraculous insights and solutions to an avid congregation of inert humanity looking for direction and meaning. He seemed to personify the philosopher King, enthroned in his palace bar among his treasures, receiving his supplicant world, where the habits of his mind could transform others. All in all he had a perfectly friendly inquiring face which, Matt reflected, meant a mask in the case of Arthur Borgen, a screen behind which his sharp devious vicious and maniacal sociopathic personality existed.

Carl had easily observed that Matt was suffering from the duality he'd seen in other young men striving for the top, that vacillation between exploration and preservation that could make one in turns seem a brilliant adventurous foresighted manager or a mangy retrograde feudal relic. He had been at his most Socratic and illuminating, speaking with him during that short time making him a second double scotch, seeming to know him thoroughly in the questions he asked about him, defining the world as he saw it through his learned lens. Matt's mind was centered as he listened to him explain reality, but not the reality with the fanaticized notions of people created by their febrile enthusiasms and imaginations over the years, describing the world's power as an inverted cone where the winds were greatest at the bottom at the narrowest point.

Matt had hung back on his bar chair with his fisted Dewar's, struck dumb by the aura of knowledge that he had walked into, that had left him momentarily to tend a gathering throng at the other end of the bar. He was a hulking giant of a man, and clever, from whose lips an unlit Sobranie eternally drooped. He seemed to have a spectacular capacity of mind to bestow a lifetime of knowledge into a matter of lucidity in moments.

A glow of contentment suddenly settled over him. Carl's Socratic notions were having their effect on him and he hoped that in the end they would find their way to the reach of his outstretched intellect. He was being instructed by this man's resplendent store of mythology and ancient civilizations. This was not the alcohol, he thought, that normally made the trivial seem important, every opinion sound convincing and every truth sound fundamental. It seemed more likely to him that the baggage he had packed for posterity was hopelessly empty and it took a bartender, philosopher, to finally put his nose up against the reflective glass.

As Carl came back down the bar toward Matt he could sense the alluring sense of his aura, smiling in a wistful manner seeming to know of the eternal mystery of everything, at last, knowing from beyond the grave from the other side of some transparent impenetrable curtain. He had a strange ability to find the right denominator, the highest or the lowest with all the stops in between that made all the rest of us just scrabblers in the muck.

Carl Pattison the patriarch of the Admiralty made Matt another scotch, placed a menu in front of him and smiled at his new patron as he saw the new thoughts fluttering over his face like restless moths. Matt had learned that Carl had owned the bar restaurant for nearly ten years, purchased after nearly twenty years of serving as a professor of social psychology and philosophy at the local state university having obtained his PHD at the University of Minnesota in the Twin Cities.

Education was one of the primary problems of the planet, he had said, Matt now spinning it once more in the orbit of his brain, having listened to him like an eager acolyte. The primary problems of the world, he had said, arise not from the poor for whom education is the answer but rather they arise from the well-educated, for whom their own selfish self-interest is the problem. Universities should be communities to rescue us from our bias and self-deception, claiming a lack of knowledge of things makes us collaborators with the forces of evil we condemn. The dumbing down of kids today is the worst form of censorship possible.

We live in an age of moral nihilism, he had said. We have trashed our universities, turning them into vocational factories that produce corporate drones and chase after defense-related grants and funding. The humanities, the discipline that makes us stand back and ask the broad moral questions of meaning and purpose, that challenges the validity of structures, that trains us to be self-reflective and critical of all cultural assumptions have withered.

Carl had told Matt of an essay written by Theodor Adorno in 1967 titled "Education after Auschwitz". In it, he argued that the moral corruption that made the Holocaust remained largely unchanged. The mechanisms that render people capable of such deeds must be made visible, he wrote. Schools had to teach more than skills, they had to teach values, for if they didn't, another Auschwitz was always possible. He wrote that all political instruction finally should be centered upon the idea that Auschwitz should never happen again.

This would be possible, Carl opined, only when education devotes itself openly, and without fear of offending any authorities, to this most important of problems. To do this education must transform itself into sociology, it must teach about the societal play of forces that operates beneath the surface of political forms.

Lost in a drunken revelry and having received the barkeep's pronouncements in boozy stupefaction, Matt ordered the battered Walleye, a basic staple in this region of the country, he learned, with a baked potato and a salad. The scenery at the bar was rapidly changing as the college crowd began to take their presence, charging in by swarms, wild and uncontrollable. It was like the reign of Pol Pot, Matt thought, when legions of ten year olds were handed carbines and put in charge of national security. Within seconds after the college gang arrived in mass, Carl and the other two bartenders were working like coal stokers, fueling the new arrivals and soon the urge to transgress would be busting its borders.

The riot of kids slowly became depictions of pinching and squeezing lads and lasses disporting among topiaries cut in the shape of sexual organs. The college boys lining the bar to his right were busy exchanging their ribaldries and as if anxious to toast his own wit he flourished his glass of Dewar's at them as they prided in discussing their sexual hierarchies of merit. The boys from the university seemed like they were about to pile on their potential love objects as randy as goats. Matt chuckled inwardly as he continued to witness their machinations, all hoping to unlock the chastity belts of their selected damsels who were a far enough distance away from the cash and stringencies of the parental purse.

They were looking for that thread hanging loose that he knew if you tugged just right an entire tapestry of restraint and reserve could unravel. All it takes is the situation, the moment, the man and the right woman, he mused, a thin smile creasing his face. He sat there placidly, trying to absorb osmotically, as if for script writing purposes, the rituals and value systems of these carnally possessed collegians.

Carl now made his way back down the bar to deliver Matt's dinner, nodding toward the raucous college crowd as he placed it in front of him. "Those kids, like most kids, Matt, are a simple lot for the most part, who have been biased by the media to think that everything is black and white which are the primary colors of arrogance and an uncaring conscience.

"The term is called Manichean. You must remember, Matt, the greatest people need to teach people like us the great lesson."

"And what is that lesson?" Matt rejoined gobbling up his newfound delight of the tender fresh water fish.

"It's just that knowing how much you are worth isn't the same thing as knowing who you are. As Plato said," the barkeep offered with a soft philosophic tonality, "what's honored in a society will eventually be cultivated there. And what have we today, my dear new friend?" he asked, turning his palms skyward as he moved along the bar to serve a new flank of the growing crowd.

"Can I get you anything else," Carl whispered past his ear as the bar was now crammed with college revelers, his Buddha-eyes staring at Matt with timeless wisdom and unblinking shrewdness

"I'll have a nightcap, Carl, and then I'll just sit here for a while." Nodding at his new philosopher friend, letting the prior consumed alcohol grease the skids of his unhappiness. "And trouble deaf heaven with my bootless cries." After a long while he finished his nightcap leaving Carl a large gratuity and walked back down the street toward his hotel under a clear black sky with a sliver of a new moon reflecting itself off the bay that fronted the shipping docks of Duluth. He was blown away by his new found local, no ordinary saloon owner, who was a beacon of intellectual rectitude, in a world that considered attitude a substitute for knowledge and opinion as a synonym for fact. He, at last, made his way to his hotel room, and, yielding to his vapors, mercifully passed out on the king size bed.

In the morning after his lubricious night at the Admiralty, Matt's mouth tasted as if the Turkish army had been on field maneuvers between his teeth, and his skull felt like a balloon filled with cement. Like a Pavlovian dog aroused by the bell, he quickly got up and put on a bathrobe, groaning, trying to reconstruct the tangled webs of his dreams. Alone with a hangover like this he was sulky and desperate, a void having been interposed between his eyes and brain. It was as if every one of his senses was pushed dunce-like to a far corner of his hotel room, the residue of his intoxication making his head whistle and buzz, his brain feeling as juiceless as an old sponge left out in the sun for way too long. He found his condition too ugly to merit mourning just as the plainness of a potential female attraction would be too uninteresting to merit affection, as he called to order room service. He passed the morning hours with his breakfast trying to decipher the local and state newspapers in the hedged garden that surrounded his lanai that overlooked the port city spreading out like a visual buffet into the glistening reflection of the azure blue sky onto Lake Superior.

Only as he drained the third fizzling glass of his hangover tonic of orange juice and club soda, did he begin to realize how struck dumb he had become the night before in the face of the feelings that had come unleashed within him like a cargo loosed in the hole of a plunging ship, as he tried to index his philosophical afterthoughts. So many questions now, bouncing like sharply thrown rocks off his brain as sore as an open wound, or was he just having one of those meaningless perambulations? He was suspended in the netherworld of unfocused exhaustion sinking free fall through his morning drowsiness barely able to move.

It was not just the hangover that was grimly imposing itself upon him, but also a fever of revelation, a drug of its own stronger than the Dewar's deluge from the night before. It was a revelation that somehow made him feel strong and emboldened, with a certain calm and peace building inside him that felt as though it could not be turned around.

From these revelations, he thought, perhaps things would come forth? The demiurge, the force of ignorance ridden, under whose power he himself and everyone else could make their blind passage through the outer darkness.

Matt could sense a building of an Othello-like suspicion that had nagged at him for the past few years that now were beginning to demand satisfaction. He made a list in his head of all the basic cuckold emotions, humiliation, vengefulness, jealousy, anger and the urge to destroy. He spun the confrontation scripts in his mind. Maybe he thought that it was best to do nothing right now and let the time and circumstance run the table.

Should he keep an emotional distance and let the future cut its own channels and run at its own pace? He preferred not to throw his disloyalty like dog meat at Borgen's feet in order to bait his ire and retribution. Off with his head would be the sentence carried out if he committed the treason of paying homage to the rival King's court. He could not escape the feeling that something malign was rising up in him, moving slowly toward the surface like a sulfurous bubble in a prehistoric swamp.

"You're entitled to interpret our activities any way you wish," Borgen had growled at him while he was working on an operation in New Mexico, Matt recalled, with a glare he felt that might find its way through the phone line and grapple his neck, using the throaty drawl he reserved only for his gnarliest desperadoes his meaning as obvious as a bullwhip, trying once again to put it over on this imperious kid. Matt had given up a hell of a salient point trying to get his contentiousness into the conversation but now paranoia began flashing a scenario onto the screen of his feeble mind that he remembered from back then.

He was beginning to sense the repercussions of standing against Borgen and his agency. He saw how the power he wielded had its own momentum and was starting to realize their contending resentments, as Borgen lapsed into unexpected vacant silences. Matt had lost the thread and Borgen was becoming successful in shutting down his synapses. "You must understand the reputation of the agency," he had said, "is like any other lens through which people see something. It's only glass, subject to distortion and it may or may not reflect the realities of how we go about our business." He had attempted to ride roughshod over Matt's half convinced demurrals at the time, demolishing the arguments he imparted, while Matt waited until his boss's malevolent vocabulary was exhausted, deciphering that Borgen had turned off his attention.

Matt's mood was restive and febrile and he knew it would be a strange tremulous voice that would make its plea to his boss. He had followed disordered circumstance, coincidence, impulse and urging so heedlessly that the logic of his business toings and froings were becoming vainglorious. He made no sense except as an agent of Borgen's.

Matt would receive his response to his concerns in silence; he was certain, mystical and cryptic as ever, he thought while the hangover banged its base drum in his head. How long must I continue in this man's dotage? he wondered, part of the gentry responsible for this massive hall of mirrors he would ask himself as Borgen blathered on in a hard humorless almost furtive spirit. Listening to Arthur Borgen, Matt would again give no evidence of suppressed contumely and he vowed at least for now that he would not chafe under his servitude, but he was beginning to see himself as what he had become.

He felt a mysterious need to stay by the phone this morning and true to his forebodings the call to his hotel room rang promptly at twelve noon from Borgen's secretary, and his boss was quickly on the line. It was the toast calling the butter knife, Matt being just another parvenu that had been scared out of his own shadow, by the cynicism Borgen used to anesthetize him, rewriting the script of people's lives. His smug contempt and disaffection were immediately evident, the air abstracted and crepuscular.

He was mercurial as always, his obdurance remaining a constant presence, as were his chuckles that were always laced with hints of salaciousness, like bitters in a drink. The solemn assurances he gave to Borgen and his commands were worthy of Dr. Zorba. It was as if a pumice stone had been taken to his mind, yet it wasn't erasing the nexus of pride and tension that had been building in him of late.

Matt dutifully listened to Borgen on the other end of the line, trying to reflect on his father-in-law in the best of terms possible, as the thinker, the contemplative ocular deliberately mysterious, revealing only the corners and the shadowed edges of the large issues and the great matters he manipulated, making sure he reserved any dollops of his suspicion, no tones of disavowal that would hint at any echo of an ongoing argument.

He was told he would be receiving an express package Monday morning and would be contacted some time that day as Borgen handed him back to his secretary with an indifferent dismissive grunt, to get his mailing address in Duluth. Matt gratefully cradled the phone, thanking the Gods that the sounds of the world would temporarily no longer be muddled by his persistent obbligato, feeling a glow of anticipation that he could now spend a quiet un-vexing evening without a quarrel or a silent barrage of recriminations and spend another evening at the Admiralty getting majestically drunk.

Matt felt like a fool. He suddenly had an unfathomable contempt for all those unsavory imaginations roused to concupiscence that reptilian daydreams could bring on by sitting still and staring into space.

The Admiralty was in full swing this Saturday night with the college throng fully enjoying the increasing carnal telepathy of consumed alcohol. The blue collar bars where politics used to percolate seemed to be quiet now because no one knew how to discharge the bile rising up in them.

Carl slid a double Dewar's across the bar giving him a wink and nod as he tended to a group of coeds who had requested fashionable martinis. He sipped his drink and unconsciously reached into the breast pocket of his navy blazer extracting the cocktail napkins he had written on the previous evening, the calligraphy of the notes bearing witness to the suggestion that they had been affected by copious infusions of scotch during his reside.

He doubled his chin looking down at his etchings, new thoughts buzzing about him like fluttering moths seeking a flame.

The sore spot in his mind seemed eased, his hurt self-esteem ceased to throb, as if some magic balsam had been poured into the open wound of his soul. It seemed as if benevolence, magnanimity, Christian charity, uxorious warmth, and human tenderness itself marched in bravely to reoccupy their rightful place in his bosom, all in perfect order and called at once by their right names.

Maybe this, after all, could be an ideal world where love could be spoken by a hand on the shoulder, a fresh drink placed on the bar, or a "good to see you," with tears welling, where what you longed for was universal and constant.

Chapter 11

Mary examined the photographs of her family and a stillness descended as though time was making a brief stop, turning memories over and over as she anxiously awaited the arrival of her family for their week-long Mother's Day retreat. Nothing was left of her mother and father so all she could keep of them was in her mind and she had kept them as one would keep libraries of rare books seldom to be touched but happy to know they had them for needed reference.

The photographs of her ancestral seeds taken from 1935 were now almost umber with age, the bitumen had in some places been completely absorbed by the paper and its edges were crumbling, the snooty patinaed faces, her father stocky and red cheeked, tweeded and flannelled from head to toe as English as plum pudding looking down from the heavily varnished portraits. The pictures of the Chisholm family were always there, a constant remonstrative presence. Mary's mother in the photo was dressed in an undeniable Edwardian fashion, while her father was inclined slightly forward in a pose that was faintly combative on the balls of his feet like a prizefighter. In the gaze he put on the lens there was just a slight suspicion of mistrust.

As Mary wandered over the pictures she remembered back then how she had wondered what the fullness of time would do and how she would look twenty years from then. Mary's father knew that women tended to outlive their husbands and thus were at least actuarially the vessels by which true community could be assured and transferred from one generation to the next. He thus specified that the co-trustees for the life of the Survivorship Trust be his youngest born child and her husband.

There were other pictures of friends and family, earnests of prestige and pictures that represented the intersections of business and pleasure. There was something present in those faces of her family back then that were present in the faces of her family today. They were really a bunch of nice genteel people then and now clinging for survival to a very thin edge of moral and behavioral superiority where the barbarians then and now were piercing the gates. How immensely proud, she thought, with a quiet calm building inside her she could finally be of all that was and all that had become and all the good that hopefully would become.

As Mary surveyed the pictures on the pine decked shelves her mental card file reminded her how much she wanted to ensure that her parental and maternal lineage would hold fast to its ancestral standards, their collective hearts would be like a pallid beach, where their footprints would forever wash away beneath the waves of sorrow that swelled and crashed, swelled and crashed, but like a rock in a riverbed, enduring without complaint, their grace of determination, not sullied but shaped by the turbulence that flowed over them.

She recalled how her father as the Oliver Mine manager had tried to deal with many of the miners' domestic issues, the red veined crusty faces of husbands trapped miles below the earth twelve hours a day, the slurred drunken talk, and the coarseness of mind now finally seeing their lives rendered more tolerable with much blood lost by a union negotiated fair and honest hourly pay rate with health care benefits and a secure pension made available by the pressure they put upon U.S. Steel in 1941.

It was not like Mary had been borne off to the social registry, but she did have instilled in her, her sisters and brother, a genuine goodness and kindness that would always be her anchor to windward, quite naturally, seeing through her thoughtful upbringing the mindless prejudice of many of the elders around her. Mary thought of her father and his character, how he had always been a man of honest dealing in his personal life and in his role at the Oliver, employing at one time in 1935 more than five hundred hard working friends and neighbors. But he had never had his reward down here and neither did Mary's mother, as her family duty dance spun in her head with increasing resonance. Never once as she remembered did her father ever talk to her as a child, always treating her as a young woman when she was with him.

Everything she had learned as a child came from her father and she never found anything he ever told her to be misguided or of no value. But perhaps the things that he and her mother held to be good and right for the time were not yet ready to be accepted. If they were then maybe he carried them out with a bit too much force or with too straight of a tongue, and because of that put men in power who were against him.

"Ah, Mary." She remembered her father's words. "I thought as a young man that I could conquer the world with truth, I thought I would lead an army, an army of newly born conscience, to shape the course of the new world, greater than Alexander had ever dreamed of, not to conquer nations, but to liberate mankind with truth, with the golden sounds of the trumpet's words. But only a few hear the trumpet, only a few understand, and the rest of them put on their Sunday black and sit in the chapel."

Mary's father had found little joy in working in ore that produced iron, for it had no will of its own. It acted as a slave to be mined and ready to be beaten into any shape one pleased, as opposed to wood where you had to work with care and respect and love because wood had a soul and a spirit. With just the slip of the chisel in carelessness or ignorance, one shave too many with the wood's plane, and the work was destroyed and fit only for burning. But with iron you shall beat and beat with only a furied flash of sparks to answer your work. If you make a mistake, back on the fire with it, more into the bellows, but there it is again, poor hard, lifeless stuff ready to be beaten a-more.

Mary's town back then was one cut out of the hardscrabble nature of mining livelihoods that were part of the heritage of everyone's lives at the time. Her old dream spun in her head as a child that had no start or end, where she saw her surrounding land stripped of its skin and bone and laid bare of grass and trees with clearness and immortal truth. As ants burrow, Mary often thought, the working fathers of her friends and neighbors labored far below the earth to bring money to their houses. She saw the owners of the mines keeping more and more for themselves and always less for the men.

She saw the riches of the earth crumble before the miners' picks and shovels and loaders, taken away by the trams on rails. It came to her then, that as with all other things, those riches the earth yielded would have to come to an end. The money would not be paid, for there would be none for the master or man. The loaders and the trams would go to rust, the mines and the pits would be left to flood water and rats and nothing would grow over it to cover our pity and outrage.

While the surrounding area of Everest was abundant with hundreds of pristine lakes that would eventually be part of the federal protectorate named the Boundary Water Canoe Area, the town itself was built on the incline of a steep grade and was very utilitarian in its function comprising just enough of the shared commons to be considered livable and pleasant.

The river, the Kiwishiwi, just a half mile beyond her back door as a kid, was so lovely, so blue and fresh acting as one of the many tributaries flowing north above the Laurentian Divide into the great deep glacial lakes of the region, and would be forever cherished.

It was the river of her childhood, the creek-wise river, the full little river of dark time and reassured history. It was their quiet, narrow, deeply flowing, uncanny in the small perfection of its size, as it went past soundlessly among the fresh grass of the fields that hemmed it with a sweep, a kept neatness of perfection. The river, Mary reflected her gaze now at the shimmering turquoise waters of the bay in the late afternoon sun, was not very wide, only thirty feet maybe, but it ran so sweet and so clear you could see all the dimensions of the rock through the bubbling water and so plenty with fish back then that nobody thought of using a fishing pole.

She recalled fondly how her father had taught them all how to tickle the pike under their fat bellies, quietly working her fingers along until your little finger was inside the gill, giving it a jerk and throwing it flapping on the green clover of the shoreline. She caught two walleye that afternoon if her memory held and she wrapped them in leaves to take home to her mother for dinner, recalling how her mother would put them on a hot stone over the fire, wrapped in breadcrumbs, butter, parsley and lemon rind, all wrapped with the fresh green leaves of leeks. If there was a better food in heaven Mary knew she would be greatly surprised.

She remembered the scent that the wind pushed in front of it those days, coming from the tall white pines, firs and the golden daffodils and all the wild flowers and the sweet grasses that grew along the river banks. The smell was strong that afternoon, as the familiar sweet scent seemed to drift into Mary's senses. Often she remembered her father would stop to breathe in the aromatics, for time after time he would say, that, "Trouble would not stop in a man whose lungs were filled with fresh air, God sent the water to wash our bodies and the air to wash our minds."

Fifty years, she thought. What is there in the mention of time to come and times past that is so quick to pull at the heart, to inflict pains in the senses that is like the stab of a knife. Perhaps we feel our youth taken from us without the soothing sense of the sliding years, and the pains of age that come to stand undetected beside us and become more solid as the minutes pass, and can be firm on an instant, and we sense them, but when we try to assess them, they come back once more in their places ready to meet us in our time to come once more.

Fifty years ago it was, but as fresh and near as the present. No bitterness was in her to think of her time like this. Mary Chisholm Davies she was and contented inside herself, but sorry and uncomfortable for what was still outside, for it was here she knew she had failed to make her mark for her family. It was an age of goodness she knew of her childhood, but badness and evil as well, but more good than bad. She knew good food, good work through the labors of our sweat and the goodness in men and women. But they have gone now all of them that were so wonderful and important in her life. Yet they are not gone, Mary knew in her bones, they are still a living truth inside her mind.

So are you dead, my father and mother and older sister, and all of you I knew, when you live with me as surely as I live with myself. Is her father dead when she still hears the mild thunder of his wise words echoing within her? Are her many friends dead then and can she not hear the glory of their voices in her ears? Is her friend Dorothy Theno dead, perhaps at the hands of the evil Arthur Borgen? It was Dorothy who had taught Mary the strength of hope, as she suffered for many years with her sclerosis, and her father Henry still dead, buried under the ore of the earth in which he worked. Is Socrates still dead when we can still read and hear the golden nuggets of his wisdom?

Are they all dead? Those mentors and friends who gave her so much and loved her unconditionally, the tears now gathering wet on her cheeks her throat choked with emotion. For if they are all dead, she was dead, we were all dead and all sense of their legacy would become a mockery. No, Mary said softly, admonishing herself, no and no again forevermore. But could she be wrong about her mother, could she be wrong about her father? How much of family life she thought could be a vast web of misunderstandings. Was it a tinted and touched up family portrait she gazed at, turning from her view of the bay, to again study the pictures of her parents, or was it indeed an accurate representation of the facts that omits only the essential truths?

As she gazed at her family and the shards of over one hundred years of family history, her mind was studiously attentive to voices no one else could hear and the memories that flowed were instructed not visceral. She thought how happy they were then, for they had a good house and good food and modest employment. She recalled how there was nothing to do outside during the winter at night, church or choir or her readings. But even so she mused how there was always plenty to do until bedtime, if not studying or reading then helping with housework with her mother and sisters or making something out in the back shed.

She could remember no time when there was not plenty to be done. What had happened in the fifty years to change it all? She could recall nothing but death to account for it. Gaslight seemed to make people want to read less, for comfort perhaps, and electric light sent them to bed earlier because the darkness became much dearer. But when did people stop becoming friends with their mothers and fathers and desiring only to be out of the house, going manic with the desire for other things to do, a kind of an asthma that had come upon people with no notion that they had it and nothing to seemingly cure it?

Oh, the dear little house that she had lived in with her four sisters and brother, flashing a visual now back to her as her mother sat in her rocking chair knitting something, perhaps a sweater for one of the children as a Christmas gift, and looked up through the open back door past the fields of rich grasses and flowering shrubs that grew along the shores of the river, her cheeks pink as young roses.

It's strange that the mind will forget so much, Mary thought, and yet hold a picture of the flowers that had been dead for fifty years and more. She remembered the flowers that were on the kitchen windowsill of the white clapboard two-storey home while her mother was talking that morning, and she could still see in her mind's eye the water dripping from the crack in the red pot at the bottom.

She remembered her mother and her superior smile of someone who was ennobled by true suffering, talking of the world that Mary had come to learn that was hidden in every woman's journey of pain, for the words were not easy to tell of, and to use the words that there are is only a telling on uneven crutches. Ordinary things like tea kettles could be talked about because we knew of them and they are tangible and solid and of utility under our hand. She remembered the kettle that always sat on the stove in her home that unconsciously gave her a respite from all the mysteries piling one on top of another, these last days for Mary.

The kettle was black from its utility and work and its puffing black cheeks, at the ready to go about its business any time of the day, with a will and always at its best, waiting only for a pail of well water and a little fire before it would boil and blow and spew its steam. Her mother and father had never taught her to expect too much from life so it was not in her instinct to see each day as an endless parade of unexpected pleasures. She was of course still cautious, but as her father had said with a kind of amazed gratitude, "Enough was as good as a feast."

Mary had always envied the simple life, and then she felt shame for she was a woman with responsibilities, though with little thought of it for so long now, and yet here was a little kettle in her flashback, always doing its job and living its life. A kettle, nothing but a kettle, born in the image of a kettle, constructed perhaps by the very ore taken from the hallowed ground on which they had lived. It was a kettle pretending to be nothing else, and on its purpose every moment, to fulfill its responsibilities as it was created. So long ago it was, but these memories were as fresh and as near as now.

There had been much happiness there even before she was born. In you is my life, the orbit of her thoughts told her, and all the people she had loved were a part of her, and had so long ago gone out of her, to leave her now to herself.

"There is patience in the earth." Mary heard the words clear from her father echoing off the ancient pine studded cabin walls, as if they were spoken, him present standing next to her. "To allow us to go into her, and dig and hurt with tunnels and shafts and beams, and if we put back the flesh we have torn from her and so make her good and strong once again from what we have weakened, she will be content to let us bleed her. But when we take and leave her weak where we have taken she will have a soreness and an anger that we should be so cruel to her and thoughtless of her comfort. So she shall wait for us and finding us bear down, and bearing down make us part of her, flesh of her flesh, with our clay in the place of the ores we thoughtlessly have shoveled away."

Taking a final gaze upon the pictures of her family, Mary did not feel at all smug in her memories, neither smug nor at last snug and secure beyond the reach of others, like one who felt impregnable, with un-purchasable redoubt, praying that she and her husband possessed the attributes necessary to serve and protect the traditions embodied in the faces of her mother and father.

Walter and Mary hoped to personalize those feelings and give them an effigy, poignant and grand like carved tombs in old vast cathedrals. They felt destined to create perpetuities for the afflicted citizenry and the mechanisms of society that cowed them that they might suddenly come upon to know and be awed into conscious transformation.

Chapter 12

Mary looked out the living room window of the lake country home as the impending squint of an eerie thin light of dawn approached. Day break seemed to emphasize a certain strangeness and forgiveness, rendering the night's fears impotent but not forgotten. It looked to be another beautiful day and Mary looked forward to her family arriving in the afternoon. Two spring robins had arrived at their northern Mecca, hopping on the front lawn, their tiny gray beaked heads cocked low to the ground, as though they were listening for subterranean secrets.

The sun that gives without expectation or a possibility of return, its generosity manifest, was a painter's rouge blush on the dawn sky as she opened the front door of the Davies' home on Bearskin Lake and walked down the semi-circle drive to get the newspaper, Gabby at her side frolicking in the grass, barking at scented but unseen dangers, then darting after a rabbit in a frenzied chase, that had just broken from a nearby coppice, bravely attempting to bring it to death and dissolution.

The morning was ghostly, utterly still. In the gradually brightening eastern sky, Mars and Venus glittered coldly in the constellation of Leo. What portents were these? She thought, grimacing her brow. She was happy to be there and watch the banners of the spring season, the greening of the trees and the blossoming that was all around her. She was comfortable at the lake, especially now that she had beaten back the evils of her cancer. It was truly her ark in a sea of turbulence and chaos. She had a wonderful family and wonderful friends and tended her two gardens at home and at the lake, her sturdy peasant love of the earth, which was as close to God as she felt she could ever be.

It was here in the pristine pine wilderness that sweetly surrounded the lakes that the behavior of nature was religiously reenacted. The instincts of the insect or the animal naturally took place. The spider that repeatedly repairs its web, the birds and loons that fly the same atmospheric lines to their former nests, the bears, that slow their blood for winter's slumber and take to bed each recurrent season, the trout and walleye that lay winter low and still in pockets of found oxygen.

The world at the lake resembled the peace of the night sky, all the stars shining together, existing on the same plane, as though painted on a plate, bringing us their light from far different times, thousands of light years away. Awestruck we gaze at them, and we see the mottled past, and wisely try to connect with their radiance to gain sublime understanding. But, the stars may not signify a heavenly society, Mary mused uncomfortably. Maybe the stars or the light we admire in the stars' stead do not constitute a heavenly society, but stand in a vast chill of indifference, and send out for no reason their wholly lonely and utterly meaningless beams.

She had come to the cabin on the lake that abutted the Boundary Waters Canoe Area wilderness, a million-acre non-motorized preserve along the Minnesota-Ontario border, a day ahead of the rest of the family to tend to the domestic requirements of her beloved getaway and prepare for the week-long Mother's Day family reunion. The Boundary Waters had always been her masters, they had surrounded her life. They were the waters of her reality, beyond growth, beyond struggle and death. They were her absolute unity in the midst of eternal change.

Here one breathed hope, as one breathed in the sweet aroma of the pungent pines, with the comforting smells of the sauna fires in the drift of the wind. Indifferent to the illusion of magnitude, Bearskin Lake rightly viewed as vast as an ocean, the pine and poplar woods as inexhaustible as the great continent itself. Here, one returned to nature to become more cultivated and civilized, discarding the crudities that man had created. She recalled what Socrates had said, that the ideal habitat for men was a village surrounded by fields and forests, and never a great city where men could not think among the press of multitudes of other men.

It was here and in the surrounding Boundary Waters Canoe Area, that one discovered the nature was peacefully indifferent, not just to our fate or the fate of the trout, the walleye, the moose or the beaver or bear, or the great northern pine forests, or to life of any kind. Nature here stood indifferent to the indifference of its plundered minerals, to the careless meandering of its streams, to the fecundity of its own mothering nature, allowing man to become the prime suspect.

Here, evil seemed to be remote, no longer the mosaic of petty little pieces placed in malignant positions mostly by circumstances in company with the mediocrity of the bureaucratic mind and empowered by the gunslingers' technologies.

It was here away from the city that grew confusion, madness, disordered imaginings, grotesque forms, perversions, excitements, and fevers, mindless currents of men, upheavals and vehemences. It was here at the lake that thoughts grew large and steadfast and philosophy could flourish as the vine and produce the fruit that gives exhilaration to the thoughts of men. To Mary and her family, it was at the lake that nature held all the manifold qualities of being, a living, loving essence, a natural and national preserve.

It was here at the lake that the themes of good conscience seemed to always drift toward one, as we were happy just accepting the comforting incoming waves from the bay into our receptive shorelines of life.

She walked back into the rustic Lodge Pole Pine logged main house. This was indeed her sanctuary, the picture of her soul, the garment of her will. It was in this pastoral lake-side setting that man was enabled to loaf comfortably through luxurious and indolent periods of their lives. Set on three acres with approximately four hundred feet of shoreline, the four thousand four hundred and thirty-five square feet included five bedrooms and four baths; a chalet front great room with two-storey tall windows, a massive two-sided stone wood-burning fireplace, with five full glass doors that opened to a seventy-foot lakefront deck. An all-wood kitchen with cabinets that were hand-scraped pine, were washed with a light stain to give the wood a golden glow, opened to a great room, dining room and three season porches, all lakeside. The main floor master bedroom with a private bathroom had full glass doors that opened to the lakefront. Upstairs, there was a spacious loft with four bedrooms and a lounge with lake views. The walkout basement had a huge family room, a workshop and potential for more bedrooms. Settled along the lakeshore were four boat slips and a large wood-burning sauna.

Mary grabbed her coffee from the kitchen counter and padded out to the back deck overlooking the lake west, her heart filled with uneasy premonitory misgivings, as she fell into the deep receiving belly of the green plaid divan, giving herself to meditation.

She looked out through the living room window as the thin light of approaching day break seemed to emphasize a sort of strangeness, although she could feel a sense of forgiveness in the oncoming warmth it would bring, like a homemade blanket that could surround you and bring comfort and peace. The day would be stellar, she sensed as she looked out upon the open waters of the bay just taking on the flickering beams of the dawn's light. She stared into her coffee, into the little world reflected on its dark surface. She took a deep healing breath of the fresh lake air, as loons crooned an early season mating call just west of Enchanted Island. She watched as Gus, the local lake trout expert, rowed his boat serenely toward his secret spot, his silent vigil, as the great curve of his fishing line trawled behind him in the great crystalline cool waters, his bait threaded on its hook, in hope of ensnaring, the delectable creature of the fresh water deep.

Mary, the Davies matriarch. Her smile was always tender, her ministrations always fruited with love. All that was Mary was graciousness and serenity, even in the midst of sorrow and suffering. She had never made a vicious remark, never had she been pettish, or disagreeable or mean or small. She had never complained.

She sat in quiet repose for a time as the morning sun broke over the eastern horizon, and placed a glory of red-orange fire beams on the waters to the south of the Davies' lakeside sauna, knowing that this would recharge her, sipping at her coffee, while Gabby combed the docks and the lake shore in search of varmints and any excuse to plunge into the chilly spring waters.

This was part of a world, settled on the outskirts of the Boundary Waters Canoe Area, a federal protectorate that many people had christened as the eighth wonder of the world. It was an enormous place of ungoverned beauty that held an ideal for all seasons. In the summer the lake became a pool of dark coniferous forest poetry reflecting a green palette of deep dark viridian to pale olive of the pointy silhouettes of pines and other trees that bordered it. In the fall it was a time of invigorating walks and boat rides and picking blueberries. It was a season at its best for older people, Mary thought, now gazing out at the eleven-mile long lake fed by seven natural springs, dotted by over fifty islands, for the secure of heart and a spirit for contemplation, rustication and renewal.

The house smelled wholesomely of fresh baked pastry, garden tomatoes and fresh pine-scented lake air undisturbed by fans or air conditioners; old-fashioned spring and summer smells. She rose now to refill her cup, the sitting room now becoming flooded with clear spring sunshine, pausing at the bookshelves along the pine paneled walls that displayed the photos of her family past and present. She picked a framed picture of her mother and father that was engraved with the recumbent C for Chisholm. Mary's mother had always told her that her mission would be the mothering of greatness in her husband and the children she would bear him. Mary was proud of her mother for not talking to her and her three sisters about sex and men in censorious ways, the way many mothers did then and still do.

Taken in the 1930s, she focused now on her father hoping at the very least that she could give him the posterity he hoped for, that she could render him a kind of permanence. She was pretty certain she and the family would be doing the right thing, the only thing they really could do to preserve her family's self-respect. It had taken some doing but Mary had finally been able to subdue most of her apprehensions with Walter's steady hand of assurance, yet she did not want to betray the secret trust he had bestowed upon her and possibly earn her father's eternal glare from beyond the grave.

It was, to be sure, a brave little light she and Walt had secretly harbored all these years, she thought ruefully, yet now right up against it, it seared as painfully as acetylene, still finding it difficult to put aside a foreboding that it was her family's destiny to sacrifice their own children and their families at the altars of a universal indifference that this evil man and his business represented. They would have to deal with the paradox of the favored and fortunate in a world in which no matter how sterling our characters the only mintage that paid the piper was hard cash, so that our talents and moral principles ceased to be strengths and became shackles so that we found ourselves not exalted but enfeebled by our best and noblest qualities, left by the roadside to scavenge among our memories while the rest of life rushed by noisy heedless and hoggish. And yet at the going down of the sun what have you got but more money?

She thought of her parents, and how strong and formative they had been for her four sisters and brother. They had been like rocks in the riverbed, enduring without complaint, their grace not sullied but shaped by the turbulence that washed over them. There was something in the faces of her mother, and father, that was present in all the faces of her family today. How immensely proud she was of all that was and all that had become and hopefully all that would be.

She placed the tip of her finger below the image of her teenage face in one of the pictures, and held it there, as if she was summoning her younger self to return. Her fingers wandered over the images of her family, sliding them clear from one another as she took them up slowly to study them. Her glasses hung at the end of her nose, and her eyes were beady and dark in a face that, although now vibrant again, had dimmed with time, yielding to age.

Life at that moment was an arrested gesture in photographic abeyance. Memories were like running broad jumps, she heard someone say once, a visual and verbal chain of recollection, that took you back only to launch you further forward, as a childhood memory made a replay in her head. They had so many friends in those days and with many friends, so too many bedsides, as she remembered the Sunday calls of courtesy, that Ile De Rigueur of course.

The family was everything in her world in those days and it was everyone's social position, equally secure at the time was the domination of religion, the role of the patriarch, and the fisted grip on ones place as controlled by the Steel Trust. There was the reliability of routines to be admired, and the tyranny of tradition to be wary of, the moral clarity culturally brought about through dogmatism and bigotry, the self-sufficient tillers of the soil and earth, wanting desperately to be independent of the city's sort of world and end being merely indifferent to it, while their own community squelched freedom like the way it squeezed juice from a fruit.

In a small town, nothing was private. Word spread with the incomprehensibility of magic and the speed of plague. Small town Everest, where every whisper was a roar. Her old life had come up from the wilderness, the buried past, the lost America. The potent mystery of old events and moments passed around her and the magic light of dark time fell across her.

The nation was beginning to articulate the engines of war, engines to mill and print out in hatred and falsehood, engines to pump up glory, engines to manacle and crush opposition, engines to drill and regiment men. The coming war seemed to unearth pockets of ore never known to the nation. Beneath the earth's skin the minerals were to be professionally taken advantage of, in the same manner the preachers and priests attempted to mechanize man's soul.

The faint signal awoke him from his dream or was the sound in his head just part of his dream? His eyelids fluttered awake and he arched his ear up off the pillow toward the south of town. It would be the eighth disaster warning at the mine for the year of 1928, now that the mine was operating twenty-four hours a day, six days a week. He listened intently and there it was again, a plain haunting shrill, like a scream in the night, a foreboding sound and emissary of imminent danger and death, the savage, brazen tongue, calling the sleepy town to action. He quietly pulled the bed covers back on his side of the bed and rose hearing the creaking of his knees. He softly shuffled to the closet to begin getting dressed.

"What are you doing?"

"Well, your breakfast," she said, switching on the bed stand light. "For land's sake," she said, seeing the clock.

"Oh Dottie, go back to bed, I can pick something up in town."

"Don't be ridiculous," she retorted, grabbing her bathrobe quickly, tiptoeing down stairs to the kitchen, but not before instructing him quietly to bring his boots and put them on downstairs.

He watched her make her way out the door wondering what she meant by saying that and was suddenly taken by a chuckle of silent amusement. She had looked so stridently serious about the shoes. It was just one of those thousands of little kindnesses that a woman kept thinking of every day in the care of her children. Hardly even thinking, he thought to himself, smiling as he pulled a thermal undershirt over his head. It was practical, automatic, like breathing and they were right most of the time. They're so much in the habit of it that sometimes they can overdo it, but most of the time if you think for a second, before you get annoyed, buttoning his undershirt, there is good common sense behind it.

He unbuttoned the top of his wool trousers, slid them on and tucked in his flannel shirt and sat on the bed reaching for one shoe. Oh, yup, he remembered, and took his shoes and jacket and started to leave the room, noticing the bed covers rumpled and turned back. He put his things on the floor and smoothed the sheets and bedspread and plumped the pillows. The sheets were still warm on her side of the bed and he drew up the covers to keep in the comfort of the warmth, and laid them open a wee bit so it would look inviting to slip back into. He gathered his shoes and jacket and made his way down to the kitchen, making sure he passed the children's bedrooms quietly as he moved down the hall.

She was dropping the eggs into the steaming water. Poached was both their favorite. "Ready in a second," she told him as he popped into the bathroom to shave, wishing for the millionth time they had a bathroom upstairs. Dottie heard the lavish noise of leather and with just a mild catch of impatience turned down the water where the eggs were basting. A few minutes later she walked to the bathroom door. "David," she said softly, "I don't mean to rush you but things 'll get cold."

"I'll be right out," he said, buttoning the top of his flannel shirt, glaring into his reflected weary eyes, making an unscrupulous part in his hair quickly padding into the kitchen. "Ah, dear!" There were poached eggs, bacon and coffee in front of him and she was griddling pancakes as well.

"You've got to eat, David, it'll still be chilly for hours." She spoke in hushed tones unconsciously because of the sleeping children. He caught her shoulders where she stood at the stove, and she turned her eyes hard with wakefulness and smiled. He kissed her richly on the lips. "Eat your eggs now," she said, "they're getting cold."

He sat down and started eating, as she turned to the pancakes. "How many can you eat?" she asked.

"I'm not sure," he said, downing one of the poached eggs, before he answered. He was not quite awake enough to be hungry, but he was touched, and willed himself to eat a big breakfast. "Just maybe two or three," he said. She covered the pancakes to keep them hot, and dripped more batter onto the large pan. She was pleased, not more than half consciously, because it would not be until the afternoon that he would find the time to eat the pasty she had warming in the oven. For that reason she made the coffee unusually strong. For the same reason, she felt pleasure in standing over the stove while he ate, as most mine workers' wives did.

"Good coffee," he said as she turned the pancake. "Come sit down sweetheart," he said.

"In a minute," she responded.

"Come on, I imagine two are good enough." He took her hand and drew her toward her chair. "You sit here." She sat down. "How about you?" he asked, pushing his cup of coffee toward her.

"I couldn't sleep," she said, shaking her head.

"I know what." He got up and went to the icebox.

"What are you, oh no, David, well thanks." Before she could prevent him he had poured milk into a saucepan, and now that he had put it on the stove she knew that she would like it.

"Want some toast?"

"No thank you, dear, the milk just by itself will be perfect." He finished off the eggs, and as she started to get out of her chair he pressed down her shoulder as he rose. He returned with the pancakes.

"They'll be mushy by now, let me." She began to get up again and once more he put a hand on her shoulder.

"You just sit there." Trying to attempt to sound stern. "They look great." He knifed on the butter, poured on the molasses and sliced the cakes in a series of triangles and began to eat them.

"There's plenty more butter," she said.

"Got plenty," he said, forking four pieces and putting them into his mouth. He chewed them up, swallowed them and speared four more. I'll bet your milk's warm," he said, putting down his fork.

This time she was off her chair before he could stop her. "You eat," she said. She poured the white, softly steaming milk into a thick white cup and took her chair with it, warming both hands on the cup, watching him eat. Because of the strangeness of the hour and the deprivation of normal sleep time they were both experiencing a kind of weary exhilaration, they found it peculiarly hard to talk, though they wanted to. He realized she was watching him and looked back, his eye serious yet expressing warmth, jowls busily at work. He was more than full, he thought to himself. I'll polish off these pancakes, he told himself, knowing it would make her happy. "Don't stuff, David," she said as if reading his mind.

"Hm?"

"Don't eat more than you have an appetite for." He thought his imitation of ravenous hunger was carried off with success.

"Don't worry," he said, spearing some more and finally finishing.

Now there was nothing to take their eyes from each other, and yet for some reason, they had nothing to say. This did not upset them; both were experiencing a kind of shyness of the early stages of a courtship. They continued to look in each other's tired eyes, yet their eyes sparkled as the beams seemed to reach into their hearts very distinctly.

"Well, Dottie," he said in his gentlest voice. He took her hand. They smiled very thoughtfully, thinking of the miners working at night, and their families living in the community. They both knew in their hearts now for so long, that there was no need to say anything. The two of them got each other. "Now where is—" he said in frustration. "Jacket," he said, starting for the stairs.

"You wait," she said, going by him with haste. "'Fraid you'd wake the children," she whispered over her shoulder.

She was a bit delayed coming down, seeing that the children were covered, he thought. He stood by the stove idly watching the repetition of dark and bright squares in the linoleum, realizing that Dottie had been right as always, the plain black and white did look better than the colors and all the fancy patterns. He was glad he had eaten all the breakfast at last.

He heard her on the stairs. Sure enough the first thing she said was that the children were all snug and not awakened by the siren coming from the mines nine miles south of town. He got into his coat that she handed him and then she reached suddenly at his heart, that by sheer reflex made him back away, the eyes of both becoming startled and disturbed. With a scowling smile she teased him, "Don't be frightened, it's only a clean handkerchief." He pulled in his chin, frowning slightly as he watched her take out the crumpled handkerchief and arranged the fresh one. Being fussed over embarrassed him and, even more sharply embarrassed by the discreet white corner his wife took care to peep from the pocket, instinctively his hand moved but he caught himself and put his hand in his pocket.

Dottie went to the stove almost forgetting and retrieved the warm pasty, wrapped it in paper, and placed it in his lunch box. After all, she thought, it's going to be a long dreadful day most likely. He put it under his arm. "Thanks, honey." He put his other arm around her shoulder and they walked to the back door. "Okay, Dottie, got to go, that damned mine." She opened the door and led him through to the back screened porch. They walked to the edge of the porch now. The moistures of May had drowned out all but the most ardent stars, and remitted back to earth the sublimated light of their little prostrate iron range town. Deep at the end of the back yard the rich green of the fir trees shone like celestial sentinels. The chilly northern spring air lavished upon their faces the tenderness of lovers' adoring hands, the dissolving fragrance of the opened world, which slept against the sky.

"What a glorious night, David," she said with a sense of dread in her voice that crossed over the back yard like an ominous mist. "I hope everything is all right," she said. They stood for a moment in silence bemused by the depth of the darkness that surrounded them. They kissed and her head settled against him.

"I'll let you know," he said, "as quick as I can, if it's serious." "I pray it won't be, David."

"Well we can only hope."

The moment of full tenderness they shared was dissolved in their thought, but he continued to stroke the round back of her head. He patted her back as they parted. "All right then, David."

She squeezed his arm. He kissed her just beneath the side of her nose and spotted her disappointed lips. They smiled and he kissed her deeply on the mouth.

"All right, dear, goodbye." "Goodbye, my dear."

He turned abruptly at the bottom of the steps. She could hear him walking as softly and quietly as possible in the gravel driveway. He silently lifted and set aside the bar of the garage door and opened it taking care to be quiet. She knew he would try to be quiet not to wake the neighbors and the children but she knew it was impossible to start the auto quietly. She waited with sympathy and some amusement familiar with the habituated dread of his fury and of the profanity she was sure would ensue spoken or unspoken. She finally heard the hrrumph of the engine kicking, and released a long breath very slowly and went into the house.

There was her milk, untouched, forgotten, barely tepid. She drank it all without pleasure. She decided to leave things until morning, ran water over the dishes and left them remaining in the sink. If the children had heard so much as a peep, they didn't show it now. Mary as always was absolutely drowned in sleep being the youngest, as were Lucy, Ruth, Florence and Kate only to lesser degrees. They had scarcely stirred as she adjusted their covers against catching cold. David junior, the oldest at twelve, had kicked some of his covers aside that she quietly replaced.

She quietly entered her bedroom and saw the freshened bed. Why, the dear, she thought, smiling and got in. She never got to enjoy his intention, of holding the warmth in for her, for that moment had soon departed from the bed. She prayed deeply for those working the night shift at Oliver Mine, and cried silently and long, as if she were made only of tears.

Mary's orbit of reverie returned to the present as her muse faded away. The year of 1928 was the worst of all the years for mine disasters, she remembered. They had lost twenty-six miners that year, her friends' fathers, her friends' uncles, her friends" lives destroyed, with no support, no insurance, no benefits whatsoever to the wives left behind in the grips of the injustice of death.

We need a new declaration of conscience, she remembered her father used to implore, for, it is moral authority, that is the source of true power, recalling how her father had been a great lover of Thomas Paine and the enlightenment period. For humans to have a responsible relationship to the world, she remembered her father saying, looking up and to the left where her visual memory was stored, they must imagine their place in it. To have a place, to live from a place, without destroying it, we must imagine it. Mary recalled her father wondering if all men kept a dream within them even to a great age, a secret island where their limbs were free and they looked upon other suns and stared at other moons. If they did not, he had said they had truly died.

Mary remembered the ancient story of creation that her father told. That men were mild and good before the age of iron, which had corrupted them, and the age of gold which followed, corrupted them even more.

War and greed, these were the monster crimes of humanity. The challenge between gods and men would never end, until the gods repented their disgust and hatred and man repented his bestial enormities. Yet, it was rare that the gods intervened in the affairs of man in the name of justice and truth. Like many men of his birth, and station in life, her father was the victim of a fatal fallacy: that the majority of mankind, if given an opportunity, would rise to great and selfless heights, that man was naturally good and preferred virtue to evil, that man's heart was inclined to the noble, and that only circumstances and environment distorted the heart.

Mary was suddenly shaken from the trance of the past by the chimes of the front door bell playing the tones of St. Matthew's Passion. At the door was Lois Anderson Miller, Mary's dearest childhood friend who she had asked to stop by this morning. She and husband Bud, a local attorney, lived year round on White Iron Lake. Lois had met her husband in college and when she brought him up to the great northland and canoe country to meet her parents he knew instantly where he was destined to open a law practice. That was thirty years ago now and having successfully raised two daughters they continued to call the lake region home. Mary had wanted to speak to Lois before all the family arrived, she needed to confide in her and wanted to get her thoughts and hoped for support. Lois still maintained a beautiful physicality with a beautiful dark complexion with flowing dark hair, carrying herself in her tall frame like a queen. She could easily have become a concert pianist but chose to return to her ancestral keep after college and raise her family.

They chatted back and forth with each other in the kitchen drinking coffee as Mary squeezed some oranges for fresh juice and made their way out to the deck. "Thanks so much for coming, Lois. I hope you and Bud can make it for the barbecue and dinner on Saturday," Mary gently pleaded.

"We would never miss it, Mary, you know that. I could sense a tinge of urgency in your voice the other night when you called. Is everything all right?" Mary let go a deep anxious sigh and began.

She and Walt had agreed that Lois and Bud Miller should be brought in on the Chisholm family's secret story, as they were the closest of friends and Bud could quietly manage the legal issues locally if all worked out in the end. As Mary detailed the story of her secret, Lois listened with astonished interest.

"My God, Mary, how did you keep this from me all these years? We told each other everything back then."

"I really wanted to, Lois, but I had promised my father I would tell no one but my future husband," she pleaded earnestly. "Over the years I guess Wally and I thought the whole issue would just fade away."

"Until he shows up at your doorstep," Lois smartly surmised.

"Does that explain Dorothy's death back in the early sixties?" Lois asked upon reflection, Mary's fierce grief over the incident back then having in a normal way been subdued by the press of time and life.

"We're not sure but that was the same summer that he had stopped in to pay us a visit at the lake," she responded, her face looking strangely vacant. "Fifteen million is what he had said to us that day," she whispered as much to herself as to Lois, a look of shocked disbelief shadowing her face. "We wanted you and Bud to know, for if we go forward with the endeavor, we want you dear friends with us, hoping that Bud could handle some of the legalities if we get that far."

"Mary, we would be more than happy, honored really to help, you know that, my dear friend."

"Oh, it's all still very preliminary and remains very hush-hush," Mary exasperated as she took Lois's hands in hers. The two old friends sat in solitude as the morning sun began its slow golden grade toward the noon hour reflecting the deep blue hue of Bearskin Lake. They gazed out over the beautiful calm, while beyond two loons vanished and reappeared in startling aqueous sleight-of-hand. Out on the lake a motor kicked in a couple of hundred yards from shore. A boat began to troll gently, wrinkling the perfect surface, leaving a wake that rolled away from it like a blue silk flag on a listless breeze. The women's faces reflected a resigned composure, yet petrified and abstract, on the threshold of an unimaginable new life challenge.

Across Bearskin Lake through the cedars near the shore, over grass still greening under the May light, came a breeze that smelled of the boundary waters and the northern lakes. Of evergreen and deep clean lakes. Of sun warmed earth, of desiccated autumn leaves, of the cycle of dust to dust. Of things seen and half seen, things unseen but sensed. They were fragrances that had graced the two friends all their lives that had become as common as the scent of their own bodies.

Pay attention to what blows across the water, Mary thought, remembering the old Ojibwa admonition.

Chapter 13

It was an excited crowd of about twelve hundred that had assembled for the noon rally and fundraiser, and Ryan and Nan were honored to be standing there with Winnie and her husband and other close friends as the hopeful new senator prepared to address the gathering. Ryan and Nan stood just off stage left with the Duncans overlooking the beautiful gardens of the landscape arboretum in full aromatic spring bloom. It was the hopeful new senator's idea to run her campaign with a politics of consciousness. No more Stepford citizens. She planned to conduct informative issue to issue discussions with her electorate, to educate first and to win their trust and their eventual vote of confidence.

Ryan and Nan stood arm in arm as Winnie stepped back after being introduced by the former governor of the State and bowed in a genuine display of modest humility, like Callas at her farewell. She was dressed casually in khakis and a navy blue blazer that gave her a graceful understated countenance, holding an inner and outer beauty that radiated warmth and wisdom. She always stood so trim and erect, you had the feeling that all her grace and softness was caught in the rigor of an idea which you could not define. She looked out at the gathering and surmised that all the leading lights of the State's political power structure were in attendance.

She seemed to Ryan to burn with an inner radiance of piety and purpose; as long he had known her she had never been mean or eruptive. She looked like a woman in a kind of waking dream, as she walked out on the platform before she began talking. Her face looked purified, lifted up and serene, like the face of someone who had just pulled out of a hard illness. America preferred its intellectuals to be on the mild side, better an Einstein than a Beethoven. It would be her voice, the voice of an ever vigilant social conscience, born of but not enabled by background to impart a new form of transcendent knowledge and awakening. She saw clearly and saw it whole. She was an intellectual ocean whose waves touched every shore of thought. It was as if she could sell rain or moonbeams or leftover wind. She would be a beautiful testament, Ryan and Nan and all her friends hoped, to the transforming power of martyrdom and the pursuit of truth, the transformation of the heart and mind.

She was here to give politics, at least her politics, a new reality, not the politics of wealth that seemed to license many of those in Washington today, to prescribe for the problems of the rest of us, but the politics of new moral dimension, a political philosophy of moral suasion. It was a process of alteration of the public mind, attempting to puzzle its way out of its own shadows moving from unlearned certainty to thoughtful reconsideration to clarifying self-knowledge. It was the act and the task of clarifying that was the ultimate challenge, the challenge to change the power of what is. It was part of her campaign strategy not to convince the electorate that all you needed to know about a candidate could be done in half a minute, the speed not of thought, but of emotion, the media being the message was the gnomic injunction.

Rather, her strategy was to push the buttons of the reading public, and bring the public that wished to be informed baying forward. Winnie and her husband and her staff hoped to find those to whom truth and beauty were after all quantifiable and not merely empty abstractions. She would most assuredly infuse those lower subjects of humankind, the necessitous man, with a wonderful sense of larger meaning, finding them in her conversations with highly serviceable metaphors for more significant considerations in our culture's conscience, knowing that the most indisputable tenet of public speaking was that it was not what you said but what your audience heard.

Winnie didn't have any impoverished lower-caste history to worry about sinking back into, which paradoxically gave her immense strength and popularity with her egalitarian proposals for justice and fairness. She realized how these days in Washington its influence could make a cur out of the finest bred greyhound. She swore privately and publicly that this would never ever happen to her. She sincerely believed that the jam belonged on the lowest shelf where everyone had a chance to reach it. She had seen first-hand the suffering of others at the hands of the clever, exigent and ruthless, and had the highest regard and appreciation of those who were kind and pure of heart and generous. Kindness to her was more than beauty, gentleness more than elegance and clarity nobler than breeding.

Winnie was building up a strong following and importantly she wasn't malleable like most politicians who were possessed of their infinite self-importance. She was proud of her friends in high places but she was not dependent on them for direction. She avoided the gossip in her business, instead, taking on the issues with a sensible clarity that rankled some but was revered by most. She instinctively understood that gossip wasn't just gossip anymore and hadn't been for a long time. It had become part of public relations and all the vacuous goings on had become part of a public bulletin board of trivialities.

Winnie had a philosophy of the everyman that she religiously held to, and she would be fighting against a culture of people who could have all the money in the world, where all they do is end up at the expensive tables in the spotlight looking somewhat ridiculous in tuxes and five thousand dollar evening dresses with paid for friends.

Her language was not of the lowborn, the gawky servant of thought and feeling. It was needed thought, prescient perception, and feeling. The shape of her sentences, were a song in its syllables, the rhythm of the movement was a movement to move the imagination.

Her own past had taught her how imprisoned much of the middle class could be, especially women, incarcerated in existences, indentured to cleaning and car pools and junk food nights in front of the television. She knew all there was to be to know of her female electorate and the mandated necessaries of both the inner and outer woman. She would not attempt to diffuse a difficult question or a loaded situation with amiable boobery or by reaching into the deep resources of feigned jocularity like her male competition for the senate seat. Above all, her issue to issue campaign had a point of view and was highly learned and educational as well. She knew she would be fighting a political nexus in thrall to craven wealthy interests and outdated ideas. She also knew the stark reality that confronted her successful efforts, that no money meant no way.

She was going up against the paradoxical notion on the right that said no government was good government, and the current president and his partiality for cracker barrel anachronisms and intellectual simplicity. America had compliantly watched this president and his administration paper over scandal, racism, economic bigotry, spiritual decrepitude and hypocrisy.

Winnie had ingrained an ideology within her politic that deplored the nation's economic divisiveness, that despised the speculative fads and furies developed and unleashed by Wall Street's geniuses of paper storms which had deflected the nation's creative fiscal energies and resources into eddying useless channels. It was rather surprising that the only adverse reaction so far to her campaign agenda, speeches and meetings, had been a mere spate of editorial small arms fire.

After the healthy ovation finally subsided, Winnie stepped to the podium, brushed her light brown shoulder length hair behind her right ear, her face radiant with fervor, with the light of her dedicated and unselfish spirit, as she thanked everyone for coming, and began. Nan moved closer to Ryan as if pressed close by the weight of the crowd, and put her arm through Ryan's.

"Our early American leaders all read Montesquieu who wisely differentiated between the three forms of government rules: despotism, monarchy and democracy. He discovered one governing principle for each. For despotism it was fear, for monarchy it was honor and for democracy it was virtue. Freedom and democracy were practically synonymous with virtue. In my opinion, we do not produce leaders like our founding fathers that established our constitution as a sacred and principled document. As Plato said, 'what is honored in a society will be cultivated there'. We idolize our wonderful athletes." Winnie paused for a second and offered a "Go Vikings" chant that seemed to clear the atmosphere of any residual misgivings with a prolonged roar of cheer and laughter. "But," she continued, "to have inferior politicians because we have sadly separated freedom from virtue. The reason this is so, to my mind, is because we have come to define freedom and justice in morally inferior ways. We have now what Herman Melville so wisely stated in his book *Moby Dick*, reached the 'dark ages of democracy, a New Jerusalem', he wrote and America would experience the 'arrest of hope's advance'.

"We must continue again today to fight off the same atavistic forces that our constitution was intended to contain and thwart forever. Those eternal forces are the power lust of those who wish to be kings, the greed of those who wish they were aristocrats and the relentless malice of those ideological priesthoods that wish to force their creed on all humankind. We must begin to challenge the power of what is.

"The twentieth century," she continued, "has been characterized by three developments of great political importance. The first came with the growth of democracy as designed by our founding fathers, second we had the growth of corporate power, followed thirdly as we are witnessing today by the growth of corporate propaganda used as a means of protecting corporate power against democracy. We need to remove the power of wealth from the political process. All of our vigor is needed to uphold the right of self-determination, for ourselves and all other countries and no longer be lethally linked to a money sequence system, which forces its co-dependence upon us, of new markets to dispossess, intimidate, imprison and kill, with access to everything of priceable value. The forces we must contend against may be powerful and ruthless, they may have the ability to throw us into a sinkhole of terrifying dystopia, where our freedoms could be curtailed and widespread deprivation put upon us. Yet no tyranny in history has ever crushed the human capacity for love. This is a love that both you and I carry in our hearts and souls. It is often unrecognized and irrational but it propels us to carry out acts of compassion that can potentially compromise our existence. It is this power of love that we all share that is most subversive and is feared most by those who wield power."

When the thunderous ovation subsided, Winnie continued with her compelling dialogue. She was leaving certain moral inferences in the faintly perfumed air of the gardens with the evanescent hints of higher calling and nobler values that were sugar to the ear and agreeable to the mind. She was delineating a future illuminated by a hard golden gleam, against a horizon dominated by a Stonehenge of giant dollar signs, even though she knew that to do so may be like affixing a lead weight to a nightingale. The crowd was foursquare behind her in their early sense of what she was delivering, as she was beginning to turn their attention.

"Our country was founded in idealism," she continued, "which had not been attempted since the Athenians three thousand years before. We must now, and I will carry this mantra to Washington, make it a reality to promote democratic values over commercial values, substance over form, virtue over prestige, achievement over money, character over charisma, the enduring over the ephemeral, and God over Mammon, and all of our shared religions and beliefs that teach us who we are all required to love instead of a creed of who you intend to hate."

The throng roared with approving applause and cries of agreement and nodding heads, as Ryan put his arm around Nan and brought her close, feeling the mounting emotion that was starting to build. Her words stood in poignant isolation. They stood as oasis islands in the ocean of information that flooded by the populace unfounded.

Winnie's nearly forty-minute presentation was a beautiful, prescient litany on love, and truth the most powerful political persuasion that mankind could possess and honor. Winnie was in actuality a spiritual caseworker who patiently and politely pointed out to her listeners that the world wasn't what it should be, because men who held power weren't what they should be.

"We must, in the end, decide after all that something is right in our democratic process. Power is an instrument of government, but it is not government. Any more than lust and a need to possess define love. I would like to suggest that there is no such thing as right or left, only up or down, up to man's age old dream, the ultimate in individual freedom consistent with just law and order, or down into the ant heap of totalitarianism. Only when our democratic process moves up to include all fairly, will it then give way to a degree of free imaginative expression, that we can then hope for the aroused witness, the manifold reportage, the replenishment and the flourishing of knowledge, that will restore us to ourselves, and awaken the dulled sense of our people to the public interest, that is our interest, yours and mine and all of us together," Winnie stated, spreading her arms wide in front of her, "only then can we begin to vindicate the genius of the humanist sacred text that embraces us all.

"I ask for your support in this challenge, dear friends. I ask for your vote so that I can represent you, my friends and neighbors, to carry out our common gospel of love. Please remember that our constitution was written as sacred text just as the Athenians had done before. They believed that your god, no matter who you feel that spirit may personally be, works through people, and no matter how large the anger and frustration is that builds inside us, we must make that anger ennobling, productive and powerful instead of embittering.

"We are all instruments of that spirit of love that implores us to become better instead of bitter. For where there is light there is hope, where there is darkness bring joy, where there is injury and fault bring pardon, where there is despair bring hope, where there is doubt bring faith, where there is sadness bring joy, where there is darkness bring light, and where there is hatred bring love, for to be consoled is to console.

"As Jesus said, when he spoke to Zacchaeus in Jericho, 'make the world better because you are in it, for when they see you they see me,' and as in Matthew 25, 'what you do unto the least of me you do unto me.'

"Kindness is a conversion," Winnie said moving away from the podium, a kindly smile flowing over her face that seemed to encompass all in attendance, "for many of us Americans, dear friends, justice and mercy will flow from changed hearts. In the world of tomorrow the highest honor will go to those who provide the deepest service to humanity. Our human family will be deeply aware of its single identity; the suffering of one will be experienced as the suffering of all; and the joy of all will be the objective of all. No one will be on the outside, looking in; no person or group will be excluded; nor will any segment of the population be marginalized or ignored.

"Let us all imagine a world in which love is lived as love itself, where love is the form and the content of relationships. This is what the future holds for us, this is the world we will live in. Our relationships will be wild new flowers blooming in this luminous garden that surrounds us today.

"As St. Theresa said, 'it is not great deeds that will save the world, it is great love, love, love, love.'

"Thank you all for your kind indulgence and I sincerely ask for your support in the coming election. God bless us all."

There was nary a dry eye to be seen amidst the collective brace of adulation and applause, as the crowd rose to its feet in unison, pulled erect by its own new sense of spirit, of community and mission.

Chapter 14

They began the un-indentured four- hour spring sojourn to the lake following Winnie's speech, Ryan seeing now an hour into the drive that Nan and their boys in the back seat were asleep, suddenly felt ennobled by a sense of love flooding over him. Going to the lake as a boy, he realized he had entered a domain of new and gorgeous wonders. It beset him with a serene force he never believed to exist, the brilliance of creation laid out in front of him. He reached across and gently touched Nan's hand, and hoped the agenda they had to deal with would bring a positive and enduring storehouse of virtue and strength which he may need to call on in the future.

He recalled as he glanced at his wife in a state of sweet repose, as the noble peace and dignity of the great pine forests passed by, how they had first met, two, solitary people piecing together the intricacies yet simple puzzle of a new relationship. He was a senior at Cornell finishing his studies in business administration and she was at Villanova getting a double major in environmental science and a Masters in Art History. A bunch of his fraternity brothers had decided to make a long trip from Ithaca to Philadelphia to the concert of a young man named Bruce Springsteen and haunt the re-known bars of the city for carnal opportunities. From the moment he had been introduced to her at a bar called Peggy's just off the main line near the Villanova campus, all systems had seemed to be on go. Out of the depths of the nameless and unfathomed weavings of a billion-footed life, out of the dark abyss of time and duty, blind chance had brought these two together. Their first meeting had been upon the timeless and immortal sea that beat forever at the shores of the old earth. They were a perfect match. Her looks were those that he liked in a woman, about five-feet-four, beautiful blonde hair the dropped richly below her shoulders, vibrant blue eyes, a firm mouth, luscious full lips, slender, with the trimmest pair of ankles and smallish rounded hips, which looked like they had been turned on a lathe, with good nicely rounded breasts, and a delightful laugh that was contagious, like a cascade of wind chimes.

She seemed to wear a perpetual expression of barely concealed amusement, as if she was in the grip of a wise inward chuckle.

At the time they met Ryan was full of all his business school badges of knowledge and the ways of American corporate trade and commerce, while she was currently studying the culture and the artistic creations of the Renaissance and the Enlightenment, experiencing the intense nostalgia for the bucolic peace of 16th and 17th century Europe. Since the selection of an object of desire was to some extent a function of one's current emotional affectation, there was no way Ryan was not going to fall in love with a charming, lovely and knowing woman who could speak so graciously of the art and life of those ages and all the beautiful images of that idealized, spacious, good hearted late afternoon harvest of the world. Their emotional cultures seemed very much in sync and her ideological feet seemed planted squarely in the past, giving her solid ground from which to sniff curiously at the oddities and pretenses of the present.

Nanette Louise Braddock was the second child of John and Barbara Braddock, from Harwich Port, Cape Cod, Massachusetts. Her older brother Mark was a Boston College Law graduate now working as staff lawyer for the ACLU of Massachusetts, and also doing conveyance work for a family owned law practice in Brighton. Nan's father and mother Ryan would later learn had been born of a certain established strain of eastern aristocracy, not quite the Plymouth Rock or Murray Hill cliques, but of that long lineage. Her father was in the Army Air Force bombardier group during World War 2, a group that bombed targets in Berlin, Czechoslovakia, Hungary and in April of 1945, participated unknowingly in the first use of napalm, in Royan, western France killing more than one thousand French civilians, as well as some German soldiers hiding near Royan.

The bombing had been ordered by military officials looking for advancement rather than specific military objectives. This had sensitized Nan's father to the ethical dilemmas faced by GI's and the endless atrocities committed by the U.S. Following the war he enrolled at Columbia earning his BA in 1951 and his MA and PHD in history and political science. His Master's thesis examined the Colorado mine strikes in 1914 and the fight to become unionized and had done his doctoral dissertation on, La Guardia in congress, the study of Fiorello La Guardia's congressional career, who represented the "conscience of the 1920's," who fought for public power, the right to strike, and the redistribution of wealth by progressive proportional taxation.

He did a post-doctoral fellowship of East Asian studies at Harvard

University, before taking a position of Professor of History at the University of Georgia in Athens in 1958, where he was subsequently dismissed in 1963 for siding with the black students of the south in the struggle against segregation. In 1964 he joined Boston University as a professor of Political Science, where today he had earned emeritus status with his writings and teachings, honing in his students a deep sense of fairness and justice for the underdog

In the first hour they were together, Ryan with his Rolling Rock and Nan with her Chablis, they discovered that their tastes and humor were very much the same, liking and laughing at all the same things, seeming to use the same lens from which to see life. So congruent were they with each other, not to have fallen in love it seemed would have been a venal sin against nature and God's divine plan, so powerful was their mutual compulsion. It was not possible that they may be filling each other's transitory emotional requirements, that they might be role players cast by coincidence to fill up phased empty spaces, as so often happened in Ryan's past love life, where the reliance on bed became the ultimate panacea, where when things went rocky, they would still have at each other as groaningly and as juicily as ever and convince themselves, for at least a half hour or so, that things were as they had been trying to sustain for themselves the initial rapture that had come over them. It got to be tough and exhausting, Ryan mused as he cruised up 35 North and it was difficult to devise a steady output of new intimate excitements and private passions.

Their tastes meshed and matched so perfectly, and in a world in which style counted for so much, they were both foolish enough to take for granted that a common taste for the subjects they talked of, from Art and literature to some of the vile goings on of the business world, would be a reliable earnest of a deeper perhaps a final, once and forever entwining. They told each other identical tales and exchanged similar sorrows and commiserations. She was coming off a long intense relationship since her junior year in college, into which she had put everything and had been emotionally savaged for her earnestness. Ryan was coming off a series of six month stands, which in speaking with her, he elevated to a sort of intense emotional hegira.

They seemed inseparable that night as they continued the early stage of their relationship talking long into the night, Ryan bidding his friends from college adieu as they left for other establishments, in carnal pursuit. It was one thirty Ryan recalled now a smile of the memory reflecting back to him in the rear view mirror, when he offered to drive her back to her off campus apartment.

Ryan pulled his car into the parking lot behind her apartment and stopped. "Well," he remembered saying. "I'll stay in touch, okay."

"Okay," she barely whispered, and then without thinking he leaned across and kissed her ever so gently and sweetly on her supple lips, she eagerly returning with an ardor so genuine that it seemed they might melt into one another. Ryan cupped her face in his hands and their kisses deepened lips a-part tongues finding each other in the electric mesmerizing throes of love making, a temporary palliative for their mutual isolation the lonely pilgrimage of their hearts. "Ummm," they both said in unison, Ryan mentally telling himself that he would keep this to only a little light necking, teenage stuff, or teenage at least was the way he thought of it, not allowing his hands this early morning to find a life of their own.

This was too special, too real, to subject their initial stages of intimacy to a free roam of carnal pleasures. They weren't kids any longer so their kisses intensified, Ryan outlining the rims of her ruby red lips with his tongue, both knowing where the treasures were to be found. Ryan paused his passion for a moment to look into Nan's eyes and saw tears begin to rise and kissed them as her mascara began to run, taking her now into his arms and holding her close as she let go a soft sob, the seeds of their mutual adorations having surely been sewn.

Ryan walked her into her apartment and up the two flights of stairs to her third floor flat, and as she unlocked the door she turned to him and asked, "Kiss me once more okay?"

Their kiss was romantic and as meaningful and full of enduring purpose, as they had ever experienced, they would both later confess. Nan blew him a sweet kiss, an almost visible sacred mist that skipped off her fingers directly into his heart. The door closed behind him. She left Ryan breathing like a hard run horse. The taste of her mouth remained like a sweet communion cracker unbroken before the bitter wine. If and when he thought, the story of all our lives, if and when we can sense and seize the opportunity and take our lives out of desperation, anxiety and loneliness and forge the chains that will make our lifetimes something more than we ever knew.

The two of them went through the attenuated minuet as Ryan became very familiar with I-476 south from Ithaca and the Pennsylvania Turnpike to Phillie. Their first date that following Saturday was lunch at Wingers on Lancaster Avenue and a stroll through the Philadelphia Art Institute which Nan informed him was the second largest gallery of art in the United States. She guided him with grace through the works of Jasper Cropsey, one of the key impressionist figures of the luminist tradition of American landscape painting in the 19th century, who had created at least nine series of the four seasons. In Europe she had explained to Ryan the turning of the seasons was a long established allegorical motif evoking the progress of time and issues of morality and transience and how he used this to infuse the landscape with deeper significance.

Ryan remembered how she had explained how he created landscapes infused with moral meaning, a meaning reinforced by its place in the cycle of nature. Ryan smiled inwardly as he recalled how they had paused at Cropsey's haunting winter landscape of the Simplon Pass a long strategic passage dating to Napoleonic times that linked Switzerland with Italy. He depicted the pass as a glacial landscape of knifelike peaks and a deep valley combining the grandeur of landscape and the intimacy of the genre painting, placing two hooded monks with a dog between these two elements, caught in the golden rays of the setting sun as they radiate over the frozen snow covered landscape. He found the divine in nature and in this work Nan had explained. Man is being balanced between the snowy vertiginous peaks reaching toward the heavens and the dark abyss warmed by fading sunlight.

They were each feeling their way through the other's delicate condition, appreciating the gorgeous sensitivity that was building, then sharing a final soulful, silent, inward sighting pause aquiver with a mutuality, as Ryan took her hand now as they stood mesmerized before Durand's, "Kindred Spirits."

Then the next weekend they had a second date for dinner at the Abbey Grill near campus, both of them feeling highly sexed but knowing that the rules required prolonging the torture at least one more time, so nothing more than a little light necking. Ryan returned to Cornell while she made a weeklong excursion to the west coast with four of her classmates in the Art History Master's program to visit galleries in Los Angeles and San Francisco. Ryan found her absence curiously tearing, the two of them exchanging multiple phone calls per day requisite to fanning the flames of their mutual amorousness.

When she returned they had a third date, a long boozy dinner at Elio's, now as sacred and refulgent of deep right feelings to both of them, as Combray of the Ritz. When Ryan parked in the lot in the back of her apartment, he took her into his hands and they kissed deep and luscious, Nan taking Ryan's hand, seizing the hint finding its way under her skirt, and by itself it closed over her. She felt like fine silk, like syrup. "That's right," she said. "Oh please just keep that right there, keep that going, just like that. Oh yes, just like that. Oh my God!" she whispered, fearing someone might catch them in their levantine desires.

How much he wanted to be inside her he remembered, he felt he would shatter like a crystal if he couldn't. He knew he couldn't break the rhythm of what they were doing, their hands on each, the two of them breathing in unison, long heavy breaths and moans that seemingly rose directly from where they touched each other.

Ryan wanted so desperately to be above her, to be in her, to get for himself that sweet, slick long release he knew she could give him. They kissed with a height of passion he had never before experienced, as he felt her slide away into a rippling series of jerks as she pushed her pelvis against his hand, and felt through her lips her breath now coming first bullet like and then dying into sighs. Ryan felt all of that in her and through her, felt it for about a microsecond that lasted about as long as the history of all time, and then it was his turn to gather behind himself stiff as a steel shaft and blow apart like a balloon.

Afterward they lay back against the seat softly gasping for air, the moonlight splashing through the windshield catching her blond angelic profile. She reached out and touched him again and it was like being caressed by an electric feather, making Ryan shutter. "You shouldn't do that," he whispered, "death by ecstasy is punishable by something." She took her hand back and looked at it with sweet curiosity.

"My goodness, what have I here in the palm of this pale little hand?" She laughed quickly, a cute coquettish chuckle not at all weighted with any faint regret. She reached up to kiss Ryan's face, her hand moving to help him zip up, whispering in his ear that her roommate was gone until Monday night. Here he was, Ryan thought to himself, a truly modern day romantic hero, twenty-two years old trousers sticky with passion as they walked arm in arm across the parking lot to Nan's apartment. They had each other's clothes off before they could get past the doorway of her flat, and this, the first time they had made love was not one of murmured civilized endearments and the intimate rustlings of silk and taffeta against skin, the discreet click of snaps and buttons something very artful and literary, but rather as Nan had later said, Ryan smiling now at the carnal memory containing an inward chuckle, that he had bedded her like a shop girl.

They dated intensely all that senior year trading excursions between their campuses, Nan staying at his apartment at Cornell nearly as much as Ryan found himself at hers. By the mere dint of seeing one another they could no longer due without seeing each other again. A tender and gentle sentiment was gradually being introduced to their souls, where the least obstacle could not become an impetuous fury, where jealousy could awaken even a greater urge of love's neediness, where discord triumphs and the gentlest of the passions receives sacrifices of human blood.

Time passed imperceptibly, then stopped altogether and lost its grip on them. They didn't leave her apartment for days. Snow melted, and fell again and they scarcely noticed. They never turned on the TV or the radio. The only sounds were the moans of love songs, and their own moans and the wind. When starving they would order food from a restaurant around the corner. The phone rang off the hook but they never answered it. They would lie on their sides for hours, staring at each other, smiling, touching fingertips, saying nothing. They would fall asleep, wake up and make love, then fall asleep again, fingers interlocked. They had no idea if it was morning or night, or what days of the week it was, and didn't want to know.

In the early spring of that year, before the rigors of finals were upon them, they made their way to Cape Cod, to make the couple's parental presentation. Ryan recalled meeting her mother for the first time that Friday afternoon.

She had greeted them at the door of their shuttered white four bed-room colonial, with the recognized tone directed toward him as that of the protective mother, exposing her child to another new man, another knight errant, not yet made sure of. It turned out to be a very harmonious weekend of great cooking by her mother with oodles of rich red wine to help palliate any imagined un-comfort. Each night after the evening's festivities and conversations seemed to wind down toward her parent's bedtime, Nan and Ryan would excuse themselves and walk around the corner and down a block to the Okemo bar and grill to meet friends and neighbors of Nan and the Braddock family. Each night it was a raucous group of young partiers present and Ryan easily and instinctively took to them, much to Nan's delight, as they drank madras with great volume and gusto, stumbling their way home just short of the 2 am closing, stealthily making love to each other as quietly as they could.

It was the week just after finals that Ryan received the phone call from Nan at his apartment at school. It was life calling in another loan. Her mother had been swept out to sea on her regular morning swim off the beaches of Harwich Port, over twelve years ago now Ryan computed in his head. A tuna fisherman heading southwest from Block Island Sound had discovered her body floating toward the great Atlantic Gulf Stream belt just before noon on May 18th 1974. It had been a little more than five months hence that Ryan had started taking Nan into his life when this tragic event occurred.

She had taken the unwelcome intrusion as strongly as she could, Ryan thought as he gently merged onto highway thirty-three, approaching the midpoint of the lake journey. She had cried quietly; she knew her mother wouldn't have wanted any excess keening. He recalled how he so desperately wanted to be a proxy for the sensations of warm tenderness and the sorrows of the world that he knew she loved so much, scattering small sympathetic noises like bread crumbs, trying to attract her, unsure of the way into her feelings.

The worst part for Nan had been the sympathy of her family friends, and those friends mostly women of a certain age in whom happiness and fulfillment had not atrophied that prized kernel of self- pity, who took up their accustomed roles wailing beside the dusty jeering road as she her mother's daughter dragged the cross of man's awfulness and sorrow to Calvary, trusting that somehow God's unbearable loss would make her loss more bearable.

Their friends were solicitous and kindly but not over anxious to have the word of deaths sojourn amongst them. The church services and prayers at St. Anne's were in fashion by all mourners and Ryan had thought at the time how entirely at our own convenience we came to God, to whom we either shake our fists or shed our tears.

How lonely they all seemed that night at the Braddock's home, there was a black crepe on the front door handle in token of filial respect to the passed matriarch. Their family and friends seemed all lonely souls, every one of them, despite husbands and children and cousins. They seemed like perennially bereaved friends, all their hopes in the end, their pairings and procreations and promises of keeping in touch, keeping track, all futile in the end keeping them from seeing that nothing they felt, after all was said, made any difference.

Ryan had tried to put out a hand, to help Nan along surrounding himself with her family knowing all along deep within himself that he didn't expect to make a difference either. It will make no difference, he regretfully knew. Eventually one after the other, would fall, and the fact of this death would be absorbed effortlessly into the life of the community, like a single tiny drop of stain dropped into a glass of clear water. It would spread outward and outward from the point of vindictive concentration, unraveling and thinning away, drawing away the central fact of the stain, until nothing was visible.

They walked to the beach that night, Ryan recalled, Nan slipping her size six feet into her mother's tan topsiders that still sat in the breezeway like a memento. Her voice began to crack and her eyes glistened as they sat in the lee of sand dune under a moonlit sky down the shoreline from the Harwich Port Yacht Club. Ryan sat with her as she cried, lifting her face to the sky as if the half- moon might warm it. What was true? A destiny that shaped our ends, was there one? Was there, ultimately and implacably, somewhere out there beyond all the prating about accident and free will? Was there a grim celestial magistrate who meted out our fates with a perfectly logical causality…?

The sudden and shocking loss of her mother and inability to make the inexplicable loss explicable had in some way cauterized her feelings and had sternly focused her somewhere within where very little presence for him apparently existed. Her mother's death had seemed to be her sole effective solace. Part of her had drawn into itself, like a sea creature backing into its shell and blocking up the entrance with its own operculum. There was no reaching her. A life had come and gone and nature had not paused for a second. The machine of time and space grinds on, and people are fed through it unmercifully, grist through the mill. Nan's entire childhood and life were stored under the eaves of the Cape Cod house where her father would now live in private pain. It was about at this tragic time that an unspoken cleavage was weaved between their emotional spirits.

Ryan somehow knew Nan had to sit with her grief and pain for a while, for our pain is not empty and can eventually inhabit a timeless eternity where loss gives birth to redemption from the deep dark places and the black under-coatings and chasms of life where we eventually find a way to climb out of to find and reclaim ourselves, hoping that she would come back to him, but knowing it would be not until the powers of her darkness told her the time was right once again. He prayed silently for her every day, hoping she would get an emotional second wind and come to understand that life is essentially a defeat, constant and steady, a losing game, and yet somehow we summon up the—the grace of courage to take what comes, and make it through.

He would try to avoid any constant solicitation of her hand, and deal with the great gray eternity of time, hoping he could traverse it with his sanity intact. He'd have to harden his heart and not succumb to the ebb and tug of the emotional and the needy, gleeful then sorry panes of love, not to be as in Greek mythology, one of Penelope's greedy guests of pursuers, Lotharios looking to get lucky with the lovely and languishing girl. Months passed and he was still awakening every morning looking for some loophole in the logic of his self-restraint that could justify his calling her.

For nearly two years after he bade Nan goodbye after all the funeral activity and mourning had subsided they led separate lives, Ryan trekking back to Minnesota and then to Manhattan to take a position at the institutional trading desk of Paine Webber that a buddy of his from school had advised him about. He found a tiny little one- bedroom flat on the upper west side, and began his solitary wander, a boat without a jib, a top without a gyro, trying like most men, to deal with his mind ache and drive home some tent pegs of reassurance, so as to make his way back symbolically to the order of things he had left behind, to repair the errors of morals or amatory judgment and whatever else lay bare. Anxiety and the loneliness of love loss had to be shoved back into farthest most nearly invisible reaches of his mind as he made way through the rigors of Wall Street and the challenges and nuances of equity and bond trading techniques.

Once hired by Paine Webber out of business school, Ryan quickly shucked his mid-western bred pacifism for the trench warfare of mergers and acquisitions, arbitraging and bond swaps. He was one of many who was thought to have a PSD degree, poor, smart, with a deep desire to become rich. He was soon to learn that though a decade lasts for only ten years, greed is both forever and universal, the avarice of mankind being insatiable, as Aristotle had observed some 2,300 years ago.

He found being a bachelor enjoyable for a time as he could find himself attached to the fluttering edges of various sorts of interesting and useful families of influence, by being available for dinner, his help in minor emergencies, his avuncular warmth and because he was the sort of person who could carry the cachet of significant enough guest and friend from one place at the table to another, as if you were a slice of something from the mutton.

He found most of these relationships with his fellow brokerage kin to be agreeable and of great value when the matters that most stirred his muse were discussed, that being the ins and outs of economic and social commerce and the hypocrisies that support manners and put a good roof on social constraint and good behavior. Social life for that period of time did not seem frivolous, even when it was extremely so, and it was Ryan's muse now, that if you have cultivated the observant, ambitious and witty, you may have attained anecdotes aplenty, ore worthy of being relieved of its roughness and rounded into impressive jewels and gemstones of cultural insight.

Ryan had the hot ichor of youth boiling in his veins and was fertile with bond market duplicities during his early years on the trading floor, still an infant at the greedy breast of Wall Street. He had enjoyed reasonable success buying and selling government bonds with the firm's capital, while establishing a handful of personal accounts of mostly friends and family. He had hit no home runs during that time, but he had belted out plenty of singles and doubles, trading floors were rife with sports analogies, and as a result he'd earned solid though not earth shattering bonuses.

Such was the long bred, insidious, institutionalized moral corruption of greed on Wall Street, and it was beginning to ware and tare on Ryan's good conscience

Friday afternoons at work on the trading floor seemed to devolve into a head start with the trader's bachelor weekends, with beer and cocktails, a generalized disengagement from their adrenalized professional selves, with discussions the last hour of why the bar they tried last Friday sucked and which new one they should lustily venture out to tonight.

Ryan could see what the market could do to a man, its ability to transform lives or ruin them. The market was like a mirror, it showed over time, who you really were, your vices and your virtues, as was exemplified by the pit traders at the NYMEX, who traded oil and gas futures and stole systematically from their clients by front-running all the trades.

July in Manhattan that year was nearly unbearable, New York had become a cauldron, hotter than hell's hinges. Air conditioners shuddered helplessly against the heat that shouldered its way through the walls of work and home. It was weather made for tension and the streets literally percolated hostility, the asphalt bubbled and oozed underfoot. Outside, the city made its rustling noises, its sighs and murmurs, its auditory offerings to the indifferent sky above it. The avengers walked up and down the street without speaking, doing three-on-two rhythms with their feet, damned determined toward their destinations. Tempers boiled over nothing and the newspapers told of angry exchanges between pedestrians and drivers that resulted in fatal shootings.

The lives of men who live in our great cities, Ryan mused, were often tragically lonely. In many ways the city dwellers in the hive were the modern counterparts of Tantalus, starving to death in the midst of abundance. The golden stream flows near their lips but always falls away when they try to drink of it. The vine, rich weighted with its golden fruit, bends down, comes near, but springs back when they reach out to touch it. It was like a painted scene of awful desolation, not unlike a desert or a heath of barren rocks that could picture man in his great loneliness, like the prophet Elijah in the desert being fed by ravens on the rocks. This was the most desolate scene one could imagine; the lonely streets walked by man in any one of our great cities on a Sunday afternoon.

Nan was always on his mind, in his blood like holy wine clearing the skies even on mornings so slimy and odiferous that the city felt like the interior of a cistern perfuming garbage cluttered streets the dismal stink that mantled the streets. Ryan had walked through the park and down Madison Avenue on his way to work after a noontime stroll, and Nan swept into his mind again with the force of a lighthouse beacon…

The oppressive weather had not kept the city's retail juices from bubbling over. The avenue was crowded, the upscale rabble was out in force, visa cards at the ready, tennis whites were now giving way overnight it seemed to Ralph Lauren corduroys and tweed jackets. The cruel Darwinism of fashion was making its power evident. Italian shoes no longer dominated the windows of the chique shops, replaced now by raggedy Japanese work-out clothes at nine hundred dollars the copy. The only constant was exorbitance.

Ryan sat one afternoon in an atmosphere of calculated gloom, weighing the problems of a long term bond issue that was in the house and having a slow sale, pondering the idea of maybe unloading the entire issue on a pension fund customer and then buy him drinks later at Harry's to salve the deception. The nature of man was concupiscent he thought, and was about to make the co-opting call, when his private line rang. It was like the clouds had parted and a two- year investment of pleading prayers to the angels of goodness and love had finally mercifully been answered. Nan had moved from Cape Cod to Manhattan one year ago, to manage two art galleries, the Frickland and the Braun, to begin to make a living out of what she loved to do.

Their first date the following day Saturday, Ryan remembered after what seemed an enormity of two years of scraping out a living of separation, was at the Plaza at 5th avenue and Central Park south. Ryan hoped this would be the last phase before the emotional point of no return, before declarations from which the turning back would be very difficult. Now was the time for taking it carefully; he kept reminding himself. He'd been in enough entanglements to know that love affairs at their outset were conducted by people in masks, that courtship could be kind of a fraud and only with time and familiarity would the blatantly true facts of personality and habit emerge to become nasty, the farting, the couch potatoing, the drinking, all those qualities and proclivities that are by turns and degrees grating, unappetizing, difficult and impossible and ultimately lethal.

Ryan knew Nan well enough to know that she was not one of those souls with an emotional circuit breaker that could shut down her heart even while her head was puzzling out the whys and wherefores of an involvement and the voltages of the infatuation both positive and negative. Over grilled sole and salad and a refreshing and spicy bottle of Alsatian wine they talked aimlessly, wandering from one subject to another moving toward the kind of reassuring intimacy that only people who know themselves could develop instinctively. There was a kind of unsecured treaty that immediately started to build between them.

They didn't try to make hostages of each other by trading intimacies, checking the urgency of curiosity and suspicion to allow certain things to remain distant and buried to trust one's soul mate or mate soul with things that shouldn't be brought to the light of day, knowing that the emotions of jealousy and envy could be so sickening and corrosive and compulsive that we don't want to leave them raw, wallowing in them for years and getting nowhere in them.

Understanding that these emotions have a kind of special shadow in them Ryan had come to realize the germ of creativity shrouded in a veil of repulsion, in a culture that prizes materialism and individual freedom and choice, the desire to possess is a piece of the shadow but it is also a very real desire, an obsessive compulsive neurotic need to know and the control the mysteries of life and the deep ocean of secrets we all have.

Envy like jealousy could eat at the heart of the ego and is the object of the envy's corrosive power. It is really the hyperopia of the soul that the Greek mythologies had taught, the inability to see what is closest to us. He was past the first worst stages of learning to love, past the sexual jealousy and the inclination to drill for one's own emotional oil in the psyche of another.

After lunch Ryan took her as he helped her into a taxi to pay a visit to one of her galleries. The late afternoon sun was just beginning to turn golden as they walked to the Frickland. When they reached the Frickland Gallery it seemed as if they had come upon a perfect oasis of peace and order. It was a needed medicine for the soul in a city addicted to adrenaline and action.

The gallery host, an aesthete young man waved at them as Nan led them directly to the Isenheim altarpiece that they had on loan from a museum in Rome she had talked of at lunch. Nan had seen it many times, but it was still too strange and cruel and poignant not to be fresh even to her sophisticated eye. She stood to the side as Ryan walked around it, examining the shutters, the wings, stopping to admire the bursting, blazing aureole of the Resurrection, finally returning to stand aside her looking up at the central panel depicting the Crucifixion. Nan took his hand now as they both stared up at the torn and scourged figure of Christ, at the pained gaping night frozen agony of the images. Golgotha looked like it was the surface of the moon, Christ's agony being transformed into a frozen stalactite of pain and grief.

The two of them stood in awe of what they were seeing, unaware of any other presence around them, Nan now sensing the experience of the painting in a direct way that she had not experienced before. It was as if they had both physically wandered into Grunewald's frightening tableau.

She realized that what they were feeling was beyond words, that there was something spiritual going on inside them. They found it hard to breathe as if all the air had been pumped out of this moment they shared. Finally,

Ryan shook his head as if to clear the mist from his mind orbit and the immense feeling that gripped him, and brought Nan's hand to his heart, tears welling in both their eyes. "My god Nan," he softly muttered looking at her both immersed in their mutual sense of the moment.

As they walked out of Nan's gallery both were charged with a frustration that made its own electricity. Both were determined to seize the days and nights and to start to bring their separated lives into a new phase and make their divergent orders coalesce. They had not made love since they had cadged a weekend at her home on Cape Cod while her parents were in Boston for the week. It had been a reptilian form of gutter level love at the shank of one claret soaked evening spent at the yacht club watching the winners of the annual yacht races from the Cape to Bermuda and back over two years ago one week before her mother had died.

Their first true embrace, their first real kiss that day outside the gallery and the kisses after, they knew should be invested with a rare special feeling and wonder, so they each tried to put a special delicacy into this long awaited initiation, as if they were entrusted with very fragile, incomparably fragile and rare, eerily delicate emotions to clutch onto too tightly or to be the least bit rough with.

They proceeded carefully at Nan's fourth floor flat in Soho, sometimes as if in slow motion not because they wished to prolong sensations or to attenuate their feelings, but rather for fear of bruising, of scraping, of leaving the tiniest scar or messy imprint on the perfect patina of what was happening to them.

He slowly undressed Nan as she unbuckled his belt and unbuttoned his shirt. When he unhooked her brassiere and slid it off she could stand it no longer and reached out to take his head to her bosom. When Ryan began to make love to her it was as though nothing had changed. Nan had thought the same, kissing him, feeling for his tongue with her lips and thinking that whatever they did couldn't come within a galaxy of what she felt in her head and soul.

She opened herself to him and felt him slide down and begin to fondle her with his tongue and lips bringing her to an instant rush of ecstasy, and when he reversed himself she happily took him into her mouth, feeling all his earnestness that was building up inside of him. Then Ryan moved on top of her and kissed her lips gently as she reached down, still like stone, as if all his feeling had been gathered frozen in this burning stalactite she grasped. She guided his way into her, feeling him go in so naturally and easily. He started a rhythm that made the frictions begin to work for her once more, letting herself go as he took over, and just slip away into pure sensation, drawn down like spinning uncontrollable into a beautiful blue eddy of tropical island water, into the vortex of excitement the was spreading electrically from where they were joined together.

She felt the familiar tingle starting in her legs, felt her skin flush, felt him withdraw until just the tip of him lingered within, felt him do that again and again, slide pause, slide pause, and then she was busy with her the sensitivity of her own nerve ends, and she heard something that she could have sworn was her own voice, and just as he she, he did, he eased on top of her, and she knew he was coming and she was in perfect sync with him. He made no groans or grunts as they both released their energies, but a sound like a sigh, and inside her she thought she felt him coming forever, flowing and flowing, and then their whole world coalesced and coalesced again and sweetly coalesced again for a last time.

When Ryan slid off her and lay beside her and their breathing slowed and their vision cleared they were both thanking themselves for the voices they heard by the saints in ecstasy. Was this what Bernini saw in his Baroque of St. Theresa's transport Nan wondered, bringing about real love and not just romantic love?

"People like us," she had told him during the first wonderful two weeks they spent in Manhattan, "could not put up with all the pushers and shovers, the dynamos and dominators." They both thought of themselves as edge type people a notch off from the crowd, always a shade more the observer than the participant. "We were strictly back of the bus sorts," she had said, Ryan smiling in her sleeping direction, who could find solace with each other. They spent a glorious romantic two weeks in New York, in the full flood of the summer, swelling slowly like a great fruit, into the full tide of feeling, in which they drifted in a breathless ease, like a strong massive, deep current, which come with an onrush, but which had an irresistible luscious weight of water behind it, feasting on good out of the way dining and drinking wonderful wines, making magical love and exploring art galleries.

At work Nan chose to present a blonde bespectacled weediness which suited her work and she had a figure kept as lissome as a flame. Ryan liked her conversations as she led her gallery visitors, infusing the more- subtle subjects with a nice sense of larger meaning, finding them in serviceable metaphors for more significant considerations. She had not acquired the supercilious air and the strange strangulated diction that at the time seemed to be a prerequisite for employment in the art world. Museum jobs went begging then because no one had an "eye" anymore and "eye" was still the core, the kernel of the vocation, where knowing what someone paid and the artworks worth, were not synonymous.

The big new money being made on Wall Street wanted art that was easily understood, visual rather than bookish, as long as it positively exuded expensiveness. Ryan smiled as he listened to Nan make her pitch, at her choice of words. The art world spoke in the three genders of the big money spender, men, women and the Arabs.

These people who had millions and dreamt of billions were as trembling, fresh and fragile as spring buds, Ryan had intuited. They wanted to keep up with whoever or whatever was in fashion with the finer boned society of museum people and the old line collectors, who perceived the virtues in themselves and their collections to be other than a string of zeros or personal pride. Rather it had to do with educational connoisseurship and the broad culture which art historians prided themselves in.

New York however always gave herself over to the newer and richer suitors because life was too complicated and too inconsistent manifesting a voracious art market that was always after new collecting fashions to promote, very willing to over esteem in order to create new gee-gaws of merchandize for its depleted counters, seeing to it that even the most modest trifles were priced way out of proportion.

At work this evening Nan was pumping the cultural pretensions of the gallery to a packed clam tight group of people eddying about in irregular whirls about a number of vortices, as Ryan drifted around in a slurry of acidic white wine and clever finger food. She had developed the expertise of subjugating her inherent distaste, knowing that one day the Dutch and Flemish flower pictures she was adorning would one day return to the price levels suitable for the botanical curiosities that they were. To the rich in New York women and their Long Island estates they were the current fashion of passports to instant respectability and price was no object.

Artists' careers had become phenomena and in and of themselves, almost separated from the actual body of work Ryan had noticed, as relationships between lovers often seemed to be aloof from passion, and were evaluated by a public in terms of the money and celebrity, brought to fruition by hype and marketing as much as by accomplishment. Artist's names had become currency as socially useful as initials on luggage.

Ryan remembered Nan explaining to him, how, "art was the daughter of freedom that took its orders from the necessity inherent in our minds and not from the exigencies of matter, and how throughout history material needs had reigned supreme and had bent a degraded humanity beneath centuries of tyrannical yoke.

Utility was the great idol of the ages to which all powers were in thrall and to which all talent must pay homage. Weighed in this crude balance, the insubstantial merits of Art scarcely tipped the scale, and bereft of all encouragement, she shuns the noisy marketplace of our time. The spirit of philosophical inquiry itself was wresting from imagination one country after another and as the frontiers of art contract, the more the boundaries of science expand."

Nan and Ryan recaptured the essence of a Manhattan which many thought had been lost during the vulgarity of the 1970's. Old particularities re-awoke their memories and stimulated their heart strings; the lights on Park Avenue denoting a path amid the dusk like buoys, midnight piano at the Carlyle, dinner parties where no one drank too much and conversations were good. Piece by piece, like a jig saw puzzle they put back together the fragments of their old happiness. Memory was a large part of the scheme of things and the future seemed to be becoming more dependable. They had restored each other like old paintings in which the first colors had been brought up from under the concealments and discolorations of old varnish, better even than what had been.

They felt that they were as nearly perfectly suited now as their relationship had aged over the last three years. They drank in the life of the city, day and night, spending glorious romantic weeks with one another feasting on good out of the way dining, making magical love and exploring art galleries hand in hand. They were co-conspirators in love, arm in arm they conquered cocktail parties where the fey young men named Spalding and Xavier passed trays of figs slathered in almond dust. They went to the opera and heard Il Trovatore Architempo, the famous tenor, singing Manrico. They walked in the Park on Sundays, dodging dogged unhappy looking joggers and aggressive cyclists. They went to the theatre and the ballet. Nan introduced him to Rembrandt and Rauschenberg, and they ate

Dim Sum and caviar. They kissed on the steps of St. Patrick's at the top of the Empire state building and in the rows of dozens of movie theatres.

Nan moved into Ryan's upper west side flat, keeping her apartment in Soho, over Ryan's mild objections. She had tried to reassure him Ryan remembered glancing over at her sleepy repose, "it's just a bolt hole and someday you may not want me anymore and when that happens if it ever does, I want a place where you can't chase me, where the doorbell won't ring in the middle of the night with you drunk and lonely on the steps. That's all. Let's not discuss it anymore," he recalled her saying with a sigh in her voice.

There was forever this thing between them, in their two-person world. They had been together for six weeks. New York was the ideal setting for new love affairs, it could distract from the potential unfolding of small aggravations and incompatibilities that might occur between two people who impetuously gave each other their hearts. "We match perfectly," she had said to him with charmed delight, her blue eyes sparkling, as the Christmas season was approaching, "I cook and you make the bed and we share the kissing and hugging chores equally."

They both felt childlike and rejuvenated. "Color and context, milk and memory," she quoted to Ryan as he chased her through Saks two days before Christmas. They were two yous, the one you yourself create by loving and the one the beloved creates by loving you. If you loved and were loved perfectly, Ryan mused as he glanced at Nan's repose, then there wouldn't be any difference between the two yous or any distance between them. They could coincide perfectly, there would be perfect blending, a perfect focus as when a stereoscope gets the twin images on the card into perfect alignment.

Nan and Ryan spent New Years' eve alone together, begging off on numerous party invitations, for an evening of Champaign, caviar and artichokes, listening to the selected poetry of Van Morrison. They spent the evening, this annual Janus-faced moment, in each other's arms saying everything that they ever hoped that they might someday be able to say to someone, making unembarrassed commitments and declarations, secure in the certainty that they were the only people in the world. And so midnight came and went and finally they had exhausted every emotional and physical resource and had nothing special left for the first day of the New Year, except each other and a long and rounding sleep.

Ryan's proposal after permission was granted by her father was made at Rachael's Italian restaurant in Soho and Nan amorously accepted to join him in indissoluble love. The October wedding on Cape Cod was to be organized by the wedding planners with week-long arrays of parties, lunches and dinners, with the ceremony taking place at St. Anne's in Brewster.

Nan's father and Walt had become immediate good friends, as they were men of a common kidney and they looked at their post war days with shared similarity. They were two men, kindred spirits really who surveyed their own domains, suffering from the same grievances railing in their souls against a world that should be done better by them. It was a busy world that they both found morally and intellectually intolerable. They repulsed at the thought of a coming society where culture would become the dominant currency with which social ambition would be able to purchase satisfaction, anesthetized to the country's noblest traditions.

They were both of a World War 2 hero generation, Ryan remembered as he drove through majestic white pines and firs, who accepted that the past and future were intimate to the present and that all levels of life interlocked and that the job and the man flowed together. They had talked of how peace and prosperity had a way of erasing memory and that brought about an atrophy of civil action that was very difficult to overcome.

How ironic Ryan thought that this nation which had grown and flourished and defended itself and the world thanks to the mutual concern of its citizens, their sense of teamwork, their near automatic acceptance of the other man's flank needs and dignity, should be seen to have lost most of that in less than two decades. Here was a great nation formed and fused in a spirit of independent community which had stood against kings and emperors and Kaisers, split up now and fractionated by greed and resentment to anyone who didn't think like they did. Nan's father would be well prepared morally for what he eventually would be told of the family's direful endeavor, he was certain, as he watched his family in the comforting throes of a deep snooze.

The wedding was wonderful with a full church of celebrants nearly half of which were part of Ryan's family and friends. But the reception was even better. At the country club they stood in the reception line with their backs to the windows overlooking the 18th hole and the tennis courts. The faces slid toward them along the line, facetious, solemn or weepy. But when one of Nan's bridesmaids Diane or 'Dinny' as Nan called her, whispered something past their ears about Ryan's aunts, his dad's sisters' mustaches as they moved past us in the line, they all nearly dropped to the floor crying in laughter. What she said or asked rather has since become a sort of wedding day secret confidence that they still roar over.

Their two-week honeymoon in Europe began in London for one day and a tour of the Tate Gallery, but they discovered that even the old city had all but capitulated to the general high priced cheapness that had oozed with the new petro money. Then it was on to Paris where they did all that tourists did, especially those whose heads were full of the magic of romance. They climbed up the Sacre Coeur late at night and watched the city go to sleep, seeing the lights twinkle out one at a time. Staying at the avant-garde Hotel-du Petit Moulin they reveled in the aesthetic appeal of Paris touring the museums and galleries rich displaying the works of Monet and Picasso and all the other artists Nan introduced him too. They visited the artful delights of the Louvre Museum, The Orsay, The Rodin Museum, The Centre Pompidou, and The National Museum of Modern.

From Paris it was on to Venice. From the air remembered Ryan marveled at how Venice resembled the heads of two reptiles attempting to devour each other, the jaw line of the top most, lunging in from the right that followed the east San Marco bank of the Grand Canal from its beginnings near the railroad depot, hinging in at the Rialto Bridge, then curving back once more to form a lower jaw which includes the city's most famous sights, the Piazza San Marco, the Campanile, the Basilica of San Marco. The upper beast's wide open jaws were set to clamp down on the other reptile's snout, a protuberance coming in from the left and shaped by the western bank of the Grand Canal. The lower reptile's vicious mouth seemed to swallow the San Marco area in whole, hinging where the Foscari canal ran into the Grand Canal, near the three great palaces of Rezzonico, Foscari and Balbi. The jaw, the so-called Dorsoduro, ran out into the lagoon and finished in a savage hook set off by the noble sixteenth century church of Santa Maria della Salute.

Below and nearly parallel to the Dorsoduro they marveled as they flew in snapping pictures from the air, was a fierce inverted talon of an island, that was the Giudecca where Ryan and Nan stayed at the Cipriani, taking lunch that first late afternoon in the fully flowered garden of their villa.

The trouble with passion and the romance of Venice was that it was eventually necessary to go back through the door back into real life. Ryan and Nan had been inoculated with the virus of Italy and it had a benign virulence. Here they were dwarfed by art and religion, not by the steel and glass fantasies of banks, insurance companies and stockbrokers of New York.

They toured all the Venice museums, the Ca Pesaro and the works of the modern Art of Klimt, Chagall, Matisse, Moore and Kadinsky impressionist artists of the Renaissance period. The artistic community of the age shied away from the verbal extra-visual ideas and symbols preferring instead the intellectual simplicity of Impressionism. The work of art was nothing, it was everything he remembered her saying, it was not this or was it all that. There was no single path to its meaning and the significance or the pleasure it gave. It was of its maker's time and of its beholders time it held woven into itself. It was what Botticelli heard in the piazza on the way to the workshop or what Rembrandt thought walking beside the Prinsengracht on a misty afternoon. It could incorporate the morning light on the façade of Santa Croce or a letter from Rubens about the English court or Cezanne's view of the corner house through the woods or a program for the decoration of the palace ceiling handed to Tiepolo by a prince's astrologer.

What they valued most Nan went on to explain in early Renaissance painting was a tenderness of feeling about the countryside, an emotive calm in the heart of what must have been the stormiest of ages giving the paintings a certain irresistible naivete. The three great Venetians, Titian, Tintoretto and Veronese and their unspeaking drama had utterly engaged Ryan and Nan.

Next they visited the three floors of the Ca' Rezzonico, the largest cache of 18th Century art with its grand staircase and the Gallery Portego that displayed the portraits and landscape paintings from Venetian artists of the Settecento, then on to the Museo Civico Correr and the beautiful marble structures by Antonio Canova and the many paintings and drawings of the old Venetian cityscape and how it had changed through the centuries.

Then it was on to the Murano Glass Museum displaying Roman works dating from the 1st and 3rd centuries AD, and the mesmerizing Gothic Architecture of the Palazzo Ducale and infamous Clock Tower on St. Mark's square, the Piazza San Marco that had once fulfilled a resolutely practical role in what was a mighty maritime empire in centuries past.

Seafarers setting out from the Grand Canal would rely on the faultless timepiece to determine the most favorable time for heading out to sea. So reliable was the clock that in 1858 it was made the official timekeeper of Venice to which every other clock would be set.

They fell in love with the other provincial picture galleries in the small cheap cafés and in churches so dark that a flashlight was needed to make out the grim apocalypses painted at the time of the Black Death. It was simply a matter of letting the artworks speak for themselves Ryan was learning from Nan during their communions of observations. As they walked down the grotto Nan pointed toward the sea coast and at the mountains in the far distance where stood the ancient Pillars of Hercules along the Straits of Gibraltar. To the 17th century mind he remembered Nan explaining Hercules was a polyvalent symbol.

The events of ancient and modern history had conspired to make Hercules a logical symbol of the Hapsburg Kings of Spain. In the course of the 16th century the virtuous and heroic Hercules was appropriated as a symbol of the prince, incorporating the paintings' symbolic aspects. Hercules had been instructed by the Delphic oracle to indenture himself to King Eurystheus for twelve years. The labors for which Eurystheus set him were the price of immortality and Hercules carried out the labors as a token of his affection for the King.

From Venice it was on to Florence and the Basilica of Santa Croce the largest Franciscan church in the world, which was the burial place of some of the most illustrious Italians, such as Michelangelo, Galileo, Machiavelli, Foscolo, Gentile and Rossini, known as The Temple of the Italian Glories. Ryan remembered the absolute awe they experienced touring the sixteen chapels, many of them decorated with frescoes by Giotto and his pupils, and its tombs and cenotaphs.

Then it was on to Olga's gallery and the masterful works of Leonardo da Vinci who Nan informed him was the embodiment of the Renaissance ideal of the universal man, the first man to attain complete mastery over all branches of art, being a painter, sculptor, architect and engineer, besides being a scholar in the natural sciences, medicine and philosophy. The short drive to Assisi was like nothing Ryan though he would ever experience as they explored the Upper Church and Lower Church of the Basilica of San Francesco decorated with the Gothic frescoes by numerous late medieval painters, works by Cimabue, Giotto, Simone Martini, and Pietro Lorenzetti.

The works of Giotto particularly moved the newlyweds. The work perfectly expressed the naturalism, the sense of real volume, the realization of space as tactile which had been Giotto's triumph by which Giotto had directed European painting away from the flat hieratic frontality of the Byzantine tradition Nan had explained. His work was a row of five panels showing the birth of the Virgin, the Annunciation, the Nativity, the Crucifixion and the death of the Virgin. Each was a masterpiece and Ryan and Nan were in breathless awe sharing the moment of orgasmic intimacy of living art together. They both felt like particles suspended in a fallen sunbeam. Nan was to Ryan's aesthetics as Phidias was to Pericles, for as long as there was art to love and a supply of jesters for amusement life was bearable he mused as he smiled in her direction.

They spent the last night of the honeymoon just outside Paris at Barbizon, in a lovely old inn. Earlier in the day they had visited the Hospice de Beaune, where they toured the wine cellars and in the courtyard at Fontainebleau. They dined gloriously at the inn with the best wines and slept all night in each other's arms.

Upon returning to New York after their wondrous three- week art tour of Europe in early November they found themselves within the full forces of the coming holiday season. In the United States Ryan thought as he glided smoothly along the two lane road of highway 53 to the north country, the period from Thanksgiving through Christmas to the Twelfth Night was a time of national mental stress, especially hyper-active New York city. The suicide rate soars the alcohol business and the purveyors of psyche-deadening drugs do their best commerce of the entire year. Unlike primitive cultures, whose great annual festivals are springtime celebrations of rebirth and renewal, post industrial culture chooses a dark cold season for its great rite and emphasizes penance and depletion, guilt and spending.

Modern day unction is sought through expenditure, the flashy wrappings swaddling the gifts of the season, seeming a metaphor for multiple layers of contrition, so said the critics of the American way of Christmas. Ryan and Nan both loved Christmas, the angst and the agro claimed for the season had never really affected either of them. They loved the whole production, the sumptuary behavior, the decorations, rounds of relentless parties, the perfectly wrapped parcels given and received. Their solid Catholic upbringings had been steeped in the Dickens myth of the fat goose on the dinner table and portly men dancing reels with beribboned ladies.

But the nigher Christmas drew this their first year of celebration together the crazier the Manhattanites became, the congeries of social climbers, stock market paper mongers, many of whom Ryan knew personally, real estate shills and other assorted virtuosos of hype and blather had seemed to increasingly dominate the public awareness of the city.

In the nearly two years Ryan had worked on Wall Street he had done quite well establishing some very profitable institutional accounts, while exhorting the proletariat around the country as instructed to own your own share of America, as if buying fifty shares of IBM or GM in 1976 was as much as a civic duty as buying a $100 dollar war bond in 1943, following the May 1 ruling of the previous year eliminating the Buttonwood Tree gentleman's agreement on fixed commissions one hundred and twenty years prior. He hesitated to call it a career he had confided in Nan, thinking of it as more of an involvement, not sure he would be able to develop the anti-communitarian moral opacity that was the key to real success on Wall Street.

Smart New Yorkers under the bombardment of stimuli, lunched where their mood of the season shaped by the trendy magazines and the sultans of sheik instructed them to dine, craving all the while inexplicably for the deference of head waiters that was part of Manhattan's manic drive. Being born and bred in New York Ryan and Nan had quickly come to learn, was like a tropical fever born in the blood and impossible to purge.

This was the new America, the largest of the shining thrusting glass cities which had come to the fore as the old manufacturing regimes of the Northeast and Middle America slid into sooty decline. Something within them both had indeed changed for the softer and wiser that holiday season, they felt they were no longer suited, if they ever were, for the hard -nosed rat-tat-tat, twenty- four a day world of New York business.

They both knew that the nightly nightmare of the Holland Tunnel, the pinch point of the world, was not to be a part of their future. Ryan's country boy roots and Nan's Bostonian Cape Cod Brahmin instincts had taken control during that holiday season. New York, with its twin towers of the World Trade center, the gold hoard of the Federal Reserve, the tombs of the Stock Exchange and City Hall and across the harbor the distant Liberty in her skin of green oxide, wasn't something you merely put up with or tolerated, to really make it there you had to relish it, crave it, truly get off on its sharp elbowed style.

For over two years Ryan had worked the trading desks of Wall Street, recording the daily scene usually in a far from acquiescent spirit, while his conscience continued to gnaw at him. A month after the New year, he had finally forsaken his trading desk broker position for its moral inadequacy. That following March the couple purchased the cozy colonial on Lakeside Avenue, in Minnesota, Ryan joining a mutual fund and insurance company as Vice President of marketing, and in August, due to their affectionate cooperation which blessed them, Nan gave birth to their first child, Thomas Christian Davies, making Ryan feel jubilant, invincible, an illustrious father of the race.

Mary watched as the Davie's transport came to a stop in the circular drive, and became instantly a-brim with high spirits while with a rush of noise and laughter the two boys as blonde as butter bowled out onto the expanse of the lawn waving at their grandmother and following the spaniel down to the shoreline of Bearskin Lake. The boys of Nan and Ryan were rambunctious as all children of that age, but they were also bright and gracious and respectful, and Mary hoped dearly as she smiled and waved at them that the best of both she and Walt's namesakes would endure forever within them, and not wake up forgotten one day, their tickets to Valhalla canceled by ill temperament.

  The late afternoon sun was becoming a deepening gray pocked with a blush scud of clouds as Nan and Ryan rustled with the bags of the family from the back hatch.

  They entered the front double doors to warm hugs from Mary as a Haydn flute quartet was whistling softly in the background just as the grandfather clock that had kept time for three generations of Mary's family chimed the five p.m. hour. Ryan bustled their things upstairs followed by Nan.

  Nan hopped quickly up the stairs into the bathroom of their bedroom overlooking the lake. She splashed water on her face and examined herself carefully in the double mirror. The woman looking back at her seemed more tired than she should even after her afternoon snooze and also older than she should. Or does she really? She ran a tentative hand over her cheek. Does her hair look right, does she see new wrinkles at the corner of her mouth and eyes? She spun around and examined herself over her shoulder. Are her hips too big, is she putting on weight? She stepped back and took a second look and decided that all was fine, and that what the scales are telling her is the truth and the mirror is kidding her.

Chapter 15

The blue olds cutlass with lights off moved slowly down Harbor Street along the shipping canal past one of the gigantic eastern bound tankers holding a full load of low sulfur content bituminous. Since the closings of the ore mines twenty years ago the primary cargo now was coal from Wyoming and Montana, shipped via rail by the Burlington Northern line that traversed the old iron range on the same railroad line that had once carried iron ore and taconite down to the Duluth harbor loading port on Lake Superior. The once thriving docks that supported thousands of hard working iron miners' families were now held captive to the old economies that continued to use and pollute with the resource that represented the last hour of our ancient sunlight.

It was just past three a.m. Saturday morning. The call had come through a very cryptic series of mysterious contacts from a distant government field office in south Chicago. The instructions were to pick up a package at an obscure warehouse just west of O'Hare airport in the city of Des Plaines. They were then to proceed north directly to Superior, Wisconsin and onward over the Blatnik Bridge that connected to Duluth, Minnesota.

The driver of the cutlass turned onto a pitch dark road along the most distant road east of the harbor and came to a stop along the slip between two tankers. A man dressed in black removed the heavy plastic bundle from the trunk and unzipping it quickly deposited the contents along the dock's edge below the footings of the huge vessel. There lay the body of Arab descent with a sole bullet hole piercing the middle of his forehead. The plastic body bag was quickly and quietly placed back in the trunk, the lightless driver now moving through the shadows of the darkness to make his way back to his lair on Chicago's south side.

Five hours later at eight a.m. sharp Matt exercised his dutiful obligation and made his call to the agency for instructional updates. He had been "on location" now for two days at the downtown high rise hotel over-looking the bay and loading docks of the port city. With no specific instructions from his bosses he had been re-reading the brief and familiarizing himself with the area and its rich history. Borgen quickly came on the line speaking with his usual air of dismissiveness staring right through Matt with his voice. "Stay on hold there a couple more days. We should be all systems go by Monday. My secretary will provide you with further directions when operations can move ahead."

Matt cradled the phone and felt a glow of anticipation that he could now spend the rest of the weekend without a quarrel or the silent barrage of recriminatory stares of phone silence that pierced his psyche when speaking with his boss. He could spend yet another evening at the Admiralty with his new mentor the new found philosopher King, in the wonderful lubricant of his Dewar's to enjoy the distillate of the bar keep's wisdom a-more.

Chapter 16

It was a typical sunny and honey-vivid day that afternoon, one of those days the family had that always held them in a luminous, crystalline stasis, beyond time. A southwest breeze fretted the blue plate of the lake, while the kids swam, dove and frolicked, wearing themselves into an enervated frazzle, and the water spaniel retrieved the endless tosses of the tennis ball into the lake. The family that collected on the deck all seemed to take a collective deep foreboding breath hoping to release it only when the horrific omen building had passed into oblivion. There was a distinct sense of uncertainty in the air that surrounded the deck as dense as exhaust fumes as Mary's internal muse was stated outwardly for all the family gathered that afternoon to hear. "Sometimes, dear family, when confronted with what seems like certain failure, with the benefit of hope, God does his best work." All most of the family could do was give the moral equivalent of a shrug of agreement.

Only six people now had any idea, any small sense of each of the strands that would make up the afternoon's filigree of conversation on the deck overlooking Lake Bearskin, but Mary and Walt, Ryan and Nan and Colleen and Dan had no hold on where those strands would take them. It would be Dan's obligatory role at the request of Walter, using the mainframe computer at Northwestern for research, to take his pupils through an equation unsure whether the students at hand were to be stubborn and obtuse or compliant and full of the need to truly understand. This would not be a time for a disquisition on the difference between being serious and looking serious. They would need to plunge in with both feet, hands and head and anything else that would report for muster, hoping for moments of mutual lucidity.

The dark Sophoclean overtones of family strife seemed to loom over them as the sweet pine scents of sauna smoke drifted in the wind over them. They were already beginning to feel the clammy touch of uncertainty that was in the offing. Ignorance might sometimes be courage, Walt thought to himself, as the sauna steams drifted off toward the bay in a gentle westerly breeze. Perhaps they would pick up the right signals from the ether of their conversations this Saturday afternoon that would guide them through. Perhaps those signals lingered directly in front of them at this moment, like the radioactive blinking of otherwise invisible stars in the streaming sauna mist.

Mary and Nan and Colleen had prepared a sumptuous tray of fruits and vegetables and cuts of the walleye that were left over from the previous evening's inaugural dinner feast. Pitchers of homemade lemonade and sun tea and an iced tub full of bottles of Leinenkugel were provided for the wanting. The stairs off the long enwrapping weathered pine deck resounded all of a sudden with the tread of heavy young feet of the four towheads coming running up the stairs, the red bandage of sun patched across each of their noses, as below along the lakeshore Gabby closed over the scent of a chipmunk, her snout poking into the brush, haunches low, her quivering stub tail wagging out of control. The boys poured themselves cups of lemonade and tumbled back down the stairs for more shoreline frolics.

Walt made a parody tug at an imagined forelock and whistled and smiled in Dan's direction in what seemed a surety of his respect, and unthinkingly touched his forelock in a fleeting salute for Dan to begin. Walter's eyes, Ryan noticed, seemed as alert and as assimilative as ever and his arching eyebrows finished his suggestion to Dan without words.

Ryan watched his father as it seemed he was building a mask of quiet concentration as Dan was about to start his dissertation. He just for a moment closed his eyes and steeped his fingers and began to nod almost metronomically in time with the beginning flow of Dan's hypothesis as if to the beat of his own inner music. It was going to be a hard slog up country he knew and the sharpshooters would most certainly be moving in behind the hedgerows and he hoped the realization of Dan's research and historical background would make him feel better and the ulcer that seemed to be building inside would become emulsified into submission.

Dan began by giving the background of the Office of Foreign Asset Control and the acquisition department that Arthur Borgen had been the head of for over thirty-nine years. OFAC was the successor to the Office of Foreign Funds Control which had been established at the advent of World War II following the German invasion of Norway in 1940. The FFC program, Dan explained, was administered by the Secretary of the Treasury throughout the war. The FFC's original purpose was to prevent the Nazi use of the occupied countries' holdings of foreign exchange and securities and to prevent forced repatriation of funds belonging to nationals of those countries. After the United States formally entered the war the FFC played a leading role in economic warfare against the Axis powers by blocking enemy assets and prohibiting foreign trade and financial transactions. OFAC itself was formally created in December 1950, following the entry of China into the Korean War, when President Truman because of the supposed national emergency had blocked all Chinese and North Korean assets subject to U.S. jurisdiction.

The Treasury Department had a long history of dealing with sanctions, dating back to the War of 1812, when the Secretary of the Treasury Gallatin administered sanctions imposed against Great Britain for the harassment of American sailors. During the Civil War, Congress approved a law which prohibited transactions with the Confederacy and called for the forfeiture of goods involved in such transactions, and provided a licensing regime under rules and regulations administered by the Treasury.

Dan went on to explain how most of the world now was being digitally x-rayed using satellites, through a government surveillance program called the star-set system, using seismic data and computers that were originally used in the process of locating oil fields after the theories of Calouste Gulbunkian and the infamous Gulbunkian Line, that delineated oil reserves in the Middle East and the great Caspian Basin. The U.S. space command now, via bases called down-link stations, receives signals from orbiting satellites. It is a star wars control of declining natural resources, via the militarization of space. It is a net-centric warfare tactic, with first strike pre-emptive action. This satellite star-set system could today easily pick up the resident signature of all elements be they gold or platinum or palladium or coltan, which likely explained Borgen's agency's new found interest in the Chisholm family claim. The U.S. Government, Dan had learned, is still taking lands and private rights from dozens of tribes and private citizens in order to transfer and monetize those to corporate contributors to political action committees, while people are being displaced on every continent of the world, brutally and mercilessly.

"I'll tell you," Dan pushed on taking a healthy swish of his lemonade, "that I felt something very ominous early on as I researched this, something like the people must have felt at the Duchess of Richmond's ball before Waterloo, or at Nebuchadnezzar's speech." Grinning wryly, tooting a little flourish of his erudition. Dan sounded oddly valedictory, Ryan thought, as he was making himself very helpful with each bit of background information one after another until all these odds and ends of historical usefulness accreted to indispensability.

As the sun began its downward tract over the western horizon of the lake, Dan continued his research but on a different track regarding the dubious relationships Borgen apparently had with certain international money contacts and transfer agents. His brother Tim who was an institutional trader on Wall Street had filled him in on some very interesting, "deep graveyard," information, as he termed it. Dan had contacted his brother, giving him no background on the family secret, and he had agreed to run a test pattern on Arthur Borgen, who he was vaguely aware of through the back channel trading and the lore of whispered illicit activities. The graveyard of his thesis would be deeper than the Marianas Trench but it was, Dan believed, part of his insidious on-going operation that would need to be punctured.

Dan went on to tell a story he had learned from his brother, about a certain financial wholesaler of note who had leveraged himself to the financial armpits and caught the big post-OPEC commodity boom using the newly created very dubious computer model of Black-Shoals option pricing to perfection and then moved into the financial markets just in time to catch the surges of the recent faux bull market. The guy in recent years, Dan's brother had confided, became a mysterious figure only whispered of in Wall Street circles who was said to move multi-billions of dollars of nefarious monies all around the world.

Dan put down the notes he had made and reached down from the thickly padded couch chair in which he sat, and uncapped a Leinie and gazed out over the azure calm of the bay as the others stared intently in his direction, with what Ryan sensed was a slight sense of dread, and turned to the family seated on the deck. "My brother said" Dan's tone cautionary "that this guy was hardly visible but it was understood that one of his key business contacts" as he lowered his voice to a near sub-aural pitch "was none other than Arthur Borgen." They had all heard it and were slowly taking in its meaning, the family now lapsing itself into a menacing silence. Mary looked at the pine flooring of the deck and shook her head and, her face looking perplexed, she turned to Dan for further elucidation.

Dan, sharing the disquiet and sensing the prior confidences voiced were in suspension, took a purposeful pause and a healthy gulp of his fresh beer, the hops and barley flowing over his tongue now seemed to be nothing but a mere bottled solution of uncertainty, and finally continued. "My brother told me that it was most likely that they would never meet, if they ever met at all, but the guy would 'lay out' to Borgen the 'number' that would be available for 'investment'," Dan said, motioning with an up down gesture of his two fingers on both hands, "for over the next three to five years. Tim suggested it was thought to be as much as three to five billion per year," Dan announced with arched eyebrows. This was the kind of money, and there was so much of it, that it hated the limelight and had its hat pulled down over its eyes.

"This guy was one of those guys," Dan continued, his voice hushed, "that you saw in the TV documentaries up in a glass air conditioned booth looking at an electronic display board and pushing buttons. Except that instead of a subway system or a chemical plant or hydroelectric grid, what this guy had put together was a wonderful machine that was fed very dirty dollars on one end and turned out clean and shiny ones at the other end. It was like the oil refineries, Dan interjected, that turn crude oil into all sorts of different end products; except instead of filter valves and catalysts his system was made up of Panamanian banks and Lichtenstein trusts and Texas thrifts and Ohio insurance companies.

"As my kid brother said." Dan moved forward. "It was 'technology' responding to the rising volume of money. The business that had once consisted of a bunch of 'mustache Petes' lugging satchels of used bills up to bank windows has grown a billion fold." Walter grinned at him as he caught the illusion of his satyriasis.

"But back then," Dan continued, "you were talking about five hundred big ones a year out of maybe something like the New York State gasoline tax scam. Today the big New York banks have developed an electronic daisy chain that they deployed at the turn of the eighties to handle the flight capital streaming out of places like Mexico and Nigeria and the eventual countries released from the Soviet bloc. With the kind of cash that's being thrown off now there aren't enough pizza parlors, trash haulers, building material wholesalers and heating oil distributors to handle the money pouring in."

"When you get close to a big money deal such as this," Ryan quietly advised in a solemn voice, attesting to his own years on Wall Street, "and with fees that are so large a kind of hysterical momentum takes over that becomes uncontrollable."

"Instead of beat up valises," Dan continued nodding knowingly in Ryan's direction in agreement with his comment, "today we are talking about 747 cargo jets flying paper money by the ton into Panama or Liberia where a couple of keystrokes transform the illicit green into an electronic blip and shutter it to Zurich and wherever else."

"Welcome to the new age of cyber-crime," was Ryan's wry comment. "Money has now acquired its sought after electronic anonymity."

"My brother Tim said the sums of money that flashed across the settlement and transfer wires might represent the economic distillate of genuine goods and services that benefited all mankind but he and all the other traders doubted it, but who really knew. He also told me that the piles of nefarious money would also use the banks, where the thrifts would take the dough and lend it out or buy into equity deals and thus it would not get into the financial bloodstream but also be backed by the full faith and credit of Uncle Sam. That would be you and me." Dan smiled with grim irony. Dan's locutions and the deep knowledge he was imparting on these subjects was quite impressive.

"They would also pass it through the insurance industry via big single premium annuities, bought for benefit plans that would never pay off," Ryan added.

"Absolutely," Dan returned, giving another knowing nod in Ryan's direction. "My brother told me they would also buy product liability insurance for products that didn't exist and the weird thing is," Dan continued with a turn of his palms skyward, "is that my brother said, nobody asked."

"Nobody asked because nobody wanted to know," Ryan added quickly, having seen first-hand the craven broker greed and client disregard, "not with the kind of money there was in middle-manning all the illicit deals."

It was becoming frighteningly clear Borgen's rogue agency had become part of a criminal extortion and seizure racket of property jurisdiction and acquisition and that here was a man of a criminal mind made up of seemingly infinite parts lavishly well connected in matters of finance and money transfer.

"I'm afraid any moral qualms would take second place to the financial compulsion," Colleen softly included, shaking her head in revulsion.

"The financial calculus of all this type of business is made intentionally devoid of all human feelings," Ryan stated, his head hanging low after a truncated pause in dialogue. "It's as if in order to be in that type of business and make money you have to accept and participate in a jihad on the war on conscience."

"Let me finish with this on the subject of Borgen," Dan conspiratorially intoned, taking the long neck of his beer for another gulp of fortitude. Dan's face seemed suddenly drained of good feelings, in the glimmering light of the afternoon, the shadow of his thick brows masked his eyes, his high cheekbones and the arch of his nose covered the play of his thin lips. "My brother discovered that one of his agency's operations overseas used a Lichtenstein nominee trust that was known in very private whispered circles to be silently run for the business of the Vatican in Rome." As Dan explained this new twist of information, there was a moment of puzzled silence followed shortly thereafter by a moment of silent assent.

Walter nodded gravely and turned his fingertips upward as he tapped at his heart. "Oh this is too much." Mary sighed heavily, finally breaking the silent impasse. Walt's eyes started to rise to the sky and he exchanged a quick glance with Mary, the usual pantomime of skepticism that Ryan was long familiar with.

Ryan nodded in the direction of his father forswearing the opportunity in the offing and like the first rumblings of an oncoming subway they could all sense with dread the question that must be asked. They all bowed their heads now before Dan in hypothalamic agreement with everything he had discovered.

The family sat in a charged silence that surrounded the lakeside deck like the mist of a shroud with the sun showing its waning golden rays in the western sky. Over the course of Dan's disquisition a general sense of duty slowly but assuredly alchemized, so that they would find themselves bound in their cause, no excuses, no evasion and no more lost dreams. Mary turned to Walt sitting next to her and nodded to convey comprehension, fright or sympathy or whatever emotion might be called for as she continued spinning out her past and its current impact.

"What about the current administration?" Walter asked Dan after the prolonged silence, Dan nodding, understandably not at all disappointed to have the conversation pulled away from his discourse.

"Tim told me that anyone who has ever known him sees him as a racist, a liar, a homophobe and a fool. According to the head of our political science department the guy finked for HUAC while in Hollywood. Back in the late forties and fifties he sold out the screen actors' guild in order to get a better contract for himself."

"He was never a great actor, not even a decent one." Mary laughed aloud. "So there could be nothing genuine about what he says or does, it's all artifice. His simplistic worldview is a pastiche stitched together from Hallmark greeting cards, Currier and Ives lithographs, Benjamin Franklin aphorisms, Hollywood epics and Chinese fortune cookies."

"Yes we had one of those types when Mary and I were young," Walt added for historical measure. "William Harding was his name and he was handsome, he spoke well and he sounded more American than Buffalo Bill."

"Oh God," Mary added quickly, "he was so shallow it made a thinking body ache. I had seen plenty of vapid vacant men in my time," Mary continued, "but this was a shallowness of a transcendent kind." Mary's face became less resolute during the course of her comment, her expression seemed tempered by resignation, but for an instant.

"James Watt," Dan continued, "Reagan's Secretary of the Interior perhaps exemplifies best the culture of greed of the 'I got mine,' mentality that envelops the current administration. He pushed hard for mining and timber interests to have greater access to lower cost minerals and timber on federally owned land because he said Jesus will return to earth at any time and everything will then be made new, as suggested in revelations."

Why, Ryan thought, in our country, are those who are driven by personal greed and narrow self-interest empowered over those who extol social values like kindness, generosity, compassion, sharing empathy, and community building? And why has it become so hard for the great majority of Americans to imagine a different, much better future than the one defined by current policy initiatives and social values?

Upon the extended silence and reflection and contemplation that followed Dan's superb research, Mary finally offered through the cover of the accumulated hush a summation of the moral challenges ahead. "It would be terrible to be crushed by one's own virtues. Can you imagine any attitudes more self-destructive than the ones our sort were made to venerate. It's like being born with a fatal disease and made to think that Noblesse Oblige is passé."

"Like good sportsmanship," Walt added to Mary's soliloquy, "that true happiness is something that money can't buy, that character matters, that the other fellow counts and there is something called shame in a shameless world."

"We were made to believe," Mary taking the baton from Walter, "that we were the American norm. What fools we were. The American norm seems to be men like Borgen or the guys laundering money or all the LBO guys or anyone else who thinks a social compact is something you can carry makeup in."

Walter merely nodded his pursed lips as the only evidence of inner calculation and laid a gentle hand on Mary's knee. He began to summarize the afternoon's learnings and visibly began to choke up, but generations of inbred professional poise stiffened him, his eyes filling with the remnants of rage and deep sorrow. Ryan was certain as he took Nan's hand that his father and mother would both perform on the flaming pyre of values they had both been raised to love and adhere to.

"Just as in World War II," Walter quietly intoned, staring out at the fan of sunlight on the water, a certain sense of finality in his voice, "our total obliterating victory and the nobility of the cause will excuse any of our strategic duplicity. I am for moving wisely forward" Mary reaching over to take his hand "on our collective project and succeeding in the end, for a lifetime of hell can be the condition of knowing through eternity what your children might think of you."

Like Canute, the great King of England, Walter would play the great leader to carry the quest successfully forward. He would shed, he reminded himself once more of whatever fogginess real or imagined, like a snake and enlist in the fight. Ryan knew his father well enough to know that no grass would grow under his sturdy brogans when he was determined to get something done. They were all beginning to see this as an opportunity to strike a purgative blow for the shared values of family and close friends. The least fracture would be like a name engraved with the point of a pin on the tender rind of a young oak; the wound would enlarge with the tree, and posterity read it in full grown characters…

They were all a little bleary, from what Ryan gathered, by the long session of woes and worries and challenges as the family gazed out from the lake deck and watched the boys while they played with Gabby and frolicked about in and out of the water, their faces considerably orchred by the sun. The salute of the late afternoon's sun clarity was beginning to muzz over with haze. The turning dull light that slanted in through the translucent panels along the deck gave the lake home's interior a comforting soft glow of yellowish varnish, Ryan noticed, as he walked toward the wet bar to wheel out the cocktail cart and commence the evening's activities.

The wind had fallen with the day and it was a truly majestic northern night as Ryan dropped down to the lake front lawn to stoke the sauna. The night was blessedly silent, the air crisp, the moon high, the sky clear, the stars assailing the lake residents with celestial revelations and everywhere there was an impression of tallness and expanse, with only a couple of moving lights on the distant waters west, to signify the presence of other humans.

It was like living in the fifties that never ended up here, Ryan halfway dreamed as he gazed out at the reflective glass of star light the lake held. It was a place where everyone still liked Ike, a place, as the old hymn said, "where every prospect pleases and only man is vile". But this was a country now, Ryan knew, that had once promised such a good foursquare fortune that was now devolving into a truculent unthinking, uncaring, uncivilized clawing crowd. Ryan took a bit of cedar bark and added it to the sauna fire. The wind rose suddenly and the fire stirred and grew brighter. The cedar bark flamed up in a small explosion of embers that quickly rose up the stove pipe on the sauna roof and lifted on the wind and scurried into the night like fireflies.

Nan joined Ryan now with fresh cocktails and they stood arm in arm along the dock rail as they watched baguettes of light strung along the far banks of Oliver Island to the southwest and a lone timber wolf, as if on cue, made its foreboding howl against the darkened forests of aspen and firs beyond. Was the creature calling his warning or sadness, for a world gone so wrong? Beyond the rising sheets of gray aromatic sauna smoke rose the pale patterns of northern lights, shimmering, rising and falling. Ryan reached out as if touching the night display. Everything is connected, he thought, like the threads on a spider web. And time is like the wind. The wind blows and the web moves, but the connections do not break. He felt something tearing though, something big. Threads were breaking and he didn't know why.

They enjoyed a wonderful night of good viands, salmon and asparagus and a blur of good white wines and needed idle conversations and late night cleansing saunas and reborn dips in the curative power waters of Bearskin Lake. It was here, like the cleansing force claimed for baptism, that they could shed any animus in the cool waters, floating and looking up at the picture painting of stars and constellations, all back dropped by the phenomenal northern lights.

"Ryan come to bed," he heard Nan whisper as he sat out in the cool air on the lanai sipping brandy that he and Nan were sharing, "tomorrow is going to be a big day."

Yes it is, he thinks happily, yes it will, and the day after that and the day after that.

They both understood that a discussion of the day's revelations would be an exercise in over-exasperation, so they were both hoping to happily throw themselves into joyous moist oblivion. But it seemed they were a little out of sync, unaware of their unease, as she guided Ryan's hands between her legs willing to accept his engorgement for passion, burrowed deep in their sensations but yet separated slightly this night in their fantasies and fears.

As Nan succumbed to sleep in his arms Ryan laid there a while hoping osmosis would implant something into his mind to support his own wavering certitude from the sleeping mind beside him.

Four hours south of Bearskin Lake in the darkness of the early morning, two men dressed in black stealthily approached the back pond level door of the home of Walter and Mary Davies. It was just after three a.m. The taller man produced a key that easily opened the door and the two entered the house. In the dark a small leather attaché case was placed on the dining table outside of the kitchen. Disposable gloves were pulled and stretched over their hands each taking a small flashlight from the case. They worked quickly dealing with phones first. The receiver from the kitchen phone was unplugged and laid on the table. The microphone was unscrewed and examined. A tiny drop-in transmitter the size of a grain of rice was glued in the cavity of the receiver and held firmly in place for ten seconds. The microphone was then replaced and the receiver was plugged into the phone and re-hung on the kitchen wall. The voices or signals would be transmitted to a small receiver to be installed in the attic. A large transmitter next to the receiver would send signals across town to an antenna atop the Foshay Tower that housed a small office leased to an obscure Washington DC cut out. Using AC lines as a power source the small bugs in the phones would transmit indefinitely.

The attaché case was moved to the couch. Above, along a wall in the dining room, they inserted a tiny bard into a ridge in the paneling and removed it. A thin black cylinder, one twentieth of an inch by one inch was carefully placed in the hole. It was cemented in place with a dab of black epoxy. The microphone was invisible. A wire the thickness of a human hair was gently fitted into the seam of the paneling and ran to the ceiling to be connected to the receiver in the attic.

Identical mikes were hidden in the wall of each bedroom. The men pulled down the attic hatch in the hallway and climbed up the ladder into the attic. The shorter man removed the receiver and transmitter from the case while the other man painstakingly pulled the tiny wires up from the walls. He gathered them, wrapped them together and laid them under the insulation and ran them to a corner where his partner was placing the transmitter in an old cardboard box. An AC line was spliced and wired to the unit to provide power and transmission. A small antenna was raised to within an inch of the roof decking.

Their breathing became heavier in the confining heat of the flashlight lit attic. The small plastic casing of an old radio was fitted around the transmitter and they scattered insulation around it. It was in a remote corner and not likely to be noticed for months, maybe years if ever, and if it was noticed it would appear to be only worthless junk, picked up and thrown away without suspicion. They admired their handiwork, descended the stairs, meticulously covered their tracks, finishing their work in less than ten minutes, quietly leaving by the back walkout door.

Chapter 17

Ryan woke the next morning to a stirring outside the open slatted window shades facing the western waters of the lake scarcely louder than the drift of leaves in the wind, with a premonition that something somewhere was askew. Next to him Nan breathed softly, hugging her pillow, clinging to the darkness behind her closed eyelids, chasing a rainbow in the remnants of her early morning dreams. He sat up quietly and collected himself, the clock on the pine bedside table telling him it was just after seven. He dressed himself in his usual lake raiment, threading his pale white legs through khaki shorts stretching his arms into an old golf shirt and slipping his feet into a twenty year old pair of topsiders. He looked out the window upon the new day as the early morning sun was just becoming streaked with the first fiery fingers of dawn turning the lake into a blazing mirror stretching along the eastern bay in front of him from north to south. He parted the cobwebs that shrouded his awareness and remembered that it was Sunday.

Home is where you know what to do with yourself on Sundays throughout the year, he mused. Sundays were, thankfully, a day of rest from the reckless abandon of entertainment. At home this day was the time for established routines with predictable options and familiar local rules and traditions.

On most Sundays in Manhattan on the upper west side during the period when he and Nan were leading separate lives, he would rise early and depending on the ravages of the previous evening put some Bach or Palestrina on the stereo as a gesture to the notional holiness of the day and pad over to his apartment door and gather up the *Times* and the *Daily News*, which he read in sequence. Living alone, Ryan had come to quickly learn, could provide a nacreous selfishness, a carapace of self-interest that really looked better than it felt. The New York papers no longer took up a full mind in the morning of those days so after he had finished, it still being early, he would dress and wander over to seventy-second and Broadway for a supplementary injection of ink, *Newsday* and whichever out of town papers caught his attention, he would skin at his coffee shop of preference.

Today Ryan padded his way quietly down the oval curved stairs, keeping the fall of his footsteps silent, as he made his way toward the front double doors to retrieve the Sunday papers from Duluth and the *Star Tribune* from the great metropolis to the south. It was a breezy early morning as a feathery barrier of gray clouds made their way over the eastern sky, beginning to turn milky white as though a celestial eyelid were opening as he scraped up the regional tabloids enwrapped in their plastic sleeves.

He made a pot of coffee hoping the aroma wouldn't awaken any of the rest of the slumbering family as he made his initial perusal of the papers. It would be some hours this Sunday morning before the claims and prospective calamities of the coming week would begin to assert themselves. By seven-thirty he had completed his routine more quickly than usual. The state of the world seemed to continue to be in a dismal form. The papers read of bombings, famine and of missiles and riots. The obituaries included a former Minnesota football player, an old college friend's mother, an all pro former football player and an abstract impressionist painter. The sports pages were as per usual principally concerned with contract disputes and litigation, with stories of franchise financing and television ratings and declining audience shares. For the real blood and guts and the current action now and the thrill of victory and the agony of defeat all you need do is turn to the business section and read about the latest throng of corporate takeover wars that are ongoing.

Ryan sipped at his coffee and made one more sortie through the Duluth news to make sure he hadn't missed anything. He hadn't missed a thing, he thought. He now knew how things used to be in Finland and their plans to invest in cell phone technology, what some lackey editorialist thought the president should do about depreciation and individual tax policy, why the Twins were in last place, how to create magical cuisine with red peppers, whether George Bernard Shaw was gay and Mozart a depressive, and our apparent next pre-emptive strike at the tiny island of the Falklands. Then, like suffering an unforeseen electric shock, he saw it, and read it two then three times his hand holding his coffee trembling, as he pursed his lips as if pursuing a second line of inquiry in the back of his mind

A body of East Asian or Arab descent, the article read, had been found in the early hours of Saturday morning along the docks of the harbor in Duluth with a bullet in the middle of his forehead. There was no identification on the male body and police could offer no explanation of how the body got there and where it may have come from. The body was currently at the Duluth police morgue and the case was under further investigation.

Ryan poured himself another reflective cup of coffee and walked quietly out to the deck and asked himself if indeed with this strange news from the Duluth harbor if all hell was about to break loose, as the morning sky to the west seemed to be turning to a shade of brimstone. Ryan looked up and was surprised to see his father swimming laps inside the marker buoys in front of the boat docks.

It was one of those days when Walter found his rhythm right away and didn't have to make himself feel the water or picture himself riding up high. Everything just seemed to happen this spring morning, that serene lazy crawl, his round arms lifting and dropping, lifting and dropping, swimming with even untiring strokes through the medium of time, a medium more inert than water, without ripples, pervasive, colorless, odorless, dry as paper, freeing his mind to wander. Soon it wandered to a painting he had once seen at a museum in London, *the Fortune Teller*, by Caravaggio. A fortune teller is reading a man's palm. You can see in her eyes that she has a big premonition about his future, be it good or bad. Walt could never make up his mind about that, he had gazed at the painting so often that his mental image of the fortune teller's eyes matched what was on the canvas. Today, gliding along uncounted laps, he felt that the young man's future was good.

Walter took one last lap, going all out on the last length, lungs bursting, then, ramping down to a breaststroke glide on his last lap. He climbed up the ladder at the end of the dock still breathing hard as he wrapped himself in an oversized pink bath towel and saw Ryan sitting on the chaise lounge. Ryan handed his father a cup of coffee that he had gone back to the kitchen to retrieve as Walt had finished his swim.

"Glad you're up, Dad, we had something happen in Duluth early Saturday morning that is rather rum," he said, a severe grim look creasing his face, as he handed the section of paper to his father for edification. Walter read the article and looked up at Ryan and instinctively read it again, and a third time, trying to make the yet unconnected appear relevant, looking less at the information than for auguries of some course of action. Suddenly as he peered into Ryan's eyes their eyes met with a strange effect like that of a collision followed by a recoil that resounded all through them, Walter's eyes becoming dark, cold and stony, producing yet another sense of uncertainty in the morning air that surrounded the docks of the lake shoreline as dense as exhaust fumes.

As the family household came astir around nine o'clock, Mary threw herself into her Sunday routine of cooking her infamous scrambled eggs just the way her patrons loved them. The family ate in silence for a few moments as they could overhear the boys and the family hound outside for a morning frolic and continuing games of retrieval, trying to determine just what the developments of the morning and the disturbing news of the body found on the shipping docks forebode.

Never, in her lifetime in Everest, had anything like this occurred in Duluth, Mary had said. They ate again without a word, the sound of their silverware seeming to echo in the mounting morning gloom like the rattle of old bones, trying to perhaps escape the potential impasse and the very thought that this event could somehow be related to Borgen and his agency and the family drama currently at hand.

Ryan nodded in the direction of his father as the six of them sat in silence, forswearing the opportunity in the offing and like the first rumblings of thunder from the oncoming storm he could sense the dread of the question that must be asked. Ryan realized as he hoped did the others that they must have a pact, a pact of mutual advantage and a pact with God. What would happen along the way, how would the cause and effect and the ramifications of the actions they may be required to take affect all the loved ones here and now?

It would be some hours this Sunday morning before the claims and prospective calamities learned would or could begin to assert themselves. The rooms plunged into shade by the rolling clouds, and a sense of dread hung over the breakfast dining area that was palpable. Finally through the silence Mary let go of the eternal thought orbiting her mind, reminding them that, "What we must do is really an act of grace upon the future of mankind and the flourish of modest wealth and care and comfort that we can help bestow upon this community of man." All they could muster were weak smiles, nervous returns of serve back into her impassive brown eyes, with nods of agreement.

Matt's mouth after his extensive evening at the Admiralty tasted as if the Corsican army was on field maneuvers between his teeth and he pitied for the agony of his condition. Like a pavlovian dog he aroused at the bell of his alarm clock and quickly got up and got dressed. He found his condition once again too ugly to merit mourning.

He passed the morning with coffee and juices and the usual bromides hoping to cure his unrelenting hangover, reading the local and state newspapers on the porch overlooking the harbor under gun metal gray skies. Suddenly Matt was struck dumb in the face of the feelings that had come unleashed within him like cargo that had become unloosed in the hole of a ship that was plunging deep to the bottom of the sea, upon reading of the news of the middle eastern male found along the docks of Duluth harbor during the early hours of Saturday morning.

So many questions now, bouncing like sharp pebbles off a brain as sore as an open wound, or was he just having another one of those meaningless perambulations? He was suspended in the netherworld of unfocused exhaustion, sinking free fall through the shreds of his latent drunkenness, barely able to move.

Only after he had drained the last glass of his hangover tonic did he remember Arthur Borgen and the whispered deeply guarded graveyard secret about the agency and its access to something called the "dead bank." Borgen took masochistic pride, Matthew knew, in being in charge and many of his victims tended to compare boastfully the relative ignominies they'd suffered at his hands. Was it now his turn to be next in that long line, he asked himself?

There seemed to be an undertone of apology in the gathering at the lake that afternoon as Jim Theno made his way around greeting everyone with what appeared to be mildly reluctant hand clasps, retreating back into the shell he seemed to carry through the door when he arrived. It was the sad ongoing threnody of the Theno legacy that still haunted him and it seemed the dim pictures of Mary's family and childhood lurked in the background like spectral creatures in the shadows. Time and sorrow, Mary thought, had made his persona just a little thicker and coarser. The sudden and shocking loss of his mother had in some way cauterized his feelings and regulated his deportment and seemed to have sternly focused him only ahead on his career. Mary felt he had locked up his childhood within himself and imprisoned its carefree innocence behind bars of gravity and purpose. Indeed, after his mother's death and his grandfather's death long before in the mine explosion, medicine and books had become his sole effective solace. After medical school at the University of Minnesota he had joined the staff at the University Hospital in general medicine, but after a few years of dealing with the very delicate, byzantine and complex pecking order he decided to return to his small town roots and practice medicine.

Lois quietly unseen had released from the side of her husband Bud and settled at the ebony baby grand piano, her back as straight as a ballerina, as beams of afternoon light came off the lakeside deck making the silhouette of a halo above her rich black hair, that swirled around her like a Botticelli painting. As she began to play the slow movement from a Beethoven Sonata the bright pure vapor of her kind soul illuminated her face and her deep innocent brown eyes. The breathtaking and rending tone seemed to instill an impeccable unity of peace and oneness in the gathering. The crystalline piano notes, the clarity and beauty, were played with an ease that was without haste or urgency, anonymous in a way, as if Beethoven were not an individual, but a mere man, a mortal who had died centuries ago, but the voice of humankind itself, refined of all that is crude, gross, debased and ugly. The music hung above them sealing and cocooning them momentarily from the careworn fractious world. Lois was spinning its attenuated sorrowful song like a rope around the heart of each listener.

It was as if, Ryan thought, his arm around Nan, that they were standing surrogate for the entire older generation represented here, official mourners of needless death deputed from the netherworld to be here, now at this moment to finally begin reconciliation. Walter and Mary and Lois and Bud looked the way Ryan hoped to look when he got to sixty or seventy, their faces were living proof that life couldn't lick character no matter what it threw at you, the sort of people around whom had once been matriarchies and patriarchies that were civilized, discreet and as tough as they were gracious.

Represented here were the three archetypes of the American generation and World War II, the G.I. generation of rising adult soldiers, the can-do heroes born from 1901 through 1924 represented by Walter and Bud, who for the most part had given up arguing with the young agreeing with their kids that they were wrong to some degree, but maintaining their life-long credo of optimism, teamwork and community, taking pride in the immense prosperity machine they had built, yet not at all happy as was the ethos of the G.I. generation present today as they witnessed the acquiescence of many of their brethren to the pan generational ethos of self-indulgence that had ensued.

The silent generation, the artistic silent children and deferential helpmates born at the tail end of the depression and before the war, reeling and suffering from a sort of cultural and technological vertigo, off balance with an inner ear reverberating to the sounds of both Patti Page and the Rolling Stones, having been raised to live for one era yet forced to live in another, represented by Jim Theno, who was born in 1942. The silent became the stuff in the middle of a generational sandwich, just younger than the can do G.I. yet just older than the self-absorbed boomers.

Like the silent generation attorney, Sam Yasgur, who persuaded his farmer father to lease their family property at Woodstock for a youth festival, where the Silent drove the magic bus while the boomer kids got to party, where silent activists and artists like Jerry Rubin and Abbie Hoffman, who lent expression to youth fury, became the pied pipers of revolt, and Ralph Nader launched the opening salvo against G.I. style mass production by attacking the U.S. auto industry with his book Unsafe at Any Speed, of delivering death, injury and the most inestimable sorrow and deprivation to millions of people.

From 1969 to 1975 the number of American public interest law firms quintupled. It was a generation where the silent youth felt the need to break away from gravitational conformism and were the least immigrant generation and yearned for more diversity. They were the most uniform youth culture in living memory, the youngest marrying generation in U.S. history, where the worst high school discipline problems were chewing gum and cutting in line. They were youths coming of age believing in sweet sentimentality, as kids who sang Elvis, "just want to be your teddy bear." They were growing up just when a hungry society wanted to invest, in an era when individualism was discouraged but economic success guaranteed, climbing the corporate ladder with many going to Washington to staff the New Frontier and Great Society agencies, coming of age with How to Succeed in Business Without Really Trying.

The Boomer generation, the post war children, the prophet generation, the narcissistic, the victory babies of returning G.I.s, inheritors of G.I. triumph, coming of age as mystical militants, their mission not to build or improve institutions necessarily but rather to purify them with righteous fire in a search for resacralization, seeking to be "together people" not together like G.I. uniformed corps of the 1940s but together as in a "good vibration," a sort of generational kinship like the necklace of Shiva in which every diamond reflects every other and is itself reflected.

In the boomer new youth culture, purity of moral position counted most, and verbal terrorism silenced those who dared to dissent from dissent, where most campus riots of the time assumed that the instant they deigned to do so, they could drop back into the American Dream machine.

The Boomer New Left pressed moral and cultural causes asking how to live individually within society, rather than how to change it collectively. The most memorable of Boomer youth symbols were direct affronts against the construction of G.I. men, from the two-fingered peace taunt, adapted from the old G.I. V-for-victory, to the defiant wearing of khaki, the G.I. color of uniformed teamwork.

The emerging Boomer agenda was a deliberate antithesis to everything the prototypical G.I. male had stressed during the High: spiritualism over science, gratification over patience, fractiousness over conformity, rage over comity, negativism over blind positivism, and most importantly, sadly, self over community. When the tempest of the Awakening began to calm, and as the anti-Vietnam fever cooled and the economy became an issue for the first time for Boomer college graduates, the aspects of life Boomers had once deemed spiritually empty, consumption, careerism, family formation, were now temptingly available, having at last been resacralized by their new values.

They were at the end of a second turning, Ryan intuited, he and Nan from the tail end of the sixties who didn't like the front end of the eighties as Lois played so sweetly at the keyboard. It was an awakening period where the heroes of his generation were entering elder-hood, artists entering midlife and prophets entering young adult-hood, toward an inevitable unraveling period, if history was true to its cyclicality, an equinox period, a transition toward shorter days and longer nights, where the old heroes disappear, artists enter elder-hood, prophets enter midlife, and the nomad archetype, the children of the Boomers, the thirteenth generation of American citizens, the nomad generation, that, if cycles held, would be the only U.S. generation aside from the Gilded, to ever suffer a life-long economic slide.

As Lois played the sonata, Mary sipped her iced tea, her mind a-spin with thoughts as she watched Dr. Jim, as he was called locally, wander off among his thoughts, hopes and memories. She saw him begin to disappear into them as if among the cool and leafy bowers and the alleys of a peaceful summer garden along the lake where the noise and trouble of the world were held at bay, where hope could be reborn and time frozen.

Both Jim and Mary knew that his grandfather, like most of the miners, drank during those hard years in Everest, but it was known that when he drank he tended to talk and let loose some things that should have been locked inside. He had sworn up and down to Mary's father that the secret that only the two of them shared would never leave his lips, but by mid July 1935 after Henry's death in the mine explosion the potential accusatory reactions were building across a no man's land of suspicion. One rumor differed from another only in the labels affixed to the assumed belligerents. Yet as the rumors slowly drifted about the town that summer they continually seemed to affix Mary's father as the most likely belligerent until that day in May of 1944, that with a terrible sigh of resignation, David Chisholm the family patriarch fell heavily to earth and was gathered to his ancestors.

Life at this moment, Mary thought, seemed like a haunted house of might-have-beens as Lois ended the beautiful Sonata with a long hold on an A-sharp. Mary murmured a silent prayer as she hoped Jim Theno would not betray the sacred trust of her family legacy and he would earn his grandfather's eternal smile from beyond the grave, when they brought him into the confidence of their family trust of knowledge.

It was a breezy afternoon, the western sky bright with heavy deep pinks and oranges softened intermittently with fingers of cirrus, as they drifted along the deep azure waters of the spring fed lake in the west bay, the lingering smoke of the unrest from the previous day's conversations seemed to be smoldering anew with a fresh kindle of flame as Bud began to familiarize the group with the takings clause of the fifth amendment.

The takings clause, he explained, has to do with the appropriation of private property for public usage. The Fifth Amendment, he explained, provides that no person shall be deprived of life, liberty or property without the due process of law. Due process was the overarching concern of the fifth amendment, that then goes on to recite the so called takings clause, which holds that private property may not be taken for public use, however defined without, as the law states, just compensation.

At issue here, Bud went on sipping his iced tea with the rapt attention of all but the kids swimming and diving off the stern, was what was called eminent domain. This is an extension of the takings clause whereby the government can condemn and seize private property in the interest of what is called the "greater good." The question in many of these cases recently that have come to the courts has centered around whether the government has the power to use eminent domain to transfer land rights or property from one private owner to another, as opposed to a public authority for the broad public use, like a park or highway which has been the traditional purpose of eminent domain.

"Now here's the rub, my dear friends." Taking a deep breath of the pristine lake air looking directly at Walt. "Although the grounds here for all intents and purposes are judiciously unplowed, the courts have recently ruled that the general benefits a community enjoys from private sector economic growth qualifies as permissible public use under the takings clause of the fifth amendment." Lifting his eyebrows and turning his palms skyward as he finished. "We need to insist," Bud added, "that we demand what de Tocqueville called self-interest properly understood, so as to avoid any court driven injunctions."

"Thanks Bud," Walt said after a short pause while the gathered ingested the information just heard. "What we need to do in my opinion is to soon begin a rational disquisition of all we have learned and of the impending course of actions that may need to be taken if there is sufficient buy-in by all of us. But there is one more piece of information I want to share with you," he nearly whispered to them as he sat in the swivel captain's chair of the pontoon boat, his face suddenly ashen with age.

"Almost as an after-thought," Walt said, his tone mysterious and grave, "I asked Dan to do some research on the Bureau of Mines in Washington DC and investigate their employment records in 1935. Much to his surprise all the employment records from 1934–1940 had been scrubbed clean." Mary squirmed in her seat along the aft of the houseboat as she looked askance at the boys floating on rafts on the calm waters. The sun was lower now and it fell full in their faces, a rich glow of amber warmth.

"When he told me of this interesting dilemma I phoned the Iron Mining Historical Center in Hibbing hoping they might have records of the mine inspectors the bureau employed back then. To my surprise they had all the records intact for the years of 1935 to 1936."

Walter paused for a moment to look upon everyone, as if an uncertain yet visible palatable omen was about to overcome them as they sat bathed in the royal reflection of the cloudless sky of the lake, a smile was playing around the corners of his mouth, but his voice had that edge in it that could make people grave with attention, a tone that would brook no rejoinder. He glanced at Mary, a quick knowing glance, so sensitive to each other, as they had become over a thousand dinner tables. Walt let go a deep inhale of anguished breath as he announced that, "During the summer of those two years, one Arthur Borgen was in the employ of the Bureau of Mines as an inspector's assistant."

"Oh my God," Jim Theno said, nearly convulsing on his words, dropping his face into his cupped hands. There was a prolonged period of menacing silence as the intake of this shocking new information was being metastasized organ by organ into the marrow of their bones. From far off to the south there came the low mutter of thunder and a breeze stirred in the high branches of the pines and aspens, setting their leaves trembling like strips of silver.

There was a palpable feeling of common shame as human beings that they all shared. To be of the same race with this one man who could so unnecessarily steal the last un-begrudged years of their lives. Everyone seemed at a loss for something to say; as if they were distant members of a family gathered at a funeral who discover they have nothing in common with each other beyond kinship with the departed. The dark opaque wall of a coming storm had risen higher until it bridged the entire horizon, blotting out the western shoreline of the lake.

"Where there's a heart there's a Rubicon," Mary finally muttered silently. "God have mercy on us all," she whispered. "Where there's a heart there's a Rubicon, of what hath God made men's hearts?"

The sun sank away to the west in a gibbous red ball and the sky deepened in strokes of rose and magenta over the rippling water of the bay, as they tried to enjoy cocktails on the deck. A medium wind blew freshly against their faces, and the thread of a new moon forced its way through the sinking dusk, beyond the north arm of the lake. In the lake's summer night there was a kind of solemn joy, a hush of peace and light and human happy resignation.

Dinner was to be a sprightly affair as Gus, the local fisher-king for engaging lake trout and walleye, had agreed to drop a share of his daily catch into the wire mesh live well built into the south dock of the Davies' lake home. All agreed after their sobering afternoon adrift to retire back at the lodge to eat, drink and enjoy the spring's mantle spread across Bearskin Lake.

The smell of the wood-chips in the grill along with sweet steam of the cooking sauna drifted up over the docks the way perfume hung in the air at a cocktail party and the shadows were lengthening across the lake, fashioning a painter's milieu of azures, indigos and emeralds as Ryan gathered the day's offerings, denizens of the deep, emissaries of the crystal clear waters, four nice sized walleyes and two five to six pound lake trout, the fish's gills flaring with mortal indignation as Ryan took them from the live well to be cleaned.

As he knelt by the water, he became curiously aware of something in the woods beyond his left shoulder, which caused him to straighten and peer through a clutter of foliage at the lake's edge west of the boat docks. Ryan didn't know why he looked because he hadn't heard anything over the hum of the sauna fire and the musical tumult of lake waves. But there about twenty feet away in the dusky undergrowth, staring at him with a baleful expression, was a moose, full grown and female, or so he presumed, since it had no antlers. It had evidently been on its way to the lake for a drink when it was brought up short, by Ryan's presence, undecided what to do next. They stared at each other for a minute, neither of them knowing what to do, Ryan noticing the haze of flea-like insects floating in circles about its head.

There was a certain obvious and gratifying sense of adventure in this, but also something more low key and elemental, a kind of respectful mutual acknowledgement that came with sustained eye contact. It was unexpected, the sense that there was in some small measure a salute to their cautious mutual appraisal. He remembered his mother's stories about the Ojibwa Indian star cluster system of Pegasus, Lacerta, in the constellation Capella Sirius. The moose, as represented in the winter night sky part of the moon of spirits, they say was used as a locative memory device to avoid getting lost in the deep winter woods. In the Ojibwa myth of folklore, the moose was revered for its hearing and wariness.

Stealthily, so as not to alarm it, Ryan crept off the docks and up the walkway to get the rest of the family. When the family silently returned, the moose had advanced to the water and was drinking about thirty feet away along the lakeshore. "Wow." Tommy, Adam, Jeff and Tony breathed nearly in sync. The moose looked up at them all, even Gabby frozen in wonder, and decided they meant no harm and went back to grousing and drinking.

They watched her for nearly five minutes, as the moose drank and groused, slowly moving west down the shoreline. Slowly the moose turned her head to look at them once more before she clumsily plunged into the lake and swam cartoon like out toward Oliver Island as the ever fearless springer spaniel barked out a wistful farewell.

They returned to the house up the flagstone walkway feeling considerably elated. It seemed like it was a gratifying and commensurate reward for their day of disconcerting mental toil.

The sun dropped away to the west, after the mild storm had passed, in a gibbous red ball and the sky deepened in strokes of rose and magenta over the rippling waters of the bay, as they tried to enjoy cocktails along the deck. A mild wind blew freshly against their faces, and the thread of a new moon forced its way through the sinking dusk, beyond the north arm.

Outside now, the air was cool and still, and the stars shone unchallenged by the thinnest sickle of moon swung low over the pines, and the glowing specks of the newly released fireflies dotted the edges of the shoreline, as they dined together that evening on the deck with cocktails and torrents of white wine, attempting to lasso the loose ends of the days findings and research into something manageable and mutually agreed upon.

They were a Gideon's army, small in number, but unflinching in their commitment to the good cause. All they could hope for now was that the forward stretch of unused days could somehow be easing.

Chapter 18

Ryan and Nan, Walt, Mary and Coleen and Dan stood backstage overlooking the waterfront of Lake Superior as Winnie stood stage right reviewing her notes.

Ryan had called Henry Grover, their neighbor, on Lakeside Avenue and had discovered that a security hold had been placed on any autopsy of the Middle Eastern male found along the docks of Duluth.

Through back channels as head of forensic medicine at the University he had called Ryan back to inform that through his contacts at the morgue in Duluth it appeared the body had been dead for at least 72 hours prior to being found. The following day Mary received a call from her sister Catherine, a bank officer with Peyton Bank in Duluth that a certain individual by the name of Matthew Winslett with some government agency in Washington had presented her with the veracity of a domestic threat search and seizure warrant in order to inspect safe deposit box records.

Mary's sister had explained to her how she found it odd that he had only focused on accounts with the last names starting with the letter C.

It was then that she found after putting back in place the disorder and haste of his search the records removed notating the existence of the old Chisholm lock box that was closed in May of 1945, giving credence as the Davie's family feared, to a plot that was eerily thickening.

Winnie had been building up a strong following, as she was becoming the truth telling tongue of her unuttered brothers. She was the language of man's buried heart. She felt confident in knowing her electorate and the proper order of battle, understanding, she and her staff, that it was a slow process like the re-kneading of previously risen bread.

She had learned as she began her campaign how things grew more real when put into words, how without story telling the past would pale beyond even the pale of the paper, that with the proper order of releasing meaning to arrive at the rhythm that determines the diction and measures the pace, turning the reference of certain words into symbols, via the marvelous march of metaphors, establishing connections with companionable paragraphs and if granted good fortune achieves not just this or that bit of luminous or suggestiveness, but her own unique lines of narrative that provide the desired restitution of the self, as they drew their shoulders forward listening in earnest to the sublime senescence being created. It was Buddha, after all, who had said that the greatest thing in life was the illumination of the human spirit.

Winnie's speech this Wednesday the third in her campaign series of issue to issue subject material was to concern the commons, education and the moral basis of knowledge of the American culture dealing with the devolution and degeneration of basic human emotions, in the face of aggrandizement by values based on enclosure, expediency, competitiveness and greed.

She understood fully that the labors of her compositions and speeches had to put certain threads of thought into a loom and weave them into a continuous whole, to connect, to introduce to her electorate, to blow them out or expand and carry them to a closure, hoping success to be found, as she reconstructed events from otherwise scattered facts, the way the broken lines of a sketch invite the eye to complete their intended course and see a complete form or finished pattern where knowledge and understanding are reached.

In the ranks Winnie could see faces lined by liquor, harried by hard work, wasted by worry and stamped invariably by disappointment, as if it was meant to prove that life was a force of crushing compromise.

It was a mongrel compost in front of her, thousands of faces of descendants, the Fins, the Slavs, the Irish, the Swedes, the Germans, the Lithuanians, the Russians, the Czechs, and the nameless hodgepodge of the Balkans.

Winnie thought as if they were left in the desert, maddened by the site of water they could never reach, and all the juices of their lives had turned to gall and bitterness, to envy and malignant hate.

They belonged to that great lost tribe of people who were more numerous in America than any other country in the world. They belonged to that futile, desolate and forsaken horde who felt that all will be well with their lives, that all power they lack themselves will be supplied, and all the anguish, fury and unrest, the confusion and dark damnation of man's soul can magically be healed if they only eat bran for breakfast, secure an introduction to a celebrity, or get a reading for a friend, by a friend of Ken Follett, or to win the multi-state lottery.

Their impulse, Winnie understood, was generally not to embrace life and devour it, but rather to escape from it.

"It is difficult for us to realize," she began after thanking the crowd of at least three thousand for attending as they gathered in Canal Park overlooking Lake Superior along the harbor ports of Duluth, "that the powers of the mind we call rational intelligence were actually invented by Plato in the 2nd century and the thinkers who followed in his path.

When it comes to critical thinking we find it hard to understand that at one period in our human history, this capability of the human mind was non-existent and had to be deliberately invented. It is also a challenge to understand that humankind's capability of critical thinking is a skill proficiency that can be lost. That is, reason and reflection can become alien to a particular culture if the potential for critical thinking is destroyed or abandoned."

The gathering seemed attentive Ryan thought and he and Nan both knew that the last thing Winnie would allow herself to do was talk over their heads. It was her campaign's intent to help to create mini-epiphanies for her followers, an attainment of new or re-learned knowledge that would bind their loyalty to her long term enduring cause.

"In western culture," she continued, "we define intelligence as the ability to learn or understand and to deal with new or unfamiliar situations using our skilled use of reason. We all have the ability to apply knowledge to manipulate our environment and to think abstractly as measured by objective criteria.

We define intelligence in its essence as the sublime understanding of our own comprehension that then develops a culture of common consciousness and distinctive set of values. This ethos that we live under today is embodied in verbal expressions, such as our constitution, our laws, our literature and our drama. I am a constitutionalist she proudly stated, constitutional law fascinates me and I will admit it is my secret pleasure that I feed on like binge food.

The most ancient form of democracy is found among virtually all indigenous peoples of the world. It is the way humans have lived for more than 150,000 years.

There were no rich and no poor among most tribal people, everybody was part of the commons of the middle class and there was little hierarchy. The concept of chief is one that Europeans brought with them to America, which in large part was what produced so much confusion in the 1600's and 1700's in America as most native Americans tribes would never delegate absolute authority to any one person to sign a treaty.

Instead decisions were made by consensus of the people as it related to the commons, in these most ancient cauldrons of democracy, that didn't even have a word for war in their vocabularies.

When I mention the commons, I am referring to our vast public lands containing minerals and forests, our communities, our schools, our libraries, our urban spaces, the broadcast airwaves that TV stations use for free and the human genome.

The commons are also our wonderful community festivals, the gift economies of public donation systems, and our greatest commons of language itself.

Then there is the commons of our fisheries, farmland and water, that two billion people around the world manage as commons to meet their everyday needs.

The founders of the Nation, and the Framers of our Constitution were greatly influenced and inspired by the democratic displays they witnessed all around them. A great part of the U.S. Constitution is based on the Iroquois Confederacy and the six tribes who occupied territories from New England to the edge of the Midwest and our great state. It was a democracy with elected representatives, an upper and lower house and a supreme court, made up by the way entirely of women, who held the final say in the tribes.

As Ben Franklin noted to his contemporaries at the Constitutional Convention" 'It would be a very strange thing if Six Nations of ignorant savages should be capable of forming a scheme for such a union and be able to execute it in such a manner that it has subsisted for ages, and appears indissoluble, and yet, a like union should be impracticable for ten or a dozen English colonies.

The commons of the media is the only industry written into the constitution because the founding fathers of our country realized that a free unfettered press is the chief instrument of ensuring our freedom.

As Thomas Jefferson said in 1786, our liberty depends on the freedom of the press and that liberty cannot be limited without being lost.

Today the commons of the freedom of the press has transformed in this country, into the ability of one to own all the printing presses.

There were fifty media companies twenty years ago and today there are five companies that control and monopolize our industry. The corporate media has essentially engaged in the censorship of our shared commons of knowledge, counterfeiting the truth by the monopolization of the means of distributing information.

This censorship of knowledge through the cartelization and enclosure of the media is a direct reproach to our means of information and is the subject of my presentation to you this afternoon.

"Before I continue on this subject let me say this to you, good hard working people of Duluth and the Iron Range, for this will always be my overarching goal and mission statement that I pledge to you.

The machinery of politics will never force me to be an agent of injustice to others, for if the machinery of politics requires you to be an agent of injustice to your fellow man you have forsaken yourself and the people you are elected to represent.

I will never bring to you and all the people of this great state; a system that brings the dominion of the few to rule over the many." A huge roar of applause waved through the crowd of the sturdy iron etched proletariats of Duluth and the range. It was like a comforting balm, as Winnie returned a broad smile clasping her hands together in front of her.

Winnie gazed out over the harbor as an ore tanker with a full carry of coal slowly spun its props out of the port for eastern destinations as the roars and applause finally came to an end.

Her audience was becoming serenely absorbed. Their minds were beginning to swim upstream, their spirits Winnie hoped were out of the box, bringing about death to the old mindset. The holiest spot she reminded herself was where the ancient hatreds so long present and loud were now served by love and kindness.

It seemed to Ryan, as if Winnie rose before the audience transfigured, the apostle of truth, with shining hair and the fearlessness of one of God's own angels, battling for truth and the right, battling for the succor of the poor and lonely, the suppressed and the oppressed.

She seemed the consecrated spirit of regnant labor as she stood there, her hands outreaching to tend and nurture her electorate, leading them from theories of life, to life itself, appealing aesthetically to the Pharisees.

"Thomas Jefferson understood that human evolution can mature in either of two forms, one being a debased plutocracy turning humans into robots and the other being an enlightened commonwealth enabling humans to reach their full potential.

Winnie went on to explain to her growing adoration as Ryan and Nan and the rest of the family listened intently backstage as she explained how, prior to Plato the pre-literate ethos of the Greek culture had to be preserved and transmitted to and by each generation and how an individual Greek citizen memorized the dramatic formulations of Homer and Euripides and all the other Greek poets and dramatists, so as to retain in their memory the verbal tradition on which the Greek culture depended.

This was done in Greek culture through lyric and epic poetry, music and drama. Greeks called this phenomenon mimesis, which is defined as art's imitation of life. It is the imitation of life or nature in the techniques and subject matter of art and literature."

As Plato pointed out," Winnie explained, "such enormous feats of memorization that were required resulted in the total loss of objectivity. The Greek citizens of the time did not think about the drama; they merely memorized it."

Winnie was making the audience aware that just as the visual media today, this was a cultural indoctrination procedure that the Greeks were involved in, an entire way of life inimical to reflection and reason.

She pointed out Plato's momentous contribution to the evolution of the human mind was in replacing the oral state of mind or memorization through association with his conception of the process of reasoned thoughtful reflection.

"Plato's contribution," she proceeded, "to humankind's development was in creating or expanding the activity of sheer thinking and rational thought, using words and concepts to facilitate critical autonomous thinking, developing the concept of a personality who thinks and knows, and developing the notion of an independent, invisible, timeless body of knowledge which is consciously thought about reasoned with and known.

Our study of Plato's concern with the oral state of mind and the struggle to replace it with a rational mind set is very timely with our current culture of the twentieth century," Winnie opined, "because this century is experiencing precisely the opposite trend of the ancient Greek culture. We today in my opinion are experiencing the deliberate destruction of the rational mind-set and the devolution of the oral state of mind.

In the new oral tradition that has overwhelmed our culture we have today a new Homer. This new Homer, this new cartoon character serves as a clear representation of the current imitative, anti-intellectual, whatever feels good, anti-mind, where all truth is relative as the media conducts its incessant barbarism.

Plato saw the oral, non-literate state of consciousness as a crippling or poisoning of the mind, and the creation of a false reality which people are made to believe in. In our current TV-movie-music culture a total counterfeit reality is created and people do not see what is really going on, but only what the monopoly owned media tells them is happening."

Ryan and Nan arm in arm now could see the swarms of people nodding their heads in agreement to what Winnie was making obvious.

One example of such a benevolent era, that I hope every Minnesotan becomes very familiar with, was the 17th century Enlightenment period which encouraged humans to develop broad understanding in all areas of knowledge.

Highly educated, intelligent groups in Europe and America developed toward a more democratic way of life, created constitutions, and founded institutions for public education. Our signers of the Declaration of Independence, who developed our constitution, were the direct descendants of the brilliant minds of those of the European Enlightenment Age."

Winnie was letting her love and understanding of the constitution and the founding fathers shine brightly now and she seemed to gleam now with a new inner radiance Ryan noticed. Standing back in the shade of the podium they watched the faces in the audience grow more rapt as she spoke, the air crackling about their heads as if something was effervescing in it.

"During this Enlightenment Period words and phrases such as liberty, freedom, natural rights, pursuit of happiness, consent of the governed, informed citizenry, came into being for the first time and were first understood by humans through their own experience.

Through our founding fathers, the designers of our constitution, America came to serve as the beacon of these Enlightenment ideals, maintaining its faith in the power of knowledge and reason in self-determination.

There is no question that the Enlightenment promoted the cause of freedom, more widely and more directly and positively than any other age before it. It not only asserted but it demonstrated the power of knowledge and reason in self-determination and made obvious the choice and realization of the human purpose. For the first time in history it carried out a concerted attack on the vested interests that opposed the diffusion of the commons of knowledge and the free exercise of reason.

As thinkers the men and women of the Enlightenment were conscious free thinking rational revolutionaries, very much aware of a new method of philosophizing that amounted to a new living faith that provided the basis for a new social order.

It was the Enlightenment of Western Europe in the late 18th century that gave birth to the modern idea of the commons of distributive justice, based on the notion that a minimum standard of living should be attainable by all members of society.

It seems however that the idea died a slow death in the public consciousness for the next 170 years, staying alive however in scholarly writings. In economics around the turn of the 20th century, Alfred Marshall (1890) was asking in the opening pages of his Principles of Economics, "May we not outgrow the belief that poverty is necessary?"

But the re-awakening of popular awareness-the second Enlightenment period-did not arrive until the 1960s, and it was particularly striking in the United States.

Culture as a creation of humankind is a neutral element, it can be used for positive or negative ends. Through the process of acculturation, which begins at infancy by which human beings acquire the culture of their society, individuals are stamped with social norms. Monied interests have however constantly sought to demolish the American traditions of democracy, plotting to destroy the enlightening diffusion of knowledge and the free distribution of the exercise of reason.

Their method is not by the consent of the governed or rational discourse, but rather by arbitrary dictate of tyrants, fascist tactics, just as happened fifty years ago when the dedicated miners of the Range tried to unionize the U.S. Steel."

A roar of applause waved through the crowd as the memories of the anti-union sabotage of the Steel Trust jogged memories, recalled, taken in by the sturdy proletariats of Duluth like a comforting balm.

"Winnie was fast becoming," Ryan proudly whispered to Nan, "her electorate's favorite son of a state of mind."

Standing just below the stage and to the far left was a looped jawed young man whose broad dull face perfectly mirrored the mind that slowly revolved behind it. He was chubby and blond and his face was set in what seemed a constant expression of thick lipped wonderment and awe, as he listened to Winnie's learned dissertation.

Matt had heard the roars and applause from his balcony at the hotel and had wandered down the hill to take in the would-be senator's presentation. He had done what he had been ordered to do following the scenario plotted out for him following the discovery of the body on the docks after having received the federal documents of emergency execution allowing him access to local bank records and access to safe deposit boxes. He had found the record at the 1st National Bank of Duluth of the Chisholm family having had on file a deeded document that had been stored in a safety deposit box back in 1941 at the then Peyton Bank of Duluth. However he had reported back that no record of the leasehold document existed and its whereabouts remained unknown.

The once resolute agent under Borgen's maniacal hand was no longer certain of where his next move may be, as his last instruction was to hold firm and await further instructions. He corrected the fashion of the single Windsor knot of his tie as he tried to clear his mind of a whole host of unknowns, and continued listening to this wise woman, unaware that the family his employer was trying to steal their heritage from were standing two hundred feet in front of him.

When the applause subsided, Winnie continued. "As our contemporary American culture devolves to the Homer Simpson oral frame of mind, people are beginning to lose the very capabilities which have distinguished us from the lower animals, namely the power of language and critical awareness.

On every level it seems today, nonsense is replacing good sense in our once thoughtful and pragmatic nation. This is also accompanied by a distortion of thinking that weakens our ability to distinguish truth from falsity, which is the basic skill of a civilized society. Humans today are rapidly losing the intellectual ability to comprehend that their lives are threatened by the loss of the ability to use language to understand and communicate. As Thomas Jefferson said so emphatically, no people can be both ignorant and free."

"A culture cannot evolve without honest, powerful and enduring storytelling. When a culture repeatedly experiences glitzy, vacuous, hollowed out pseudo stories, it begins to degenerate. We must have our stories brought to us as truthful meaningful satires and tragedies, dramas and comedies that radiate a cleansing light into the shadowy corners of our human psyche and our society. If not, as Yeats has warned us the center of society cannot hold.

Flawed and false storytelling is forced in substitute spectacle for substance, trickery for truth. Weak story, desperate to hold audience attention, degenerates into multi-million dollar razzle-dazzle demo reels."

Winnie was slowly giving her audience a new reality and a new moral dimension, a great leap in understanding and the potential for social change.

She continued with her story of Charles Dickens as a great entertainer and lesson giver of his era. "Dickens entertained millions of people as they waited for his next installment of Oliver Twist and when little Nell died all of England mourned. Dickens in Victorian England wrote about such horrors as Tiny Tim in A Christmas Carol, in need of medical care that was unavailable without a wealthy patron like Ebenezer Scrooge. It was entertainment but with a point of view and in its way it was educational on any number of levels. It was showing millions of people throughout Europe just exactly what the selfish "bottom line" mentality meant for their lives.

During the great age of the novel, that of Dickens and Thackeray, of Tolstoy and Dostoyevsky, the relation to the writer and his readers was widespread, intense and warm. Authors were intellectual and moral leaders. They were honored and attended to, often persecuted in consequence, but always significant.

Their novels reached out to their audience the way movies do today, and regulated the beats of the cultures heart. Fiction's imaginary characters seemed more real to its readers than the grocer down the block, their human sympathies were wrung by the plight of poor David Copperfield. They laughed when Trollope skewered hypocrites like Mr. Slope, and they nodded with understanding at the relations of Mary Anne Evans, who used her pen name of George Eliot so her works of the Victorian era would be taken seriously. The great novel could actually create a community among its readers, a place where their spirits if not their bodies might live, laugh and love with security.

"Aristotle approached the question of story and meaning in a manner that asked, why when we see a dead body in the street or along the harbor docks of Duluth," Winnie added striking a quick glance in the direction of the Davies family off stage to her right, "we have one reaction but when we read of death in a novel, or see it in the theater we have a quite different reaction.

It is because in our lives ideas and emotion come separately. Mind and passions Aristotle posited revolve in different spheres of our humanity, rarely in sync with one another and usually at odds.

When we see a dead body, we are struck with a rush of adrenaline, my god he's dead we say to ourselves and perhaps we then drive away in fear. Sometimes in the reflection over time we may reflect on the meaning of this stranger's demise and on our own mortality, on our own life in the shadow of death. This contemplation may change us within, so that the next time we are confronted with death we have a new perhaps more compassionate reaction.

Just as in youth we think deeply but not necessarily wisely about love, willingly embracing an idealistic vision that takes us into a poignant but very painful romantic experience. This may and often does harden our hearts creating perhaps a cynical person who later in life finds the idea of love's idealism bitter, as the young continue to think it is sweet and enduring."

Aristotle declared that all humans by nature desire to know, and thereby helps to justify the way that a relatively new human type, the philosopher, or the lovers of wisdom, rank their activity as the best choice worthy of life. What makes it most desirable," Winnie asserted, now moving along the left edge of the stage, "is its contemplation of the primacy of thought, the first causes of being that are not subject to human action, but which make all human thought and action possible. To know such causes is therefore to have in the highest sense, self-knowledge.

Our intellectual life prepares us for emotional experiences that then urge us to look for fresh perceptions that then re-blend the chemistry of our new encounters.

The two realms influence each other, beginning with the first and ending with the other. In life, moments that radiate with a fusion of idea and emotion are so infrequent that when they happen we may think we are having a spiritual experience. Our lives separate meaning from emotion and our stories unite them. Our life stories are instruments from which we can create epiphanies at will, as Charles Dickens did, creating aesthetic emotion in readers of his stories all over the world."

Winnie's charges were loving this wise dissertation Ryan sensed and he thought he could almost see the little moths of new found knowledge encircling the heads of the audience seeking the warm radiation of the new flames of gained insight.

"The source of all art and story," Winnie continued gesturing with her hands lifting skyward, "is the human psyche's primal need, pre-linguistic need for the resolution of stress and strife through beauty and harmony, for the use of our creativity to restore a life deadened by routine, to create a link to reality through our instinctive, sensory feel for the truth.

Just as with music and dance, painting and sculpture, poetry and song, our stories are first, last and forever the experience of our aesthetic emotions and the simultaneous encounters of thoughts, emotions and feelings.

When an idea encloses itself around an emotional force it becomes all the more powerful and all the more profound and all the more held in our memory.

Winnie moved back behind the podium to retrieve her notes as the Duluth lift bridge rose vertically to invite another ore tanker to the docks of the port.

Winnie paused for a moment and took a sip of water and stood to the left of the podium. 'It may be useful for us to think of the situation I speak of in this manner. Changes in the symbolic nature of our culture like language are like changes in our natural environment, they are both gradual and additive at first and then it all comes together and a critical mass is achieved, like the farmer who doesn't really see his corn grow, but one day walks into the fields and it has grown over his head.

A river, or God forbid, the beautiful bay of Lake Superior that serves as our backdrop, and our pristine shared commons, that may become polluted suddenly becomes toxic, most of the fish die off and swimming becomes dangerous to our health. But yet the river or bay may look the same and we may take a boat ride on it. In other words, even when life has been taken away from the body of water, the river or the bay does not disappear, nor do all its uses, but its value has been seriously diminished and its degraded condition will have harmful effects throughout the countryside.

Men who know not wisdom and virtue and are always busy with gluttony and sensuality, go down and up again as far as the mean, and in this region they move at random throughout life, and they never pass into the upper world, because they neither look nor do they find their way. They are truly filled without being able to taste anything of pure and abiding pleasure.

Like cattle with their eyes always looking down and their heads stooping to the earth, that is, to the dining table, they fatten and feed and breed in their excessive love of these delights. They kick and butt at one another with horns and hoofs which are made of iron and they kill one another by reason of their insatiable lust, filling themselves with that which is not substantial and the part of themselves which they fill is also unsubstantial and incontinent."

Winnie stepped forward toward the edge of the stage and looked up once again over the azure waters of the bay and continued. "The point in this analogy I am making is that the river or the body of water, like the bay that glistens in the afternoon sun behind us is just a mere reflection of the vast expanse of 370 mile long glacial lake is part of our public commons, public discourse, that is our political, religious, informational and commercial forms of conversation.

What I am proposing and I will take this point of view to Washington if you give me that ability, is that our television based sense of messaging pollutes public communication and its surrounding landscape, yet on the surface just like the St. Louis River to our south and the bay of the port of Duluth in front of us, all continues to be in order.

There comes a point at which profit has to defer to the commons of decency and the commons of morality must take precedence over the demands of marketplace economics. I will not stand still as our lobbied congress attempts to traduce the constitution handing America over to a mongrelized world-state.

My commitment to you the proud citizens of Duluth and the Iron Range is that I will take with me as my pedagogy and governing guide to Washington, the sacred principles of Matthew 25, where Jesus told his disciples when they asked him how they could find their way to heaven, "that what you do unto the least of me you unto me."

History is not just made up of just facts and events. History is also a pain in the heart, and we repeat history's injustice until we are able to make another's pain in the heart our own.

With the birth of Christ and the teachings of his Apostles, there came a new concept of man and society. It was structured mostly on the tenets of classic Greek tradition, especially those relating to the works of Plato. The major idea was that man is not an animal. You and I, unlike any other species, are capable of purposely enlarging our species power over the entire world. This is possible because we have the immense power of cognition. Cognition gives us the capacity to discover and prove correct universal principles and to apply those principles in manners which enable us to increase man's power in and over the universe and to improve the conditions of life for all human beings.

Perhaps the greatest of these universal principles, is the righteous principle of reciprocal altruism. Reciprocal altruism states that what is best for an individual must also be best for the whole of mankind. Once through cognition we understand our nature, we are made in our Creator's image, each of us equally. We must cultivate or redeem that quality which is within us, given to us at birth. We must relive and rebirth our commons of the acts of reason, the discovery of universal principle which has been passed down to us, but forgotten. We must relive, reexperience and reabsorb this in ourselves. It is our common and ever enduring duty.

I thank you for your time and God bless us all."

The crowd roared and stood with approving applause, a sincere outpouring of tutored emotion from her beloved, their faces burning with the pure blue flame of faith.

She stepped back and smiled, overwhelmed for a moment with a feeling of the purest, highest and most glorious happiness that life can yield, the happiness that is at once the most selfish and the most selfless, the happiness that the artist must see when her work has been found good, has for itself a place of honor, glory and proud esteem in the hearts of men, and has wrought upon their lives the spell of its enchantment, to snare the spirits of mankind in nets of magic, to make prevail through her creation, by creating a living, single moment of life's beauty, passion and unutterable eloquence that passes, flames and goes, slipping forever through our fingers, with time's sanded drip, flowing forever from our desperate grasp, as a river flows and can never be held.

Winnie walked along the podium shaking up stretched hands, her eyes beaming with a beauty that seemed not of the flesh but of her spirit, as the Davies family and Will moved from backstage out on the stage to congratulate her for the great deluge of knowledge she had bestowed.

Chapter 19

Armed with new research from her staff at the *Progressive*, Sophie flew down to Washington on Saturday for the joint conclave of the IMF and the World Bank that began on Monday. The biennial meetings in DC were a high spot on the calendar of every financial leader in the world; ministers of State, bankers, the world's money elite and every assertive financial hot shot with a deal in his pocket and enough money would be there in an attempt to hype their deals to the right gatekeepers.

Her first stop for the weekend was to be the annual spring gala and dinner dance that her father had nearly ordered her to attend at the Chevy Chase Country Club. It would be the usual overdone affair, she knew, as she had been to so many of these conspicuous extravaganzas before. College girls, in party frocks and their mother's pearls and diamonds and earrings, were being twirled by young men, whose smooth confident faces bespoke a life without problems, as she bore witness to the dancing throng sipping on her flute of Champagne. The girls were convinced, Sophie mused, that they were the reigning basilisks of fashion, each with a retinue of desperately clever young men, seldom looking at each other as they just appraised each other's parure. They were for the most part a pre-packaged pap put together by fancy catalogs, from which ordered their Champagne cocktailed lives.

Here was a generation, Sophie thought, reluctantly designed to bask into an endless summer of afternoons of ease and entitlement. She watched as the party goers cantered about with their petty social calibrations fraught with a distinctly visible cosmic insecurity. Sophie's dance partner earlier had released her with a supercilious smile as she quickly made her exit from his sweaty grasp. He was part of a long line of types she had little time for, with numerous roman numerals after their clubby first names. She knew all too well people like most gathered here, who gave an ache to the old bones of old money, that defined real society with astronomical precision, never confusing the fixed stars and the true comets, with people the likes of these who came on like fireworks over the river climbing high and splendidly popping all their colors and drawing an instant's worth of oohs and aahs before fizzling down all spent. She herself had long ago passed over to the other side of the river, the safe shore where old money and immutable respectability dwelt.

Sophie and her brother in law Matt sat on the porch of the club house and shot the breeze for few moments as spread out below them were the last of the golfers playing in the season's first match play tournament, the golfers' bright clothes forming cheery blots of color against the grass and sand traps and the greening oaks and elms.

In the far distance west clouds of cumulus were fluffing up over the Potomac, as Matt's wife, Sophie's step sister Darlene, joined them sitting down next to her husband. She was ascetic and down mouthed, lit by the unwavering cold fire of social zealotry. She was pretty in a standard all American way, appearing a little used around the edges. She had been very carefully put together in the latest expensive trappings designed to distract from a personality that would befit a boa constrictor. She was a Stevens College graduate, who held a Master's Degree in whining and a Doctorate in shopping and a PHD in being a self-indulgent, hedonistic bitch. Her gimlet eyes darted around the rooms of the country club, alighting on this object and that, looking like a greedy spoiled child making up her Christmas list, running on envy the way a car runs on gas, easily displaying her all too familiar quicksilver bitchiness. As the white gloved waiter filled their flutes with Champagne she rose and gave Sophie a weak grin and returned to her whining antiphony in Matt's direction.

"I always tend to overdo the back story, Matt," Sophie implored after his wife had left, "as all good journalists must, so what is yours these days my boy? You look so grim. Did a bolt of lightning knock you off you and your agency's high horse on the Damascus Road?"

Matt motioned to the waiter standing nearby to refill his flute as well as Sophie's. Taking a deep nervous breath feeling insecurity flooding in upon him from all angles of the afternoon sun, he began telling Sophie what he was involved in up in Duluth, Minnesota. She listened with an intense focus of interest as he explained to her how it was Borgen's bid to rid this Chisholm/Davies family of its legally entitled heritage. Matt kept his voice low as if speaking in a manner that had the explicit tone of conspiracy and treachery. "He told you he offered the family fifteen million for the leasehold, Matt, are you sure of that?"

"He said the family has always denied any knowledge of the mining discovery, but now having seen that some sort of deed was filed with the bank in Duluth back in 1942, by David Chisholm for keeping in a safety deposit box, it seems that there may be something to this mining leasehold he claims they own. Our research team at the agency is quietly looking through the files of U.S. Steel for verification," Matt informed Sophie. "How did he know of this strike in the first place?" Sophie asked, draining her Champagne. Matt gave a grim smile at Sophie, raising his hands up from his side.

"You got me, I have no idea."

"And where did this dead body come from that gave you access to bank records?"

Matt went on to explain that again he had no clue about the body, but explained to her about what he vaguely knew of the dead bank. They both sat in silence for a time as a cheer rose up over the porch from the eighteenth green as one of the members dressed in green and pink, looking like what resembled a pimp, holed out a chip from the deep fringe.

"Will you work with me, Matt? We can put a major chink in his quite unreal continuing unaltered order of things," she whispered to Matt with a determined lock jaw glare. Sophie could see a tear building in his eye as he stared back at her.

"I will, I will," he said. "I've been thinking about this for a long time and I think I finally had my epiphany while I was in Duluth. I will," he said once more. "I think I have to save my soul, Sophie." Sophie reached over and placed her hand on Matt's knee.

"I think he is off his feed," Sophie continued unbroken by the fear that was building inside of her, knowing that her father was somewhere on the country club grounds, "and he seems to be taking his advanced age rather badly, and I'm afraid he's becoming bored and boredom ages and decays a man more than anything."

Matt was suddenly feeling ebulliently liberated, as Sophie instructed him to continue to show himself receptive and continue to be the dutiful agent and align himself with the agency's siren songs.

"You must continue to be the pied piper of the man, Matt, and show the respect of the big money that buys him and the rest of his agency men, the dream that they have sold themselves. His agency and its corrupt activities will be the lever and his anxiety about his position and his direct involvement will be the fulcrum. We must find a way," she whispered toward Matt's right ear, "to enlist that anxiety and to make it our channel and our tool. Can you help me do that, Matt?" He raised his head now, eyes clear and focused on his sister in law's eyes, his nerve ends dancing close to the surface. "Can you, Matt," she quietly implored again. Matt's thoughts swung back to Sophie, as the compass to the pole. He finally saw his duty, sun clear, as Saul had on his way to Damascus.

"Yes, Sophie, yes I'm absolutely with you," he spoke firmly, grabbing her arm as a gesture of resolute promise, swearing silently to himself that he would become no longer a supplicant to Borgen, and more of a judge. A judge, he tried to reassure himself, that would judge harshly and take no recourse in the stasis of having no opinion.

It was just then that Arthur Borgen appeared, walking toward them along the deck. The mere sight of her father triggered in Sophie a reflux of resentment and thirst for retribution like a sour chord, pulled on the strings of her chagrin, now that she had received the report from the investigator she had hired two weeks' ago, but she knew especially now, at this moment, that this was a reaction she would have to put to the recesses of her psyche. Borgen extended a hand, grinning as if he had something painful stuck in his picket fenced artificially whitened teeth looking down at her with raccoon like eyelids, as she rose taking his hand, repulsed at his impervious gesture, and hung something on her features which was meant to be taken as a grin, and offered a patronizing hug. He unenthusiastically shook Matt's hand and sat down next to the left across from Sophie, as if he had heard a warning shot, readied for fire. Sophie noticed that under his faux aristocratic tailored suit he was sweating like a pig.

Sophie watched him sip at his scotch, the narrow intelligence flashing from the keen eyes of this clever rogue, and how eager he was, how clearly his paltry soul saw the way to his end. He was the reverse of blind, she thought, his keen eye in the service of evil, forcing his agents into the same mischievousness in proportion to his craven cleverness. It was power he wielded undeniably, but it was not the magisterial moving of levers he had once hoped for, it was a good deal more like riding out a gale in a small boat, driving along at the mercy of a thousand willful elements that forced their own designs on nearly every action.

He was long ago constrained by fortune to become a public tyrant, a master of others when he is not a master of himself, like a diseased paralytic man who is compelled to pass his life, not in retirement, but continually fighting and combating with other men. He is a tyrant that could not be content with moderate power that could assure the power and means to live well, which he mostly had presently, without acquisition of more. He grows worse from having power, Sophie intuited, he becomes and is of necessity more jealous, more faithless, more unjust, more friendless, more impious. He is the purveyor and cherisher of every sort of vice, as a consequence she knew that he was extremely miserable, and that he made everybody as miserable as himself. Not fame but bitterness was the last infirmity of the once noble mind.

Sophie and Matt sipped at refills of Champagne, a common bond built between them as Borgen sipped nervously at his scotch as they conversed idly about the club's activities for the evening. After a few moments when the conversation had worn uncomfortably thin he rose heavily to join his third wife, Gertrude, a desiccated and faded, bleak vulture of a woman all elbows and cricks who blew kisses madly, looking as austere and elegant as a Spanish duchess in a Velasquez portrait. She was like Julia in David Copperfield, peevish and fine where nothing bloomed near her, and the air around her was poisoned by corrosive envy and want. These were the type of ladies who needed only a year or two to solidify their positions and implant themselves under the skin like tropical parasites carrying lifelong infections, living out in their ghastly green and white shuttered country estate lives trying to forget who they really were.

Her face was well past the prime that her bosom still seemed to enjoy, Sophie thought, who had long been enmeshed in a series of amphetamine chains, responding to people in the voice fawns would have if fawns could speak. She was not at all intelligent and full of airs in her tea cozy fripperies of conversation, talking about the price of things and their extravagant itineraries, with some country club friends standing near the bar in the richly leathered lounge, her practiced crystalline laugh piercing the noise of the crowd as she rushed to a new gathering group of country clubbers starting the whole Lillian Gish routine once again.

The other guests to her stepmother that she did not know directly, who had not been corralled into being among their pretentious party of friends, were merely the filler in her mind, the human equivalent of polystyrene flakes in which the China came packed. They were all rich and insipid, Sophie observed, with their accents buffed, speaking with a much practiced bloodless uppity rescission, their social personas patinated, inoffensive and colorless enough to fit in anywhere, making four for bridge and six for a box at the opera. They were all enormously rich but deep within them their convictions were all based on a series of accumulations and half facts, with few enough anchors to windward beyond stark materialism with no pilings to cling to in battering seas. They prospered and comingled with one another because of the shared insecurity and fear that their money might in fact be the only justification for their existence.

Her father remarried within a year of her mother's death and her first step mother remained less than two years and now lived in a mansion in Newport, Rhode Island with her fourth husband, the owner of a chain of coal mining operations the largest of which was located in West Virginia. The furniture of her other houses had mostly been exiled into storage because of the relentless trading up of the environs that surrounded her. Sophie had reluctantly attended a dinner party at the audacious estate overlooking Newport Bay adjacent to the grounds of Newport Country Club, greeted at the door by the prescribed English butler with jowls like abalones. She had viewed her first step mother and new husband then as confederates in vanity, a quality they thought set them apart. They made each other feel good about being rich, she had mused at the time, about the conspicuousness with which they consumed the world's goods including the lives of others. They both believed that wish alone made right and that their money was an instrument of that rectitude.

The southern plantation style house was stocked from floor to ceiling rooms throughout with the expensive doodads and trifles manically collected by such wives and girlfriends. I buy things, therefore, I am, Sophie imagined was her step mother's mantra, the Latin version reading "tenero ergo sum." It was her form of social anxiety. Sophie remembered how she had laughed to herself as she watched her stepmother interact with her wealthy guests, their faces written with armoring certitude of vast wealth, how she attempted to exhibit a sense of the old Southland's glory in her bones with that special brand of courtesy that was such an integral part of the Southern aristocratic culture.

But Sophie understood that this newly discovered contrived pose her step mother was putting forward, was not the paradise of courtesy it seemed, but rather it had a crust of sin atop it, that this cult of politeness served also as a daily reminder to blacks to keep their place, a sinister cultural matrix structured by images of the virgin on her pedestal keeping up with kinfolk, cooking big Sunday dinners, and the savage black rapist whom she needed constant protection against.

Sophie knew Newton's third law of marriage, that to every action there is an equal and opposite usually angry reaction. And for her first stepmother there had apparently been three of those angry reactions. Yet she continued on going to any and all lengths to put her in advantage's way. She hardly expected to foresee being all wrapped up in herself if there existed, a legal means for extending her mania for extravagant wealth beyond the grave of marriage dissolution.

The $30 million from number three following her divorce from her second husband, Borgen, was about what she had budgeted in her dreams. She could somehow instinctively find pollen for exactly whatever financial male bee was buzzing around. She would be nimble and ready, Sophie intuited, when the timing was right to take the next big step, trained and well-schooled to deploy her next man's wealth at whatever level of discretion and flamboyance seemed within her selfishly stretched bounds.

Borgen paused before entering the lounge, his gray eyes hung in senile impertinence, an unmistakable malignant gleam, like points of steel, reminding Sophie that he would see her Tuesday noon, at his office, offering no please that could possibly mitigate. "I'll see you then, Father," she said trying to sound the dutiful daughter. Sophie and Matt both watched as Borgen, it seemed, moved uneasily into the room, trying to quickly become as amiable and off hand as possible, as if relaxing with an ingénue, a tribune for the good society.

She enjoyed another harvest of her grievance as she watched Borgen move to the interior of the party, despising how the actual family system worked and its methods of operation, its smugly narrow stupid views which infected their children, the monarchy of men posturing and pompous and its stifling so called moral grip, its hypocrisy concerning women, courting them like queens and breeding them like sows. If a man were not a ruler of a kingdom, even not the owner of all he surveys, at least he was the master of his own household, where he made the decisions, chastised deviations, doled out the dough, did the deep thinking and got the mail.

CHAPTER 20

Monday morning, the annual spring meetings of the International Monetary and the World Bank commenced at their headquarters, bringing together central bankers, ministers of finance and development, private senior executives and academics to discuss issues of global concern, including the world economic outlook, global financial stability, poverty eradication, economic development, and aid effectiveness.

About ten thousand people were expected to attend this year's proceedings. Sophie listened patiently as she sat next to her business partner from the *Progressive*, Margo Malone, in the last row of the auditorium seats, as the meeting opened with the speeches by the Chairman of the Board of Governors and the heads of the two institutions, to be followed the next day by meetings of the International Monetary and Financial Committee and the Development Committee.

Following the speech by the IMF head, Sophie was to conduct a breakout session sponsored by her magazine and other accredited civil society organizations and their representatives, the likes of Transparency International, the Washington watchdog NGOs Food and Water Watch, Fifty Years is Enough, Jubilee USA Network, the Development Group for Alternative Policy, and the African corruption investigator John Githongo, all of who at various times had, "drip fed" Sophie's magazine with IMF and the World Bank's nefarious operations around the globe. Her thirty-one hour session was part of the Annual Meetings Program of seminars designed to foster creative dialogue among the private sector, government delegates and Senior Fund and Bank officials.

The Per Jacobson Lectures on international finance were sponsored by a foundation set up in honor of the Fund's third managing Director and Sophie was to speak in one of the adjacent meeting rooms about the urgent need for reform of the institution's activities.

"The debate over how, or even whether," Sophie began to a roomful of nearly three hundred, "the Bretton Woods Institutions can be reformed has taken on a greater importance in recent years, thanks to the apparent fusion of neoconservative geopolitics and neoliberal economics under the leadership of both the World Bank and International Monetary Fund.

Attempts at democratization and governance restructuring has failed, even as greater attention to the bank's corruption on projects has emerged over the past years. Debt relief has been scanty and little or no success has been recorded in moving the World Bank and IMF away from environmentally destructive and economically painful projects and policies.

While civil society co-option was one of the World Bank and IMF's specialties, the approach was both exhaustive and fruitless soon after it began and protests against the new Bank president put on much greater pressure.

The basis thus exists in our opinion for a full-fledged decommissioning strategy, one that has been adopted by leading Third World social movements and think tanks that have joined us here today."

Sophie paused for a moment to mentally measure the emotional gauge of those in attendance. "Can the World Bank and International Monetary Fund be reformed? Or should they be rejected outright and closed?

What kinds of analysis, strategies, tactics and alliances allow us to even pose the question of defunding and decommissioning the BWIs? Does the advent of neoconservative control of the World Bank that we have recently witnessed along with the 'anti-corruption' posturing currently make any difference?

"Let me begin by considering these factors, give a history of these organizations and then take measure of the first few years of the current regime, and end with some key arguments about the global justice movement and its capacities and priorities.

Sophie took a deep cleansing breath and looked at her partner Margo in the audience, giving her a wry half-way grin. She looked at her 12 pages of submitted prepared script and put them aside.

Now she would tell the delegation of diplomatic "banksters" what they really needed to hear, regardless of whether they liked her damning, incriminating message about Nightmare America.

So she began:

"On April 4, 1967, Dr. Martin Luther King Jr. delivered his famous "Beyond Vietnam" speech at Riverside Church in New York City."

Sophie took a quick glance toward Margo, receiving her affirmative nod and sly smile of approval.

"Citing a "very obvious and almost facile connection between the war in Vietnam and the struggle I and others have been waging in America." King said, he had moved into "an even more deeper level of awareness," through which he realized that he could "never again raise my voice against the violence of the oppressed in the ghettos without having first spoken clearly to the greatest purveyor of violence in the world today: my own government."

"The speech was considered treachery by America's controlling elites, and exactly a year later King was dead. He was assassinated allegedly by a petty criminal, a "lone gunman" who had been paid by a cabal of mafioso and Southern racists, while under 24-hour a day surveillance by the FBI, CIA, and local police forces.

On May 7, 1970, the eminent British historian Arnold Toynbee put his life on the line like MLK, when he said in the New York Times, "For the whole world, the CIA has now become the bogey that Communism had been for America. Wherever there is trouble, violence, suffering, and tragedy the rest of us are now quick to suspect the CIA had a hand in it." Toynbee was responding to Henry Kissinger's barbaric invasion of Cambodia. "In fact," Toynbee continued, "the roles of America and Russia have reversed in the world's eye. Today, America has become the world's nightmare ."

Only one percent of the ruling elite need to be organized to install a fascist regime in the United States. This is the ultimate objective of the greatest covert operation ever, one in which the oligarchs steal everything you own, via the murderous machinations of the criminal, never audited CIA and the National Security State.

Those who resist like President Kennedy, Senator Robert Kennedy and Dr. King, were murdered and subjected to "compromise and discredit" operations like the forged letter the FBI and CIA sent to Martin Luther King Jr. encouraging him to commit suicide.

False rumors will proliferate and ruin the reputation of anyone who refuses to comply and accept the myriad of lies and corruption of American empire.

Every minute of everyday, through the National Security mechanism, the oligarchs that own America and through it cravenly seek to own the world symbolically transform themselves from murderous beasts into a "force for good," that protects us from them.

They call it "America," but what does that word represent: a shining city on a hill above a fruited plain, or a segregated oligarchy with a murderous dark side?

The answer is obvious. We and the world are all victims of a massive criminal enterprise and the key to its success is its ability to keep its crimes and corruptions secret. The secret rulers have made it illegal to blow the whistle on what they are up to. There is no freedom of speech or public right to know how our government is really run.

It doesn't matter that the FBI, CIA and the National Security State have an accommodation with the bosses of organized crime, they ARE organized crime. The CIA runs the world's illicit arms and drug business, while the Pentagon illegally invades and destroys sovereign foreign nations, using the immoral tactics of depleted uranium and more, so corporations can steal everything the people in those nations own. It doesn't matter that the corporate crime bosses and their petro-dollars get away with savaging the world of anything of priceable value.

The mafia is not an outsider in this world; it is perfectly at home. Indeed, as an integrated spectacle of corruption, it stands as the criminal expedient model of all advanced enterprises.

The establishment and its security chiefs know what they are doing. The legal criminality of the social system and its institutions, of government, and of individuals at the interpersonal level, is tacit violence. Structural violence is an unregulated systemic daisy-chain of the vertical integration of stolen wealth and the enclosure of our shared commons, that has brought only exploitation, social injustice, and the denial of our Constitutionally guaranteed human rights.

Politics and business are said to be mutually exclusive and the Big Lie of "democracy," freeing the world to death, enables the greatest criminal covert operation ever. Business people, and now newly created un-regulated private equity funds of no good conscience manipulate political and social movements, through financial instruments and institutions of behavioral engineering like the age old British Tavistock Institute and the CIA, so they can greedily make even more money.

The police keep resistant poor black and Hispanic neighborhoods in lockdown through the CIA's distribution of narcotics. The FBI manipulates lost, insecure, and even intellectually disabled individuals into attempting crimes and acts of terrorism which they then jump in to prevent.

The CIA conducts false flag operations all over the world in their MK-ULTRA mind control "sleeper-cell" operations to enhance public fear, even as they arm and train them to overthrow progressive elected governments.

Emanating from the super-secret CIA, which informs every other government bureaucracy, this criminal enterprise corrupts every social and progressive political group in America, forming consumers of myths and commodities into a dystopian moat of "true believers" that surrounds the establishment elite that oppresses them. It's a perfect diabolical enterprise, stabilized by manufactured crises du jour, and ineluctably heading into a predictable direction of dumbing down.

I would like to finish by making a statement about the power of truth, a treatise on truth made by a famous theologian and prescient writer.

"Yet, with a Gandhian faith in the power of truth mankind continued to hope. Every slightest effort at opening up new areas of thought, every attempt to perceive new aspects of truth, that puts the power of freedom and justice in the hands of the people, is of inestimable value in preparing the way for the light we cannot see."

These were the prophetic words of the religious monk Thomas Merton, made shortly before he was electrocuted in his hotel room by more of the murderous machinations of the CIA.

Here, Sophie was at her best, her essence, confronting the diluted, diminished and amnesiatic Washington get-along-to get-ahead consensus.

Her winged words hunted out her persecutors, stinging them where they wallowed in beefy complacency, and fettered to smugness, arrogance and hubris. Her words were an angelic scrubbed antidote, a strong, heady, disconcerting dialectic to personal indifference, social hard heartedness and spiritually corrupted introversion, that America was forced to suffer.

CHAPTER 21

The meeting room where Borgen would join them was a bare Spartan space that gave off a harsh penitential kind of sanctity. Here, around the great oaken conference table, sat the recreant Pontius Pilates, his agents, covert action specialists in the shadows, accountable only to their own shadows. They sat in rich leather high back chairs, an assembled congregation of a somewhat select list of superannuated executives, de-gunned military generals, un-shipped admirals, pastured lawyers and celebrity seeking corporate chieftains or egocentrically self-commemorative individuals, willing to barter their own, or preferably some-one else's, money and resources for status, on their own vestigial power trips, hoping to scotch the others' stake, who all enjoyed a whole host of executive entertainments and privileges which was the duty of the American taxpayer to fund.

Their malefactions might be extreme vanity and profligacy and the heedless stewardship of stupidity even, but these were explicable and sentence-able only by the luxurious pensions they would enjoy, and generally disregarded by the puppy dog financial press. There seemed to be no sense of fierce justice, as over the ages, older dying men, as were most of his agents, were to be seen as noble kamikazes willing to yield the remnants of their lives in grand apocalyptic apotheosizing gestures, exemplifying the worst conditions of selfless public service. His staff incarnated the vast potential for sleaze and opportunity, the notion that the point of public service was not to steward or improve the general interest but to prepare a man for a prosperous afterlife in corporate America.

Most of his agents didn't really need the money, rather it was just the further hegemony of them maintaining their spheres of influence, and Borgen had indeed milked them very handsomely, living off their efforts, like a prince of the company coffers, which was the accepted fashion of the day.

All of his hoplites were congealed around the conference table as in a George Price cartoon of subway riders into a single enervated glob of flesh and neuroses. They had been summoned for a light brushing over with truncheons and hoses.

As Borgen entered the conference room to take his seat at the head of the table, all around him rose, a thin steamy mist of uneasy sycophancy, fawning obsequiousness and servile compliance. Not an eye touched him without fear, hatred, dislike or servility. There was nothing about him that seemed rarified or epicene, having a lapidary presence cut and polished from base matter, making him shiny and obdurate as gemstone. He could bark out directions and answer questions in a clear eyed command no matter how violently the deck timbers shifted under his feet or raging tides beat against the hull.

He expected to be compared to everyone from Christ to Caligula, who would journey to Canossa and kiss his ring. He was the throbbing heart of influence and manipulation, deluded enough to think that all would savor his vigor and bask in the radiance of his malevolent grin. He exuded a brand of greed and calculation the way other men exude cheerfulness and confidence, with a well-worn expression of personal outrage, but yet somehow also looking intent, reflective and solidly visionary.

He wore his ego like antlers and any ethical, moral or sentimental second thoughts were not reactions native to him. They would have hindered his mad dash to theft and acquisitive asset gathering, from his shamefully inelegant background. He had hammered into the deep sands most of the pilings of his life, forbidding himself from remembering how he had blustered and loud mouthed his way out of a possible cabinet spot under Reagan that he thought he had a lock on. It was his paranoia and a terror of being tested that drove him, which brought with it an immense compulsion to cheat. His career since being rubbed out of the Kennedy administration had been one of continuous nimble adjustment, and like a good courtier he had bowed before the throne no matter whose buttocks it cradled. He had been living in the dark for so long, that he was morbidly afraid of stepping into the light. Gone for him was the antique notion of his vocation as a matter of hushed discretion as a respectful prodigy, existing as a diligent intermediary.

Borgen knew he was merely a servant in the plantation mentality that governed Washington, a servant, however he felt so much more perceptive than those he served, but he was still a servant now and always. His mobility up and out of the agency he knew deep within him had long been determined by those with whom he held no sway. He was a valued presence he knew but somehow always to be vaguely apologized for. He had been assigned a role in the affairs of others that practically ensured his cancerous dissatisfactions and resentments. He liked real power like he had during the war and liked his actions to have acknowledged positive consequences. He wanted the power to the degree to which its effects would simply be too transcendent not to surrender to.

Borgen stood for a moment like a great crane being repositioned to peer over his marshaled servants, having made his emergence from his chrysalis of total secrecy, reaching behind him to twitch the double vents in his Huntsmen suit into precise alignment, before shaking hands with one of the chosen few, who happened to be a recently retired cabinet secretary, now pillorying private sector cash. Everything seemed to have an intense throbbing immediacy as he stood for a moment in front of his leathered high back chair. He was like a reptile stirring in the sun, the first stirrings of hunger pricking his lassitude.

From his Hermes briefcase he produced a thick sheaf of computer printouts which he proceeded to thumb portentously. "We have done our homework," he said as he glared menacingly at his men, "and I have a clear view of the direction we are going to take," while his agents nodded in agreement with lugubrious gloats and gurgles. During the meeting Borgen would proffer bits and pieces of his new plans turning up edges and corners here and there fueling leaks and gossip and surmise, setting the stage for exhortations to the troops, getting ripples of ingratiating supportive nods. With the recent development of the new satellite technologies, these had been glorious years for Borgen and his clandestine group of G7 employees. This was now a time to create due bills and to extract from others for the years of gentlemanly disparagement. For in the end, all the old partners kept silent sullenly accepting that the men of the moment and the hour have as their privilege immunity from the hauntings of history, as any thoughts of Borgen's evil misdeeds had long been swallowed up in his unplumbable abyss of forgetfulness.

The meeting commenced with reports of field updates from his agents, many militaristically and heavily testosterone driven, and he listened with a dead-pan scholarly interest, his dark eyes glancing this way and that, his thin mouth set in a faintly downward curve of disapproval of the world around him. His agents' reports depicted the ichthyological food chain of small fish that were being eaten by the larger ones, and so on, around the country. The agents nodded consensus at Borgen's declarations and instructions that he regurgitated under stress with an irritating twitchy geniality.

Although one or two of the older men seemed to fall short of genuine ebullience, he had a way of making it unspokenly clear that heel-dragging dissenters of any kind could expect to begin the next week selling insurance. He after all preferred error to indecision and, for Borgen, it was a small price to pay for the incidents of insolence and disrespect that could be heaped like ash and offal in his memory. He began, in his fierce quick way of turning his herd, to bark out his directions and responses to questions in a clear eyed command, his vindictive reverie interrupted by no one, making his points as he jabbed the air with a flat spatulate middle finger, looking around the table with a bully complicitous smirk, pitting his influence against an existential set of facts.

Borgen buzzed his secretary, remonstrating her vigorously, giving her instructions with the benign severity of one who had discovered the other's utter irrelevance and worthlessness. She immediately came down the hallway through the double thick oak doors of the conference room and distributed the nineteen copies of Borgen's computer printouts she had made to the agents as Borgen sat silently, smiling at his gray skinned ghouls who operated in the shadows, druidically, as they read with avidity the revealed bits and pieces of new plans from the reports and the aligned strategies and potentialities brought forth to further scotch the stakes of other people, using the powers of new found digital technology.

When after a period of ten minutes one of his agents posed a question that hinted at the lack of moral integrity of the operation, it was as if Borgen depicted him as a sightless marble knight standing with his vigil shield at his side before him, grasping his broad righteous sword, he immediately affected an expression of deep indignation, at the same time attempting to sound lofty and spearingly superior, with the full weight of opprobrium and a self-assured casual air of menace. It was all part of the showings of his vestigial power trip, in the continual process of atrophying the psychological ligaments of his players and staff, subjugating everything and everyone to the short term results dosed with prevarication and the managerial egotism of Arthur Borgen. After a few moments watching his agents peruse the reports he stood up with a heavy air of authority and moved to the door and down the hall back to his office, trying desperately to keep his evil nature of unyielding severity and malice to himself.

Sophie arrived at the lobby of OFAC at noon just as Borgen's agents were breaking for lunch into smaller working parties convening to formulate high sounding resolutions to cosmetize various aspects of the new illicit endeavors in the arena of intellectual property and patent rights acquisition. Her father met her in the office's glass walled lobby as his personal driver waited patiently outside in the limo to carriage them to lunch.

Sophie was mildly surprised that she was able to convince him to take lunch at Joe and Pete's, a small bar and restaurant at the eastern fringe of Georgetown that served up the best and greasiest burgers in the metro, and not the usual worm-wooded posh restaurant in Georgetown she knew he preferred, with its cut crystal decanters that held vintage gall, or Clyde's that he suggested as an option, that was a popular attraction for locals and tourists because it was connected to the big three-storey shopping mall in the center of Georgetown.

They traveled in a strange silence as the limo turned left onto H Street. Sophie looked across Lafayette Park, as the light of the early afternoon sun brightly lit up the White House. Now, Sophie looked out the window at the Jefferson Memorial, as they crossed Fourteenth Street out of the city toward Georgetown just west of downtown Washington. The afternoon sun was creating an eerie orange blaze that highlighted the magnificent monument.

Georgetown overlooked the Potomac River high up on a bluff that rose from the northern shore. It was a high-end enclave of mostly expensive boutiques, restaurants, bars and pricey townhomes, much like Rodeo Drive in Los Angeles, except that it was done mostly in neo-colonial motifs as opposed to chic. It was also home to Georgetown University, the dark spire of the university's gothic cathedral was a readily recognizable landmark used for power boaters and sailors during the summer when they anchored just north of Key Bridge, which connected Washington to Virginia, on the wide calm section of the river.

They sat on stools at the bar, as all tables and booths were taken, Sophie sipping at her beer while Borgen worked on his second scotch, plainly disturbed to his daughter's delight to be in such an uncivilized dive. Unlike the more upscale establishments closer to the center of the area, Joe and Pete's catered to a younger, less affluent set, mostly Georgetown students who were at least twenty one as well as younger kids who enjoyed the work of the artisans of design of fake IDs. The place was dark and stale and smelled of stale beer and peanuts, a dive compared to most other places nearby like Morton's in McLean, and Sophie loved it. It reminded her of a place her sorority sisters and fraternity friends had frequented in college.

Sophie ordered another Moosehead, her second in fifteen minutes and chuckled at herself inwardly, as Borgen ordered another scotch, taking it from the sticky aging dark wood bar, trying to rid himself of the tiny seed of doubt that still nagged him, that she could be working for the other side. "I know some men," he said staring into the amber auguries of his drink, "who were very unhappy about your speech yesterday, very upset, I would say, to rephrase the contempt they expressed." It was spoken with enough poisonous intent to wipe out a regiment Sophie thought.

There was nothing that became so completely implacable as an originally good man turned by some circumstance to enraged resentment against the world. Arthur Borgen, Sophie mused, did not know that a man cannot approach God save through his own humanity. But he did know, she surmised, that man approached hell through his own pride, his own vanity, his own hunger for power. It appeared to her as she gazed steadfastly and with dread, at her father, that he had taken on the very aspect of Lucifer.

For the moment she looked at him with only a slight tremor around her jaw betraying the rage that was a mere synapse away from contorting her face with ape-like fury. Such a display of emotion however would be a surrender, she understood, to femininity and she had built her young empire on stronger pilings than womanliness. She stifled her anger and disappointment and told him in that strange upper class diction in which the vowels pursed in upon themselves, an indication that she quite understood.

Sophie knew, although he may have a cool if not rather shrill exterior, the rage of pure hatred that convulsed and filled him with his maniacal sense of mission. His hatred spoke to her with the cold harsh voice in which madness often tries to instruct its adherents.

Borgen's hatred and his red faced diatribes had become his best friend, she surmised, even closer to him than his third wife, a man that was the master of appearances, fascinated by the gap between deception and detection, a man living in a time when men were becoming cynical enough to imply that truth was a relative thing.

He had come through at the University of Chicago, the General Motors method of statistical accounting of Robert McNamara, counting everything that could be counted and comparing everything that could be compared, void of any human considerations, devising coldly eerily rational solutions to the problems thus revealed, fulfilling his fondest dreams of aptly dealing with the corporate Pauls and the labor union Peters smiling knowingly across the bargaining table as his minions amicably divided a nation's bounty, with nobody taking from anyone else and no one left out, unbeclouded by political calculation, a hungry bidder for immortality.

Sophie realized that Borgen had figured out that any potential risks were assumed to be mitigated by the magical incantation he had developed through the status of his various NGO cut out agencies and organizations. He was sure that he ran an impenetrable schism of accommodating legal domiciles stretching from Liberia to Lichtenstein that her researchers had uncovered.

She knew of the evil sociopathic nature that possessed him, and that his urge to win had a way of turning into a kind of paranoia, a terror of being tested, which brought with it an immense compulsion to cheat. Here was a craven man, Sophie thought watching him as he chewed his sole and greens carefully and industrially, a teuton martinet happiest in a military hierarchy, who took his pleasure as he liked from a world he believed was his own personal oyster.

She had heard some call him a "compensated schizophrenic." Like Hitler and Stalin he appealed to the unconscious sadism and hostility in the average human being, well, deluded about the line between fantasy and reality. In some of the circles she traveled, people, knowing her as Sophie Nichols, called her unsuspecting father many nasty things, from a weasel, to a hyena, a shark, a barracuda and a piranha. From an ornithological species to an ichtyological he had been called a vulture or buzzard or a vampire or a leech. From the herpetological species they chose viper, python, cobra, asp and adder. It was a veritable zoology of vituperation, for he was a peremptory angry person. Sophie knew first-hand that Borgen was unhappy and angry with his own life and angry men don't always stop to count to ten, and who knew what a person under stress was capable of?

She was beginning to thoroughly understand Borgen's disparate enterprises and the private mystery of his relationships to it and that what he controlled and promoted were part of a cryptic system of global forfeiture and theft. He and his agency men were merely that latest line of what the press liked to call the "crime world controllers", differentiated from its vocational forebears only by an increment of zeroes.

This was a group of very secretive men, the *Progressive* staff had surmised, who believed that surprise was to financial strategy and acquisition as presentation was to French cooking. Some people bought friends, some people bought fame and what Borgen bought was more money, illicitly gained for the most part. She understood how for his kind of people nostalgia operated as a cure for moral neuralgia, all draping themselves in the appropriate clothing in order to convey an impression of genteel old money respectability.

To Borgen, Sophie figured she was just an abstraction, although a gnarly one, thinking she barely understood what was reality, confident in his stereotyping, of womankind's opacity to the real world. He was incubating enough confusion and hatred for a dozen lifetimes, his mind so occluded with hate that even when the doctors told him about his cancer, years ago, he felt that it was just as if a little piece of the bug hatred had broken off and had become lodged into his bloodstream somewhere.

Their conversation had turned desultory and difficult as Sophie finished her surprisingly good pecan salad with a sweet cranberry dressing. "Umm," he grumped at one of her inquisitions, staring implacably at the amber of his scotch, in the authoritative tone used by men of his type when addressing inferiors, a tone she hated. She could sense the depths of the rancor in him that could surface at any moment. He was not in a state of union, she understood, most given to introspective self-evaluation. But at this moment Sophie could also feel the exhilaration building inside.

There was no other word for it, of that moment of pure focused hatred toward her father. She had rejoined morality and the righteous plight she spun in her head, yet she knew how her father's mind worked and any failure would beget paranoia. She had an instinctive feel about what people liked least about themselves and what they feared most, which was ninety-nine percent of the time, about losing their money. Mammon was the straw that stirred their drink, to have more, or at least not less, was their creed and money being dreadful for friendship was the essential basis for enmity. She looked forward privately to pouring gasoline over the slow burning cinders that she would begin to stir, creating after all the scandal that was the era's opiate for the masses.

Just before they were about to leave the pub, Borgen leaned in close to Sophie, his face drawn and deeply lined, the face of a man on the thin edge of ungovernable anger, the odor of his three scotches nearly making her gag, breaking the news to her manfully that the doctors recently discovered he had liver cancer and likely a year, two at most, to live. He touched her right shoulder but his hand might have been a fly alighting there for all she cared. Sophie sat silently for a moment looking directly at him, with a curious combination of hatred, fear, surprise and a kind of furtive awareness, trying to muster sympathy, finally reaching out to touch his forearm.

"I'm so sorry, Father,' she heard herself say, slightly surprised at the sincerity she felt. "Have you had second opinions? You know that you must."

"I'm scheduled at Bethesda Medical next week." A distinct sadness in his voice, hoping all the while that news of his new found malaise, might somehow overrule any of the stormy impulses of his daughters disgruntlements.

Chapter 22

On Wednesday, before returning to New York, Sophie met with a private investigator in Prince Frederick, Maryland, about the death of her mother all those years ago, near the Golden Gate bridge on the banks of the Potomac River. He reported to Sophie that the records at the police station there were a bit antiquated but he had dug up some interesting facts. The police report said that her car was hit sometime between ten and midnight by a drunk driver in a one ton truck but oddly no such driver was ever found. The pictures of the car show a large impact dent on the driver's side of the car that had plunged into the river. When the cops got there the truck was empty, no sign of a driver. They ran the plates and found that the truck was stolen in Philadelphia three days earlier.

They dusted for prints but there was nothing that turned up. The investigator knew the detective who had originally investigated the case, now retired, who had talked. He said they were suspicious but had nothing to base anything on. There was a broken bottle of whiskey on the floorboard, so he said they just blamed it on the drunk driver and closed the case. "There was no autopsy, Ms. Nichols, as it was pretty obvious how your mother died. But it was suspicious to me as I read through the files and that led me to look through some of the ancillary files the station has on dead cases, and that's when I came upon these papers." He handed three type written dog-eared pieces of eight by eleven manuscript over to Sophie, placing them gently in her hands.

Theresa Borgen raced along the Georgetown Pike in her black BMW sedan. She was racing through the early darkness toward the small upscale town of Great Falls, twenty miles west of downtown Washington DC. Twisting and turning along the narrow road through the heavily wooded area just south of the Potomac as fast as she could, praying she wouldn't spin out of control on one of the small patches of ice left from the snowstorm that had passed through the mid-Atlantic two days prior. She had to get home before her evil husband did. She had just been to a private detective's office in Prince Frederick to discuss what she suspected were criminal activities that her husband's agency was involved in. She had recently found papers in one of his suit jackets that told of operations of a system of forgeries and thefts of ownership conveyances to resources owned by other unsuspecting parties and transferring them to agency cut out operations and other private parties.

Theresa had made copies of the documents she had found at the local library and given a set to the private investigator. He said he would look into it and get back to her with a report in a few days. It was February 1970, and she grimaced as she steered the BMW through a sharp turn over a bridge and a small frozen creek. She took a meandering right turn down the gravel road along the creek and traveled another two blocks until taking a left turn into the four car-wide driveway of her home, a sigh of tension release and a grin of relief creasing her face as the garage doors opened and his car was not there.

Sophie read the papers as a dark cloud of rage and indecision flooded through her. The date on the documents was February 12, 1970. "She died on a Wednesday, February 18," Sophie whispered to herself as if no one else was present. It stopped her dead, as though it was now an incontrovertible fact, like the moon and its pull of the tides. Finally she looked up at the detective she employed, her blue eyes without a compass point, fathomless and cold in their slate, concentric rings-on-rings, unwavering, pitiless and malevolent. Sometimes a single sentence with such a momentous truth was all one needed to read.

Chapter 23

Sophie, Walt and Ryan had choice tables at the third avenue restaurant where the Knicks and the Yankees hung out. The restaurant was the current class act in a fickle city which changed enthusiasm as often as neckties, the current Mecca of dining for people who otherwise haven't got much to dream about. After Sophie had called them at the lake that Sunday from the country club with the contact information she received from Matt, Walt had specifically requested that she make a reservation at a noisy place where their voices would be less likely to be overheard. The waitress, actress in waiting, quoted the menu to them with the ingratiating unctuousness of a Beverly Hills waitress describing the day's vegetarian special. They all ordered mixed pasta dishes worth about fifteen cents and eighty cents worth of blanched vegetables and olives for the round sum of twenty-four dollars per portion.

It was a new regime that had recently stormed into New York City in a cloud of famous attorneys, razor minded real estate brokers and blue chip advisors of every sexual and social persuasion. The new operation had caused not only raised eyebrows among the older guard but also a painful revision of an opinion widely held in the city's Anglicized gentry, that the British may be many things but pushy and commercial they never were. This new feckless group of Manhattanites now competed for the big items as did Christie's and Sotheby's backed by a bottomless pit of Kuwaiti and Venezuelan oil money.

Both Ryan and Walter immediately noticed her striking good looks, finely boned face with thickly textured beautiful blonde hair and a sharp calculating face that was backlit by confident self-awareness, a steely self-assertion that New York demands. What collision of inscrutable genes had made her so astonishingly beautiful? She transmitted a nascent feminine judicious consciousness. She was smoothly sheathed in a classic blue blazer and white blouse and a tan skirt that fell just below her knees, her carriage firm and straight.

During the first part of lunch they exchanged chatter like insects encountering each other on a vine leaf, each flicking and probing with their antennae fine-tuned to establish identity and territory. She was like so many of the youngsters now, Walter thought, with that wary appraisal of the world they had so little confidence in, the middle class baby boomers who could not stand being in a social mansion surrounded by a global ghetto. It wasn't surprising that they were somewhat tentative, understanding the potential stake on the line. Walter and Ryan were both mildly uneasy without being nervous. Sophie was obviously up to something as she had initiated the call to them at the lake following her visit with Matt. In her complex dramaturgy of life as it related to her, things had to be arranged in the most optimum manner. She wasn't family and there were no closed accounts between them. She had an easily distinguishable freshness of spirit that seemed to be uncontaminated by hustle or by money or egoistic calculations. She displayed an astonishing assurance that she wore like a diadem.

The initial conversation was meandering and inconclusive but Sophie displayed a mordent asperity, which struck a sympathetic chord with both Walter and Ryan. They shared a common bond that their talents and worldly desires had been compromised or circumcised by the fatuousness or the envy of powerful men in big offices. Sophie specifically seemed to divide her desire almost equally between the doddering eastern praetorians who claimed to have inherited the right to govern America and the incompetent unlettered bumpkins to whom an exhausted unhappy electorate had most recently conveyed that right.

As Sophie told of the hard stories and very little of the peripheral matters about Borgen's agency, Ryan began to feel he was being told of an energy and influence of a reach, magnitude and variety that he could never have imagined from afar. He felt like an outsider once again to a world where he could have never guessed at the power of this Washington institution nor had he wanted for an instant to entertain the thought that such power might exist. He began to sense the repercussive possibilities of these entities and the way they amplified greed and ambition and the inherent defects of individual character and ego that resonated with them and sent them crashing down on families like his. Looking out now for the first time and getting a glimpse from inside the monolith he could begin to understand, in a way both real and graspable, what might flow from the presence of this man's agency in Washington.

For the first time as he listened to Sophie, he was getting close to the exercise of real power, evil humming, a glowing deadly radiant core of institutional cause and effect that sent its immoral reverberations across continents and through people's lives. For the first time, he perceived, in ways that weren't conceptual or theoretical, but real. He could perceive, from his own days on Wall Street, how people become intoxicated by the experience and the association, how they become arrogant, self-involved, hubristic and dangerous. He could see now how power had its own momentum in and of itself. This was the real thing as Sophie was describing it, and it was downright scary.

As the conversation evolved, Ryan and Walter were like two praying Mantises circling the stems of their senses around Sophie hoping to finally establish confidence. While her bona fides couldn't yet be established with absolute certainty, the sense of right and moral indignation she projected toward her father was beyond doubt.

Sophie told them everything over lunch, both men warming up to the implied flattery of her confidence, all she knew, suspected, theorized and connected, even the fact that she had recently turned over evidence from her DC and Maryland visit that her father may have had a hand in the death of her mother. In finance, she had told them, which is essentially what Borgen's agency was all about, everything ultimately regresses to the mean. White though his collar may be the financial activity he is involved in is criminal and in crime the mean is violence and murder.

She took them through the deductions and speculations, led them through the behavioral arithmetic of the agency and laid out the mental sums she and her *Progressive* magazine had arrived at. Walter and Ryan listened quietly and intently, much of her information jiving with the research of Dan, asking questions here and there for clarification.

She talked of black money, fleeting regulation taxation and disclosure in the relatively new void called cyber-space, dirty money implying drug money and embezzlement seeking anonymity offshore. Her larger point was that just as water runs downhill, money and the potential for turning hard assets into money, as was the Davies intent with their secret will, tend to head for America. The U.S. did revere money as much as the Swiss, she reported, but the markets here in the U.S. were far more capacious.

Wall Street constituted the single largest money hotel in the universe and the "vacancy" sign was never extinguished, there was always room to accommodate another fifty or sixty or a hundred billion dollars into the electronic underbrush, as digital technology nimbly rose to respond to the ever rising volumes of money.

As a result she went on to explain, as had been the case in legitimate financial markets, a host of exotic investment products had been developed for the sole purpose of getting money into the United States from overseas, producing straw borrowers, shell companies, Hindi chits, Dutch sandwiches used as fronts for agencies such as Borgen's and many of his NGO cut operations.

"Borgen's procurement operations," she went on to explain, "were playing in the Luciferian world of the invisible hand of offshore cyberspace where its cartography was digital. They were walking a fine fiber optic tightrope between the legal and the illegal, the benevolent alliance between drug traffickers and politicians in Central America carrying over directly to the United States through their various operations. He was involved with businesses, to paraphrase Mao Tse-tung, that swam like minnows undetected in the great sea of consumerism, where the Icarus syndrome of American hubris ran at its ultimate despicable heights where until the lions had their own historians, history would always be told by the hunters. Wall Street dealt in money actually in hand whereas Washington dealt in the money of the imagination and its possibilities were limitless, but its exposure to risk was large."

Sophie went on to explain, as her researches had discovered, how her father's agency and its cut outs were part of the new "technology" responding to the rising volume of cash flows being thrown off. They were part of a shadowy electronic daisy chain the big New York banks had deployed at the turn of the eighties to handle the flight capital streaming out of places like Mexico and Liberia, taken by 747 cargo jets flying the paper money by the ton into Liberia or Panama, where with a couple of keystrokes and a quick cyber run through the exchange stabilization fund at the U.S. Treasury and with the New York Federal Reserve as agent, it was magically transformed from green stuff into an electronic blip of anonymity and shuttled to Zurich and elsewhere.

"Money laundering," she explained with the researched knowledge from her staff, "had become a regular way function of the global capital markets with South American Central Banks taking over as the agents of exchange, changing the institutional characters of drug finance. Flight capital from Eastern Europe, the Balkans, the old Soviet Union and the deposed nomenklatura had been busy emptying coffers, generating flight capital of billions, a half dozen dialects and many nationalities, most of it taking time in Switzerland, awaiting more creative lucrative employment.

"This is the Orwellian Pentagon driven economic operating philosophy we are dealing with when we confront Borgen's agency, akin to the ancient Greek philosopher Thucydides who believed in the permanence of war. It is part of the nexus of a craven plan, we believe, to centralize the political and economic power not via privatization to private investors at the market price, but by piratization, the transfer of government assets dubiously obtained to private investors and political cronies at below market prices. This is all a process and now you find yourselves smack in the middle of it," she said, arching an eyebrow at Walter and Ryan, "using the government apparatus to centralize economic power and wealth that leads to shrinking the total pie for everyone else.

"Think about it this way." She paused to sip her iced tea and munch her spinach salad. "The average taxes per resident household is about five thousand dollars and eighty five percent, or forty seven hundred dollars, goes to government agencies who refuse to provide audited financial statements or any reliable financial systems. By studying the black budget operations, which our researchers did, and the provisions in the NSA Act of 1947 and the CIA Act of 1949 that sanctioned and allowed for the 'crawl' of money from outside agency budgets and spend it on non-transparent purposes, you find that the money is going to support private corporations and private banks who are using those resources to basically steal community assets such as yours from under the people. We are financing, as the tax-paying public, an operation which is stealing our political power and economic wealth.

"When I was in Europe recently attending the IMF World Bank meetings, I overheard some quite off handed talk about the agency my father runs when at a party in Paris that they held. I overheard a conversation over numerous cocktails by two world bank executives about the latest 'scavenger hunt' that the agency was involved in, something about the attempts to gain control of a 'yellow brick' lease as they termed it, in an old mine on the iron range of Minnesota that had been abandoned. I then made some quiet inquiries about him in Basel, Geneva, Berne and Zurich and was met with a silence I recognized from my experience," she nearly whispered, "that dripped with intimations of conspiracy and intrigue."

Ryan and Walter flashed astonished looks at each other. "It was that special silence," she continued, "that the Swiss reserve for large sums of money of very shady and questionable pedigree. It had a particular quality to it, so thick and deferential I felt I could reach out and touch it and you could feel a certain faint tremble of apprehension. I soon discovered, through our avenues of research at the *Progressive*, when I returned to New York, that many of the assets were held by AB Foster, a Swiss holding company which in turn was a creature of a Luxembourg shell corporation whose shares were registered to a half dozen Bahaman trusts for which the sole trustee was a Netherland Antilles nominee for none other than Arthur Herman Borgen. This is no garden variety trust fund scheme, Walt and Ryan.

"I thought you'd like to get a close-up look at the thunder of battle," Sophie said softly as she eased leaning on the back of her chair, "before we get into the cut and thrust of ideas. Borgen is a virus, and his operating philosophy is one of a Promethean model of vindictiveness having led an active front line life of ill treatment via his superiors, who kept him out of any of the future administrations since the Kennedy administration had him removed from the NSA.

"It was not a virtuous cycle but rather a vicious cycle in which he trod, with extortion and larcenistic tendencies and a protracted act of vengeance on the world of his former bosses and associates that had sold him out, and if he eventually sensed that one of his major gambits was beginning to sputter and a seamless weave of manipulation was starting to fray his venom and desire for retribution, I guarantee you, will be unfathomable.

"Let me say again that he is a virus, think of what the Germans did with Lenin." Both Walt and Ryan writhed in their seats just a smidgen, looking mildly perplexed. "They sent him to Russia sealed in a railway car just so he could make mischief. The czars were ruling Russia for a thousand years and one man was finishing them off. The German general staff understood what they were doing, they were transporting a virus, a tiny virus that would cause a plague and destroy the dynasty of the Romanovs. They got it right, they saw what the right man in the right place at the right time could do, knowing that the world of man had always been in bondage. Our American business headquartered right here in this city on Wall Street, acts as the host for that virus. There are poisons today so tiny that just one drop can poison lakes and reservoirs.

"There are men like that in business today, in the right place at the right time with the right power. Lenin was one such man as was Napoleon, a supposed leader who made other men into fools and fanatics, like in the fourteenth century when the plague came off a boat in Venice as a germ no bigger than a pin head in the blood of a rat. That rat found another rat or a person to bite and within ten years a third of Europe was dead from the black plague. I have come to understand," she said solemnly, clasping her hands together as if in a form of prayer, "and firmly believe that Arthur Borgen is a form of that deadly virus. Greed and ambition has dulled the man and his agency's perceptions both moral and numerate and even though he might wash his hands for hours and scrub them with a wire brush, just as Lady Macbeth and Herod discovered, some stains are indelible. Certainly few individuals, below the level of great captains of State and their immediate lieutenants, could have contributed as much to the decline of private morality and responsibility as a man like Arthur Borgen." Sophie sipped her iced tea for a moment and watched her lunch mates as new thoughts seemed to be fluttering over their faces like restless moths.

Sophie knew that Borgen's assumed financial noblesse would fail to oblige, but there was now, she heard from the rumblings of his staff meeting, a hint of disquiet at the heart of his agency's machinations and that any spasm might be greatly magnified. Her father had a great sense of being reassured as his potential ungovernable minions toiled in varying degrees of preparedness as their nefarious business steamed on with a diminished sense of purpose and direction. By now she knew he was in such a state of distinction between hope and probability like a line towed in the desert during a sandstorm that was completely obliterated and his disgruntlement and alienation was festering soon coming to a vile volcanic eruption of a cancer of vindictiveness.

"Their newest asset acquisition game they are playing," she continued, "is now in the field of intellectual property, which for years has been the softest part of the corporate shield. Corporate greed is purposely made institutionally pervasive and once you get a taste of the sadism and fascism it breeds on itself it becomes uncontrollable. So now, the recent changes in copyright and trademark law, being lengthened to ninety years or a lifetime, whichever is greater, from fourteen years, is tantamount to performing intellectual genocide, creating a new humanity of two point zero for the uber-wealthy and continues to feed that greed. There is a point at which profit has to defer to decency, but today it seems that integrity is trading at an all-time low, with the happy conspiracy of greed and self-deceit driving the train."

Ryan and Walter were beginning to understand Sophie as their Geiger counters for insincerity, phoniness and half-truths were registering zeros. She could dismantle a pose with a single glance and deflate the most romantic notion with a single word. She sought truth so single mindedly that under her steady gaze, exaggeration, self-delusion and bravado simply dried up and blew away, as did any lack of knowledge, or nonsense and ungrounded giddiness. Her philosophy of life seemed to be to get to the bottom of things and from there to seek to sway away any passing that might becloud the hard won clarity of her vision.

"In other words," Walter said when she was finished, "in addition to all his other misdeeds you think he is guilty of contract killing."

"Absolutely," Sophie responded quickly, "including my mother, damn him. He was not a man any more but only a force holding other men in bondage." Most men she knew reinvented themselves three or four time in their lifetimes, but Borgen and his agency were revisionists who edited their own histories, but this would be a history where no revisions other than the stark horrible binding truth would take place if she had her way in the great scheme of retribution that now ruled her life, a more than apt recompense for his evil misdeeds.

Walter motioned to their waitress with a prearranged knowing nod and she appeared with a decanted bottle of red wine. "I thought, Sophie," Walter explained, trying not to sound presumptuous, "this being our first meeting of hopefully many we should have a go at a fifty-seven Mouton." "Mmmm, very good," Sophie commented, swirling the bowl, admiring its ruby legs. Ryan sank his nose into the snifter as they all flashed conquering smiles and joined in a silent toast. It was indeed a magically complex and powerful Bordeaux.

"Well, Sophie, let's do a little brainstorming," Walter said, being careful not to appear officious or unctuous, understanding intuitively that it was a dangerous fallacy to expect others to accept ones subjective conclusions and experiences as objective fact. "Before we finish," Walt politely intoned, "let me ask you if you feel your father has an advantage over you in any way, or has a way of controlling you?"

Walter's keenness and Kentucky wind-age were on full alert, like the only small fraction of the napping cat that is asleep, and the antelope that is on high alert as they graze, the buffalo that stands still to listen, the horse that lifts its head to catch a scent, and the wildebeest that remembers to be careful while approaching the watering hole, and to be scarce at evening when the lions hunt, and they become a flash of fleeing limbs when smoke is smelled or when a white hunter has sullied the air with his odor, dragging his gear through the brush for a better shot.

The neighborhood swimming pool is full of snakes and alligators, and every bird worries about the whereabouts of its next meal, and pecks the dirt, bark, berry bush or the buggy air for protein. Flies can bite the flanks of a moose till it runs amok, where constant grooming is required to combat ticks, mites, lice and fleas. The glorious happiness of a mindless browse in the gentle sun is never to be enjoyed by these creatures, their peaceful kingdom is a world at war, at hunting and being hunted, at alarm and incursion, at lessons learned through pain and maiming, death being the only else. They were creatures uncontrollably immersed in the life of the Dionysian beast, not able to partake of the Apollonian that represents the specifically human self-conscious and the detached mind of man. It is the Apollonian self-regard that separates man from the world, like the solitude and honor of the mountaintop, where our thought can see so far and delve so deep that those depths, when seen, see him, and not the Dionysian passions of the crowds and the bestirring martial air.

Ryan could detect that his father was sensing something, and those that knew him well had come to understand that he had evangelical faith in his sense of smell, his ability to take cognizance of prevailing conditions, and to study and take advantage of what may lay ahead. He recalled the story now as he sat in the restaurant, told by his older brother of how when Walt was twelve years old he'd cut across a marshy field near his family farm in Wisconsin along the shores of Mississippi River on his way home from school. Perhaps it had been an infinitesimal shiver in the marsh grass of the path, he would never know, but something tingled down his spine from his cortex and, without sensing why, he jumped backward holding back his brother, just as the open fanged mouth of a rattlesnake sprang out from a clump of mud and rock and gnashed a weed patch just where his ankle would have been.

Then when he was twenty-three, on his second day after having jumped into Normandy, he quietly dropped into the high grass near Ste. Mere Eglise, directing the three soldiers with him to do the same as they approached a hedgerow. Something told him there was danger directly in front of them, although he saw or heard nothing. They lay there silently for twenty minutes at Walter's command, when finally four Germans walked out from behind the hedgerow and were promptly dispensed of by the Americans. Now Ryan sensed his dad's cortical quiver was making its presence known once again, just like the undersea world would freeze, all life and activity sucked out of it by a vacuum, when a great white shark would appear. His world was frozen now, Ryan sensed, his old instincts alerted, the same instincts that made birds flee for ground cover, before a tornado or gales of winds began to make their way to the trees that nested their homes.

Sophie took a contemplative sip of her wine and seemed to cock her head just slightly to the right, as if trying to decipher some inaudible high-pitched tone being sent by a metronome from afar, unconsciously rubbing the St. Theresa medallion, the emblem of her mother, that she had given her at the age of seven, on the necklace she wore.

"Well there is one thing," she said after a lengthy stream of thought orbited inside her head as she rubbed the base of her nose with her forefinger as though to avert a sneeze: a child's gesture, ingenuous and charming. "He does in some way appear to always know where I am here in New York or even when I'm traveling, like he has someone constantly tailing me."

"Say that again," he asked Sophie, looking at her evenly and appraisingly, his eyes bright blue piercing poignards fixing themselves on her face. Sophie repeated, seeming mildly befuddled, that she thought her father always knew where she was.

"What do you make of that?" Walter asked leaning forward toward her on both elbows, his antennae now vibrating with a force he had known only a few times before. He felt the graying hair on his neck begin to stand on end and a flush and rush of apprehension under his skin so intense that it bordered on elation.

Walt decided to circle the principal matter on his mind that bestirred him regarding Borgen, taking another sounding of the man. "Look at it this way, consider the possibility, Sophie," Walt continued, his eyebrows asking a question, with not an atom of pleading or parenting in his voice or on his face.

Walter Davies was the tablet carrier, he viewed his opinions, received or personal, as his truth, no matter what anyone else may believe. "When your father paid us a visit this past spring he had planted a bug in the pot of a plant Mary had blooming just inside the front door, and I noticed an unmarked service van parked down the street that I am sure was there to pick up our voices. We just left the tiny bug there not wanting to tip our hand and in the morning the van was gone, and Mary replaced the plant the following day. Could he have placed a tracking device on you somehow Sophie?"

There was a protracted period of silence as they enjoyed their wine while Sophie pondered the newly posed possibility of Borgen's evil tactics.

"Get an MRI," Walter softly suggested, "have your apartment and office swept, we do it every six months at my business, and,— he reached over and gently touched her forearm "—have the medallion you wear on your necklace checked as well."

Walter knew that they couldn't play with a marked deck, that luck was the residue of good design, that one was not able to predict the accidents, but must be prepared for the incidents. Sophie looked at both of them and shook her head slowly up and down, the gesture having an ancient finality to it as though it dated from the dawn of humanity, the unvoiced confidence from all of them seeming to have a hollow ring suspended in a solution of uncertainty and foreboding.

Sophie proceeded to explain how her mother, the first wife of Arthur Borgen, was Theresa Nichols who died when she was twelve in a car accident in rural Maryland when her sedan skidded off an icy road and fell forty feet into the frigid waters of the Potomac River. She told of how she adored her mother and eventually had her last name legally changed to her mother's maiden name of Nichols shortly after she graduated from college with her multiple degrees and was about to enter the workplace.

A light compost of respectability, they all agreed, would be an essential first stage in preparing the ground for a truly first class defalcation. Months ago Arthur Borgen was something rather to be feared but in an abstract manner, but now after Dan's research and today after what Sophie had disclosed and the warning of the danger that may lay ahead, it appeared now that a jackal had definitely drawn up a seat at the dubious feast.

Walt intended, as he explained, to draw the agency head in by appealing to his most piercingly felt inadequacy to what he perceived to be the great raw hole at the seat of his being, he explained with what seemed like, Ryan thought, the fatigued dignity of a man who had spent the last hours discussing indentures with demanding clients. Walter understood that old wounds were useful when it came to getting new business, and he had seen this as an opportunity to strike a purgative blow for the values his family, and now Sophie, as well held dear. They all agreed they needed to cut one by one the strings which make this marionette and his agency dance. No grass would grow under their sturdy brogans once they were determined to get things done.

"We need to dismantle his cardboard temple of Mammon," Sophie added as their lunch meeting ended in a final toast to their collective mission, as a dusky urgency seemed to come upon them, a certain universal grimness.

Outside the beginnings of the late afternoon were starting to turn toward a gray dusk, as a dark and lowering sky hung threateningly overhead. Madison Avenue was dotted with gesticulating cab seekers, as they bade each other goodbye with warm hugs of new found friendship of a common bond.

Ryan and Walt jumped into a taxi, both sensing the first rhapsodic rush of the unopposed march through the open fields was over, Walter finally saying, staring directly ahead as if in a daze, that, "From now on it was going to be a hard slog up country and the sharpshooters would be moving into position behind the hedgerows." His voice brave but with the courage of his hopes.

"As one of the great philosophers once said, Dad," Ryan offered, "even losing on the right was vastly better than winning on the wrong." Walter shook his head inwardly contemplating the needless destruction of something harmlessly trying to make for a better society. Well so it be, Walter thought, the winds of "free enterprise" blew fierce and changeable, the devil didn't sleep and wherever he was, there was Mammon, and it appeared wherever Mammon was there would be Arthur Borgen.

He leaned back hoping against hope the interim hours and days would find answers and a way out. He had a lot to answer for, he thought, it was no fun being this age and feeling about your life's work the way he was beginning to feel. He wanted desperately to redress this account and pay alms to posterity and make sure Asclepius gets his cock. He didn't want to die with this matter still on his conscience.

"This is the point, Ryan, where we have to run on our own pedigrees," he finally added, breaking the silence, as the taxi turned and sped up the FDR on the way to the RFK Bridge and LaGuardia Airport.

Chapter 24

When Ryan woke they were circling Palm Beach, preparing to land. It was his annual business duty-dance, to attend and speak at the investment symposium in Florida's sun baked Wall Street event circus.

From the air the city looked much more pleasant than it actually was. The sea beside it shone gorgeous light green, the uncanny surface shivered under the faintest of breezes, as a flight of black ducks crossed toward shore flying in a V wedge inches above the shimmering water, while the beaches down the coast sparkled in crescents of golden autumn sunlight. Ryan frowned at the commercial abundance adjacent to the beautiful beaches, recalling his dream, a variation on one he had been having intermittently for many years. It always made him feel the same.

Palm Beach was one of those locales Ryan had hated on principle, but winter up north had worn on in a skein of unrelieved gray frigid dampness making the meetings at least climatically of value, making ones attendance there a near reflex action. Palm Beach was Vienna in reverse, an air conditioned Hades, but for its citizens' leathery political troglodytes and their sun embalmed wives. Everyone here seemed born seventy years old and retired. The season here was down to butt ends, people who had little enough to say to begin with, now had nothing to say. As Ryan rode along in the taxi to the hotel he could see that the upscale rabble, were out in force, credit cards at the ready, the cruel Darwinism of fashion powerfully evident.

All around him, millions of newly minted American millionaires were engaged in the identical pursuit of feeling extraordinary, snared in the toils of mortal compulsions, by buying the perfect Victorian mansion, of skiing the virgin slope, of knowing the chef personally, of finding the beach where no footprints had ever tread. There were further tens of millions of young nubile Americans who had not the money, but were nonetheless chasing the "perfect cool," who believed in the importance of their destined selves, young paragons of bloated self-esteem, in an endless sea of sensory adventures, till right up until they disappear or die, dissolved in their collective consciousness; and to what purpose all those things and all that adventure? The sad truth, Ryan mused, was that not everyone could be extraordinary, not everyone could be super cool. Who would this leave to be ordinary? Who would be about the thankless work of being comparatively uncool?

He watched the joggers and their numbing runs along the beach as his taxi made its way to the hotel, wondering if they exercised their heads or understood what the diet of their minds does to their consciousness, their character, to the body they pray to, and the salvation they seek.

Most people came here reflexively, Ryan mused, as the cab traveled slowly in the congested traffic along Worth Avenue, the local retiree drivers obeying barbiturate speed limits as they crawled to their destinations. It was called being rich together, similarity breeding affection or at least reassurance. He hated the place really, as it incarnated everything that was most repellent and contemptible about the country's materialism and social ambition. It was a sink hole of money, a gilded cesspit, the capital of blind valueless wealth worship, as he watched the female slaves to fashion coiffed in what the style setters had decreed the fashion of the season, a "lacquered out-doorsiness," adorned in the latest styles with the men looking like fibrous pansies heftily gaudy, dressed in their peach silk jackets and lemon trousers, luxuriating in the delusion that wealth was synonym for wisdom and good character.

It seemed that there was no life beyond the moment. There was only the insane flux and reflux of getting and spending. They were all drowning in their own obsessions. These people were like Saint Francis of Assisi in reverse, he thought, all having taken a vow of wealth, acquiring all sorts of gear needed by newly insecurely rich people who craved the visible reassurance of other people's taste, even other people's names and symbols, plastered, appliquéd, carved and incised on everything they wore or carried. This was the other side of the coin of the New Prosperity, white minked, open collared, gold chained, blow dried, down and dirty, peel off c-notes America. The insecurity of wealth acted as a powerful emotional adhesive, all part of the mysterious implacable biogenetics of wealth.

Entering the main ballroom of the Palm Beach Gardens hotel for the annual investment symposium that the major Wall Street firms sponsored, Ryan suddenly felt as if he had gotten on the wrong carousel and the music had faded away and the centrifugal pull had dwindled and it was as if he had to get off, feeling depleted, by a sense of anti-climax. Ryan looked out upon the gathered, all seeming somewhat forlorn, hunched and huddled amid the noise and chatter, gross insects drawn into the alien glare by wives and mistresses, lured from the shadowy recesses where they hatched their vast complex schemes. He saw them sadly as just another few cubic feet of flesh and bone competing for a fraction of personal space and recognition within the throngs of others that care a hoot about who that "other" was or will end up as. His time around Wall Street had convinced him of its basic intellectual dishonesty and most of the business he had witnessed had proved him right.

Ryan stood in silence just inside the doorway on the ballroom closest to the stage, smartening his tie as he listened to a Wall Street firm's senior vice president speak, waiting for his introduction. The man's shameless self-promotion and insouciance before such a large group struck Ryan as downright disrespectful. His presentation was typical, becoming nine tenths bravado, the technical palaver being as tiresome as ever, in the perpetual effort to sell motion as progress. He was skating on a tenuous veneer of pretense and blather, attempting to deliver a high minded persiflage intended to distract from the gutter action. The bullshit was piled high but Ryan vowed silently to himself to keep his shovel leaning against the barn.

His industry was becoming in large part a culture that looked and babbled at each other that constantly seems mentally into a new hustle. The speaker, who Ryan had known while on Wall Street, had probably popped a couple of tranzines to dull his apprehensions and had took aboard for the three days of meetings enough Columbian to maintain a self-deceptive state of confident elation. Ryan knew the guy preferred to get out of tight corners by talking faster and faster like an attempted seduction, letting his machine gun glibness for which he was famous carve an improbable escape route from his adversaries.

Present here in this crowd, as it usually was in these presentations, existed that irrepressible market animating fear that they might be missing out on the latest new hot thing on Wall Street. The markets in their infinite power had cast a seductive rosy glow which tinged the financial news with a fine positivism as opalescently rosy as the first beams of sunrise. Wishful thinking and its adolescent step child of optimistic forecasting by Wall Street were now showing their faces to the warm sun every day now, hoping to gorge the fickle investor to the point of euphoric loyalty, eager investors willing to put their money where their worship was in order to buy another piece of their retirement dreams.

Finally, being introduced, Ryan forced a smile hoping that his ambition wouldn't be far exceeded by his talent. He stood behind the highly polished mahogany podium and began his thirty-minute presentation to a throng of nearly one thousand in the grand ballroom, on the new product iteration his company had recently pioneered.

"Adam Smith presciently described the characteristics of today's corporate and institutional managers with these words: 'Managers of other people's money rarely watch over it with the same anxious vigilance with which they watch over their own…' they very easily give themselves a dispensation. Negligence and profusion must always prevail. In short, the managers of our public corporations have come to place their own interests ahead of the interests of their owners, exploiting the powers of their agency yet unchecked by traditional gatekeepers such as directors, accountants, and regulators and even the shareholders themselves. For the true owners now play nothing but a small and rapidly vanishing role in our investment world. Our now dominant money manager transfer agents have happily accepted the new environment in which management self-interest is in control. Indeed they have fostered it by accepting as the holy-grail whatever earnings our corporations report, and by for the most part generally ignoring corporate governance issues such as proxy access, executive compensation, board composition, and mergers and acquisition and dividend policy.

"I believe, as do the other principles of our marketing company, that we currently have a crisis of ethic proportions. That is ethic not epic," Ryan repeated for clarification, his voice rising with his plaint. "Again, relying on Adam Smith's 'invisible hand', through which our own self-interest is said to advance the interests of our communities, our culture has come to rely less on strict regulation to govern conduct in the field of free enterprise, in commerce, business and finance, and to rely more on open competition and free markets to create prosperity and well-being, adding value to our society. Today, that self-interest seems to have gotten out of control and it has spread to the very core of our national culture, the result being a marked change in our society, where the traditional standard of conduct in which there are some things that one simply does not do, has taken a back seat to a modern standard of, if everyone else is doing it I can do it as well. I would describe this change as a shift from moral absolutism to moral relativism, and it has been the driving factor in the investment iteration my company puts forth to you this day. The moral themes of virtue, loyalty, fidelity, faith and honor have been debased and we feel not truly engendered in the traditional investment products. Business ethics has been a major casualty of that shift in our traditional societal values, and the idea of professional standards has been lost in the course of activity.

"Back in 1934 in the aftermath of the great stock market crash Supreme Court Justice Harlan Fiske Stone warned:

"'The separation of ownership from management, the development of the corporate structure so as to vest in small groups control over the resources of great numbers of small and uninformed investors, make imperative a fresh and active devotion to the principle that no man can serve two masters, if the modern world of business is to perform its proper function. Yet those who serve nominally as trustees, but are relieved, by clever legal devices, from the obligation to protect those whose interests they are purported to represent; corporate officers and directors who award themselves huge bonuses from corporate funds without the assent or even the knowledge of their stockholders; and financial institutions which, in the infinite variety of their operations, consider only last, if at all the interests of those whose funds they command, suggest how far we have ignored the necessary implications of that principle.

"'Most of the mistakes and major faults of the financial era that has just drawn to a close will be ascribed to the failure to observe the fiduciary principle, the precept as old as holy writ, that a man cannot serve two masters. The resulting loss and suffering inflicted on individuals, because of non-adherence the principle and the harm done to a social order founded upon business and dependent upon its integrity, are incalculable.'

"Justice Stone's words, excerpted from his 1934 essay in the *Harvard Law Review*, are very relevant at this moment in history, where our fiduciary duty, as expressed in the provisions in the Investment Company Act of 1940, requires investment companies to be organized, operated, and managed in the interests of their shareholders, rather than in the interest of their managers and distributors."

Ryan could sense his listeners seemed attentive but unenthusiastic, giving him polite bland nods and dead eyes. It made him feel uneasy, as it always had when a presentation seemed it wasn't going over, but he would resist the urge to attempt to make the sale, and not begin to intone a series of dubious verities, having no intention of starting the hard sell and not about to do the diffident routine. Ryan could sense that some qualitative initiative had to be taken like the notes establishing the key to a musical composition. He realized not to expect those listening to keel over in a transport of appreciative ecstasy, but to rather make them comfortable investors through the familiar vocabulary of profit.

"We seem to forget," Ryan continued after taking a mental read of his fellow advocates, "that the driving force of any profession includes not only the special knowledge, skills, and standards that it demands, but the duty to serve responsibly, selflessly and wisely and to establish an inherently ethical relationship between professionals we all claim to be and the society we serve. It's the old notion of trusting and being trusted, which was once not only the accepted standard of business conduct, but the crucial key to success in the marketplace, which has now come to be seen as a quaint anachronism, a relic of an era long since passed.

"Here again, we can't say that we hadn't been well warned in advance. Speaking before the 1958 Convention of the National Federation of Financial Analysts Societies, Benjamin Graham, who you all know as the legendary investor and the author of the classic, *The Intelligent Investor*, described some contrasting relationships between the present and the past in our underlying attitudes toward market investment and speculation.

"In the past, the speculative elements of a common stock resided almost exclusively in the company itself; they were due to uncertainties, or fluctuating elements, or downright weaknesses, in the industry, or the corporation's individual setup... But in recent years a new and major element of speculation has been introduced into the common stock arena from outside the companies. It comes from the attitude and viewpoint of the stock buying public and their advisors, chiefly us as security analysts. This attitude may be described in a phrase: primary emphasis upon future expectations... The concept of future prospects, and particularly of continued growth in the future, invites the applications of formulas out of higher mathematics to establish the present value of the favored issues. But the combination of precise formulas with highly imprecise assumptions can be used to establish, or rather justify, practically any value one wishes, however high... Given the three ingredients of optimistic assumptions as to the rate of earnings growth, a sufficiently long projection of this growth into the future, and the miraculous workings of compound interest and lo! the security analyst is supplied with a new kind of philosopher's stone which can produce or justify any desired valuation for a really 'good stock.'

Mathematics is ordinarily considered as producing precise and dependable results; but in the stock market the more elaborate and abstruse the mathematics, the more uncertain and speculative are the conclusions we draw therefrom... Whenever calculus is brought in, or higher algebra, you could take it as a warning signal that the operator was trying to substitute theory for experience, and usually also to give to speculation the deceptive guise of investment... Have not investors and security analysts eaten of the tree of knowledge of good and evil prospects? By so doing have they not permanently expelled themselves from that Eden where promising common stocks at reasonable prices could be plucked off the bushes?"

Ryan watched as his statements floated across the room hoping to transfix the gimlet eyed intellectual cattle in their Paul Stewart suits, standing in the back of the room that ran the various firms' trust departments and hedge funds, who functioned as the ultimate gate keepers, hoping they would scramble to his company's product concept iterations and bite into the apple as if it were a saltlick. "The obvious reference to Original Sin," Ryan continued, "reflected Graham's deep concern about quantifying the unquantifiable and doing so with false precision. The implications of that bite into the apple of quantitative investing were barely visible when Graham spoke in 1958. But today, this new form of investment behavior has become in our opinion a force that continues to be a major driver of the securities speculation that has overwhelmed our financial markets.

"Consider for a moment." Ryan pushed toward his closing, as he surveyed his audience, thankfully, he sensed, seeing the nodding heads of acknowledgement and clear eyed attention. "How the erosion in the conduct, values and ethics of business has been incubated and fostered by the profound and largely unnoticed change that has taken place in the nature of our financial markets. That change reflects two extremely different views of what investing is all about, two distinct markets. One is the real market based on intrinsic business value and the other is the 'expectations market' of monetary stock prices. The British economist John Maynard Keynes described this polarization as the distinction between enterprise, forecasting the prospective yield of the asset over its entire life, and speculation, forecasting the psychology of markets. Keynes was deeply concerned about the societal implications of the growing role of short term speculation on stock prices.

A conventional valuation of stocks which is established by the mass psychology of a large number of ignorant individuals, he wrote, is liable to change violently as the result of a sudden fluctuation of opinion due to factors which do not really matter much to the prospective yield, resulting in unreasoning waves of optimistic and pessimistic sentiment. Then, prophetically, Lord Keynes predicted that this trend would intensify, as even expert professionals, possessing judgment and knowledge beyond that of the average private investor, would become concerned, not with making superior long term forecasts of the probable yield on an investment over its entire life, but with forecasting changes in the conventional valuation a short time ahead of the general public.

"As a result, Keynes warned, the stock market would become a battle of wits to anticipate the basis of conventional valuation a few months hence rather than the prospective yield of an investment over a long term of years. Just as Keynes had predicted, speculation came to overwhelm enterprise, the old ownership society became today's agency society, and the values of capitalism were seriously eroded, as professional institutional investors moved their focus from the wisdom of long term investment to the folly of short term speculation, where the capital development of the country became a by-product of the activities of a casino. Just as he warned, when enterprise becomes a mere bubble on a whirlpool of speculation, the job of capitalism is likely to be ill-done, and that is one thing we can't allow to endure.

"It is amazing that long ago, these present warnings were proclaimed. Justice Stone's words in 1934 and Keynes words in 1937 and Graham's in 1958 all warned us. So, yes, now it is time to reform as best at least as the company that I am part of possibly can. Today's agency society has not served the public interest in the most ideal manner. The failure of our money manager agents represents a failure of modern day capitalism.

"That is where we are today, and in response to the enduring principles of the long term honest stewardship of investor assets with the shared goals between ourselves and our clients, we bring to you today, what we hope to be an artistic and a commercial success. It is a product offering we bring of simple arithmetic, a reflection of the words of Sophocles: 'Remember, O stranger, that arithmetic is the first of the sciences, and the mother of safety.' Yes, arithmetic and engineering. The SEC's approval and review of our filing documents stated that our plan was consistent with the provisions, policies and purposes of the 1040 Act, stating specifically that our fund complex furthers the Act's objectives, enhances the funds' independence, benefits each fund with a reasonable range of fairness and provides substantial savings from advisory fee reductions and economies of scale and promotes a healthy and viable mutual fund group in which each fund can better prosper.

We have designed and bring to you our best effort to align the interests of fund investors and fund managers under the established principles of fiduciary duty, designed with three simple principles, of being structurally correct since we will be owned by our fund investors, mathematically correct, since it is a tautology that the lower the costs incurred in investing, the higher the returns, and ethically correct since we will exist only by earning far greater trust and loyalty from our shareholders than any of our peers. Thusly, we bring to you the industry's first client driven, low fee, an operating expense ratio of twenty basis points on average assets, tax advantaged, no load, no surrender charge fund series of index funds, tracking all sectors of the market, that compensates the financial advisor annually on a fee based structure, providing for a more ethical long term retention of client assets.

"As William Parsons wrote in his nineteenth century masterpiece, *The Merchant of Probity*, the good merchant, though an enterprising man and willing to run some risks, he is not yet willing to risk everything, nor put on all the hazard of a single throw. Above all, he makes it a matter of conscience not to risk in hazardous enterprises the property of others entrusted to his keeping. He is careful to indulge in no extravagance, and to live within his means. Simple is his manner and unostentatious in his habits of life, abstaining from all frivolities and foolish expenditures. He recollects that he is not merely a merchant, but a man, and that he has a mind to improve, a heart to cultivate, and a character to form.

"I thank you for your kind attention and indulgence. We will be having our investment symposiums tomorrow and hope you attend to witness first-hand how this innovative offering can be a part of your future business plan and vital to the fiduciary duty we all must share to our client's investment and retirement needs. Thank you again and we hope to see you at our break-out sessions," Ryan concluded to a polite if not mildly enthusiastic round of applause.

That first night Ryan attended a variety of sponsored cocktail parties by brokerage firms and asset managers of dubious reputation, drifting through a slurry of acidic white wine and finger food. He had steered himself through the events of the evening with tact and agility, answering questions about his company's new offerings, smiling noncommittally as others made counter arguments and offensive parrys with their intellectual swords practicing the studied neutrality of his profession, eventually venturing out away from the constant propagandizing and squeezed his way outside and down the street through a crowd at a plastic palmed joint in Vero Beach, where perspiring ephebes in bun tight white ducks poured drinks. Ryan sipped an absolute in slow fashion as he watched a man have a mercifully unconsummated flirtation with a skinny divorcee at the bar, before making his blessed retreat back to the peaceful sanctum of his hotel suite and a call home to Nan.

The orator after the break-out sessions the next afternoon at two o'clock was Henry Grover, the chairman by inheritance and the CEO of the second largest investment banking house on Wall Street, the third largest in the country and the ninth largest in the world. Grover spoke in a practiced ocular manner which he felt suited the leader of such a great institution, inflecting his prose so that certain words seemed to be capitalized, the vocal equivalent of the typeface of the old moral stories which his ancestors had papered in the libraries of Ivy League colleges. The ballroom collapsed in applause at his perma-bull bias and the forecast of up markets. This was a savvy audience, very capable of instant recognition of its own best interest. The self-satisfaction on both sides of the rostrum from which he spoke was thick enough to spread on a bagel, glutinous, almost tangible. In the last fortnight, the market had suddenly burst out of its lassitude and had brought about a nice two hundred points on the Dow with huge volume. People were talking of a major bull market. Everyone was suddenly richer and just as suddenly feeling smart and confident. Ryan could smell it and he recognized the scent from his own stint on Wall Street.

The people who had been assembled on the stage behind him and at the rostrum were surprisingly young, Ryan thought, mostly in their early thirties, neatly dressed in the uniform of the day; three piece suits for the men and dress for success matching blazers and skirts for the women. Almost to a person, everyone wore a cravat of some sort, the women favoring floppy bow ties of Rembrandtesque proportions, the men subdued in four-in-hand neckties. Here and there among the youthful, confident faces, a grizzled head could be seen, nose and cheeks finely webbed with the evidence of too much drink and pressure and disappointment, eyes that had seen far too many markets ups and downs, flashes and fizzles, veterans of the sixties, who'd somehow kept it together and hung on in the brave new age. They were few and exceptional however, Ryan knew, the game again belonging to the new breed, the young trading tigers from the hot new money management firms, the analytical cool eyed boys and girls who now ran the mutual funds and bank trust departments, the specialty analysts who called the tunes on the largest capitalized stocks.

Ryan was sitting about half way back at the end of a row next to Richie, an old chum from his trading days on Wall Street, in the packed grand ballroom of the Palm Beach Plaza Hotel. "It is our mission and our responsibility to bring economic stability to our brothers and sisters in the Third World," the orator continued. He had a flat, parson voice which suited his priggish, sanctimonious face.

"Bullshit," whispered Richie, easily audible to others around, to needle any believers in that delivered tripe. "I bet you will," he said in the sub-voice tone schoolboys use to drive their teacher apoplectic.

The moderator that had introduced him earlier was back at the podium, echoing the audience's dutiful applause beaming rays of deferential approbation at Chairman Skoglund. "We are now open for questions and of course we are grateful indeed for Mr. Skoglund's lucid remarks on matters much on the mind of everyone here this morning. Are there any questions?"

"Mr. Skoglund." The moderator pointed to a man who had risen in the front row. Ryan recognized him as a stockbroker who he knew sucked up the tail ends of business from the big institutions like Skoglund's firm. The question he would ask would probably be just another creative corporate inoculation by the plant initiated by the banks relentlessly active unsleeping public relations machine.

"Mr. Grover, in the course of your sage analysis—" the broker giving a mock tug to his forelock "—you have alluded to certain present day alarmists who have publicly asserted that the American banking is de facto bankrupt. They claim that a run by OPEC and certain entities in South America on its overnight deposits, combined with a series of defaults on outstanding loans to the lesser developed countries would wipe out the capital and surplus of our major banks."

Skoglund's obfuscating answer took almost fifteen minutes and made no sense whatsoever as Ryan listened to it. He said that the facts were that the banks had gotten in over their heads, not with OPEC depositors. The Federal Reserve would freeze those deposits if they tried a run on his bank or any other bank. His words were accompanied by a series of charts, unreadable from more than five feet, which were generated on signal by a bean thin young man with a complexion reminiscent of a naval field bombing. "These charts," Skoglund was finalizing, "and the figures which I have adduced demonstrate the unshakable solidity of the banking system, and I am happy to be able to say, the Bank considers itself a cornerstone, morally, ethically and financially."

"The beatitudes as written by Wall Street public relations," Ryan whispered to Richie.

"With music from the Messiah and arranged by Marvin Hamlish," Richie retorted, both of them trying to hold their laughter within.

Onstage the moderator and Grover and the assigned panelists were bobbing and bowing like supplicants at a Japanese cocktail party. The session which wrapped up the investment forum portion of the conference was adjourned and the true purpose of the shindig could now unfold. Richie turned to Ryan with a look of mischief now overcoming him like a shroud.

"After listening to all this bovine fundament, my boy, we have to get a drink, right now, a free drink, perhaps many free drinks."

"There are hundreds of hospitality suites, where would you like to start?" was Ryan's reflective retort.

"Let's begin with Barney Hutchins, the largest institutional trader at Freidman, they have the largest jackass quotient and you need to be reasonably drunk to cope and take and take advantage of it and if worse comes to worse we can live off the all-beef cocktail sausages." Richie smirked with a roguish grin.

"Okay," Ryan heard himself saying, in a flat voice which wasn't quite his own. "Okay"

About two years before Friedman Partners had been merged with Mouser and Tescombe, a marriage joining one of the country's oldest Jewish investment houses with an old WASP firm which had in 1654 traded fur pelts at the bottom of Manhattan, now Battery Park. A series of ill-advised bond trading positions had all but wiped out the capital of Mouser, forcing its partners to seek a merger before their wives sued to protect their capital. The marriage had been happy for a very short duration, only after six months Charles Freidman, whose principal private benevolence was his work as chairman of the Holocaust Committee of the Federation of Jewish Philanthropies, had initiated the systematic liquidation of the Mouser partners. It was a process which was variously celebrated in the demeaning mythography of Wall Street as, "the Jews versus the Gentiles". It was the classic example, as Ryan saw it, of two plus two equaling one.

Still Freidman was respected on the street and was known to serve decent first rate cocktails, and as Richie had stressed, there was one hell of a girl at the meeting who worked in the bond department. Richie was pretty sure she'd be there and Ryan knew his old friend would be planning some sexual Armageddon in her direction.

"Christ," Richie had said as they made their way to the suite, "every self-proclaimed expert in international finance and money brokerage was at the conference." Including me, Ryan thought half in amusement half in rue. "And they always brought along their office's hottest talent." Ryan smiled nodding in agreement.

Richard Cummings was one of Ryan's best friends in the business. They had known each other since college fraternity had brought them together at Cornell. His family came from boat loads of money, his mother from the Poors family of Standard and Poors. Richie was funny, hilariously funny really, and for nine months of the year he was fat, and then urged on by some thick wagers with a group of clerks on the trading floor who didn't know what determination was, he would proceed to drop fifty pounds at a thousand buck a pound. It was a handsome supplementary and undeclared income he didn't need but loved the challenge. He was a man who had prospered almost entirely as a by-product of being pleasant and obliging, in the old fashioned sense of his ancestry, no matter how repulsive and vulgar the client. Ryan never begrudged Richie his success, these days nice was a hell of a lot harder to be than smart.

Richie was dressed in a variation of what Ryan called, "Wall Street self-important chic," shoes both tasseled and buckled, a dark suit with side vents that seemed to come up to his arm pits, a Hermes tie wide enough to sleep in and suspenders needle pointed with his initials. By contrast Ryan had dressed the same way for fifteen years, black or burgundy Cole Hahn loafers, navy or black sport jackets and quiet club ties. He wore a great, thick Swiss watch that he claimed was guaranteed for accuracy under three hundred feet of water or when dropped from the roofs of tall buildings. It had a stopwatch attachment and all sorts of dials. It did everything but play the Swiss national anthem, Ryan scolded him, half kidding.

He was a manic egocentric, Ryan understood, and he possessed an inflated sense of self-worth, an easy sociability, with an air of imperturbability with a cool indifference to social responsibility and the welfare of others. He may have a facile and superficially charming personal style, as noted by a seeking of praise and attention, as witnessed in his exhibitionist and self-enhancing behavior. Ryan knew his interpersonal relationships were sometimes characteristically self-indulgent, demanding, shallow and fleeting, with a penchant at times for exploiting the naïve, taking a measure of delight in defying and challenging convention. Easily capable of feigning an air of dignity and confidence he was skilled in deceiving others as was the demand of his business. His histrionic over activity and stimulus and his exhibitionistic and excessive talents manifested in his rapidly changing, short lived and superficial affects. He tended to be capricious, easily excited and intolerant of frustration, delay, and disappointment, but in short doses Ryan loved his riotous company.

Ryan knew, however, Richie was considered a degenerate by the pursed-mouthed dinner table types who in many cases would have sold their wives and children to get in on Richie's financial and erotic action. For a living he pedaled stocks and bonds to oilmen and other entrepreneurs who'd made it and like Barney Hutchins at Freidman he liked to swing. As long as Ryan had known him he had lied like a small boy who feared that his luxurious life was nothing but a series of reproach punishments, and like all avid adulterers, he hoarded free evenings like gold nuggets. His falsehoods in the past, mostly little self-glorifying exaggerations, had over the years expanded into important risky fabrications, bubbling freely from the inventive springs deep inside his character. It was a tale he repeated a dozen times a year, in an industry where such men invested their libidos in business and sex that made them vulnerable. It showed itself, Ryan had witnessed, in his deceitful handling of women. His relationships with women were like fruit flies, numerous and short lived. Those who had witnessed his actions called him privately an emotional scavenger, a panhandler in the streets of the heart, knowing sorrow was the fastest way to women's genitals.

For a character of his type, as Wall Street was full of them, it was the action they loved, the psycho-adrenal rush of writing the ticket, pushing the stock up or down at will, the savage intents of continuous commission trading pumped reposefully in savage hearts, that did the trick, and the slam bam of a quick vaginal fix to make them feel good about themselves. The hotter the action the faster the chase and sometimes the two affections got confused in the mind, while their eyes whirred like slot machines. He could screw another woman or an unsuspecting client with equal ardor so long as there was a good time attached and plenty of free booze and dope. These are the type of guys, Ryan intuited, sipping on his absolute at the Freidman suite watching Richie enwrapped in solicitous conversation with Barney, who feel they can get anything they want within the compass of two phone calls. It was a strategy perfectly suited to a culture that saw every day not as a new beginning but as a manic last chance. Like swimmers sucked into the riptide, he and so many like him Ryan knew had literally disappeared into their money.

But for Richie it wasn't about being wealthy, it was about living the biggest riotous life possible, and money was just the instrument that drove his carnal anarchy. It looked as though this night, Ryan smiled, that Richie would once again seal his legend.

Good as he was he had an ape of his own that could also get loose in the streets, a potentially life wrecking itch that he felt sometimes needed to be scratched. He had to admit to himself it was a struggle some days to maintain focus, not to take his hand off the wheel and every once in a while allow that reptilian brain to go free and experience some carnal exercise. Musing for a moment on the pallor of his youthful follies, on his old loves, taking a fresh drink from Richie, Ryan recalled how in the end, finally worn out with each other, their romances became stripped to the husk of shopworn recriminations and useless memories and in short time, having played out the particulars of the psychological drama of their boomer generation, they would part for good. Ryan watched with a sort of grim avariciousness as Richie's fancies began to flow freely, no doubt leading to the penultimate of his nightly activity.

All of a sudden it seemed that the entire entourage of chatelaines from the Palm Beach houses of carnality seemed to be in attendance. It was becoming a scene of inspired debauchery.

He had been able to keep himself out of compromising situations for more than fifteen years, but he knew that if a certain fuse were lit and the sirens fetched him below the belt he could wobble and everything he'd been working so hard at could go up in flames, which was why the young blond bond trader standing next to the girl Richie was ocular pawing on the other side of the bar, had scared him to the depths of his soul. Ryan sat there mortified, planning his congenial leave as she walked toward him, her perfume drifting like angelic mist into his nostrils, stricken suddenly by the potential recklessness of his friend's potential conduct, reminding himself of where he was. He slowly backed out of the room like an ambassador leaving the presence of a volatile pagan empress, welcoming the passing of the night's enchantments, quietly seeking a route back to his hotel suite and more pedantic convention, happy in the thought that he would not suffer the sin sore hung over self-consciousness, having not fell prey to the two face Dionysian god of sensual pleasure and wake up in the morning in a groggy stupor scrambling to find his principles, understanding as he made his leave that character was much easier kept than captured.

Chapter 25

The first two days of the annual Palm Beach gathering, Ryan had spent in the dressed up company of want to be tycoons and simulacrums, were profound with bland meetings and money manager presentations, however, Ryan's two breakout sessions held the previous day had been quite edifying with a nice flurry of indications of interest, and two major broker dealers signing selling agreements on the spot. Ryan made a great show of resolution as he attended other investment forums, organizing and putting papers and notes in order, before deciding to hie himself off to the sun somewhere to labor in solitude, now that his rounds of meetings, seminars and grip and grins were mercifully over, and await Nan's arrival the next morning, in time for the dinner gala and dance that evening, to finally spend the remaining week in Palm Beach to their own desires.

Ryan and Nan had been served the latest in good red wines, burgundies and merlots that walked with a heavy tread, by a flank of hostesses with bright affability, speaking like they had just cut their mouths on the sheer edges of a beer can. They were attending, with about two hundred other men and women in the most exclusive private dining room at the Palm Beach Gardens, an invitation only dinner party hosted by Institutional Equity Associates, where a presentation was to be made by one of its hottest up and coming media corporations that it was underwriting. They watched as the broker community attending drank with parched abandon and licked their lips munching up the Hors d'oeuvres at the offer and set about them sword and buckler. All those financial types, stylish yet awkward people looking gloomily un-hatched in their brilliant plumage, a puffy over moneyed younger crowd gulping smoke and booze and buzzing back and forth into the encroaching gardens to feed their olfactories with sweet white powder. You could distinctly hear the murmurings of unadulterated greed, no different in its emotional purity from the cries of infants mewling for the nipple, on their never ending vestigial power trips forever moist with the possibility to sell as many shares as they could per day until it became obvious enough for the sheep to hear the tinkling of their bell themselves and join the rush to the exits.

These were men Ryan knew, for whom the caresses of a wife tried and true no longer thrilled, even with the newly acquired high breasts, for the crypto-erotic urge for making money was all too powerful, on uppers designed to promote that whiz-bang sense of self which seemed integral these days to the trading game, believing the alchemist's incantations of turning lead into gold, propped up by dope and delusion, two very frail supports when the going got tough and the markets reacted in their first regurgative hysteria. It seemed all in attendance were now part of a new society, where they may be doing better, but in actuality were feeling worse. Here smack in front of them was the manifestation of the culture's new declinism, where a flinty ethos of self-determination emerges, another part of the institutional cultural casino.

Ryan moved the two of them about the room in what he hoped was a graceful manner, Nan looking radiant in her sheer light blue strapless silk gown doing the mandatory grip and grins required hoping his stock, based on the personas he and Nan projected and his presentation made two days before, was climbing with no breakpoints. Everyone was full to the brim with the promise of tomorrow's money to be made and would sooner die than disavow a hand shake.

"Yes nice to meet you as well," Ryan parried back at those they were greeting, as both he and Nan began to fasten on an avenue of fashioned escape. Within a mere twenty minutes of meet and greet they became fast weary of the brittle conversations filled with the rat-a-tat-tat fast talk. As they danced in the adjoining room to a sweet rendition of "Unchained Melody" by a four piece ensemble, with an enchanting female lead voice,

Nan's humid breath in Ryan's ear was positively tropical, and they discreetly found their way back to their suite and their own private erotica, taking the love within them to share.

Light slanted through the royal bluish water in sunny columns, one which illuminated the fish swimming near the base of the reef, purple and gold, like a jewel on the move. Ryan and Nan had two exquisite days to themselves away from the flow of meetings and seminars and cocktail parties. They decided to go snorkeling as far down the beach from the hotel as possible. Nan breathed deeply through her snorkel, filling her lungs, and dove straight down with slow powerful kicks, her upper body still. Near the bottom she stopped kicking and glided the rest of the way hovering over the fish. A fairy basset or possibly a beaugregory, but she had never seen either one with gold so bright and purple so intense. It looked up at her, tiny eyes most colorless of all its parts, watching her void of any expression she could define. The fish was hovering as well, its front fins vibrating at hummingbird wing speed, filigreed fins so close so transparent they were almost invisible. Amazingly two of its front fins didn't match; one was purple and the other gold. Nan transfixed, lost all track of time, until she felt pressure starting to build in her chest. She checked the depth gauge on her wrist, twenty feet it read. She was a good breath holder. She turned back for a last look at this special fish, perhaps one of a kind. It was gone. She kicked her way back up.

Nan broke the surface, blew through her snorkel, and sucked in the rich gulf air, floral and salty. She turned toward a little coral islet about fifty yards away north of the Palm Beach Gardens. From this angle tropical paradise pared down to the simplest components, white beach, a few palm trees, thatched hut, all colors bright, as in a child's coloring version. Hadn't one of the boys brought home from school just such a painting, she wondered? She was trying to remember when something down below grabbed her leg.

She jerked away, a frightened cry rising out of her snorkel, a cry she smothered when Ryan burst through the surface, a big smile on his face. "Ryan," she said, pushing her mouthpiece aside, "you scared me." He put his arm around her and sang a few off key notes from what Nan took to be the theme from Jaws. "I mean it," she said, playfully hitting his arm. Ryan stopped singing. He glanced down at the sandy bottom.

"Hey what's that?" "What's what?"

"On the bottom," he replied.

Nan dropped her face into the water, and gazed down through her mask. She saw something black lying on the sand, something man made, maybe a box. She turned to Ryan, that big smile on his face. Ryan put his mouthpiece back between his teeth and dove down. Yes, it was a box, not too big, not heavy. He carried it back to the surface.

"What's inside?" Nan asked, a smile beginning to form. Nan raised the lid. Inside, wrapped in waterproof plastic, she found another box, this one blue marked with the word Tiffany on the top. She opened it.

"Oh, Ryan,"

"Merry Christmas," said Ryan. "But it's over a month away." "I couldn't wait."

They bobbed up and down, Ryan carrying Nan in his arms, as the swells of the ocean pushing them closer and closer to the shoreline, Nan admiring the beautiful oval sapphire aligned with diamonds as it glistened its brilliance in the late afternoon sun, as a flock of dark birds rose out of the palms far down the shoreline wheeling across the sky heading north.

They ate dinner on the patio of their cabana far down the beach south of the hotel. Nan looked down at the beautiful ring that now graced her right ring finger. "I love you, Ryan Davies."

"Ditto that, Nanette Braddock." Ryan poured Champagne into Nan's fluted glass and after tasting the sparkling effervescence shared a deep luscious kiss. Dinner included spiny lobster and conch fritters, cooked by Ryan on the grill, rich greens of a spinach salad and two bottles of Dom Perignon.

The lights of the gulf shone in the east, a fuzzy glow like a distant galaxy. They toasted their glasses, as a shooting star went by, not an uncommon sight, but this one burned very bright. Nan caught its reflected path in Ryan's eyes. "Life is good," he said. They kissed again, their bare feet touching under the table. "I don't want to go back," Nan said.

"Maybe we won't... one day," said Ryan, pausing at the thought. "When," said Nan. "Tell me."

Ryan laughed. "When, our family drama is finally resolved." "When will that be?"

"When, our kids can finally support us in our retirement." Nan laughed too, pretending to throw a punch at Ryan as he pretended to block it.

Later that night they made beautiful rhythmic love with the cool breezes flowing through the wide open sliders, drifting over their hot intense passion, like an enveloping silk sheet. Ryan kissed her mouth, her neck, tenderly, and moved down once more. Then came more of those timeless minutes, Nan spent in a place without thought, rationality, cognition or anything else but pure pleasure, growing more focused and expanding simultaneously. Their love was the ascending energy of life itself. It was the place they occupied together, a flash of pure communion, the gift they offered that knew no distance, felt no differences and had no axes to grind. Love was light, love was energy, love was life. It was the ecstatic, energetic essence of their being, infinitely translatable into millions of idioms of human social experience and relationship epiphanies. It was a higher level of experience, a concerto of exalted moments in which they recognized their perfect connection with each other, and came home to the common ground woven together by their common thread.

After all the rushes of ecstatic feeling were beginning to wane, Ryan said, "I love you."

"I love you too."

They were silent for a few moments, the entrails of their shared ecstasy floating above them as if a sacred mist coming off the sea. "Everything's going to be all right," Ryan whispered.

"I hope so," Nan hushed back. "I hope so." They drifted off sweetly lying together like spoons, intimate in every way, in spirit and in love.

Chapter 26

Sophie caught the five thirty-five flight out of LaGuardia to Minneapolis and was happy to have been upgraded to first class, where she hoped she could peacefully replay in her mind the plan of attack she had with the help of her unwitting staff at the Progressive drawn together. It was Friday, the week before Thanksgiving, and she had wisely left her beloved St. Theresa medallion on her necklace at her condo on east eighty-third street, discovering that indeed Walter Davies' sharp senses had been correct. She gazed out over the Hudson as the 747 bellied its way up over a thin skid of clouds and banked gently to the right and eased into cruising speed for the three hour trip west.

She ordered a glass of Chardonnay and opened the black binder where she had put together the plans and strategies formulated to retrieve the Davies' ownership conveyances from Switzerland. She swirled her glass of wine holding it in front of her in the window, looking due north toward Canada. What would this venture bring? she thought, taking a healthy swallow, feeling herself slowly drift into a state of sublime unconsciousness. There was a template for everything, she mistily thought, somewhere there was an overgrown head water of the original and unprecedented. You might hack away in search of it your whole life and never find it. Or, on the other hand maybe you just might.

Far below the highway lights were muted and blue and the neon signs danced like festival delights. The people, the multitude, the rabble, the great unwashed, the man in the street, the many-headed hydra, the monster, the venal herd. Who were they? As individuals, generous, selfish, impetuous, unsure, unwise. Western man, in the saddle of a runaway technology in desperate need of a contemplative center, cut off from ascetic disciplines.

The technological society, which now encloses all modern communities, after the effects of industrialism, science and the media. They, we, have all become creatures of technique, technique being the totality of methods rationally arrived at and having absolute efficiency in every field of human activity. Technique is not only the machinery we use, it is the state of mind which uses us. Technique is the new environment of man which has replaced nature.

It is an environment in which mechanics have been put upon all that is spontaneous or irrational, and in which the overriding criterion of all planning and action is efficiency. As creatures of society we do not ask, "Is it right to do?" Or, "Is it wise?" Instead we ask, "Does it work?" "Is it effective?" Sophie sipped her wine gazing down at the lights, her mind ache continuing. The ultimate in technique lies in modern weapons, governed by efficiency, which becomes the determining factor of every decision. In technique, decisions are made according to means which inexorably become ends.

Ends then disappear in the reality of technique, overwhelmed by means. Techniques are all calculated means, rational efficient means which obscure quickly all goals and become the ends themselves, as the means of modern warfare have repeatedly overwhelmed all political ends. In the din of the capitalistic, technological society, which bombs abroad and consumes at home, the basis for a way of liberation can be found, must be found.

Her mind spun. The revolution goes on; a man does not make the revolution, not a thousand men, not an army and not a party. The revolution came from the people as they reach toward God, and a little of God is in each person and each will not forget it. This is the revolution when slaves shake their chains and the revolution when a man bends toward his weaker brother and lends him his arm. The revolution goes on and nothing stops it, because the people are seeking what is good, not what is wicked or powerful or crude or rich or venal. They simply want what is good. Yet because of that the people flounder and feel along one dark road after another. They are no more self-seeing than those who govern them. It is in intention that they differ.

Man's vision had always been a vision of godliness. From the deep dark morass he had come, from the jungles, the airy mountains and the windswept steppes. Always his way had been the way of the seeker. He made civilization and he made a morality and he made a pact of brotherhood. One day, he ceased to kill the aged and venerated them, ceased to kill the sick and healed them, ceased to kill the lost and showed them how to find themselves. Man had a dream and a vision and Isaiah was one of his habitants as was Jesus of Nazareth.

He offered a hand, saying, Thou art my brother, and do I not know thee? And man began to see God, like going up a ladder, rung after rung, always closer to something that had been waiting eternally. First wooden images, then marble ones, the sun and the stars, and then a just, unseen singleness, and then an unseen one of love and mercy, and then a gentle Jew nailed onto a cross and dying in pain. Man does not stop; he will create brotherhood worldwide, because a musket was fired in a Massachusetts village.

The way of revolution, as a mob, was to use heads and hearts to secure its ends, and she'd long ago seen the folly contained in that course. There never was in this world, a technique for revolution. But, there was a technique for tyranny and strength implemented it. But it was always the strength of a few. What good lay in reaching some mythical El Dorado when the beneficiary had already been turned into a robot wound up by dogma, powered by coercion? The road she'd taken was better, she would always believe that.

Of more worth is one honest man to society, and in the sight of God, than all the crowned ruffians that ever lived. It was her abiding faith in the individual's capacity for excellence, in the ultimate solidity of the common man. It lay at the heart of the great liberal tradition and she would not disavow it. Revolt against authority which is not aimed at the common good ceases to be seditious.

Was it ever right to sacrifice ones truth for expedience? She thought of the Grimke sisters, Sarah and Angelina, the revolutionary abolitionists from Charleston, South Carolina in the 1830s. They were crusading, not only for the immediate emancipation of slaves, but for racial equality. Their daring feminist arguments in *Letters on the Equality of the Sexes* would inspire and impact women such as Lucy Stone, Abby Felcey, Elizabeth Cady Stanton and Lucrecia Flott. Their pamphlets and books were publicly burned throughout the states, even in their home town of Charleston…

She was in the Sistine Chapel looking up at the painting on the ceiling and the gorgeous woman in Michelangelo's painting, the one that God has his arm wrapped around while his other arm extends to touch the hand of Adam. The gorgeous woman was a petite blonde thought to be Jehovah's grandmother, the Goddess Sophia. In the Judeo-Christian tradition the Goddess Sophia is the beginning, the source of wisdom, and the keeper of knowledge is righteous and just. With her sound wisdom and guidance, rulers lead their kingdoms to prosper. In the darkness and ignorance that thrive in her absence, the proverbial wasteland eats away at the soul and nations perish.

Known as the Mother of All, or simply as Wisdom, Sophia was born of silence according to Gnostic creation myths. They conceived of her as an incorporeal entity, the active thought of God, who was responsible for the creation of the world. It was believed Sophia embodied the highest form of feminine wisdom, possessing a purely spiritual wholeness in which the material world was altogether transcended.

She gave birth to both male and female who together created the elements of the material world. The female she gave birth to then gave birth to Jehovah and all his emanations. She also gave birth to Ialdabaoth who was known as the Son of Darkness. When humans were created Sophia loved them all dearly.

Unfortunately, her affection for humans sparked jealousy in both Ialdabaoth and Jehovah. Hoping to keep humans weak and powerless, the brothers forbade humans to eat the fruit of the tree of knowledge. Female then sent her spirit in the form of the serpent to teach the humans to disobey envious gods. Sophia so desperately loved humans that she decided she would live among them. To her dismay they mostly ignored her, turning a deaf ear when she tried to speak to them. She would scream from the tops of the highest walls and still not be heard.

In her anguish at being so neglected, she left humans with one last thought: You have denied and ignored me, so I will do the same, when calamity comes, and you call for my help. Only those who earnestly search for me and love me will merit my love and affection. Sophia, so desperate in her desire to relate, later returned to humans in another attempt to bond with them, symbolizing herself in the Dove of Aphrodite, which later became the dove representing the Holy Spirit.

The dove appeared to the Virgin Mary in the form of the Virgin of Light, entered her, and conceived Jesus. In this sense, Sophia attempted again, to inform of a man, to be united with the mortals she so loved. A Sophia woman sees it and tells it as it is; she has no fear of the truth. She brings meaning to the human experience with her gift of understanding "the bigger picture". Only when you can stand back, gaining some emotional distance, can you see that even the most traumatic experiences can be the birthplace of your most treasured strengths. It is only in times of great stress that heroic feats are truly appreciated.

Sophia was also the mother of Faith, Hope and Charity. These are Sophia's gifts to us, Sophie's dream was revealing to her, gifts that can overcome the despair, confusion, and suffering that frame human life. Sophia reminds us of that clear vision and understanding, that line, the path that leads to the discovery of the meaning of our lives…

There came to her an image of man's whole life upon earth. It seemed to her that all man's life was like a tiny spurt of flame that blazed out quickly in an illimitable and terrifying darkness, that all man's grandeur, tragic dignity, and heroic glory came from the brevity and miniature of his flame. Man knew that life was little and would be extinguished, and that only darkness was immense and everlasting. Man knew he would die with defiance on his lips, and that the shout of his denial would ring with the last pulsing of his heart, into the maw of an ever-engulfing night.

The slight descent of the Northwest flight brought Sophie out of her dream as the announcement was made of the beginning approach to the Lindberg terminal. She gently rubbed at the lingering mists of her muse of time travel from the edges of her eyes and sipped at the wine that sat in front of her, still remaining more than half full. She whispered a silent prayer to herself that the Sophia of her mythic dream could somehow guide and protect her through the perils that lie ahead for this mortal, Sophie Theresa Nichols, of here and now.

She peered out of the dense glass window again. Fewer lights now; even as she watched them some of them winked out, the night gathered force.

"All that is necessary for the triumph of evil is that good people do nothing."

She sighed, a long, shuddering sigh, passed her hand through her blonde shoulder length hair. Was that true, that simple adage of Burke's? It had always been a favorite of hers, credo and clarion alike, the wellspring of an alert citizenry who would not accede to tyranny in any form, who would not be driven or deceived.

It didn't make sense, yet of course it did. There was a reason, there was always a reason. There was something she couldn't quite put her finger on, something that rasped at the far edges of her mind. Track down the incongruous element someone had once told her, isolate it, analyze it correctly and it will often hold the solution.

The only truths lay in contraries, in conundrums. To yield was to triumph, to lose was to find, to give without stint was to gain without measure. It was so simple. Was it so simple? Sophie asked herself, a squint darkening her brow?

Out the window, the Mississippi made a wide black ribbon through the soft maze of lights, as the plane banked, beginning its approach. The slave was freer than the tyrant, the vagabond richer than the merchant, the lover mightier than the man of war.

Chapter 27

The doorbell at the Lake Avenue home of Ryan and Nan Davies sounded just after six p.m. with an immediate bark of startlement emanating out of the deep siesta that Gabby, the black and white spaniel was enjoying, instinctively leaping off the couch to the front double doors, tail frantically a-wag. Sophie was greeted with warm mid-western hugs from Mary and Nan quickly offering to have the Davies boys trudge her bags to her bedroom suite, recently designed over the three car garage, in the ever-expanding two-storey colonial.

Nan and Mary gave Sophie a quick tour of the Mediterranean style five bedroom that was nestled at the end of the cul-de-sac. She explored the kitchen in joy, with its terracotta floor, and granite counter tops, knotty pine woodwork, stainless steel appliances and the stained glass windows in the breakfast bay that overlooked the poolside patio and a broad lawn with landscaped vegetable and gardens terraced in the backyard, a loggia overlooking state protected pine woods.

The kidney-shaped, modestly sized pool, now covered with a thick reflective white tarp, mirrored the comforting shadows of the fall colors backlit by a series of running lights through the windows off the hardwood deck that stood almost two storeys tall. Just off the formal dining and living room sat the den with a large fieldstone hearth, the stones collected from the heart of the Iron Range of Mary's youth. The pine paneled den was enclosed with two rich dark leather couches and plush colorful high back chairs and ottomans.

The girls padded up the circular stairs, the tan berber carpeting, exposing the beautiful hard pine at its edges and down the hall to the spacious four bedrooms on the second floor, and then down to the lower level, brightly decorated, pine beamed, window lined recreation room where the Davies boys were intensely involved in the latest video game escapade on the television screen along the west pine paneled wall, ending her tour in the in the library and study off the hallway just beyond the mudroom, where an antique roll top desk stately stood flanked by bookshelves along the walls from head to toe.

Sophie paused for a moment to gaze upon the gems of knowledge that the pine shelves held as she chatted with her two new girlfriends. She looked upon the sturdy spines of the books. From those pined shelves were the dense rich bindings of the great voices of eternity, the tongues of mighty poets and writers dead and gone. Some of the books had been read, studied and discerned and did not lie forgotten like the shelves of a rich man's library; to be a portion of his idle wealth, the evidence of arrogant possession.

Every book is a miracle, she mused. Each book represented a moment when someone sat quietly, and it was that solemnity that was part of the miracle. They were there to comfort those about the world, for only the wicked could be pleased by the present state of things, while the virtuous disagree about the reasons for our plight and threaten to fall to fighting over which of us is responsible for the misery of so many millions, and in that way steadily increasing the number of hypocrites, jackals and rogues. How far advanced could our culture become, she mused, without the means to organize, classify, and pass on gleaned knowledge learned in books, in books of all fields?

The neatly alphabetized indices appearing in textbooks and encyclopedias represented only part of the great gift of literacy. Here along the bookshelves existed another dimension: that of the sheer aesthetic pleasure that accompanied reading. It helped to break the confines of the shell that more or less encased each individual. It was literature that allowed readers' minds to merge into the imaginations of the most thoughtful writers who had ever lived.

Ryan and Nan's library was an earnest of a sympathetic point of view, many virtually identical to those that were on her own book shelves, not likely to be found on the shelves of the fat and sanguine. The titled erect spines of the Davies' collection, Sophie noticed, included, Martin Mayer's *The Bankers* and *the Money Bazaars*, works on the debt crisis by Makin, Delamaide, Lever and Hune, Kindleberger's *Manias, Panics and Crashes*, Galbraith's *The great Crash*, the Nader report on Citibank, popular works on banking and Wall Street by John Brooks and Anthony Sampson and Penny Lernoux's classic, *The Cry of the People*. She also noticed in her quick perusal, Kaletsky's *The Cost of Default*, and a few other well-worn classics like the trilogies of Taylor Caldwell. It was a symbolic collection she thought that faced directly the age old conflict between conscience and unexamined desire.

Here in the colorful rows that made the Davies' bookcases seem to dance, the world existed as the human mind had received and conceived it, but transformed it into a higher realm of being, where virtue is knowledge, as the Greeks claimed, where even knowledge of the worst must be valued as highly as any other, and where events as particular as any love affair, election or battlefield are super-ceded by their descriptions by the volumes of text, being banks of knowledge, examples carefully constructed of our human kinds of consciousness, of an awareness that is otherwise momentary, fragile and often confused.

Among the shelves where the philosophers tent their troops, there is a war of words, a war of the one supportable kind, a war of thoughtfully chosen positions, perhaps with no problems solved and no blood spilt, shelves where human triumph and its suffering are portrayed by writers who cared at least enough about their lives and the world to take pen to paper, creating histories that don't just happen once but repeatedly in reader after reader, every one of the books as a friend who will always say the same thing, but will always seem to mean in its virtue something new to each reader, forever living within.

These were books of prescient language, language which takes us inside, inside the sentence, inside where meanings meet, modified, reviewed and revised, where no perception, no feeling or thought, need be scanted, demonized or shunted aside.

After the wonderful dinner of a simple salad of yellow and red cherry tomatoes, harvested from the garden, and quinoa with butter and saffron and halibut steaks with a color guard of mussels and roasted peppers and cucumber from the garden and corn bread made from a recipe handed down from Mary's maternal grandmother, they gathered in the den. Mary and Nan followed the boys upstairs to deal with their bedtime ministrations.

Ryan had built the fire in the six foot wide open stone hearth in the tradition of his woodsy know how. The kindling was burning brightly, big flames swelling up with the white skins of the birches curling up, popping and cracking, before the conflagration reached the hardwood pine logs he had layered on top in crisscross layers four feet high. The fire grew as they settled on the couches, the flames reflecting through their stems of rich merlot that sat on the six foot square antique pine table in front of them, turning the rich ruby color of the wine into a flickering display of orange and gold, as fat yellow dancers of flame were being brought to form with just a scent of that sweet smoky "at the lake" aroma.

Mary and Nan joined them as they settled themselves into the couches encircling the gently warming fire like birds getting snug in their big comfortable nest. Together it seemed they were forming a new little island of love, indestructible until someday when somebody might try to destroy it, safe and secure until someday somebody might make it otherwise. They all felt a realization of the concrete necessity of this family of conspirators, its weight, destiny and location in space. Each of them dug themselves into the warmth of the den, as Gabby made a quick circuit of the room greeting everyone looking for a scratch or the unlikely possibility of a proffered morsel of one of the homemade chocolate cookies Mary had made that lay in a large red and blue flowered bowl at the center of the table, before wiggling toward Mary and Nan promptly hopping up on the leather couch to comfort herself between them.

As if on cue all reached out for their crystals of merlot and Walter looked toward Sophie offering her and all a mock toast and asked her if she was ready to begin with her findings and the potential plans of operation. Sophie sipped her wine in a genteel manner thanking the Davies for their warm hospitality and began.

"Please believe me when I say this," she began, her tone sounding almost apologetic, "but I think we all should realize just what we may possibly be confronting.

The United States was born of a revolt against corporations, which had been instruments of abusive power by British Kings. Our new republic was deeply suspicious of both government control and corporate power. Corporations were chartered by the states in order to keep them under close local scrutiny, not by the federal government. The term of corporate charters was limited, and they were automatically dissolved if not renewed or if the corporations engaged in activities not granted by their charters. By 1800 there were only about two hundred corporate charters in the United States.

Sophie paused for a moment to sip her merlot, and looked softly into the forlorn faces of her new friends as the blazed orange-red flames from the hearth brought a primal sense of warmth to the den.

"This incestuous history," she went on, "needs to be emphasized, not only because we may be ignorant of it, but because it continues today.

She looked lovingly at Gabby, who was asleep upside down next to Mary, with her feet draped against the back of the couch and her head hanging off. She appeared not to have heard anything. Then, in a moment that seemed propitious, as if prompted by the importance of the discourse, Gabby woke up, stretched and padded over to end of the couch where Sophie sat cross legged and nonchalantly plopped onto Sophie's lap, as if prompted by her canine cunning to get a closer listen and contentedly drifted off back into her siesta.

The family listened now to Sophie, with the spaniel's head happily reposed in her lap. It was as if Sophie was both the ink and blotter, wholly self-absorbed as she began her staff's research, who could read the world the way a tracker could read a trail looking for something in the flicker of the flames that might console them, a ship that would sail straight into the dreadful storm approaching them.

Sophie paused looking at Gabby softly panting on her lap and stared into the mystery of the fire burning before them, seeming to be in search of some Promethean truth.

They were all quiet for a moment as the fire cracked its whip sending up sparks, as they all passed gazes to one another, watching the fire without seeing, looking only through it, and the threatening consequences of the plans they would be making.

"Civilians think Black Ops are cloaked in secrecy," she explained, "but they have no idea what cloaked in secrecy really means. They have no idea that Gray Ops are much more clandestine, so much deeper in the shadows. The government can be very good at keeping a lid on things when they really want to and this is where Borgen's agency operation becomes very important."

Ryan made a mental note how she had referred to her father by his formal name, rather than as Dad. "As I told Walter and Ryan when we met in New York, my father was with the OSS during the war and I have recently discovered that he was for a short period of time affiliated with the Office of Policy Coordination." The silence was deafening as this news hit them with an awakening and unshackling of a whole amalgam of new fears and insecurities. Mary took a deep breath letting it out slowly, stroking the spaniel now asleep next to her and Nan, as Sophie pressed on.

"After World War II the United States inherited the imperial drug connections of the British and the French. To understand the CIA's involvement in the Southeast Asia drug traffic after the war we must go back to the nineteenth century opium policies of the British.

"It is now generally acknowledged that the CIA, like the intelligence agencies of other great powers, has used drug traffickers as assets in virtually every continent of the globe. This is an example of parapolitics, state covert actions and policies conducted, not by rational debate and responsible decision making, but by indirection, collusion and deceit. The role of deliberate governmental direction in the larger arena of deep politics, and the entire field of political practices and relationships, deliberate or not, are usually repressed rather than acknowledged.

"The global drug connection is not just a lateral connection between CIA operatives and their drug trafficking contacts. It is more significantly a global financial complex of hot money uniting prominent business, financial and government as well as underworld figures." Sophie paused for a moment and looked at the ebbing embers of the fire as if for answers. "This is where—" taking a big sip from the bowl of her wineglass, leaning over to touch Mary's arm as if asking for support "—I think the agency Borgen operates in Washington fits into this evil network. The whole network maintains its own political influence by the systematic supply of illicit finances, favors, and even sex, to politicians around the world, including both parties of the United States Congress. The result is a system of indirect empire, one that, in its search for foreign markets and resources, is quite satisfied to subvert existing governance abroad without imposing any progressive alternative.

Mafias and empires have certain elements in common. Both can be seen as the systematic violent imposition of governance in areas under governance. Both use atrocities to achieve ends, but both tend to be tolerated to the extent that the result of their controlled violence is a diminution of uncontrollable violence. An important difference between mafia and empires is that with the passage of time, mafias tend to become more and more part of civil society whose rules they once broke, while empires tend to become more and more irreconcilably at odds with society they once controlled.

"The deep continuity underlying U.S. expansion since World War II helps make the phenomenon startling, namely the deep events that have occurred. The assassination of John F. Kennedy has many mysteries surrounding it, but at its core was the fact that he was going to eliminate and render useless the entire operations of the CIA. Without understanding the details, we can safely conclude that the operations of the CIA were somehow implicated whether innocently or conspirationally in the background of the JFK assassination. With respect to the CIA's withholding of information from the FBI about Oswald, even a former CIA officer on the case, Jane Roman, later agreed that this withholding in the fall of 1963, indicated some sort of CIA operational interest in Oswald's file. The now recently disclosed fact that immediately in the day that followed the assassination all FBI agents' personal identity papers were sent to Washington to be destroyed, lends further credence to the complicity of both agencies in the matter.

"The pattern would repeat itself five years later with the assassination of Robert Kennedy. In the twenty-four hours between Bobby's shooting and his death, Congress hurriedly passed a statute, again drafted well in advance, that still further augmented the secret powers given to the Secret Service, in the name of protecting presidential candidates. This was not trivial or benign, my staff reports," Sophie stated with a conspirational tone suddenly hanging in the den like a daunting mist. "From this swiftly considered act passed under Johnson," she continued, "flowed some of the worst excesses of the Nixon presidency. In the chaos and violence at the Chicago Democratic Convention of 1968, army intelligence agents, in addition to the Secret Service, were present both inside and outside the convention hall. Some of them equipped the so called Legion of Justice thugs whom the Chicago Red Square turned loose on local anti-war groups. The presence of army intelligence agents at the convention was authorized by the statute passed while Booby Kennedy lay dying.

"Of these deep events some, notably the JFK assassination, stand out as having had structural impact on American political society. America's major wars of the last half century have all been preceded by deep events that have cumulatively contributed to America's current war based economy. Underlying every one of the deep events, such as the U-2 incident, can be seen as a contest between the trader multi-lateralist and warrior unilateralist approaches to the maintenance of U.S. global dominance. For decades the warrior faction was clearly a minority, but also an activist and well-funded minority, in marked contrast to the relatively passive and disorganized trader majority. Hence the war machine with its dominant mindset, thanks to ample funding from the military-industrial complex and also to a series of deep events, was able time after time, to prevail.

"The United States continuously intervenes, and our staff has determined, on the side of the drug traffickers. Partly this has been from a real-politic; the recognition of the local power realities represented by the drug traffic. Partly it has been from the need to escape domestic political restraints. The traffickers have supplied the additional financial resources needed because of U.S. budgetary limitations, and they have also provided assets not bound as the U.S. is by the rules of war. These facts have led to enduring intelligent networks involving both oil and drugs or more specifically both petrodollars and narco-dollars.

These networks particularly in the Middle East have become so important that they affect not just the conduct of U.S. foreign policy, but the health and behavior of the U.S. government, U.S. banks and corporations, and indeed the whole of U.S. society. The London Independent reported recently that drug trafficking constitutes the third largest global commodity in terms of cash after oil and the arms trade.

"The aim of all U.S. anti-drug campaigns abroad has never been the hopeless ideal of eradication. The aim of all such campaigns has been to alter market share; to target specific enemies." Sophie paused for a moment looking kindly upon the Davies family, gently patting Gabby's head as the golden flickers of flame began to ebb. "And thus ensure," she went on, a hint of weariness in her tone, "that the drug traffic remains under the control of those traffickers who are allies of the State apparatus and or the CIA."

"Our deed and the substantial assets we will control and the cash that it will throw off seems to fit the mold you have described, Sophie," Walt said in summation with an edge of dread to his tone.

"That is my fear," Sophie replied with a sense of agitated release, "and the forty to fifty billion at minimum that you project the mine at least initially will be able to generate, would be considered 'wrath of God' money to the agency Borgen runs and nexus of operations that surround it. In my opinion," Sophie continued after an uneasy pause, "the growth of militarism, official secrecy, and a belief that the United States is no longer bound, as the Declaration of Independence so famously puts it, by a 'decent respect for the opinions of mankind', is probably irreversible.

A revolution would be required to bring the Pentagon back under democratic control, or to abolish the Central Intelligence Agency, or even to contemplate enforcing article one, section nine, clause seven of the Constitution that states that 'no money shall be drawn from the Treasury, but in Consequence of Appropriations made by Law, and a regular

Statement and Account of the Receipts and Expenditures of all public money shall be published from time to time.'"

They all gazed now at the dying red hot embers of the fire, Sophie's thorough dissertation completed, the house fell silent except for the faint hum of the furnace from the basement, barely discernible through the floorboards, and the frightful whirring of the un-oiled gears of dread and doubt that spun in all their heads.

Chapter 28

Sophie thought she might be the first one up that Saturday morning but as she walked into the kitchen Nan was already there squeezing fresh orange juice. "Good morning, Sophie," Nan nearly whispered, hoping to keep the rest of the sleeping clan undisturbed. "How do French crepes sound?"

"Yummy, the best in a long time, Nan," Sophie said, feigning a mock cover up, pretending to bring the imaginary coverlet up to her neck. Nan poured her a glass of the orange juice, while Gabby was slurping out of the toilet in the hall bathroom next to the mud room. "Gabby no," Nan called out softly. There were no more slurping sounds, but Nan could picture her, head raised over the toilet bowl, ear cocked waiting to see if she would follow her admonishment. Sophie sat down at the wet bar as the faint sound of the spaniel's next slurp of the tongue fully floated down the hall and into the kitchen.

Then came a series of barks outside the door of the mud room. It was Gabby's running mate Colonel Popcorn, a Dalmatian from the house two doors down. Nan made her way to the door and happily let Gabby out. This was the two dogs' daily ritual. For a half-hour they would nose about the neighborhood, sniffing, scenting and smelling out any four-legged predators that may have entered their protective domain since nightfall.

Then, true to the format of her daily detective duty, Gabby would faithfully return, by nosing open the screen door, and happily indulge herself once again in her rituals of eating, sleeping in luxurious comfort, and drinking out of the toilet.

Sophie loved it!

Nan was using her secret crepe recipe, one of the family's absolute favorites and a genuine grade A amber maple syrup from Vermont. Nan poured the two of them coffee, bringing out cream and sugar. Both drank their coffee with a tablespoon of cream, and Nan poured them each another glass of OJ while she finished cooking.

Delicious French Crepes rolled up on both plates, Sophie poured a nice little pool of syrup and watched it flow over the golden-brown cliffs in a waterfall of thick amber. She sliced off a corner of the top piece and dipped it, soaked it in the syrup, and tasted it.

"Mmmm the best ever, Nan," Sophie said, giving her a big smile, her mouth in a taste bud orgy of heavenly delight. Sophie tore off a tiny piece of another corner of the bread and, looking at Nan for permission, got a non-verbal nod of "why not" and handed the desired morsel to the dutifully begging dog sitting at her slippered feet, looking for any spillage, while applying her best panhandling skills on the new houseguest. Each sip of coffee Sophie took seemed to raise a veil of warmth across her cheeks and a welling in her eyes.

The two girls talked, girls have to talk, and they did, like they were catching up upon lives they had lived separately but seeming to have much in common. Only a year separated them, and they talked like school girls who hadn't seen each other since high school graduation. Now they were looking back through their collective yearbooks sharing experiences, successes, heartbreaks and life's cruel unfairness and injustices. They sat now in the sunroom looking out at the ripening colors of fall's end and the tomato plants in their last stage of maturity and sipped their coffees and talked on, as Mary made Crepes for the rest of the family now astir, while Jackson Browne versed music softly through the Bose speakers in the family room of Lives in the Balance.

Walking the neighborhood that evening before dinner after spending a lazy rainy day with Davies family, the wet avenue beyond was lit by the orange phosphorous of the street lights, the raindrops themselves flashing black and silver in the air darkening the sidewalk and the gray street, raising the smoky odor of wet asphalt.

Sophie could feel the coming of sickness in her soul, for that greater meaning of home that she understood so easily and purely when she was a child in her mother's house. It stood as a metaphor for all possible feelings of security and of what is predictable, gentle and valuable in life.

As she walked along she could feel the limp in her life, the headache in her heart, the emptiness she was full of, desperately hoping that once this race was over she would not walk through the front door of her future like the brushman with some feckless patter and a chintzy plastic prize.

There had been no one, nothing around her for such a long time, she thought with all the activity in her life, just simply the white noise of a life she tried to make go by in the least painful manner she knew. Another bout of sadness passed briefly over her face, as the tears coursed unbidden down her cheeks.

It was like a shadow of a small cloud moving over the earth and she willed it to be quickly whisked away. She walked around the block of the Davies' home along Lake Avenue as darkness fell, as one imagined oasis after another emanated the yellow light of family life and warm love, a woman's head at the kitchen window, her arms moving in slow and steady motions as she made dinner, children passing to and fro doing homework, turning down the stereo on easy parental command, and men dozing in their big comfortably cushioned chairs.

These were houses, Sophie mused, where housewives kissed their husbands tenderly in the morning and passionately at nightfall. In every house there was love, graciousness and high hopes. The schools were good and the roads were smooth. These were homes of friends all lighted and smelling of fragrant wood smoke like temples in a sacred grove, dedicated to monogamy, feckless children and domestic bliss.

So much like a dream she pined internally. Families gather safe and whole at the end of another day, and darkness seeps into the sky second by second until the shadows no longer fall but rise from the ground and fill the air completely. Humans withdraw to their homes and surrender the night to the creatures that own it: the owls, the raccoons, the crickets. A world that hasn't changed for hundreds of thousands of years then wakes up, and carries on as if the daylight and the human race and the changes to the landscape had been an illusion. And no one walks the streets.

Suddenly a light feathery snow was falling and Sophie could see the light puffy flakes reflected in the street lights off the wet sidewalks below. It was the beginning of a big storm that was moving in from the west. In a blizzard like a nor'easter she remembered, a gale, a sudden line squall, a tropical storm, or a summer thunder shower along the eastern shores of Maryland in her youth, there was always an excitement that came over her, like no other thing. It was like the excitement of battle, she thought now, except that with the whiteness of the snow it seemed clean.

She could hear the faint sounds of the wind that was beginning its surges. In a snowstorm the wind could blow with such ferocity that it was a force full of driving whiteness, a white cleanliness where it seemed there were no enemies to be reasoned, and when the storm ended and the wind had ceased, there came a stillness and all things seemed changed, for the better. It was her childhood climatic dream, as she stood in the driveway of the Davies' home looking west up into the stormy skies transfixed by the oncoming rough weather.

As Sophie entered the Davies' home through the mudroom, she noticed another houseguest had arrived, that being Dr. Jim from Everest. Dr. Jim Theno, grandson of Henry Theno the co-conspirator, as Mary had described it, along with her father of the creative mining lease hold operation.

Mary and Nan were in the kitchen getting dinner ready, and Mary beamed a radiant smile at Sophie as she introduced Jim, while Ryan and Walter were making cocktails at the wet bar. She looked at him with her frank green eyes. There was something in them, Jim noticed, that seemed to make her ten years older than the thirty-five or so he guessed her to be, a trace of ennui, of a seen-it-all sadness.

"It's so nice to meet you," he said, "I understand you and the family are going to put a plan together to resolve this old Chisholm secret."

"I think we're close to finalizing a plan," Sophie said, flashing a confident smile. "It may be a tremendous risk for us to take, but as they say, we think the flame is worth the candle." A rueful smile creasing her face.

"We'll talk about it in great detail tonight, Jim," Walter added as they all walked their drinks into the den.

They all sat around the roaring fire enjoying cocktails and boiled artichokes with Nan's yummy dip, talking idly about northern Minnesota and the beauty of the boundary waters where Jim resided, as Mary's homemade pasties baked in the oven. There seemed to be a common bond again building with the arrival of their new friend to the deep secrets of the family's past doings. Sophie was absorbing to Jim, neat and stylish without modish little tricks to her sheathing, she wore her clothes, the clothes didn't wear her. He quickly realized in listening to her speak, that she seemed to wear her clothes the way she wore her independence, with an ease that concealed long and careful hours and years of self-study. Her eyes were cool and her voice calm, a professional award winning writer, she was here to help the Davies family complete a mission that his own ancestors had a part in creating. He found her dispassionate objectivity professionally commendable and personally intellectually compatible.

He sat diagonally from her on one of the colorful stuffed chairs sipping his vodka tonic and dipping the artichoke leaves, hoping his shaky nervousness wasn't detected. She was really a terrific looking lady, just right in every detail that counted, he thought. Her beautiful blonde hair was combed back away from her face in a pageboy, he guessed, in a fruitless attempt to underplay her beauty. Her features were sharp and composed and cool, her high cheekbones giving an effect of eastern aristocracy, and it occurred to the doctor that smiling might be something of an effort for her, a grin of impossibility. Her most compelling feature, which fed her beauty like the spring rains made the flowers bloom, was the frankness of her gaze. She looked at him when she spoke with an objectivity that somehow drew him to her, that didn't make him feel like an insect on a pin or something the dog had done on the carpet. She seemed as organized as her clothes which were plain and perfect and gave nothing away of her figure he noticed. She was neither dry nor prim, just so very interesting.

For her part, Sophie seemed to like Jim, knowing him initially for only those few hours that night. She had once been seriously pursued by a Richmond banker of an obstreperously good family, but his confederate conceit had worn wearisome, whereas she found Theno's English bred restraint and intellect he seemed to convey invigorating. She looked up at him as he talked of his life, her muse asking if this could be the man her romantic imagination had so many times prefigured, a fresh sharp face that seemed to be full of quiet humor and intelligence? He was tall and blonde and handsome with piercing eyes and a down turned nose spry and agile, a man seasoned in humanity, a character that was wise, good, honest and gentle, the very Parfit, the gentle Christian Knight, Donatello's St. George, brought to life who would take up her cause, and do battle with the dragons and nightmares that haunted her.

Sooner than he, she recognized how much they shared a view of things. Neither of them was on a normal timeline or path in life. They were about the same age, thirty-five and thirty-eight, and it seemed to Sophie that the peculiar instruments in life might somehow synchronize their lives by way of an old magnetism she was disinclined to question. Something in her was newly drawn to the burden of doubt he seemed to carry, like original sin. Something in him was beseeching her for absolution, or was it damnation? Or was it just an asking to be held in a kind of wild abeyance, amidst the dangerous breezes of the coming war against her father?

Like the rest of the Davies extended family, he too, disliked the way things were, the self-concerned, shortsighted, morally illiterate generation that had brought the world to its clustered, polluted angry state. They responded differently, of course, the years separating them, being the tag ends of the depression and the Vietnam War that had legitimized social insurrection and progressive writing and causes for Sophie and her contemporaries, while Jim took his unhappiness out in a secluded tireless work ethic of ministering to the health needs and illnesses incurred by the hard working proletariat souls of the Iron Range, and the readings of his vast library at his home on the shore of Fall Lake, next to the waters and chain of lakes of the BWCA.

Chapter 29

She fixed her stare on them, hoping her firm could bring the mining operation to the financial fruition that would be the key to her being welcomed into the bastions of the investment world she wished to storm. Big or small, these types of M&A outfits couldn't have sold their full allotment of tickets to the crucifixion. It was nonetheless part of the investment circuit rota that was mandatory to get the maximum financial kick. Their objective was to overwhelm the prospect's reticence with personnel, so by sheer weight of numbers of people, the matter at hand was complex enough to justify the fees being charged and to crowd out with the clouds of pro-forma figures in impressive logo typed folders bound in maroon lexan whatever reservations the client might have about what he was being "advised" to do.

The instant he saw her Ryan made her out for one of the hundreds of annually cloned and cookie-cut outs on Storrow Drive at the Harvard Business School. She came not merely from another generation but virtually another civilization, the new sexless yuppie feminism. She was anti-men in a sort of frozen neutered way, not at all like the sixties women's lib survivors who had handled their femininity like a slave rebellion. She was accompanied by two other MBAs from M&A, thinking they were the toughest, most worldly article ever, carrying the required artifacts of their vocation, part of the new breed on Wall Street that was pugnacious with success, part of the calculus of a buy sell mentality leached of human feeling. Though Ryan had a better sense of gutter brains, what Thackeray had called the "dismal precocity of poverty," they both could see how they all thought themselves so prodigiously self-important, that both Ryan and William knew they would be able to guide then easily with the reins of their own conceit.

Both knew what the fixed income boys represented here were thinking, what with all the money around they could put a hundred million in equity in the bond portfolio and then another one billion could be borrowed and with leverage they could make a bundle on the carry, the difference between what they borrow for in the market and what they charge the client for carrying his position. The commission tickets would be okay, Ryan knew chuckling to himself, but the real dough would be in the spreads. Ryan could see them mentally rubbing their hands over the prospect of hundreds of thousands, even millions, and even more in commissions and trading profits and financing spreads. They were dreaming of where this thing would float, tempting and succulent until it was taken like a trout finally succumbing to the sheer force of appetite.

Ryan and Will could already see this company's M&A dorsal fin breaking the water as they readied themselves to make their presentations, at Will's office downtown of McMillan and Associates. The cart first, was always the strategy of operation that hoped to then get the client to buy the expensive team of horses to pull it.

With Bud's pre-feasibility study nearly completed on the Davies' deeded mine rights, they had determined the property size to be one hundred and twenty-five kilometers in depth and width and contiguous properties and likely provable and probable reserves as quietly determined by rock chip sample anomalies that Henry Theno had acquired via his own personal exploration drilling in 1935, was 1.115,000 ounces, with resources measured and indicated and inferred of 1,875,000 and 127,000 ounces respectively, with average annual production to be estimated at 110,00 to 130,000. The granite-hosted disseminated deposit, located at longitude 47.926N and latitude -91.80W in St. Louis county Minnesota was estimated to contain a compliant reserve of one point three million ounces of gold, three point seven million of nickel, seven point four million of copper with varied traces tungsten, coltan and hard rock lithium out of a measured and Indicated Mineral Resource of twelve point nine million ounces of mineable precious ores, enough to make any potential bank providing capital drool uncontrollably as they would over a massive Saharan Oil field discovery.

As the presentation began both Ryan and Will realized without even mentioning it to each other that they didn't want her type and her sort of firm involved with the public private partnership they were to put together. They knew they needed to find just one staunch ally, one cow with whom not to bell the rest of the institutional flock, but to provide the lead financing to the private and public partners and community investors. There would be none of the requisite attenuations and edginess of a multitude of proxy fights. They would not fill the board of directors of the mining enterprise with any of William's clients or invisible stars, using the combined birthrights of he and Winnie's as some sort of stepping stone to solidify business relationships or to "cure" himself socially in a way that fine tobacco was cured in bonded warehouses. They were not in search of some new found respectability by acquired association. They had no desired prospect of joining some exclusive club or gaining some better corporate company. There would be no promotion here looking for top notch Wall Street names to crutch a shaky offering of speculative securities over the barricades of investment dubiety. This would be a pact of mutual advantage and advantage for all alike.

It needed to be a fairly priced offering with no huge spreads built in for the debt vultures that sat before them, with demand offerings going to a tight circle of friends and the public and communities that surrounded the old mining town, as Mary had demanded, being a potent source for wealth redistribution, the stones of the old town needing new sunlight and a fresh heart. With a portion of Will and Winnie's money involved, they were assured a fiscally virtuous prime participant. There would be no paper empires here which stood ready to exchange their shares for tens of thousands of vestigial non-liquid partnership assets.

Will had offered, after he and Winnie had been brought into the confidence of the Chisholm family secret, to contact a longtime friend of his who was a solid technician, first rate at things like present value and regression analysis and least squares depreciation, all the arithmetical acrobatics that so mightily impress the minds of corporate treasurers. Will knew he and his friend's staff were the good technicians needed to take care of the details while the deals were cut with the men at the top to whom the details of a bond spread were incidentals in the grand scheme of things.

Old money was William's firm natural bailiwick keeping to the ancestral standards of the past as it had always been when established by his father. This was serious money that spoke in deep tones which brooked no superficiality. This was money, that no matter how far-fetched or fantastically alluring was the rumor, for the taking, it instinctively sent the hand to the hip to keep confident the wallet was still there. This was a firm where discretion was always the rule of the day. He did not and would not operate as a social point man acting as an intermediary between new money and old clubs. He had long since made his peace with his own opportunism and the moral flexibility, as he called it, that was its correlative. His words on the market, just as his father's, had taken a theological coloration of investment banking and brokerage, were divine missions robed with moral responsibility. His firm stood as a pillar of judicious and analytical calm. It was illustrated by the three quiet hued photographs that graced the walls of his office, his grandfather Henry, his father William and himself.

William's investment advisory used the symbol of the philosopher Diogenes as its modest logo. It was Diogenes who had searched the ancient world for an honest man who would help to protect the impression that Wall Street was intellectually beneath him. There would always be a niche for a firm like Will's and Ryan was pleased to be joining his advisory as a relationship manager. The firm incarnated the old enduring values of investment stewardship. They would operate the IPO of the mining business in the manner that he operated his investment firm, where he ran trusts and had friends that ran trusts for people who still trusted, who did old money business on the stock exchange and who saw about the placid but enduring work of small foundations. A firm's competence was ratified by the company it kept and Will's family had enjoyed the heritage of being the very model of probity.

William was the product of his father's learned study and the ancestral standards of the past that held fast to the prudent man rule and the honest and enduring stewardship of investor assets. His father had educated him to understand that at the root of the problem was the banks. His father was convinced the more he read back in the fifties and sixties that the nation's economic birthright was being leveraged away. Without the complicity of the banks, Wall Street's mischief would be impossible. They were the necromancers charged with measuring out the magic portion of credit. They were supposed to be the last redoubt of economic integrity. Will's father had explained to him that the first truly giant step toward the eventual destabilization of the banking system was the invention in 1962 of the negotiable certificate of deposit. There were a certain group of impatient rogue bankers who became quite bored with the "liability side" of banking, hustling for deposits, kissing the asses of low ranking assistant corporate treasurers, performing a multitude of tasks designed to translate customer goodwill into balances, who sought at the time to do some ingenious innovating on the funding side.

As it happened, his father had explained to him, the negotiable certificate of deposit was an idea whose time had come, like the airplane, the bold new instrument seemed to have been invented simultaneously, by Wriston at Citibank, Bank America and others. The negotiable CD was an instant success on every count, as it freed banks from the traditional constraints on size and lending practice.

When it came to lending funds, a bank simply didn't apply the same microscopic scrutiny and rigid credit standards to putting out what it had "bought" in the open as it did to cash entrusted to it by depositors. Wall Street was always looking for new products to peddle and trade and it loved the idea of marketing a freely tradable ninety-day promissory note of First Bank of Minneapolis or First bank of Chicago. A new type of security meant new markets to be opened up and new purses to reach into. Within six months, a half dozen Wall Street houses were making active liquid markets on certificates of deposit of the dozen largest U.S. banks. Within a year the number of acceptable names had swollen to the hundred largest banks. Once again, Will's father had explained, Say's law had been proven, that supply creates its own demand.

As his father had explained it to him, on the surface the negotiable CD seemed a useful even salutary tool for promoting economic growth by enlarging the economic resources of the banking system. It permitted the biggest and supposedly best banking names to go into the open market and offer investors a new and desirable short term investment which, even if it was subject to stringent interest ceilings, offered the incomparable attraction of decent liquidity. That was the way it seemed to the maddening crowd, but to Will's father the negotiable certificate of deposit was the first step in a financial chain reaction. The faster the market grew, he sensed, the more dependent the banks would become on this form of financing to meet the demand for credit. Already in the early sixties bank analysts and strategists were using words like "permanentize" in the role of CDs in bank financing. The logic was, his father had explained, if a short term obligation could be successfully renewed time after time, rolled over and over continuously, as certain and rhythmic as the waves of the sea, should it not be looked upon as truly long term and as a legitimate source for funding longer term loans? If ever there was a certain recipe for disaster, it was to borrow short and lend long.

Unlike most other nations, America was instinctively habituated to borrowing, not being parsimonious, they didn't keep their stashes tucked away in their mattresses, they were used to getting what they wanted, and right away. The costs of credit were therefore in Will's father's lights a more significant factor than the general level of prices in the United States than elsewhere. These costs were restrained by an elaborate fabric of interest rate ceilings. The negotiable CD represented the first tiny tear in this fabric. CDs competed in the financial markets with other types of "deposit" security from treasury bills to savings and loan certificates. The more important CDs became to the bank as sources of loan capital, the more vulnerable the banks became too short term interest rates. If the rates should move above the levels the bank could legally pay on their CDs, the banks would be squeezed and something would have to give to avoid a crisis, which could only be the New Deal ceilings on interest rates and another nail would be driven into the coffin planked with those once energetic Charleston induced memories of 1929, and over time those marble bastions of financial solidity could be transformed into paper palaces, houses of cards. Will's father knew back then that in the circular world of high finance, the banks sold their paper in the primary market, to corporations awash in surplus cash, and frequently reloaned the proceeds to the Wall Street houses that made up the secondary market and financed their inventories of their banks CDs with call loans.

The depression, his father had explained, had driven businessmen underground as far as personal publicity was concerned, but by 1964 with the Dow in full conflagration and the man in the street throbbing with stock market buy fever, visibility was beginning to be back in vogue. Banking was glamorous now and was becoming a growth industry, the biggest banks now "managing" their industry to obtain a sustainable annual growth rate of fifteen percent of the bank's earnings per share. Where one led all must follow, or lose "market share," words never before uttered in connection with the staid business of banking. The big banking industries now proclaimed total commitment to "total return" to be a tree growing in the sky with fruit for everyone. The heads of the big New York banks now chided their colleagues in the investment institutions for past caution of what they called their nitpicking insistence on investment balance between stocks and bonds, between income and appreciation, an insistence they implored was costing them money. America was on the verge of a decade of exploding growth, and as Will's father had explained, it was time to get on board, to go into the equity market with both hands and two spades. A new institutional stock buying frenzy would be launched that would enrich

Wall Street to the end of time, and it would be license for the Street to wholesale stocks at retail prices.

Until the early 1960s, the equity ownership of the U.S. economy had been vested in a large, discreet and, above all, a patient group of individuals; however by 1965 it seemed that all that was changing according to Will's father. The post war boom had been for the most part made up of industrial growth in steel, automobiles, petroleum and chemicals and aircraft. The chosen instrument of the U.S. economy had been the effectively structured unionized public corporation. Employee and executive benefit and pension plans had been created that began to be flooded with funds clamoring for investment. These were managed for the most part by conservative men in bank trust departments, men whose sense of risk was depicted in the quiet dark suits and sturdy laced brogans that they wore. Now however stock brokers and their institutional clients were fomenting new approaches to large scale investing, launching the great decade long institutionalization of the stock markets. It was as Will's father had predicted, a bull rush stampede, a feeding frenzy fattened by corporate contributions to their benefit plans and by a massive convergence of savings from around the world, where the appetite of the institutions seemed to be insatiable. Ironically the management of corporate America hastened to facilitate a process which, over the course of time, only put itself at risk. Institutional equity analysts came to be courted, wined and dined, fed morsels of confidential information along with Chateaubriand. The institutional share of daily trading activity grew from roughly twenty percent to over fifty percent by 1970, and in time it would reach eighty percent.

Increasing percentages of major corporations came to be owned by fewer and fewer, but by larger, investment institutions. Eventually William's father reckoned this sort of concentration could convert what was now a market in shares into an active market in companies. As the activity reached a faster pace, the investment community's image of itself and its work effort morphed. Dark suits were chucked in favor of gaudy finery and body jewelry. Personality cults formed around the more dashing money managers, calling themselves gun slingers, using tough guy, male testosterone driven vocabulary. A highly profitable apparatus of publicity sprouted directed by the new found public relations gurus, and glossy fan magazines appeared. No one seemed to grasp the implications of what was happening, Will's father had explained to him as he was studying finance at

Stanford in the late sixties. Old honored bastions of interest were being displaced. The passivity of the individual investor had been a priceless asset for corporate America. The patience of the individual had underwritten the cost of research and development and experimentation. It had provided industry the time it often took to do its job properly and management the freedom to indulge itself.

The wholesale transformation of equity ownership, Will's father felt, would inevitably lead to a frenetic competition of Wall Street for accounts, which would in turn create a manic demand on short term investment performance as a marketing effort. Accounts meant management fees, and money managers' first loyalties were to their own compensation, disguised by platitudinous prattle of acting in the best interests of their fiduciaries. The institutionalization of the ownership of corporate America essentially restored Wall Street to the ascendant, the herd-like crush of such intense concentrated buying power into equities produced a raging market that overpowered and overwhelmed other forms of business. Finance and speculation far advanced all other forms of commercial activity in the awareness of the public. The nightly news reports began to imply that the true measure of the nation's economic health was the Dow Jones stock average, but by 1967, the power brokers and investment iterators had their gaze fixed overseas where new frontiers beckoned their craven machinations.

Their creation was Eurodollars and Asiadollars, his father had explained to him, dollar balances maintained beyond the borders of the United States and thus beyond the control and reserve requirements imposed by the Treasury and the Federal Reserve Board. Dollars belonging to foreigners, spent in Italy by tourists, in Germany for machine tools, in Saudi Arabia for petroleum, dollars belonging to expatriate Americans, to individuals or multinational corporations, left for overseas as a matter of convenience, or out of fear of U.S. taxes, or to take advantage of high overseas interest rates. The reasons for keeping dollar deposits overseas varied from depositor to depositor, but there was no shortage of motives, and thus there was a vast quantity of such currency in circulation or in banks, hundreds of millions perhaps billions. Without the Fed to control the process by the imposition of reserve requirements, there was no upper end to the number of Eurodollars that could be "printed" overseas. A dollar held by a New York bank customer in Berlin could be loaned on the bank wire to a borrower who placed it on deposit with the Dresden Bank in Bremen, each bank now reflecting that dollar in its deposit accounts in a manner that one had transmuted itself into two.

The possibilities, Will's father had explained to him, for further multiplication and subdivision would be inexhaustible to the business of finance itself. All that was needed now, his father had so wisely explained, was if something could be devised to precipitate an immediate artificial explosion in the value of world trade, in the price of a particular world commodity, could potentially bring about a massive hyper-expansion of the worldwide supply of dollars, which the Federal Reserve would be helpless to limit or control.

By 1970, his father had instructed, as he continued to manage his firm's clients' money in the manner of the enduring value investor tradition of Ben Graham, the counting house had been replaced by the progeny of ENIAC that had matured into a formidable brood of the latest generation of computers that could already produce and process data and transactions at a faster clip than human judgment, which the new machines did not supply, replaced by the impersonal, somehow unreal computer screen. Banks and corporations were now able to move their free cash balances in Pavlovian style, reacting instinctively to the potential of earning a fraction of a farthing more in Taiwan than in Switzerland, making a game out of the entire system. What possible difference, Will remembered his father asking him pointedly, could it be to make a billion dollar corporation to earn an extra .0003 basis points on thirty million in overnight reserves? What possible difference could ninety dollars make to such a corporation? But his father knew that was no longer the matter, it was the game itself that counted. The computer had made it seem unreal, and the generations of machines to come would only be quicker and of greater size, judgment and reality would be left further in the void, by the speed of the process and by manic thrill of it all.

Will's father had told him that in 1955, the year his grandfather had died and he took the helm of the family's investment firm, two insurance companies, two mutual funds, and a handful of bank managed trust funds had between them owned perhaps eighty thousand shares of the bank in New York that they worked with, less than four percent of the total shares outstanding. The CEO of the bank at that time was able to control the bank's two hundred thousand shares in trusts he dominated, thanks in part to the complaisance of individual stockholders content with regular increases in the quarterly dividends. In 1970, as his father had pointed out to him, their correspondent bank in New York was governed at the sufferance of a coterie of institutions, most of them unlike individuals, tax exempt and thus with very little compulsion to invest for the long term, the lot of them managed by rapid fire trigger types who rather enjoyed blowing in and out of big stock positions while watching the executives in their suites trembling in the wind.

By now all the other big to mid-size banks had followed the megabanks of New York's lead in using the Eurodollar market to mint loanable dollars at will, with no surprise to the investment creators, whose privately expressed dictum was, "put in enough of a commission for the goat and you'd be surprised how easy it is to sell the goat's milk as cream". All this done without so much as a wit heard from the Federal Reserve. By 1970 the Euro-market continued to grow exponentially and no one really knew how many dollars were in the pool and, as long as there seemed to be a supply sufficient to meet any demand, nobody really seemed to care, at least in the private sector.

In the United States as well, the Fed's iron grip seemed to be relaxing, his father had explained. With the invention of the one bank holding company, an innovation that all the major banks seemed to jump to at the same time, by a matter of days, banks were allowed to circumvent the Fed as they pleased when it came to raising money. With the complicity of Wall Street, the one bank holding companies, Citicorp, Chase and Morgan and others could now buy funds on the open market at rates that banks proper were forbidden by law to offer. The holding company format permitted them to operate without license and equanimity wherever dollar flows were to be located. The big banks were as comfortable in Bangkok as they were in the Bronx. It was now easier to pull a billion out of Bogota than in Boston. Other barriers were crumbling as well, the old honored connections of habit and mutual interest that tied depositors to their local banks suddenly seemed out of date, now that the banks were openly bidding for the funds and the increasing categories of deposits were free to track down the highest found rate. The Penn Central commercial paper crisis in the summer of 1970 had obligated the Fed to remove the ceilings on large denomination certificates of deposit, thus slyly getting another one of the financial innovators competitive camels to get its nose under the tent. Untrammeled now, his father had opined all those years ago, by government interference of any kind, "the Federal jawbone is as lethal to the aspirations of free enterprise as that with which Cain slew Abel." The forces of free finance, it seemed, had arranged themselves in response to certain stimuli as obedient as molecules proving a theorem.

Shortly thereafter, as Will's father had forecast, the OPEC crisis occurred in 1973, and the traumatic boost in the price of oil would have to be funded at the printing press, where the Federal Reserve's foot now weighed heavily on the money pedal and could grow only heavier still. This would consolidate the economic torrents and rushes that Vietnam had created into an almighty torrent of inflation. America would begin to export inflation in its money the way other countries haplessly exported fruit pests in their cases of bananas.

To the wealthy, inflation was a serious hazard, but to the poor it was lethal. Some sort of massive credit infusion would be required to get the non-industrialized world through this oil shock. No debtor ever loved his creditors, and few relationships ever survived a loan. Properly orchestrated, his father realized, energy enforced borrowing could be construed as a sort of reparations exacted from the haves upon the have-nots, a penalty inflicted upon them simply for being poor. But most of all, his father had pointed out, the coin had two sides. Commodity bubbles from tulips to salad oil, occurred when people were induced to believe that commodity prices no longer followed the law of supply and demand, when people, mostly traders on Wall Street, no longer thought of commodities as commodities. This was the delusion that lured fools, the clients of the traders into the game, pushed up prices and pushed up production costs in a manic bubbling for a piece of the action. When oil prices rose so would all energy costs, and so in time would the price of everything.

The initial shock of 1973, the second round of price increases and the embargo of a year later and the final upheaval in the wake of the 1979 Iranian revolution, produced gross suffering and misery around the world and gross inconvenience to the American consumer. From the beginning, proposals rang through Capitol Hill and Whitehall and Tokyo that some international body, possibly an adjunct of the World Bank, should assume responsibility for coordinating and calming over the terrifying financial disruptions that OPEC had brought about.

Petrodollar recycling then came into vogue at the big New York Banks.

It sounded so rational yet it fronted for a litany of outright folly committed in the name of profit. The private financial sector, revved up like zealots at the prospect of handling the torrential cash flows OPEC was generating, marshaled beneath the gonfalon of the major banks, took up the cry with one resolute voice and made it resound in every corner of the earth in which deals were made. Countries don't go broke, the bank CEO's reassured the world, as the oil billions poured in one door and were sent out another for rich fees, to Mexico, Ghana and Brazil.

The sheer velocity of financial activity and wealth creation that took place in OPEC's wake had no precedent in history. This size of everything got so much larger, his father had explained, with old frames of financial reference quickly becoming obsolete. The Eurodollar market swelled from $200 billion to nearly $3 trillion by 1980. The huge increase in volume produced a large bank led proliferation of new instruments and "financial products," reshaping and redressing the clothes of lending and borrowing packaged to take full advantage of a now totally institutionalized marketplace.

First came listed options, then options on options, then futures on options on options, along with money market funds that permitted the small depositors to move their money around as easily as an oil company treasurer. New occasions teach new duties, Will remembered his father saying, quoting the poet, and these new financial products spawned new forms of parasites and purveyors, as seen in the emergence of deposit brokers, risk arbitrageurs and discount brokerages. Along with all this nominally creative activity came widespread ethical and intellectual deterioration within the financial sector as a whole.

The face of Wall Street had seemed to change overnight, with two-thirds of names, that made up the under writing syndicates of the sixties and early seventies, no longer existing, either sunk without a trace in bankruptcy or swallowed up by the mass of the investment conglomerates that were emerging. Inflation induced disasters and near disasters became frequent, foreign exchange and securities scandals regularly convulsed the markets. The terms scandal, crisis, collapse and default, once apocalyptic words, were now regularly found in the financial pages and discussed as mere abstractions in private Wall Street dining rooms. In the minds of the CEOs mega-banks there were two kinds of inflation, demand pulled and greed driven, two fundamentally distinct reasons why the price of an economic unit, whether a BTU, an hour of labor, or a tin of coffee, would rise without a commensurate increase in its intrinsic value. The OPEC fiat pricing had been greed driven in total, and now that the industrial economies except Japan were stagnant, and the growth of the undeveloped world had been stopped cold by crushing indebtedness, the game was morphing into a new deflationary phase, as Wall Street began to create its newest fashion in the sadist world it lived in using the tax deductibility of debt and the power of leverage called the "leveraged buyout".

You could see it was the latest new trend, Will's father had warned him, because none of the guys who had brought it about were anyone you had heard of five years' prior. It was interesting how, Will remembered his father saying, new credit at the ready, made geniuses out of otherwise just normal everyday grunts, as if a new bank line adds fifty points to a banker's IQ. The corporate CEOs were now talking about doing billion dollar buy outs of their public stockholders, borrowing five hundred million from their mega-bank partners while getting a bunch of pension funds that would put up the rest. The actual equity investment would amount to perhaps $25 million if that, the banks not giving a bovine fundament about a capitalization that's five percent equity and ninety-five percent debt, using unaudited statements, showing secret asset appraisals, cash flow figures and hidden depreciation reserves, all figures that the public shareholders don't get to see, in addition to a game plan that states that in one year he is certain they can sell off enough assets to off five hundred million dollars of debt, claiming the business they would have left to be worth the original five hundred million, which works out to a nifty fifty to one return on cash equity. Nobody would be able to resist this kind of deal although its logic was so twisted, Wills father had predicted, what with a ten percent or more "carried equity" for the lead bank doing the deal. Due to Glass-Steagall, however, the supposed "Chinese Wall", between banking and investment, the "carried equity", would be termed an "equity equivalent contingent participation".

The LBO guys were now recycling the stockholders' assets into their own bank accounts, now even banking a few oil barons who couldn't find the black gold in their own crankcases, giving them a line of credit to buy oil stocks with, that, between them and their money managers who would sell their own mothers below the bid price if it made their quarterly performance shine bright, would stand the oil industry on its head when they were finished with their machinations. When the Saudis took a look at some of these "restructured" balance sheets, his father had warned, they'll need about five seconds to figure out that bringing oil back down to twenty bucks a barrel would affect a thirty to one debt to equity ratio at Arco.

Debt had become a narcotic, just as Will's father had predicted, as religion was the opiate of the masses, so too credit was the opiate of capitalism. Banking had morphed like the butterfly back to its larval stage, where "if it was once considered a good deal," bankers would find a way to lend money on it, to an ass-backwards, counter-intuitive rationalization, where bankers now thought, "if we can find a way to lend money on it, it's a good deal." Nobody used the term collateral any more, the new kids being trained on Wall Street didn't even know how to spell it, thinking it didn't matter anyway, what with the only collateral needed being their capacity to find the funds to lend. The carousel would whirl faster and faster than his father had predicted shortly before his death, thanks to the unleashed power of the computer and cyber-space, a marriage of information technology and speculation that seemed to be made in heaven to the growing heathens on Wall Street.

A new gimmick was currently on the scene as Ryan and William patiently listened to the final drones of the M&A firms' wails floating by them, not paying much attention to what they were saying in their hopeful rants of self-righteousness. Soon to be at the offing was a new trick a couple of teenage scientist types hired by one of the major New York banks had that was called program trading. An algorithmic, completely automatic, no human hands, system, that would portend that every once in a while the market would get the totally unexpected shit kicked out of it, doing to the stock market what they'd been doing to the foreign exchange markets for the last ten years.

So much had changed so fast, so many old tried and true safeguards dismantled by a financial community in which not two dozen people remembered 1929. No wonder older heads like Will's father were troubled. Bankruptcy, once a recourse of last resort, redolent of disgrace and failure, was now merely another legal ploy, used to avert a liability suit or abrogate a contract. America today was awash in financial euphemism. Home equity loan sounded ever so more palatable than "second mortgage," palatable to the extent of over a hundred billion dollars already on the banking systems books. CHIPS, the New York Clearing House Interbank Payment System, was balancing seven hundred billion dollars of bank transfers daily, the volume processed by its acronymic overseas offspring SWIFT, the Society of Worldwide Interbank Financial Telecommunications was hardly lagging as seekers of the highest interest rates prowled Wall Street and the world buying the foreign debt pools of TIGRS and CATS.

Well after all that had Schumpeter said, he recalled his father saying, that, "the essence of capitalism is change, decay and regeneration and alteration." Old industries die and new one arise, in a cycle of obsolescence, change, creation, obsolescence and change once again and so on. He called the process "creative destruction." His father could accept the idea in its nature and now Will held the same feelings. The operative word was "creative" for, despite what rags like the *Wall Street Journal* might say, he didn't think Schumpeter would so describe what's happening today, this slimy, insanely leveraged take over game being played by unethical sleaze trading on inside information. Will called it "destructive destruction," being force fed into the system by a collegiality of the CEOs of the biggest banks in America and their money hungry salesmen. Both Will and Ryan, now financial comrades in arms, were brought up to believe that if you were lucky enough or smart enough to get your hands on a bounty of money, one of the luxuries you could afford was a conscience.

The entire Davies family along with Will and Winnie understood that for far too long there had been an economic fault line running throughout the world which today's economic gurus seemed unable to explain or offer any remedy for. The widening wealth and income gap between a tiny rich elite and multitudes of poor in every country between and within developed and developing nations. With global communications, the global economy and the global environment, one could not help but feel the reverberations inside and outside national borders. The growing economic imbalances have promoted bloody conflicts, widespread starvation, international crime and corruption, depleting the planet of its non-replenishable resources, unconscionable destruction of the environment and the systematic suppression of human potential and life-enhancing technology.

It was the idea to set up the mining business model, if all went according to plan, in a vision of the twentieth Century lawyer-economist Louis Kelso, who understood the power of technology either to liberate or dehumanize civilizations. He was popularly known as the inventor of the employee stock ownership plan ESOP. It was Kelso who observed that modern capital tools and their phenomenal power to do more with less had offered people an escape from scarcity to shared abundance.

Having studied Kelso, Ryan and Will came to understand how as a lawyer Kelso also saw that the design of our "invisible" institutional environment and social tools determines the quantity of people's relationship to technology. Such intangible things as our laws and financial systems determine which people will be included or excluded from sharing of access to equal economic opportunity, power and capital incomes. Access to capital ownership is as fundamental a human right as the right to the fruits of one's labor, Kelso had asserted. The democratization of capital credit was indeed the "social key" to universalizing access to future ownership of productive wealth, in such a way that every individual as an owner could eventually gain income independence through the profits from ones capital.

The operating template of the mining enterprise as determined by Mary and Walter would be capitalized and designed and managed in what was termed in the nomenclature of the "third way." Logically, this third way would be a free market system that would economically empower all individuals and families through direct and effective ownership of the means of production, which was the guard against the potential for corruption and abuse, operating for the people of the Iron Range under the economics of ownership and justice.

The essence of what Kelso called binary economics was a single revolutionary proposition, that could legitimately create economic value through two (thus binary) factors of production, being labor, defined as all forms of economic work by people, including manual, intellectual, creative and entrepreneurial work, and so called "human capital," and capital defined as anything non-human, contributing to the production of marketable goods and services, including tools, machines, land, structures, systems and patents.

The capital raised for the Davies mining operation, would not merely enhance labor's ability to produce economic goods, but the capital, which was increasingly the source of economic growth, would also increasingly become the source of added property incomes for everyone. The ideal market system upon which the operation would operate would be based on three basic principles of economic justice, participation, distribution and harmony

Participation was the input principle that rightly posited that if both labor and capital are responsible for production, then the equality of opportunity demanded that the right to property and the access to the means of acquiring and possessing property must, in justice, be extended to all.

Distribution or the out-take principle, stated that property rights require that income be distributed based on what one contributes to production, that is ones labor or ones capital or both. Given that capital ownership is widespread, the free and open market becomes the most democratic and efficient means for determining just prices, just wages and just profits. Just profits in this case would be a just distribution on the increases in productivity.

Harmony or the feedback principle, which is called the principle of limitation, restores balance between participation or input and distribution or out-takes and establishes limits on monopolistic accumulations of capital and other abuses of property.

Under the democratized access to money which the mining venture would adhere to, capital credit and credit insurance would become instruments of inclusion, not exclusion, and the means for procreating financing of whatever capital the economy of the operation would need to move toward prosperous lives for all its employees. Monetary, tax and other capital homesteading reforms would allow the operation to finance sustainable growth through techniques that offer more universal access to future ownership.

The mining operation, as Mary knew her father would have approved of, would be a justice based management system, a cooperative community, designed for building and sustaining an ownership culture within the enterprise. By applying the principles of economic justice and the philosophy of servant leadership and the democratic financing techniques, justice based management would become the prevailing management system for not only the Davies operation but hopefully for many others of the late twentieth century, JBM would systematically anchor capital and build ownership into successive generations of its employees.

JBM, Mary had hoped as she knew her father had, would re-orient the operational and governing systems of modern enterprises from the present top-down, risk averse and conflict prone patterns of the wage system, to an operation of participatory ownership where risk, rewards and responsibilities are shared among the many co-owners. This operation template under which the mines would be run would enable all workers to be reconciled with the realities of competition, supplemented by capital incomes, workers' incomes would increasingly shift from automatic wage increases to more equitable sharing of the net profits.

The role of labor unions, Mary was confident her father would be most pleased with, would also evolve as unions moved from the economics of conflict to the economics of co-ownership, the unions regaining their original role as a democratic society's most important institution for advancing economic justice by organizing all non-owners, not just workers, to help get them their fair share of the growing capital pie.

Chapter 30

The candidate formal dinner debate had been expertly crafted by her staff, and all the right influential species, the states' most liberal divines were represented in solid support, and Winnie could see on many of them the armoring certitude of the attendees' vast wealth. Many of the women of import were strangely impressive in their gowns followed along in the ballroom by their befuddled husbands. Winnie smiled at the deferential traffic which eddied around her. She would be nothing like the senator she hoped to depose from office, giving his spoken word in that ponderous orotund manner he had always employed when describing his politically jaded view from Olympus.

He greased his dinner guests and supporters with a confident smile as oleaginous as margarine, his countenance glistening with polish and bromade blazed buttons abeam like bullions, eyes nipped and skin sanded, keeping his tan on a shelf in the bathroom along with the patently artificial auburn of thinning hair parted north from beneath his ear. He would have smiled, Winnie imagined, bringing the news of Thermopylaes to the Persian encampment. He would maintain his galling smile, in the futile hope of beating back the rage of the hungry and disadvantaged. It was a vapid smile, for certain, the painted on ivory earnest of easy self confidence that had taken him to wealth and adulation. Here was a man who even at his most effacing self resembled a large arrogant mouse and Winnie surmised that the speech he was about begin that evening would be positively insufferable, as it was his style, to stretch his large frame over the crowd and bark consensus chestnuts through his bullhorn, putting on a one page position statement on issues with phrases of room temperature prose, squishing the "morality" themes of his arguments together in such a way that was so dubious that would vitiate any power whatsoever of the appeal.

She thought he was looking even larger, his tall frame appearing more slab-like than ever. He was part of the mob that this president marched with, jackboots on society, with less than a nickel's worth of intellectual furniture, all refusing to budge from the free market orthodoxy of the pre-Hoover brontosauruses who had financed his rise to power, an intra-group homogenization of the ultra-rich, who could only really be comfortable in the company of each other. They have the same toys, look for the same things and know to the penny how much their brethren in wealth are worth. Outside their homes and the lackeys who make up their immediate business circles, they're at ease only in the company of the equally rich. It was an orthodoxy that operated with the solemn conceit of pretending to do the public's beneficial business, in which wholesale speculation using money as a commodity was considered a legitimate objective of fiscal policy as the simulation of productive competition.

Ryan was about to say something to Nan just as the lights went down and so reverent a hush fell on the attendees seated at their round dining tables that it would have been a sacrilege even to whisper. Dave Duncan and his wife Jen both flashed arched eyebrows that expressed the dread of what was about to come, as the incumbent senator was introduced on the stage one row in front of them. All of Winnie's and William's close friends and supporters were desperately hoping that she could be the one to finally replace this absolute con job of a man, who photographed well and had mastered the form of generalizing blather that the media seemed to lap up.

The senator now speaking, and his types Winnie hoped to replace, seemed to have so much taste when it came to Italian shoes or gold necklaces or money to be made but so little taste when it came to human values and morals. He had kept the press corps, journalists who had become sleepy on patrol, entertained with decent bourbon whiskey and a string of backwoods apothegms and like many of his kind she knew him to be also sly, vicious and bigoted. He had collar ad features and an imperious manner that seemed to create space around him as he walked. His perorations were now being dispensed behind the mask he used for public consumption, like the civilities of an Archbishop blessing a Cathedral of penitents, sounding like an over ambitious Dickensian father sermonizing over the Sunday mutton. The country wanted grown-ups, Winnie thought as he spoke, stretching his lips into a smile that displayed his teeth like a trophy case grin of a man who thought himself wise and witty with money in the bank and no force of man, if he could help it, would be permitted to disturb the blissful contemplation he had of himself and his future.

Winnie planned to calmly and quietly establish her incumbent opponent typologically as the epitome and avatar of political duplicity and self-interest, who had consistently sold his conscience to the highest bidder, part of a lobbied corporate society that devalued everything the least bit humanitarian. There were so many in Washington, she realized, just like the blow dried turn coat now blowing wind, who'd been running the budget, and too many cowboys and oil barons calling the tune. These types had politically changed course and done a complete one-eighty, smelling the duplicitous pollution of the profligate new conservative tide of imperial conceit. They were now in search of a new high point of greed and selfishness for the now forsaken liberalism. They had traduced the country's noblest traditions, politicians whose ethical and moral impulses tended to be much weaker than their political ones who in order not to stand out would do most anything to fit in, who would eventually find it impossible to erase the blots from their political copy books, and find life would present them a bill they would find very hard to repay.

There were too many who stood to profit from an electorate soothed into helplessness by their vapid easy spokesman in Washington. Moral money had turned the trick and it was in tune with the caveman mentality of the current meme of supply side economics that prevailed. They were collectively all poisoners, thought viruses, Winnie felt, of the mind and spirit and the atmosphere of the earth, futilely in search of moral and ethical insulation and justification. She doubted the value of their collective prolixity, as she found its costs appalling as particularly measured against what was received. She understood that like the biblical Paul, who was the great Lion of God, she would become an expatriate forced by fortune to dwell among the savages.

Far too many of these politicians humane illusions had fled and nothing appeared to have replaced them. It was very hard to have possessions and not become possessive, Winnie understood all too well, having come from extensive wealth, but she understood from her own personal epiphanies that the poor should not be left at the mercy of their poverty, just as the rich should not be left at the selfish mercy of their wealth. One of the craven attributes of power she well understood is that it gives those who have it the ability to define reality and the power to make others believe in their definition. No one is justified in keeping for exclusive use what he does not need when others lack necessities and that the sharing of our surplus was an act of justice rather than merely an act of benevolence. The question of ownership, she was rightly taught, was subordinate to the question of use.

She had long seen, as she stood backstage with her husband, that this was just another age marked by a gaudy orgy of getting and spending, times when avarice was counted as a good thing, a sign of social fitness. Wall Street millionaires were popping up all over the talk land these days offering up platitudes and palaver about deficits and social security and health care, complaining how the poor don't save enough, which was like complaining that not enough people in wheelchairs don't sign up for the pole vault. The paradox Winnie reflected on was that these senators, the one speaking before the ballroom now and the ones speaking on the senate floor in Washington, were the very ones who ran things, who accepted the political payoffs and allowed their paymasters to be able to borrow money at wholesale prices and who view the tax code as their personal profligate playpen. As they said in Washington, she recalled hearing, if everyone is lying, then no one is lying.

The growing block of conservatives in Washington looked at their bad actor President and relished being in the comforting proximity of his jack booted millionaires and billionaires. It was a coming once more of the Gilded Ages of the 1890s, the 1920s and now the revolution of the 1980s and the attempt to eviscerate the middle class. We are witness to the secession of the successful, where they have abandoned our public services losing important advocates. The uphill financial climb of the rich had accelerated the downward spiral of society as a whole, leading, she knew, to a widening inequality and a heightened estrangement and the moral amnesia that estrangement required.

"A trickle down demand trickle up economy," Winnie began, "has been the normative structure of economic operative theory since ancient Samaria and the Epic of Gilgamesh. In 1791 Alexander Hamilton, the Secretary of Commerce, developed an economic plan of trade tariffs, similar to the Tudor Plan of England in 1607. From 1793 until the Civil War all of our government revenues were derived from import tariffs. In the years between World War I and World War II tariffs were one third of government revenues, yet today, imports represent just three percent of our nation's revenues. From 1793 until 1981 our demand trickle down economy worked extremely well with supply, productivity, demand and wages all keeping a concordant pace. The end of demand-side economics in 1981 was fundamentally antithetical to democracy, leading to the gradual destruction of our commons: our streets, our highways, our libraries, our schools, our post offices, our parks, our rivers, our lakes and all the shared wealth we enjoy. This represents, in my opinion," Winnie positioned, "the usurpation of our constitutional province of life liberty and the pursuit of happiness that our founders designed.

Winnie would spend the next half-hour enthralling her devoted dominions and even many of the right wing illiterata present to the purposeful designed horrors of the new amoral regime of neo-liberal economics. She uncovered the lies and deception of The Powell Memo in 1971, the establishment of right wing "think tanks" and foundations and the warped and devilish republican strategy of the "two Santa Claus theory, and the corruption of democracy from within.

"We have been told by our politicians and economists that we operate in a free market system, but I see it as only free for multinational corporations, using their financial leverage to do business around the world. Globalization and the tenets of the free market are pandered about and promoted in the technical sense, but surely not in the doctrinal sense that has been appropriated by the 'individual rights' style of integration that is built into the so called 'free trade agreements,' with a complex mixture of liberalism, protectionism and the undermining of popular local democratic control over policy. This is merely the shrouded continuation of a legacy of poisoning the moral cultures around the world and the extension of the multinationals' division of labor across international boundaries, of imperial thuggery and a designed control grip over free humanity.

"For several decades now," Winnie pressed on, feeling a sense of a new awareness floating over her audience, "the right-wing extremists have made every effort to put in place an ultra-conservative re-education machine, an apparatus for producing and disseminating a public pedagogy in which everything with the hint of a liberal origin or taint, where the word 'public' would be vigorously contested and destroyed.

"In 1980 Paul Weyrich, The Christian right leader who founded the heritage Foundation, told a group of his flock in a speech these exact words: 'How many of our Christians have what I call the goo-goo syndrome-good government? They want everybody to vote. I don't want everybody to vote. Elections are not won by a majority of people, they never have been from the beginning of our country and they are not now. As a matter of fact, our leverage in elections quite candidly goes up as the voting populace goes down.'" Winnie stepped from behind the podium and asked, her palms turned upward pointing to the sky, "Is this the party you want representing you in Washington," she pleaded. "Is it, I ask, is it?"

A roar of "no and no way" blazed through the ballroom like a firestorm, as the republican candidate and his delegations at their tables squirmed in their seats.

"Today," Winnie continued after the commotion of spoken disgust had died down, "the conservatives' fight to limit the freedom of our votes, has manifested itself in ALEC, the American Legislative Exchange Council, also founded by Paul Weyrich and the right wing think tanks, most specifically the Koch brothers. It is their mission among others, and they are beginning to carry it to every state in the union, to make every effort to keep certain segments of our population that typically vote Democrat, from exercising that vote, through all sorts of nefarious means.

"Again I ask you, is this the party you want representing you in Washington?"

The disdainful roars of "no" were even louder, as her electorate were beginning to see the big picture of the fascist republicans and the undermining of democracy.

"I intend, when I get to Washington if I can merit your vote, to get about the business of repairing the damage and recovering the stolen assets of these craven hustlers.

"We must ask ourselves—" Winnie touched her forehead with the fingers of her right hand "—if one generation of men has the right to bind another holding the earth in usufruct to the living. American history has long been a battle between civic democratic values and corporate commercial values. We must not succumb to our collective conflicted energy and the easy convenience of our conscience. We must always search for beauty and the peaceful possibility that resides just on the other side of chaos. It is the lack of understanding that keeps us from unity.

"The best love is the love of knowledge and understanding that can empower our common souls, for it is only those who don't have all the facts, who could counsel unchecked belligerence.

"We need today to build our own version of modern day enlightenment, for it is only an enlightened society and citizenry that can bring about a reciprocal altruism and a practical utopia of an egalitarian system of social and economic justice.

"Our government," Winnie stated adamantly, looking directly at Nan and Ryan and the table of her neighborhood friends, "should be a buffer to hardship and an honest opportunity for all.

"Today, when it seems like it's easier to be smart than good, we have all the paper requisites of democracy but not true democracy. The seeds for creating the systems of enduring people power need to be formulated in the Senate of the United States where I hope to represent you.

"I will be a champion of re-enlisting and force feeding the stimulus programs of the Keynesian philosophy of economics, that has been proven to work, from the ground up, by means of trickle up demand creation, and a progressive tax policy which is, after all, the fertile soil that small business roots itself in."

A burst of applause spilled over the ballroom throng, and the chant of "Winnie, Winnie, Winnie," coursed the air as the attendees in her favor stood in adoration and pride of their would-be new senator.

"We must also have a government," Winnie finally continued, a bright almost angelic smile creasing her face, "that monitors the corporate conscience through effective regulation that benefits all mankind together honestly and ethically.

"To truly understand our economic history, we must grasp the precepts and philosophies of John Maynard Keynes," Winnie continued. "Lord Keynes died at his country house in Essex England on Easter Sunday, April 21, 1946. Keynes had shaped the intellectual and spirituality of many economists and thinkers of commerce world-wide and inspired the conviction of many, with his capacious and compassionate spirit, that the intellectual just as much as the so called man of action should take on the real world with their knowledge.

"Those who followed Keynes, and his work on the General Theory, knew how right his simple economic theories of demand creation were, and also understood how neutralizing the classroom could be. Take a look at a man like Schumpeter, Keynes would say, a great intuitive, to be sure, but his influence scarcely extended beyond the lecture hall, or the statistical maggots at the University of Chicago, he would rant, who believed themselves to be accumulating a critical mass of data from which some sort of monetarist truth must emerge. They were smart men, for the most part, but not a shadow on Keynes, whose shadow at the time of his death stretched into both Whitehall and the White House.

"Keynes was a man with a mission. He loved managed capitalism and despised Marx and Lenin. He believed that managed capitalism with government regulation acting as the quality conscience of business, as the vanguard against cancerous monopoly, was the essence of a vibrant economic culture. I wonder what he would think about our economy today?" Winnie said evenly, putting her hands up in question.

"The Army's computing machine named ENIAC was developed in 1946, the year of Keynes death, to calculate artillery firing tables for the United States Army Ballistic Research Laboratory. ENIAC as we all know was just the first iteration, like the Neanderthal, like the Cro-Magnon. It had its children and grandchildren and great, great, great, grandchildren, who today can make calculations like billions per second. There would not be a science and not an art that would not be revolutionized.

"For whenever politics and its politicians are to debauch mankind from their integrity, dissolving the virtue of human nature, they themselves become detestable, for to be a statesman of this strategy is to be commissioned a villain. For again it is peace that, to every reflecting mind, is a most desirable object, but that peace which is accomplished with a ruined character, becomes a crime to the seducer and a curse upon the seduced.

"We must remove the power of wealth from the political process and operate the national budget as a moral document. Wealth after all in the end is the measure of what we have taken out of society and those with the most monetary good fortune, who don't reflect on this fact, choose to stand within the deceit of their reified glory. In their tautological manner of thinking, the fate of the species is an abstract externality that monopoly capitalism would rather ignore. Humans have learned to split the atom and now instead of killing ten or twenty with a wooden club, we can kill a million by pushing a button. Are we to call that progress?

"Linear time tempts us moderns," Winnie stated, beginning her summation, moving from behind the podium, "to believe that we are immeasurably better or contemptibly worse than our ancestors.

"By appealing to our pride or despair, unidirectional history relieves us of the challenge of proving ourselves worthy of their example. While deprived of the challenge we are also relieved of the fulfillment.

Commenting on the matters of Rome during the early empire, the great historian Tacitus disagreed with moralists who argued that the civic virtue of a great society can only change in one direction. 'Indeed, it may well be that there is a kind of cycle in human affairs,' he wrote, 'and that morals alternate as do the seasons.'

"'Ancient times were not always better: Our generation too has produced many examples of honorable and civilized behavior for posterity to copy. One must hope this praiseworthy competition with our ancestors will long endure.' Two millennia after Tacitus we must share this hope.

"We must bend the arc of the universe, realizing that ethical principles and moral principles motivate no one, understanding that values are less 'taught' than 'caught' in the doing of important experiences, and be in concert with all other nations to see fulfilled the world around, all hope for justice, that has been so long and cruelly deferred, while doing our democracy's transformative work, for we cannot 'will the way', without 'willing the means', as we begin to challenge the power of what is, fighting those who make peaceful evolution impossible and revolution toward peace inevitable.

"Justice is the moral test of our spirituality and for that we should make the conquest of war, the preservation of nature and the pursuit of social justice our magnificent obsession.

"We need democratic distributive justice, because to find common ground we must first move to higher ground and drain the swamps of injustice through social responsibility legislation. If mental development and our increased knowledge are not counterbalanced by a corresponding growth in consciousness, then the potential of mankind for unhappiness and despair is very great. There can be no more denial of our moral responsibility, because morality is the only source of true power.

"In the prescient words of William Parsons stated in his book *The Merchant of Probity*: 'We must all be people with a mind to improve, a heart to cultivate, and a character to form.' We need to commit ourselves, and I hope you will join me in the charge, to a re-declaration of conscience, and a kind of 1776 style of insurrection.

"Many of our great leaders of the past like Jefferson, Franklin Roosevelt, John F. Kennedy, Robert F. Kennedy, Gandhi, Jesus and Allah, are honored today, but few are emulated by our elected representatives. I will not take that course. I ask you sincerely, dear friends of Minnesota, for your honored vote on Tuesday and help begin the difficult journey of rebooting our economy for the benefit and enduring well-being for all of us, our children, and the generations to come.

"As the great Greek philosopher Heraclitus said during the vibrant period of Athenian Democracy, 'Our character is our destiny. Let us move forward together to make the new possibility of our modern Enlightenment become our manifest destiny'.

What Winnie, the budding prophet was essentially telling her electorate was to "take everything you know and have learned and add the power of love and truth to it." Her words were the weapons of the side of the soft power of moral suasion and the side of doing what is right.

"I sincerely thank you for your time and attention, and may God bless us all."

The roar was nearly deafening as William walked out from behind the stage curtains to greet his wife, as she waved to her adoring throng, accepting their adoration with humbled dignity and a radiantly beaming grin.

Chapter 31

A muted, disembodied voice announced the imminent boarding of Northwest flight 361. The January 2 non-stop flight from the Twin Cities to London Heathrow was a welcome first segment of what lay ahead for Walter, Ryan and Sophie. January, the month named after the Greek god Janus, the god of two faces back to back, the god of doorways. Always looking both ways, torn between two ways of doing things, looking forward to the New Year and back to the old. He sees the past and the future. Here they were packed and ready to go, armed for travel, like Ulysses with his black ships caulked and a fair wind behind them, unknown perils lying behind the next promontory.

Days before, during the holiday week, the extended family watched Christmas movies; *Miracle on 34th Street*, *The Bishop's Wife* and *It's a Wonderful Life.* When George Bailey suddenly saw Mary Hatch at the school dance, Ryan took Nan's hand in his, and when George's brother called him the richest man in town, they all sat together sobbing. On Christmas Eve they talked with Dr. Jim and Bud and Lois Anderson at their lake home in Everest, and checked in with Sophie in New York City. They had a plan and now just needed to draw from each other, the resolve, to go through with it.

Walter continued the holiday ritual by making cucumbers and sour cream, while Mary made oyster stew, and Ryan grilled huge shrimp with Nan's luscious baste, while drinking Champagne. They watched Dickens, *A Christmas Carol*, the old black and white version with Alistair Sim that Dan had discovered in a shop in Evanston. Winnie had won the election for senate from Minnesota in a near landslide, many votes coming from the staunch legions of normally republican wealthy suburbs. The Duncans had thrown a very private neighborhood party for the new senator, the first weekend in December, and all were elated with her success. She was to be sworn in two weeks later.

Walter and Ryan, in flight to London, were both feeling like mere spectators to the world, the camera of their visions slowly leaving one scene after another of America left behind them. They were leaving one set of circumstances for another, unable to witness the fact that the people, the trees, and the water that lay miles below them actually move, while the plane that carries them blithely, flies forward in the interest of yet another place to go, other business to take care of, as the picture behind them fades to black, dissolving the mind's eye.

Meaning is never in the event itself, Ryan mused as he listened to the drone of the DC 10, but in the motion through the event. If not we could isolate an instant in the event and conclude that this was the event itself, the meaning. But that cannot be done, he thought as he dozed, for it is the motion itself that is important, in the whole tissue of phenomena which was the world he and his father were lost in, bound together under the unwinking eye of eternity.

And they were moving all right, moving East at three hundred and fifty miles per hour, at thirty thousand feet. To the hum and lull of the plane, the past unrolled in his head like a film. It was like a showing of a family movie, the kind the advertisements tell you to keep so that you will have a record of the day. He dreamed gently back over the years, as the man, in his business suit, leaned over him as he sat with crayons of the rug in front of the fireplace, and surprised him with a new balsa-wood glider from his favorite toy store, and the man who had congratulated him when he hit the game winning double, completed the mile swim and became an Eagle Scout, and the man who had roared with laughter from the Crist-Craft when he took a header as he was learning how to slalom ski. "Just one bite, now, for supper is almost ready," said the woman with the tender brown eyes and the soft cheeks as she leaned over him after prayers and kissed him good night, promising that there were no tigers, or lions or bears under the bed, and left the sweet smell, that was hers, in the dark after the light was out.

The sky began to lighten east to west over the Atlantic, like the day doubling back on itself, as Ryan and his father went once more through the strategic tactics they had planned to undertake, with the wise assistance from Sophie. Being alone in an airplane for eight hours, irrevocably alone with nothing to do but observe their own hands in the semi-darkness of the cabin over the Atlantic, the two of them had nothing to contemplate but the size of their own courage, nothing to wonder about but their beliefs, the faces and hopes of family rooted in their minds, temporarily relieved with their alien conditions, knowing they would be plunged back into it when they landed. Ryan had hoped that no new dangerous revelations would befall them as they flew over the Atlantic, immersed in the disembodied feeling he always got on airplane flights.

Chapter 32

Arriving thirty minutes ahead of schedule at nine thirty, due to a tailwind, they gathered their bags and hailed a black London cab, to the seacoast town of Portsmouth forty miles south of London. They checked into the Lysses House Hotel in town adjacent to the English Channel, met downstairs for dinner and shared a bottle of rich Bordeaux, and were off to bed before midnight, knowing they had a busy week that lay ominously ahead of them.

Walter rose just before sunrise, showered and walked out on the pier, the low even seas sliding westward under a light wind. Over the eastern horizon surrounding London, a thin line of clouds were slowly turning pink in the approaching light of the dawn. The day was overcast with a chill damp breeze eerily coming off the channel. The rainy slush that had fallen during the night had stopped, but there were still traces of the gray snowy precipitate along the port docks. It was a drab time of the year in England and the air was heavy with mist, almost a drizzle. The sky was a shade grayer than the concrete slabs of docking where the ferries were slipped. He watched the proud ships in the harbor, the proud sweep of their breasts of white, their opulent storied superstructures, like bridled horses held in reign. At nine-o-five, the two men boarded the Normandie, one of the three ferries operated by the Bretagne Ferry Line of Portsmouth, for the three hour trip to Le Havre, France.

The boat pulled away, churning the water behind it, battling the wind with a smoky roar. The distance soon pressed the English shoreline further and further into the gray horizon, like a thumb pushing into putty, until it was fully subsumed. The water slowly deepened behind them, its ghoulish gray color taking on the quality of a solid.

They took their coffees ensconced in the ship's top tier lounge looking out over the western horizon, and the vastness of the sea and the gray sky pictured before them. The ship was beautifully designed and spacious. It sliced open the English Channel, its horizontal beam slightly pitched, bow to stern. The crossing made them astoundingly aware of the immensities of sea and sky. The ship itself seemed to be a character in its own right, an omnipresent structure with smartly styled officers and crew, guiding it from bow to stern. It seemed that the transport carrier contained a different solar system, taking them into a world that moved at another pace, one that allowed time to think, look and surmise. The isolation here spun its cocoon, focusing the mind on one place, one time, one rhythm. It seemed to have an atmosphere of mystery accentuated by the feeling of suspended time and a blurring of the lines between actuality and daydreaming, as Ryan listened to his father speak reflectively of his memories of crossing this channel by air over forty years ago.

They had sat and talked with one another for almost two days now, unlike their usual routine, and it had given them real time together, getting even closer than they had ever been. They were now being confronted with something new and dangerous. They were being transported gracefully over the gun metal gray waters of the English Channel, to foreign cities and foreign lands, to unknown peril. While they approached the French coast, the town of Cherbourg came into view, and from that distance it lay like a solid pattern of old chalk, at the base of the coastal indentation. An English ship appeared off the coast, and approached with a strange, looming immediacy of powerful objects that move at fast speeds. Yet, there was no sense of continuous motion, but of gradual and progressive enlargement. Rather, the visage of the ship melted rapidly from one largeness to another, like a genie un-stoppered from a wizard's bottle, to an overpowering command of the spectator.

As the ferry slipped into the long docks of the port city of La Havre, quartering in a slow turn upon the land as she came up for anchor, twenty minutes on the other side of noon, the day had turned bright blue with only a few scattered white caps breaking the calm surface of the channel. They rented the Peugeot sedan they had on reservation and began their drive toward Caen, Ryan taking the honors of being the chauffeur. They drove slowly toward the Normandy coast, man and master returning to the throbbing heart of nightmarish memories. G.I.s like Ryan's father had landed in Normandy and fought and won the Great War. They had put the sword back in the stone after VJ Day, and had been waiting for a generation, for their progeny, with the wills of modern day chastity belts, to arrive, who could pull the sword out again.

The signs along the coast bore famous names, but for different reasons, making up an odd mixture of fiction and history. They were names signifying war, genius, honor, and the death of Kings. First Cabourg and Proust's "Balbec", then Oistreham and Arromanches and finally the invasion beaches of Sword, Juno, Gold, Omaha and beyond them Pointe de Hoc and Utah Beach. Arrows pointed to the inland towns of Caen, Bayeux and Ste. Mere Eglise.

As they approached Caen along the Orne River they could see the steeple of the Saint Pierre Church rise majestically in the distance, with the bright blue sky as background. Then the Chateau de Cain came into view built in 1060 by William the Conqueror, who then conquered England in 1066. The two Abbeys that the Pope had encouraged William the Conqueror to build for marrying his cousin Mathilda of Flanders filled their eye's lens next. The Abbey of Eglise St-Etienne was constructed honoring St. Stephen circa 1063 and the Abbey of Eglise de la Ste-Trinite honoring the Holy Trinity was built circa 1060.

The day continued sunny and bright but a chill was increasing in the afternoon as they drove over the country roads of Normandy toward their destination of Collevile-sur-Mer, and the Normandy American Cemetery, in the Basse-Normandie region of Northwest France. They stopped at Pointe du-Hoc, Walter's drop zone on that late night mission of June 5, 1944, where the fields were still cratered by the bombs of the U.S. Navy.

At Walter's request, Ryan stopped in Caen, at The Memorial Pour la Paix, pulling into the main parking lot that was, surprisingly, nearly empty. The men stood at the base of the memorial where a list of the Nobel Peace Prize winners was inscribed, along with an exhibit of conflict resolution in different cultures. At the center of the polished stone memorial, the sightless marble knight knelt, with his vigil shield at his side, both hands before him grasping his broad righteous sword. Ryan and Walt quietly reflected on the etched words of Elie Wiesel's prescient meditation. "Peace is not a gift from God to man, but a gift to man himself."

The Normandy American Cemetery was located overlooking Omaha Beach and the English Channel. It was established by the U.S. First Army on June 8 1944. It was the first American cemetery on European soil. The majestic white marble memorial was structured in a semi-circular colonnade with a loggia at each end containing maps and narratives of the military operations. At the center was a bronze statue of a U.S. soldier titled, "Spirit of American Youth." It was the home of nine thousand, three hundred and eighty-seven brave dead Americans with an average age of twenty-two. On the walls of the semi-circular garden on the east side of the memorial were the inscribed names of one thousand, five hundred and fifty-seven soldiers whose remains were never recovered or identified.

By May 1944, some one point five million soldiers were bivouacked in make-shift camps all over England. At twenty-three hundred hours on the night of June 5, eighteen plane loads of pathfinders rolled down the runways and lifted into the black night, the beginning of operation Neptune. They began jumping out at four hundred and fifty feet above the ground, from the C-47s that had crossed the English Channel, between the islands of Alderney and Guernsey, crossing the west coast on the Cotentin Peninsula. The 82nd Airborne and the 101st were preceding the main body of the 101st that followed about one hour later. Eight minutes after crossing the coast at 0015, Walter Davies, the pathfinder from the 82nd, stepped out of the C-47 four hundred and fifty feet above, and made a rough parachute landing when he hit the ground of the flooded Merderet River, southeast of Sainte-Mere-Eglise.

The 82nd had a multiple mission: seal off the Cotentin from the south, destroy bridges over the Douve River and Point-l'Abbe and the Beuzeville, occupy and hold both banks of the Merderet River, protect the southwest flank of VII Corps, by holding the line of the Douve River, and most important, seize Sainte-Mere-Eglise.

The landing of the 82nd was even more hazardous than that of the 101st. Walter and his group had dropped near the Merderet River, into an area of ersatz swamps, the land having been flooded by the Germans just days before. The dispersion of the 82nd had been so broad, that by D-Day plus two, only 2100 of the scattered paratroopers were under command control. The second battalion of the 507th and had probably the best landing Walter had recalled, of any of the battalions. Its pathfinders had found the drop zone near the connecting Nueville-au-Plain with Sainte-Mere-Eglise and had set up their Eurekas and lights to beam in the other planes to their correct drop zones.

Walter's battalion had landed outside the drop zone, but fortunately in an area free of Germans, Ryan had been told. After about half of his battalion had found each other and assembled, and started toward Sainte-Mere-Eglise, his D-Day objective. They had a French guide with them and went almost untouched into town, but once inside they ran into German patrols and guards, killing ten and capturing thirty.

Walter blinked hard and rubbed the right temple of his head, as uncomfortable war time thoughts flooded back through him. Before dawn the next morning of June 6, the 507th had captured Sainte-Mere-Eglise and over the town square mounted a U.S. flag. Sainte-Mere-Eglise was the first town liberated on the western front.

The 82nd and the 101st suffered high casualties because of the dispersed landings and the irregular drops at high speeds and from wrong altitudes and the enemies present in unexpected locations. On D-Day, the 82nd had 1259 troopers killed, wounded or listed as missing in action, the last probably captured, killed or wounded. The 101st had a similar number of casualties at 1240 lost men.

In 1944, only four years after the initiation of the U.S. airborne effort and after the largest airborne assault in history, the question continued to haunt Walter Davies. Was the airborne effort in Normandy worth the numbers of dead and wounded? By dropping behind the American forces that landed on Utah Beach, the battalions that jumped into Normandy had significantly limited the casualties there. At Utah Beach there were 197 casualties, 60 of whom were killed in the channel when their boats sank. Omaha Beach, however, behind which there was no U.S. airborne force, was where the slaughter took place. By the end of the day at Omaha Beach, the 1st and 29th Infantry Division had forced their way only a mile and a half inland. 2374 men were killed, wounded or missing.

Walter stood, his current place of mental residence, in stone silence, his eyes dark with memory, at the Normandy Memorial. Ryan put his hand on his father's shoulder as they stood in silent repose in front of the statue, while Walter became absorbed in memories, hearing the spectral voices of the murmuring prayers of his comrades, mentally transporting himself back forty years to the C-47 rolling down the runway at Witham Air Base, south of London, lifting off, the beginning of operation Neptune.

"Oh God. God help me. Help me to be wise and full of courage and sound judgment. Harden my heart to the sights that I may see. Grant me the power to think clearly, boldly, resolutely, no matter how unnerving the danger…"

All the planes warmed up at the same time and the thunder of the engines was deafening. Cutchall grabbed his forearm, "Jesus," he said, "We're going."

The sergeant who was standing next to the bulkhead by the radio room raised his voice and hollered, "Say goodbye to England, boys." Everyone nodded and attempted to smile. The motors died down to a throbbing rumble. The crew chief leaned out the door and quickly pulled his head in as a plane went by.

"There they go, there they go!" he shouted. "They're off!" It was eleven o'clock. The tail swung around in a dizzy arc, almost throwing the soldiers from their seats. "This is it," the crew chief said, buckling his flak vest. The C-47 worked its way up the runway with squeaking wheels and a heavy coughing, an all-powerful rumble until it reached the line of departure, where it stopped and waited for the signal to lift off. The pilot gunned the motors and then let them idle. It was eleven-fifteen.

The signal finally flashed from the control tower. Go! Go! It blinked, kill 'em all! There was a last terrible rattling and an all pervading roar and the plane began to move ahead. Then, gaining speed, it raced down the runway at ever more speed. Everyone held their breath and clung to the seat belts. The tail rose slowly until the cabin floor, which had been aslant, was level to the ground. Just when it seemed as if the plane would never leave the runway, the plane's nose lifted and they were airborne. The motor's roar faded to a steady drone. With a collective sigh of relief, soldiers relaxed and undid seat belts. The invasion had begun.

"Cigarette," Cutchall, asked on his right.

"No thanks," he responded and smiled. With the lift from the ground he had experienced a sudden total change of feeling. The load of brooding anxiety had faded away, leaving him light, reckless, resigned with almost a feeling of detachment, as the sheer relief of all the waiting came to an end. He looked around to see how others were reacting to takeoff. Only the smokers, who were faintly lighted by the firefly glow of their cigarettes, were visible. When they inhaled the flaring tips lit up their shadowy, blackened faces. They did not look happy.

The engines roared louder, climbing higher to the sky. The plane was bucking and slamming around now in the rough air currents above the large Devonshire hills that once seemed so lovely. He turned stiffly and staring out the window saw far below in the shifting moonlight, the dotted white perimeter lights of the field and the tiny red and green wing tip lights of other C-47s taxing and taking off getting into formation. They banked again and continued round and round in a great droning loop until the whole Battalion was formed in a long V of Vs, nine planes wide. He watched as a red light crept up on them in the darkness outside. It was a wing plane moving into position. When it was almost abreast, it throttled down and rode alongside with a bouncing yawning motion.

The moon went behind a cloud and he twisted himself back into position. Suspended in a rackety darkness lit only by cigarettes and a tiny blue ceiling light in the pilot's passageway, he felt as if he were in the worst of bad dreams, riding a nightmare to an obliterating hell. A night jump was always eerie, but this one seemed so utterly unreal and incredible and yet so final that it wrung the feeling out of him and left him passively indifferent, with impatience now becoming his greatest emotion. The crew chief left his stand near the door, stopping here and there to chat with men, slowly working his way back toward the bulkhead where Sergeant Halvey was sitting. Soon he made a return trip to the tail, clutching the anchor line that ran down the plane's ceiling and stood by the open door. He beckoned to the lieutenant, who rose clumsily from a seat nearby and looked out, then nodded and smiled.

Facing the down the aisle, the lieutenant bellowed, "Look, men, look! It's the fleet." He turned stiffly to the window again, like a rusty robot and gasped. Five hundred feet below, spread out for miles on the moonlit sea were a massive array of landing barges, destroyers, cruisers and attack transports. They were bearing the infantry slowly sailing east, like a flood of lava, to a destiny of a dawn assault on the shores of Normandy. As the battalion passed over-head, a lamp blinked up at the men from the command ship. All the planes' wing tipped lights flashed off and the blue lights went out in the pilot's passageways. His shoulders swung away from the window.

He stared at the men opposite him in the racketing, vibrating, oil reeking, vomit scented darkness. "Isn't it great?" he said to Cutchall. "Those guys are going in with us!"

There was no reply, so he turned and looked at Cutch, his best buddy, who had said for months he was going to die on D-Day, and who by comparison made himself feel like an eternal optimist, and saw that he had not heard him. He looked very scared. The compulsion to lose was universal, he remembered the commanding officer say, days before the invasion. Only a handful of people could overcome it. He had come to know it to be true. You can't approach anything in life with the thought of losing being predominant.

The airborne troops were trained to be winners. If you oppose me, I will win and you will lose. Simple bravery un-tethered with doubt. Yet fear remained. He started to tell that everything was going to be all right, but as he shouted his first words his ears tingled and the engines' pitch changed as they strained for altitude. It wouldn't be long now he knew and suddenly lost interest in Cutchall. His stomach tightened and filled with ice and an inner voice told him to get ready.

The red light flashed on in the jump panel beside the door. The plane lurched and roared as if in answer and the lieutenant staggered erect, grabbed the anchor line with one hand and snapped his static line to it. "Stand up and hook up," he shouted.

They were now flying between the Channel Islands of Guernsey and Jersey which was the point at which they had been instructed that they would stand and hook up. With only twenty minutes to go they stood and hooked up over a hostile land of flak batteries and anti-aircraft machine guns. As they passed the islands, tiny red dashes of tracer fire floated up lazily from both sides of the plane. They seemed to rise woodenly from their seats, felt blindly for the anchor line, clicked their static line snap fasteners to it and held on. They stood in one line facing the tail, so crammed together that they could hardly breathe. "Shove me," Cutchall said. "Shove me when we go." He was clinging to the static line with both hands.

The plane went slower and slower, the motors getting louder and louder. From the strain on them he could discern that they were still climbing, gaining altitude for the run to the drop zone. A stream of trace bullets floated up at them, speeding up as they passed the windows, disappearing with a rattling burrat. They had reached the mainland, it was just before midnight and the infantry was due on the beaches at six a.m. Some threw up and cursed and Cutch had to catch him from falling in the sudden lurch, as the pilot took evasive action to avoid another flak nest that opened fire on the planes ahead.

Ten thousand Germans. "Oh God," he prayed. He didn't want to blow up in the sky and burn to death. He didn't want to die like a mouse in a can in a garbage dump fire. He wanted to die fighting if he had to die. Let's jump, let's jump. Let's go, let's go, he pleaded silently to himself.

"Check your equipment!" the lieutenant shouted. He felt the snap fasteners on his leg straps. They were closed tightly and in place. How about the reserve snaps, also in place, and the belly band? Good shape. He knew his chest buckle was snapped because it had been digging into his ribs ever since he put on his chute.

Now he checked Cutchall, who stood in front of him, while the soldier behind him checked his pack. Each man was responsible for himself and the man ahead. Cutchall's backpack was all right, the chute was in its cover, the thick sturdy rubber bands still held most of the static line in position.

Burrat! Another machine gun burst crackled around the plane. "Sound off for equipment check!" Up by the pilot's passageway, the lieutenant's command sounded like a child's whisper. The pilot gunned the engines and threw the craft from side to side. An eighty-eight mm shell burst outside with a quick flash and a metallic bang. The blast tilted the plane, throwing the men into their seats. They clutched their way back up again. "Sound off for equipment check," the lieutenant shouted again. He yelled he was okay and Cutchall took up the cry and passed it on. The plane dove toward the ground passing under a string of three white flares that hung malevolently motionless in the sky. The pilot twisted and yawned and raced back up again.

He shook his head and clamped his teeth shut. He was beyond all hope. If you have to die, you have to die, and what a way this is! If you have to jump, you have to jump. A man's life and death are decided by forces he cannot fight. He can only question them and rebel against them, but in the end, he has to go with them. The plane slammed up and down, zigzagged, rattled and roared, threw everyone from side to side with such violence that several fell down. A flash of light came in the window and he glanced outside and saw wisps of clouds streaking by. Now and then a pale moon mocking in its serenity appeared briefly among the long thin, scudding black clouds.

"Close up and stand in the door!" the lieutenant screamed. Left foot forward in lock step, each man pushed hard against the man before him, as the C-47 bounced up and down and gasped for altitude. The motors began to fade somewhat and the plane rustled through the air more slowly. They were finally over the drop zone. "Go!" the lieutenant shouted. He bent over and lifted the ends of the parapaks, slid them out the door and jumped after them. The line of men surged forward. All he could see was the water, miles and miles of water.

This was D-Day, and nobody went back to England. A lot of infantry, riding open barges, seasick from the low tide beaches, were depending on them to draw the Germans off the causeways and gun batteries and so knowing this he grabbed both sides of the door and threw himself at the water.

He fell three hundred feet in three seconds straight toward a huge flooded area shining in the moonlight. He thought he was going to fall all the way, but there was nothing he could do about it except dig his fingers into his reserve of bravery and wait to be smashed flat. All he could do was gape at the water below when suddenly a giant above snapped a whip with him on the end, his chute popping open finding himself swinging wildly in the wind. Twisted in the fall, his risers were unwinding and spinning him around. He was pinned, his head down on his chin on top of his rifle case preventing him from looking up and checking his canopy. He figured that everything was all right, because at least he was floating free in the great silence that always followed the opening shock of the chute opening.

For several seconds he seemed to be suspended in the sky, with no downward motion, and then all at once the body of the water flooded field whirled up and rushed at him. He wrenched desperately at his reserve chutes snap fasteners as the first step for preparing for a water landing. He unsnapped two leg snaps, his chest buckle and the belly band. The next step would have been to drop the reserve and work himself into the seat of his harness so that he could fling his arms straight up and drop the chute when he was ten feet above the water. He didn't have time to begin the procedure.

He had jumped so low, from three hundred feet, instead of the scheduled seven hundred feet, that while he was still wrenching at the first reserve strap he saw the water twenty feet below. He reached up and grasped all four risers and yanked down hard, to fill the canopy with air and slow his descent. Just before he hit he closed his eyes and took a deep breath of air. His feet splashed into the water hard.

Walter crossed himself, taking himself out of his mental journey and gently motioned to Ryan to follow him, with an almost undetectable motion of his hand. They walked toward the American soldiers' grave sites. They passed first through the gate and then down past the visitors' center. Then Ryan saw the first diagonal rows of white crosses. Nothing had prepared him for the impact of the place and the breath stopped in his throat and he drew up short, as he felt the stab of a wordless grief he never knew before. "Oh God," he silently gasped. Suddenly he saw his whole life as if he had already lived it.

Walter, a half step behind, put a hand on his shoulder to steady him, and just as involuntarily he put his other hand over Ryan's shoulder to secure and keep it there. "I know, Ryan, it's very powerful," he barely whispered, out of respect for the dead laid out in front of them.

Ryan stood frozen, thinking of the photographs of the young soldiers, firm-featured boys and men serene in their uniforms, boys who died before the age of twenty, who live on as the embodiment of wasted promise, in photo albums and on pianos and side tables, handsome and confident, unfazed by their doom, while the living survive jobs, errands and household chores and disappointing holidays. There was no pathetic vanity here of enormous gravestones to the rich, just the simple marble stones of our fallen heroes. Here, was war brought home to him in a way he had never expected. Here, far beyond the literature of war, he stood in shock, taken up short, thinking for the first time what war was truly like, in such a way as to revolt him, nauseate him and turn him against war no matter what lofty justifications come out of the mouths of authority. Now he really understood. War was no longer just an abstraction. The numbers of dead were no longer just numbers, the numbers of gravestones no longer just gravestones. The vast cemetery of endless rows of marble headstones had an aesthetic purity of absolute moral indifference, a powerful beauty. Here was the truth of war, the immoral truth. "Oh God."

"Come on with me, Ryan, I want you to meet someone," he whispered again. They walked through the neatly rowed white marble crosses which were interspersed here and there with Stars of David. It took them a while, but finally there was the grave of the fallen soldier Ryan's father had wanted him to meet. On the simple marble cross the name of Ryan Timothy Cutchall, was etched along with his rank, his unit, the 82bd Airborne, the date of his death, June 6, 1944 and the State of Massachusetts. Ryan stared at the monument, and the air seemed to tremble with the beating wings of what might have been. Awe and wonder overtook him. He looked beseechingly at his father, the question he had for him written in the angst and despair that creased his face. "He was my best friend in the battalion, Ryan, and we always jumped together." He paused for a moment now, his thoughts flashing back to the horror he fought to forget. "He took a bullet in the chest just as he landed at the Merderet River overflow. He took his last breath in my arms after I had gathered him up and hid behind a hedgerow," Walter said, tears forming in his eyes. Ryan shifted away from the gravestone, his tearing eyes asking his father the unspoken question.

"Mary and I named you in his memory," he quietly murmured, as tears began to roll down his cheeks. Ryan was struck dumb in the face of feelings that had come unleashed within him, like cargo that became loose in the hold of a plunging ship, and threw himself into his father's arms, the two shaken men weeping the common tears of remembrance and hope. It seemed that all Ryan's life had been a prelude and preparation to this humbling site.

For reasons Ryan would never be able to explain to himself, he felt that coming here with his father had somehow squared an account on which some small balance remained due, that he was now settled in some way, for those who had given their lives in the horrors of his generations Vietnam War.

"So long, Cutch," Walter muttered softly under his breath, as they turned away, and he swore he could hear the spectral voice that answered back.

"So long, Davies."

Chapter 33

It was mid-afternoon and they decided to take lunch at a small inn that turned upon the inland road. They would enjoy the countryside after lunch driving toward Bayeux and the hundred and seventy-mile journey to Paris following the Seine.

The two men, father and son, awoke early. They were billeted at the Plaza-Athenee and as requested were given a large two bedroom two bath agreeable room overlooking Avenue Montaigne. They called down for breakfast and the papers so they could finalize plans in the privacy of their room. They ordered oeufs-brouilles, scrambled eggs made perfectly, the way only the French knew, with flaky croissants and steamy rich coffee. They perused the French papers which were full of grave situations, public outcries and serious inquiries, beguiled by the stately and intellectualized language the French papers used to describe the public life of their nation. American papers by contrast spoke of a politics of personalities and events.

After the papers, they dressed and tried to relax, but they found it difficult to focus their attention on anything but the task ahead. They knew they were moving into new, strange and probably dangerous territory. Ordinary people like himself, Ryan thought, spent their lives light years away from great events, unless they were trapped in a war or an earthquake, and distant from events created and styled by truly powerful men, unless they fell under their command. In this regard Ryan was no different. The power with which he was familiar was limited, the stakes always definable and the risks acceptable. In the end for Ryan it had always come down to money and the acquisition of investor assets. He had never presided over or had been involved with any of the great gripping decisions or actions which seemed to confront him now. Apart from books, he knew nothing of this level of life and had really no sense of how to deal with it. It made him uncomfortable, with his nerve ends dancing on his skin.

Ryan bade his father an emotional goodbye, with a prolonged hug that elicited the silent hopes of luck and safety from peril, at the front door of the hotel, Walter leaving for a flight out of Paris, the two of them going their separate ways, Ryan to Geneva the next morning and Walter ostensibly back to Minnesota. Ryan made his way back up the hotel elevator to the room they had shared to review once more the plans and directions that he would need to carry out beginning the next morning.

Feeling somewhat confident of the nuances of his upcoming task at hand, he went down to the Relais Plaza, the small restaurant on the Rue Marot side of the hotel where all the chic, the Tout-Paris gathered to make air-kisses and frank social wigwags. He had a Byrrh Cassis and took in the show. The café was jammed with elegant, highly attenuated men and women. The sweetish vermouth made him hungry and he ordered a Croque-monsieur, which he ate at the bar. The remainder of the day was at his leisure.

He spent a delicious afternoon by himself, desperately wishing Nan was at his side. He'd thought of visiting the Louvre, but he knew once you got started there you couldn't stop and that was a full day's worth of enjoyment. He dawdled along the Faubourg and then along the Seine, poking into little shops and boutiques. At a fine small gallery on the far side of the Seine, there was an exciting show of Manet etchings. He bought a nice signed work of *Le Guitarero*, knowing that Nan would adore it, and chatted with the gallery's owner. From Vitrines he picked out an Aldine Petracea and a rare French translation of Boswell.

It was little after five when he got back to the hotel and he had a near uncontrollable urge to call Nan and the kids at home, but he knew he could not, as they had agreed as part of their plan, not to call back state side for fear of their calls being traced, through the menacing tentacles that Sophie's father could call upon. He thought he would indulge himself, and called to make a reservation for a table at Chez l'Ami Louis, in the Rue de Vertbois. It was like eating off the curb, the concierge had told him, but the foie gras was the best in Paris, the Beaujolais the best in France, and the frites the best in the world. As was his custom, the old man who owned the café paid neither deference nor attention to the great clients and celebrities that passed through his eatery. He cooked well for all and was rude to all without prejudice. People from all across Paris came to be insulted by Mr. Magnin and to sample his foie gras.

He gorged himself in the non-descript restaurant. It was a splendid meal as he finished the last legs of the wonderful wine, ruing the fact that he was not sharing this with Nan, foreswearing that he would as soon as time and the order of his world allowed. He returned to his hotel by eleven, and crawled into bed where again his exhaustion dropped the curtain on his consciousness.

He dreamt he was in a vast open field pointing a huge musket at a crowd of tethered enemies. Arthur Borgen was there, it seemed, along with other newspaper familiar faces he couldn't quite identify. He pulled the trigger on the Civil War weapon firing a great spray of excrement which drenched the enemies with a reeking mess. Beyond the sounds of his musket's flatulent firings, he seemed to hear voices bringing forth a clean cheery song of triumph. He fired his musket again and again. It was an empowering dream and he didn't want to see it mist away as the alarm on his nightstand so rudely announced six a.m.

It was not until he had dozed a half hour after lifting off from Charles de Gaulle airport that his sanguine state of mind, which had been helped along by the residual entrails of the prior evenings Beaujolais had evaporated enough to let him begin to allow nervous apprehension to take him over as the tasks ahead reclaimed their ominous proportions.

Chapter 34

Approaching the city from the air, he thought of Rome, the once proud mistress of the universe that was originally a band of ruffians, plunder and rapine that had made her rich, her oppression of millions making her great. He had come to understand, through his study of Greek history in college, that the God's who dealt the cards, would even hint sometimes as to how they best be played. He was coming to Rome to meet with the Vatican's second in command, upon the vestigial introduction given him by the Archbishop back in his home state. The Vatican, the sanctified city within a city, with two thousand years of paying no taxes, with diplomatic immunity, while enjoying compound interest. He was hoping on importuning the Vatican for divine assistance.

He hoped the Cardinal would grace and bedizen his plight with his full ecclesiastical habiliments. The Vatican's second in command more importantly was the Director of the Pontifical Council for Justice and Peace, whose stated goal was for the responsibility that the common good must be given primacy over the economy and finance throughout the world. The Pontifical Council had recently released a statement, asserting that institutions like the International Monetary Fund have not been responding adequately to global economic problems. The document had grown out of the Roman Catholic Church's concerns about economic instability and widening inequality of income and wealth.

It was just after Christmas week and the worshipers were few as he walked through the public cathedral in the Cathedral of Rome, noticing that the murmuring worshipers in their habit of faith were few. The man dressed in black looked toward the back of the church and the rows and rows of pews, where in the rear pew a disheveled man wound down his muttering day in the comparative warmth that the Basilica provided.

A sudden urge to kneel and pray came upon the black dressed man and he took to an empty pew and went to his knees. Concerned, as he had always been, with the agonies of men, with injustice and cruelty and madness and fury, he had been too absorbed in his current difficulties, to withdraw into himself and indulge in contemplation. He had rarely thought of God. When certain men had spoken to him of God, he had listened with an inner impatience. What had "God" to do with the immediate and terrible problems of mankind? It was an apotheosis to be indulged in only by metaphysicians, by those who had no real regard for their fellow-man. At its worst "God" had been the fantasy abstraction of the wicked, the foolish, and the tyrants. If the man dressed in black had thought of God in any acute manner in his life, and particularly in the past few years, it had been with a building rage and hatred and detestation.

If there was a "God," how had He been able to stand by in complacent or evil silence through these years and the wars, and see what there was to be seen? How could He have beheld the degradation and violence of mankind, the torture of the innocents, the death and tears and despair of the defenseless, the multitudes who had died with hands uplifted to the mute heavens, and not moved in His eternal might and destroyed their enemies? How many countless prayers must have risen from the ghettos of convulsed countries run over by that madman of Germany, to that silent and heedless God? How many anguished cries for help must have started from the bloody cells of the concentration camps, from the burning walls of churches and synagogues, from the turgid gutters where children died in torment, from blasted homes and shattered fields?

Yet the heavens remained mute. There had been no sign from Him who had declared that it was better that a millstone were hung about a man's neck and he were cast into the sea than that he inflicted suffering upon one of these "little ones." Thousands upon thousands of these "little ones" had perished, their mouths stopped with their own blood, their arms reaching for the mothers who were not there, and yet God had slept, or had not cared. The innocent had died unscored and uncomforted, in agony, torn asunder by man, deserted by God.

Out of the man in black's thoughts, then, out of his anguish for the helpless, for whom no one cared, there had arisen in him a profound hatred and loathing for any "God" who might exist. He suddenly felt his spirit standing naked and alone on a desolate mountaintop, as he knelt in the Cathedral, silently cursing God for the horror He had inflicted on man. There was no excuse, spun his troubling muse, for the apologies and explanations of churchmen, their foolish and outrageous mouthings, the mutterings of those tortured souls, who must have their religion-magic, even in the face of the desperate agonies of the world. There were some who declared that God was "testing" mankind by this horrible spectacle of human depravity and suffering. There were some who promised that those who died helplessly, and in torture, would enter a "better world."

But to the man in black no "better world" was worth the last fluttering, dying gasp in the throat of a little child. What eons of eternal bliss could ever ease the final memory of that death, and hopelessness? If the enemy paid over and over throughout eternity for his cruelty and his madness, it would not be enough to take from the records of time the glazing of one child's bewildered and suffering eye, as it died in loneliness and pain. There was simply no explanation, no excuse, for the last pathetic lifting of a dying child's hand, for the last wild shriek of a mother searching in the ruins for her little baby ruthlessly murdered, for the last groan of a man in a concentration camp. There was no forgiveness for the men who did these things. There was no forgiveness for the God who permitted them.

Now, the man in black fixed his gaze upon the marble altar and the sculptured scene of the Crucifixion behind it. The few morning candles that were lit were like the tongues of angels that were trying to speak to him. He was suddenly overwhelmed by his pain. A universal suffering pervaded him. He felt the universal sorrow of the earth and at last all the hatred that he had felt ebbed away, leaving only tears and sadness behind. He now saw the tormentor suffering equally with his victim, that in the end he died in equal anguish. So the man in black's sorrow was now too deep for despair, too profound for words. He felt the universal aching throughout his spirit, it left a grief too enormous for anything but prayer, for anything but compassion.

The realization, all at once, brought him a solemn and bottomless peace. He watched as the early afternoon sunlight sparkled in breathtaking multi-colored radiant beams through the stained glass of the sainted windows that surrounded the central nave of the Cathedral. Now he began to hear the louder triumphant voices of the earth. He felt no joy however with his peace, no fulfillment. He could not deceive himself that he "understood." He only accepted. How frightful, he thought, to carry into eternity the memory of the horror of men, of the indifference of God, of the mysterious hopelessness of the world!

The man in black knew that a man could not approach God except through his own humanity. He knew also that man approached hell through his own pride, his own vanity, his own hunger for power. Yet, he felt an immense sorrow and grief, and an enormous fear suddenly spread over him.

After some urgent pleas to God for their collective safety he noticed what appeared to be an old leather bound prayer book lying next to him. He picked it up and it fell open at once to a certain page, as if some unseen hand had forcibly turned the pages. The printing was brown and faded and the title and author had long been obliterated from the cover. The man in black looked around the nearly empty cathedral and began to read:

"The desolate heritages of the people, they are heirs to all sadness, all sorrows, all anguishes and agonies. They steal hope and faith, furtively, mournfully, as men search ruins for food. They set out feeble lanterns through a dark land, turning their lights despairingly over meaningless chaos through which deceitful paths run into nothingness, or into pits or chasms. They cry out into the night in response to echoes which mock them; they bivouac in stony mountains. They find nothing, not even guidance, in the cold stars. They come upon empty temples whose fallen gods are nameless. They flee from the bellowing of unseen armies. In the shadows they look for faces of friends, but they find only bodiless ghosts. They wander in the mists, and cower beneath the storms. The earth is to them an unknown and a wild land, hating them as a far land hates the alien.

"And then men think in their hearts: We are strangers, and the earth looks at us with loathing. We have no home, neither in the darkness from which we came, nor in the darkness into which we go. We are lost in an eternity which heeds us not, and only our voices and prayers return to us from the slope of the heavens. In the fugitive dawn there is no light for us. In our death we are alone, and we go into the bottomless abyss without hope, and only with one last cry."

The book seemed to close by itself in his hands. He stood in the tranquil peace of the Cathedral and shuddered, as if struck by an icy wind. He experienced a deep sickness, as though he had fallen a great distance, and he heard the painful beating of his own heart, as he genuflected in the aisle, making the sign of the cross.

The man in black entered through St. Anne's Gate, the Vatican gateway closest to the Tower of Nicholas V, which housed the offices of the IOR.

The office was simple, splendor, and monastic, just as a Holy Man's cell should be, he reasoned, very medieval and pure in spirit, as it was inhabited by one of society's better angels. The white plaster ceiling was carved chastely and the paneled walls glowed richly in the early afternoon sun which poured through the tall windows, the polished glass of which was set in tiny leaded panes. As he waited for the Cardinal in his Vatican office, on the third floor of the south transept, he noticed the wide range of liturgical and patronymic commentaries on the previous Pope's autobiography and the present Pope's latest posturings; a history of the church in America and several volumes of devotional verse and, fittingly he thought, a set of Machiavelli, in the original Italian.

His eminence Cardinal Castilla, was a great figure he knew, but having done his homework with the prolific power of computer research, he knew that this Holy Man, who was also secretly in control of the Institute for Religious Works, the Vatican Bank, understood derivative calculations and knew his yield book and capitalization rates and bond spreads as well as his rosary.

In their minds, as formulated in their sessions together, which seemed so long ago now they had surmised a planned Ponzi scheme of suppositions of half facts and red herrings and the false starts of many surmises and few certitudes. But as they pondered and discussed they could begin to see each successive layer of suppositions building on its predecessor.

He turned now to see the Cardinal enter through the door and was greeted with a smile that was thin as if expressing a certain level of danger. He wasn't imposing, but exuded an inner intensity that was almost palpable. His face was a gray replica of what it might have been in his youth right out of a Catechism reader of the old church, the death mask of a once handsome delicate young priest who could quicken a pious lady's pulse with the resonance of First Corinthians. He had an El Greco lean and intense look, his gazing piercing features seemed attenuated and refined by years of striving and cynicism and ambition and fervor. He had skin that was sallow and taut over his cheekbones and dark eyes that conveyed an impression of immense cumulative weariness, depicting a sort of robed elegant fatigue.

After sharing a very gentle hand shake, the Cardinal moved stiffly around his desk and seated himself, studying his visitor silently for a moment. Walter sat in front of him in the low chair of the supplicant. The Cardinal's eyes were serious yet gentle and he raised his hand with a gesture of ineffable affection, and asked without preamble, "Well, Mr. Davies, what can I help you with?"

"I seek, rather my extended family seeks, a writ of mandamus your

Excellency, and your considered assistance with this matter." After some further conversation and rather lengthy background information being given, there was a prolonged silence.

Finally, the Cardinal sighed. "Ah," he murmured, and lifting his eyes, regarded the ceiling with languid fixity. "I congratulate you and your family on your loyalty and perspicacity," the Cardinal continued at last. "This is potentially a very grave matter." The russet of his brows knitted as he contemplated deeply, stroking his fingers, turning his left hand so that the magnificent ring upon it sparkled in the golden streak of sunlight. The golden shadow of the muted sun chased itself vagrantly over his rigid still features, bringing a deathly aspect that crossed his face. The cardinal remained silent and his fixed smile had something spectral and morbid in it, like the grimace of a corpse. Now he stirred in his great chair and gazed directly at his visitor, and the latter could not read the expression in the Cardinal's eyes.

Sunken in his thoughts, the Cardinal forgot all else. He sighed deeply and there was a floating and dimness in his vision. The visitor now suddenly saw the Cardinal's face swimming before him. The Cardinal inclined his head toward his visitor, lifted his brows and smiled gently. "I have heard rumors of this man of whom you speak," he finally said as he nodded with sympathetic understanding.

The Cardinal's visitor laid a piece of paper gracefully in front of him with sets of geo-coordinates and metallurgical documented yield estimates.

The two men rode down the elevator together and parted, it seemed, in good company. As they entered the public Cathedral, beggars and poor worshipers seemed to creep out of the shadows of the church to intercept the Cardinal. In the darkness of the Cathedral, they were tiny, barely human, figures it seemed, small wads of cloth appended to upturned palms, uttering soft wails, seeming to seek the only moral recognition they ever required, as the Cardinal gracefully shook their hands, bestowing felicitations, blessing them all, putting his fingers to his forehead, as God's blessing upon them. The Cardinal and his visitor watched in silence as the figures enriched now by the blessings of a member of the Pontiff's council returned to the habit of their prayers.

It had been a cordial meeting and Walter hoped it would provide some sort of celestial insulation to their cause, as the two men shook hands and bade each other farewell. The Cardinal watched the Davies patriarch leave and walk across the square. He then turned sharply and carried himself back inside and up the elevator, he didn't stop at his third floor office, but continued higher up in the south transept into his direct access office with his highly sophisticated electronic and digital paraphernalia.

On the wall to the right of his enormous desk he studied the portrait of Richelieu, the Cardinal's model and idol, and thought of the young boy who wanted to become a priest to serve God, the young boy who wanted to become a priest and serve justice. How long had it been, he tried to recall, since the slow crumbling of his conscience had begun, in favor of self-interest and the resulting corruption of his soul? He hesitated for a moment, plunged in the nagging tumult of his thoughts, and then he plugged the coordinates his visitor had given him into the computer, through a secured Vatican web site and waited.

The man in black, now back out on the street walking along the Tiber river which Shakespeare had insisted Caesar had swum with all his armor on, hoped that perhaps the exemplary research and knowledge provided by his family members and co-conspirators had paid its dividend. Only the nearing of time and the coming of their next maneuvers would tell.

Chapter 35

As Ryan flew into the Geneva airport in southern France bordering the Swiss Alps, the clouds were thinning with breaks here and there that disclosed dark pine forests dotted with necklaces of blue-black lakes. To the east the towering spires of the peaks of the Alps rose into a row becoming as pristinely blue as an angel's eye sky.

Ever since the first time he had seen the Swiss Alps on one of his family's vacation trips, the image had never been entirely absent from his inner eye. He gazed out now upon the beautiful Alps and the new fallen snow wondering when his family's duty dance would end. It was as if another six inches of snow had fallen on a hundred-inch base of his-own personal insecurity. He felt as if he was like Oedipus in the Greek myth brought here to solve the riddle of the sphinx, who was then blinded by the Gods for solving a mystery that should be kept beyond the scope of our reason, or could it be more like the myth of ancient Greek God Phaeton, who tried to drive the chariot of the sun across the sky, but fell to a fiery crash upon the earth? Or perhaps he was more like the earthly personification of the young pure Icarus, who in Greek mythology escaped the complexities of the Labyrinth, by putting on waxen wings made by his father Daedalus and then flew, despite his father's warning, too close to the sun and fell tragically to earth.

The late afternoon sky was a deepening gray pocket with a bluish scud of clouds, the skies becoming dreary once more with snow making its way upon the region and it looked as if the entire area of the Matterhorn almost five thousand feet high was curling in on itself like a dying leaf. The wind whirled and cut through the leafless trees and sleeping winter pines, skidding gustily along the wondrously arched Alps, the frozen lakes lying below under skies as gray and lifeless as dead skin, eerily prefiguring perhaps his personal storms in the offing.

Taking in the immensity of the Alps, he a gave resolute head shake, in an effort to detach the mental cobwebs, that seemed to drift back and forth, his silent voice brave with the courage of his hope, wishing to transform assurance into certainty, knowing in his heart the game here was worth the candle and worthy of the demanding patronage. It all came down to this point in the drama, on his earthly sojourn, an unraveling period, Ryan thought, an equinox era and a transition toward shorter days and longer nights, at a time when he would have to rely on his pedigree and run metaphorically uphill with a full heart.

He had simply run in place it seemed for so long now, merely treading the lake waters in the beautiful Indian summer of his Minnesota homeland. Now here on the edge of the Swiss Alps, overlooking the resort town of Sta. Marta, he hoped the cool early winter high altitude air would bring clarification as he was a-swim with ambiguities. They will have seen plenty like me before, he mused as the Air France DC7 made its descent, orphans of the storm, like Tristan in the epic Greek myth traveling on the sea without an oar or a rudder, making his way by playing his harp, driftwood washed ashore by the complex tides of life, looking like everyone, for love and explanation.

It struck Ryan, as he drove his rented Peugeot to Geneva along the shores of Lake Le Ban, that he was a persona absolutely at one with the deeper idiom of his own culture, which was America's preoccupation with the success of winning, as opposed to the European's Proustian exercise in the mourning of loss. Here Ryan found himself separated by culture, geography and focus, haunted by the inability to face down his mounting anxieties that he may have to be forced by his own lights, to consider himself a failure. As he drove toward the edge of the French Alps and the Hotel Auteuil in central downtown Geneva, near the La Perce-Du-Lac Park and the Jet d'Eau Fountain for the night, he realized he needed surcease from the danger dancing on his nerve ends for the last thirty-six hours.

He parked the Peugeot along the Rue de Lausanne a half block away from the hotel, checked in under his own name, and took the elevator to his twelfth floor room, grabbing a Kronenbourg from the minibar and a bag of French pecans. Well, here he was, he thought, as he looked out upon the majestic peaks and caverns of the Swiss Alps, finally able to relax. He suddenly felt the restoration of those feelings that told him they were doing something worthwhile, something that made transcendent his own dissatisfaction with the world. It was as if this battle was somehow the last redoubt, the final test for the rejection of the new religion back in America of unbridled greed and the abandonment of thoughtful consciousness. He finally fell asleep into a maze of troubled and uneasy dreams.

There was a voice in them that called for the vengeance of heaven, the compassion of saints, the retribution of the whole world. Like Genghis Khan, the powerful had spread their banquet cloths upon the dying bodies of the helpless, and had feasted loudly above the groaning poor. Surely there was a day of liberation coming, and let those beware of who stood in the path of the bloody deluge. He heard it again in his dream as before, the shrieking of a multitude of voices, the rushing of millions of liberated feet. For, when that day came there would be no mercy for the oppressors, for the smug and secure in their gated estates, sitting comfortably next to the warm fires of their own indifference, for the mitred despoilers of the people, for the thrones and kings.

I fear no man, he heard the spectral voices in his dream resound, and fear nothing except man's wickedness and depravity and lack of heart. I sing the songs of the people so that the deaf ear of power may be touched and the heart of majesty be moved. I sing of pity and justice and mercy, not the artificial and dainty songs intended to please the decadent ears of the idle, the soft and the rich. Now, dimly for just an instant, it became clear and powerful, a liberation for all men, a liberation from slavery and oppression, from suffering and exploitation, from serfdom and starvation and cruelty. It was the coming of age of countless multitudes, bent under whips, sightless and tormented. He felt the stirrings of universal compassion, of impersonal anger and indignation. Toward dawn, these dreams of mysterious excitement had drifted and faded and become nightmares filled with angst and pain.

Chapter 36

The plan for the following day, as designed by the family with Sophie's input being invaluable, was for Ryan to travel the southern route to Zug, Switzerland, going around the Northern shoreline of Lake Geneva, through Lausanne, Montreux and Matigny and on to Sion for the night, checking in with his conspirators that evening via the secret codes of numbers they had devised with an answering service they had set up in Nova Scotia.

The morning was gray and cold with a new three-inch snow blanketing the city streets and the Alpine Valleys that appeared in the distance of his vision, as Ryan took the Rue de Lausanne, leaving Geneva, known worldwide as the capital of Peace, to route one taking the third exit off the roundabout to the A1 toll road, showing the vignette toll sticker that he had purchased earlier that morning to the attendant as he passed through the toll booth. The countryside off to his right was breathtaking, dotted with family farms, dormant now for the winter, with cattle here and there grazing on hay, with Lake Geneva serving as the background, like the palette for a painting. He could see on the slope below a small village with its white wooden-steepled church. Beyond and below the village was the lake, gray and lifeless without the sun. A steamer churned its way to Geneva. In front of him the jagged white peaks of the Alps stretched everywhere like white cathedrals in the distance.

The towns he passed were clean and orderly, the fields geometrically precise, the buildings, with their great barns and sweeping slanted eaves, were witness to a solid, substantial, peaceful life, firmly rooted in a prosperous past. It was a landscape for peace and continuity and one could not imagine armies charging over it, fugitives fleeing through it.

It was difficult, Ryan mused, forcing himself not to allow the stunning views, as he drove through the canton of Vaud, to keep him from remaining conscious of his family duty, to convince his father that he should be the one called to duty to this phase of their strategic set of plans. Ryan would act as the decoy, the bait, the goat tethered to the rope in the open field, as Sophie had described it, ostensibly making his way to Zug, Bern or Basel via southern Switzerland and then northward through the dangerous Nufenen Pass.

As he drove east toward Lausanne in light mid-morning traffic, he imagined himself to be part of a highly ironic version of the success story, a redemption plot, in which the protagonists pursue values that were once esteemed, money, renown, career, love, winning, success, yet with a degree of compulsiveness and blindness that would carry them to the brink of destruction, standing to lose if not their lives, their humanity, stooping before they went over the edge, throwing away what they once cherished. Would this protagonist, he asked himself, as he played out the drama of the movie spinning in his head, sacrifice his dream, in the carrying out of his blinded courage, or would he gain, in the end, an honest, sane and balanced life?

Ryan stopped in Lausanne, as it was still early in his itinerary of travel, and took lunch at the Les Trois Rois café on the Rue du Simplon, that the concierge in the Geneva Hotel had recommended, in the Ouchy waterfront area. He enjoyed a light salad of local farm raised greens, with slices of local range fed beef and home grown cheeses. He enjoyed the view from Lausanne, that was called the San Francisco of Lake Geneva, and the Lavaux Vineyards that covered the slopes that drifted majestically in front of him to the edges of the lake below, imagining Nan was with him to take in the splendor of the beauty that was given to him.

He remembered now the telling of the history of Arthur Borgen as told by Sophie at his home two months prior. The stock market crash of 1929 and the resulting depression also bankrupted the Wall Street backed German Steel Trust. When the German government took over the Trust's stock shares, interests associated with Konrad Adenauer and the anti-Nazi Catholic Center Party tried to buy the shares. However, the Union Bank run by Averell Harriman and Prescott Bush working in concert with Montagu Norman the governor of the Bank of England and a vocal supporter of Hitler and fascism, made certain that the German Steel Trust, operated by the Thyssen family and Frederich Flick, regained control over the trust shares.

In May 1933, after the Nazis consolidated power, an agreement was reached in Berlin coordinating all Nazi commerce with the United States. Under the agreement Harriman International, headed by Oliver Harriman, first cousin to Averell, would lead a syndicate of a hundred and fifty firms and individuals to conduct all exports from Germany to the United States.

By 1934, with Hitler in solid control of Germany, the profits from the Thyssen-Flick union soared to more than a hundred million. Both Union Bank and the Bank voor Handel en Scheepvaart were overflowing with money. Prescott Bush became managing director of Union Bank and took control of all the daily operations of the German plan.

Instead of divesting himself of Nazi money and activities, Prescott Bush hired Allen Dulles to hide Nazi assets. Dulles' client list from the New York law firm of Sullivan and Cromwell showed his first assignment at Brown Brothers Harriman, to be June 18, 1936. The entry, Sophie's researchers had discovered, listed his work at Brown Brothers, to be the "Disposal of Standard Oil Investing Stock".

Standard Oil was another of Dulles' clients who hired him to cloak agreements with the German industrial conglomerate IG Farben. By January 1937, all of Standard Oil's Nazi activities were conducted in one account, "Brown Brothers Harriman-Schroeder Rock." Schroeder was the Nazi bank in which Dulles served as a director. The Rock referred to the Rockefellers. In May 1939, Dulles handled another problem for Brown Brothers Harriman listed as "Securities Custodian Accounts".

On July 31, 1941, the New York Herald Tribune ran a bold headline, "Hitler's Angel Has $3 million in U.S. Bank." The article described Thyssen as that angel and reported that the money actually belonged to "Nazi bigwigs," including Goebbels, Herman Goering, Heinrich Himmler or even Hitler himself. The account was deposited in Union Bank.

Shortly after the bombing of Pearl Harbor, leaks from Washington suggested Prescott Bush was under investigation for aiding the Nazis in time of war. Once again, rather than divesting himself of the Nazi accounts and his pro-Nazi activities, Prescott Bush wrapped himself in the flag. He became the national chairman of the United Service Organization's annual fund campaign. The subterfuge didn't work, however, as the government's investigation continued.

On October 20, 1942, under the authority of the trading with the Enemy Act, the U.S. Congress seized UBC and liquidated its assets. The seizure was confirmed by Vesting Order No. 248 in the U.S. Office of the Alien Property Custodian and signed by U.S. Alien Property Custodian Leo Crowley. The Vesting Order listed the stockholders and all those listed were directors of Union Bank.

Government records showed that Bush and Harriman not only hid their

Nazi activities from the government, using bearer bonds and stocks to conceal their ownership, but also continued dealing with the Nazis unabated. These activities included financial dealing with the city of Hanover and several industrial firms while Averell Harriman was serving as President Roosevelt's personal emissary to the United Kingdom.

Shortly after the United States entered World War II, through key contacts at the University of Chicago where Arthur Borgen had earned his master in economics, he became a property control agent of the Alien Property Custodian that the Roosevelt administration had established. The APC and its agents quickly seized twelve thousand, three hundred patents, five thousand of which covered chemicals, pharmaceuticals and munitions. The APC was part of an operation directed by the Foreign Economic Administration in coordination with the Department of U.S. Treasury's Allied Control Office, to recover assets looted by the Nazis, under the clandestine direction of Allen Dulles. The ACC had the legal right to all German assets under the Vesting Decree. It was the U.S. Treasury, Sophie's research team had discovered, that insisted the Swiss government recognize the ACC Vesting Decree and agree to return to the Allies for reparations an estimated $378 million in looted gold by the Nazis.

The allies used various methods and programs to recover Nazi gold. Poland took the first measures against Nazi looting by moving their gold reserves to Romania before they were invaded. Unluckily, the Nazis soon overran Romania too, and seized their gold. Several other countries in Europe made similar efforts. The French officials at the National Bank shipped their gold to the United States. At the end of 1939, Belgium entrusted the French with $223 million for safekeeping. Soon after the German invasion of the Low Countries, Belgium urged France to ship its gold to London aboard military cruisers. However, the French transferred the gold to Dakar, its West African colony of Senegal. After the fall of France and negotiations with Vichy, the Nazis got their Belgian gold. Other European Nations who failed to take any precautions found their gold seized as soon as they were overrun. It was in this manner, Sophie's research had explained, that most of the gold reserves in the central banks of Europe fell to the Nazis, except for those of France and a portion of those of the Dutch.

On January 5, 1943, the Inter-Allied Declaration against Acts of Dispossession Committed in Territories under Enemy Occupation or

Control, better known as the London Declaration, was announced. The measure declared that the Allies would no longer recognize the transfer of property in occupied countries, even if it appeared legal. The allies were aware that the Nazis were forcing people in occupied countries to sell or transfer their property to them. Up to that time, the Nazis had painstakingly created the illusion that such transfers were legal.

On February 22, 1944, the United States announced in its Declaration on Gold Purchases that it would no longer recognize the transfer of gold loot from the Axis, nor buy gold from any country that had not broken relations with the Axis. England and the Soviet Union followed with similar declarations.

In July and August of 1944, the Bretton Woods Agreement was reached, calling on neutral countries to prevent disposition or transfer of assets in the occupied countries. On August 14, 1944, the U.S., UK, and Swiss War Trade Agreement was reached, requiring the Swiss to reduce trade with the Nazis.

Then on December 6, 1944, Operation Safehaven was organized and just four days later the State Department released a paper urging a soft line toward Switzerland. This was the first step, Sophie's research had explained, in sabotaging efforts to return assets to Holocaust victims. In essence it continued the long standing feud between the Treasury and State Department regarding peace terms.

It was into this milieu of agencies that Arthur Borgen operated during World War II, becoming eventually connected to the OSS. It was the OSS directed by William Donovan that collected and evaluated most of the data for Safehaven. Within OSS, Safehaven was confined to the SI (Secret Intelligence) and X2 counter intelligence divisions. It was X2 where Sophie discovered Borgen was involved with assisting the German effort to transfer looted assets to foreign countries.

The Safehaven operation however was dependent on the personalities of the various OSS station chiefs. In Switzerland, Allen Dulles was the station chief, and he had already been exposed in an earlier operation, a joint program with the British, on spying on America and he was suspected of being sympathetic to the Nazi cause. Roosevelt had deliberately sent Dulles to Switzerland, where he would be most tempted to help his clients. When Dulles reached Berne he was aware that he was being watched, thus knowing he could not use official channels to help his clients in the United

States. So he used his Vatican connections to help the Nazis and couriers with diplomatic immunity. The Vatican readily agreed to help Dulles in its zeal to regain its assets in Germany and further its fanatical anti-communist philosophy.

Dulles and his comrades, of whom Borgen was a part, exerted a good deal of influence to ensure that U.S. investments in Nazi Germany were not seized for reparations. In Switzerland, the German SS bought a large amount of stock in American corporations and laundered money through the Chase and the Corn Exchange Banks. Even more brazen, her magazine's researchers discovered, was the case of Pan Am clippers hired by W.R. Grace Corporation, to transport Nazi gems, currency, stocks and bonds to South America. These operations were the product of Dulles' money laundering for the Nazis. Several American officers readily admitted that much of the Nazi gold was never returned over to them. One officer told of being in a huge vault filled with gold, gems and currency that never appeared in any U.S. files.

Dulles and his agents, to whom Borgen was directly linked, backed Germany for a long time, viewing it as a bulwark against the Soviets. The young Lt. William Casey was another OSS agent, Sophie's staff had discovered, who shared this view of Germany. Casey served in the SI division in France and the Lowlands following liberation. In a report from Paris, Casey wrote that Safehaven was a valuable field of endeavor, especially because of the potential for leverage with German financial circles. After the war, Casey worked on Wall Street before becoming Reagan's CIA director.

In 1946, Dulles' men, including one Arthur M. Borgen, simply changed their OSS uniforms and became the War Department Strategic Service Unit. Sometimes they were the War Department Detachment; other times the Document Disposal Unit. In effect as Sophie had explained, there were two factions left from the OSS, a liberal faction that took orders from the President, and the other under the control of Dulles. The latter faction was hoping for a conservative victory by Dewey so it could unleash an émigré army against the Soviets.

Due to Dulles' close association with German industrialists, he was unwilling to give the attention to Safehaven that Washington expected. In November 1944, with the Allies now in control of France, a land route to Switzerland was reestablished, making it possible to send an X2 agent to

Bern to help run the Safehaven program there. By April 1945, X2 in Bern had unearthed a great deal of information on Nazi dealings including: gold and bonds looted from Europe that was received by certain Swiss banks, and additional funds that were sent by the Deutsche Verkehrs-Kreditbank of Karlsruhe to Basel. They also discovered stocks and bonds held in Zurich by private firms for the Nazi party, along with hoards of Swiss francs credited to private accounts in various Swiss banks.

This information gleaned in less than four months by the X2 agent, only confirmed other information that surfaced over the years that Dulles was working hard for the Nazis to hide their loot. Dulles was a friend of the American director of the Bank for International Settlements and top Nazi banking officials.

After the investigation into his money laundering, Dulles resigned from the OSS and returned to New York to seek out Thomas McKittrick, the former head of the Bank of International Settlements. The Nazis by that time had moved many of their assets from Switzerland to Argentina. Dulles soon went to work for a staggering number of Argentine clients, Sophie's research had discovered. He and Donovan agreed that every effort should be made to sabotage Truman and the liberals. To this end, Dulles inveigled Donovan into serving on the board of the World Commerce Corporation, where Dulles was the lawyer. Nazi money flowed in a circle, through Germany, to Switzerland, to the Vatican, then on to Argentina. Argentina's economy boomed from the influx, the so called economic miracle of the 1950s came from the same money, her researchers had found, the Nazis looted from Europe in the 1940s.

Then in the early sixties, Dulles and many of his henchmen including Borgen were fired after Kennedy discovered he was duped after taking office as related to the bogus "missile gap" that Dulles had manipulated.

And here he was, Ryan thought, in Switzerland whose main "industry" was regimentation and a commitment to secrets and complicit silence, a nation restrained by the trusteeship of other people's money, that highly addictive OPM, guardians of the neutral ground for the World Trade police. Here he was, in the middle of some worldly ramifications he still couldn't fully get his head around. His cerebrum ached, the warning signal of his psyche on ultra-high alert, even as he looked out over Lake Geneva and the snow-capped Alps that flanked her southern shores.

Ryan finished lunch, and stopped at a little gift shop along the rue and purchased a postcard of the city with its backdrop of Lake Geneva, slipping it into the jacket pocket of his blue wool blazer. It was two o'clock as he began the second leg of his journey around the northern and eastern portions of the lake traveling on E62, through the idyllic countryside flanked to the left by the Alps fashioning their snowy presence in the distance, through Montreux and Matigny, and to Sion, the home of Anzere Ski Resort.

Merging onto A9 from E62, Ryan took the first exit to Sion and then the third exit off the roundabout, to Av. des Mayennets and the little city's quaint downtown. He parked along a street off the river-walk and, with his daub kit as his only companion, stopped at a payphone to code in his whereabouts, bought a six pack of Appenzeller bier and checked into the Hotel Des Vignes. Later that evening he had a nerve driven light dinner of veal and salad at a nearby restaurant, Enclose de Valere, busy with groups of skiers visiting from Italy. He returned to his room by ten thirty hoping the warm sheets and blankets that covered him would provide some needed sleep, against increasing restlessness.

Chapter 37

The street was still unlit and at this hour empty of traffic or pedestrians, so the figure dressed in black was able to discharge his task in his customary matter-of-fact way. He did nothing wasteful, made no movement which was not precise, economical and efficient.

Crouching at the curb, beside the Peugeot, he molded the clay like substance into short, plump rolls about an inch long. There was enough for just four such rolls; the rest of the slab brought from Chicago had been deployed earlier, on a bigger job. It was new materiel, the latest thing, more powerful and workable than the stuff the Irish and the Mossad were using, and eminently more stable. Expensive stuff indeed, there were only ten plats in existence. It had cost a half million Deutsche Marks to purchase the unauthorized exit of five of these from the closely watched experimental laboratory of the Hoechst plant outside Duisberg. Five slabs were made with one going to London, one to Paris, one to Bangkok, and two to Baghdad. It was one of the latter that had been flown in a diplomatic pouch to Chicago, to rendezvous with the man kneeling behind the front right tire, who himself had just arrived from Damascus.

The man was well traveled. He was given to making painstaking estimates of the trivia of his life, estimating that the ink used in the entry stamps in his four passports would aggregate nearly half a kilo. This was not his first trip to France or Switzerland.

He didn't go in for gadgetry, no tooth darts, grenades made up to look like shaving canisters, or cars that flew. Good stuff for the movies, but unreliable in the strange hotel rooms or dark roads where he got most of his work done. He wasn't a mass bomber, trying to pinpoint the blow-off of kilotons of TNT to vaporize a passing car. He killed chosen people one at a time and alone. He didn't scatter his inventory of death. Besides, working as he did, hundreds, thousands of miles away from Damascus, he couldn't possibly cope with the paraphernalia his associates insisted on lugging around to their latest mass outrage.

He could shoot, if necessary, but better he knew exactly how and where to hit a man and send him down the short road to eternity. He always worked alone, figuring that his own wits would stand him best if not responsible for the conduct and safety of anyone else. He didn't care where the battlefield was pitched. He wanted only first tools and a margin of flexibility. He would have none of the headline grabbing stuff. He was a careful man and he would take on any assignment. A wife and three daughters buried in Lebanon, charred by Israeli flamethrowers had cemented his purpose. A small store of technical knowledge, six languages, five passports and an American Express card were all he needed to get on with the job. He intended to meet the Prophet Shod, smiling and at peace in the heat of his beloved desert.

He finished shaping the explosive, taking from his pocket a pair of standard circular, half volt camera batteries. Each had a hair fine copper filament soldered to its surface, the last sixteenth of an inch shielded with plastic winding. One by one, he pinched the middles of the explosive sausages flat and then with his thumbs very gently and carefully, pressed the batteries into the rolls. Taking a bottle of clear nail polish from his jacket pocket, he coated the joining of the plastic and battery case, leaving the filament loose and clean.

Using a penlight, he examined each battery for the numerals one to four which he had scratched on their surfaces earlier. Placing number one carefully on the pavement, he felt under the right front tire fender of the Peugeot, reaching around the back of the tire, to the groove which signaled the meeting of the rubber and the rim. He left his finger there to mark the spot and with his right hand brought out a tube of special epoxy cement. From his finger down, he squeezed what he had judged to be a half inch dab along the tire rim. He gave it thirty seconds to set, then picked up the explosive and pressed it gently into the hardening epoxy. It was fixed hard and the man in black smiled.

Slab number two went into the same place on the right rear tire. He loosened up the trunk in the rear and placed number three on top of the tire. It had taken forty minutes and only twice had he been obliged to flatten himself into the night as a car passed. The street was not much visited this time of the early morning.

The job finished, he walked down the hill to the rented car he'd left parked at the bottom of the street. No one would notice a middle-aged man walking briskly to his automobile even at this time of morning. His car displayed a set of "M.D." plates purloined at the Lyon Airport. The man made a U turn and drove back to an all-night self-service petrol station he'd noted during his survey of the area. He parked on the far side of the self-service island, which screened the view of the drowsy attendant in his glassed booth. He pumped a tankful of gas and while the meter ticked changed the license plates back.

Stopping just after passing the outskirts of the city of Sion, he threw the other plates into the mouth of the Sionne River and the Rhone River that lie below A9 highway. He headed for his hotel near Sierre to the east where no one would notice or care at the sight of his car pulling up in front of his room at nearly five in the morning. It had been a long day and he was thankful he could sleep at least for a few hours.

Chapter 38

Ryan did not sleep well at all, awakening from a confusion of dreams, although he lay in bed until dawn, feeling alone and lost in the outer darkness without friend or faction, in a frightening place until the slant of the angle of the new sun flashing through the wood slatted shades finally made him rise, under the weight of his fear and exhaustion, driving him toward his mission. Part of his confused state which assaulted him was due to the struggle between his inner conviction of his natural invulnerability, and reality, the realization that for the first time he had been catapulted into the tempestuous world of craven adult men and their murderous adult acts. He had clung to boyhood in the manner of all men who naturally hated responsibility and the necessity to think and reason. Consequently, to some degree he had played at all things, and in that measure, had been the secret of his former invulnerability, though he had failed to know this. Did he truly believe that one such as him could have the true sternness and fortitude to engage in anything of such a formidable nature?

But now, to his secret dismay, he discovered that he stood in the raw and blinding lightning of this dangerous mission, which he had entered out of a degree of sheer light-heartedness and restless exuberance. Until the night before, he had still felt himself invulnerable, a player in an exciting melodrama. But now he saw death or ruin before him, in ruthless and violent colors that darkened his heart. His father had spoken of them to him, on many occasions, and he had listened patiently and respectfully, loftily declaiming that such contingencies could never induce him to turn back. Now, in horror, he saw that Ryan Davies was not invulnerable.

It was not that he was afraid, as much as it was that all his life he had tried to avoid anything disagreeable or final, and now he found himself confronted by both.

He sat now on the edge of his bed and thought deeply and fully, it seemed, for the first time in his life. It was a painful process and he felt ashamed, as he blinked at the inexorable light that dawned blindingly before him. He was dismayed at the realization that he could not withdraw. All noble reflections vanished, as they always do in the final awakening of a man to the maturity of his task. Only grim resolve and duty remained. He could not withdraw because, in his thirty-fourth year, he had at last become a man, and had broken through the bright and vari-colored brittle crust of delusion, and stood now on the black and iron ground of reality. It was a dreary awakening that he had not expected, as the chill wind off the Alpine mountains entered his room. His past life was forever behind him.

He stood up and looked about him, and felt a strange emotion as he suddenly remembered, and he felt nothing but compassion.

It was just past nine a.m as he traveled on A9 to E62, proceeding east for twelve miles taking the second exit on the roundabout to Rte. 19 for seven miles, moving left onto the Quatiere Quartina Airole, three miles to Rte. 2 for four miles and to Rte. 51 which began to track the deep treacherous caverns of the Alps. Ryan's fingers uncontrollably increased their grip pressure as his eyes reflexively blinked twice in near disbelief, as the sign foretold of the presence of the Nufenen Pass that lay four miles ahead, between the summits of the Plaza Gallina to the north and the Nufenstolic to the south.

He was to stop two miles before he reached the beginning of the pass, and engage the vehicular computer drive system that Sophie had so ingeniously developed with the help of a brilliant engineer friend of hers at MIT. They had put together an exact computer model of the contours of each yard of the eight mile stretch of the most dangerous hair pin turns along the pass, where Sophie had discovered in the papers that the detective uncovering her mother's suspicious death had discovered, where Sophie's mother had found that Borgen had conducted at least six mysterious fatal accidents in the past.

Through Sophie's own private research she had discovered at least nine more such accidents along the other dangerous passes, such as the Simplon Pass, the Gothard Pass, the Grand St. Bernard Pass and the Splugen and Goiden passes, that had Borgen's and his agency's footprint all over them. Sophie had verified through cross referencing the Vesting Orders that were cryptically registered with the Treasury Department, showing the acquisition of patent rights on pharmaceuticals, chemicals and mineral rights and the previous owners registered names in the Swiss banks where the property was held in secrecy and the dates in which the accidents in Switzerland had occurred. In every case there was a direct link to the previous owner's mysterious death and Borgen's agency in acquiring the Vesting Order.

It was what they were going on, for there was what you thought, there was what you know, and there was what you could prove, and Sophie was sure it would be the snare that would bring about the proof they needed: satisfaction for her and the Davies family and eventually the law, for her father's grave misdeeds, once and for all.

Ryan slowed the car to a stop, thankful there was no one behind him and engaged the VCS computer system he had affixed that morning to the steering column, plugging the electrical circuit into the lighter socket, set the speedometer to thirty miles per hour, put his driver's license and the rest of his ID into his wallet leaving it atop his daub kit, put the Peugeot in drive and rolled out the door, kicking it shut behind him as he fell to the slick pavement of the pass.

He frantically ran along the other side of the road at the base of the high arching Alps away from the deep caverns south of the Pass that lay eight thousand, one hundred and thirty feet below. He ran as fast as he could, taking cover along the way down outside the western edges of the pass, among the Alpine firs in the cold crisp January air. There was no traffic thankfully, as he waited breathing heavily, his heart racing as it had never done before, his breath forming a faint gray mist in air around the pine boughs that encircled him. Four, five, then, six, seven, eight minutes passed, he estimated, nervously glancing at his wristwatch. It was eerily quiet, the day having turned from blue skies scudded with heavy white clouds, now turning darker with icy snow beginning to fall, in the chilly silence, as he watched the snowflakes nestle upon the pine boughs. Then in a horrible moment everything presented itself to him and suddenly he knew, and saw his whole life as if he had already lived it.

There was a thunderous crack and then in a microsecond the universe across the Nufenstolic Valley four thousand plus feet below, and the universe seemed born all over again in a frightful burst of noise and incandescence. The earth seemed to rock and there was a momentary whirlwind visible in the air over the valley ahead. A plume of smoke rose in the distant sky to Ryan's right across the valley, as the Peugeot burst into pieces and was turned into a piece of scrap and fell nearly a mile to the base of the valley. Ryan shivered, feeling the nervous chill of energy flowing menacing along his spinal cord. Suddenly he felt the vast isolation that every man endures, alone in his flesh, the world as he knew it sent wobbling on its axis.

Further down the pass, a man dressed in dark clothing, standing outside his car hidden on a service road winced at the explosion. He counted thirty seconds slowly by as the pillar of smoke had reached what he estimated was twelve stories high. He grinned, knowing there wouldn't be anyone left within a hundred yards of the burst, to fill a measuring cup. Ryan stood in shock watching the scene from the other side of the valley. His life now suddenly seemed lost and lonely upon the mighty breast of the earth. It was the cold and terrible loneliness of man, every man, and of the lost America, who had been brought forth naked and under immense and lonely skies to act for himself, to grope his way blindly through the confusion and brutal chaos of life, as naked and unsure as he, to wander blindly down across the continent, in search forever for a goal, a street, a dwelling place of warmth and certitude, a light, a door.

The sirens from some distant town, perhaps Airolo, finally broke him out of his hypnotic trance. Now, he felt oddly free and clean suddenly, as when you come to see that, after being paralyzed by ignorance you can finally act. He felt on the verge of the act. A man doesn't make a decision to swim when he falls into the lake, he simply starts kicking. He turned smoothly and as quietly as he could and began to make his long trek back to Visp, the nearest town, and his way back to Geneva, taking shadow in the heavily pined landscape as he progressed, as the staccato sounds of the sirens of police and ambulance passed directly in front of him.

It took him about an hour to make his stealth return to Visp, just south of the Nufenen Pass, where he paid thirty-seven dollars in U.S. currency and boarded the fast train just after two p.m. for points west and Geneva.

He felt nearly pulverized with excitement at the prospect of victory, and yet terrified as he had never been before, feeling the mortal exhaustion in his flesh, as he sat in the upper level viewing through the panoramic windows of the modern train, the stunning views of the valley below checkered with the red roofed farmhouses that sat along the Rhone river and the spine, the exoskeletons of the snow coated Alps that glowed radiant and bright, in the afternoon sun. It all passed him rapidly, as did the stations of man, changing ruthlessly, like the fun house barrel that always turned but never slowed. He was frightened, that scooped out hollow, distending fear, the flutter of the huge black wings, the old aboriginal dread of a pitiless universe. Once a man felt it, is he never the same again?

His imagination became acute and paranoid and found fresh terrors in the inchoate monsters appearing along the alpine forests. As the train sped by he felt a universal and diffused agony creep up on his nerve endings.

Was he to believe now that evil was more powerful than good? That it is a distinct entity, pure and unsullied, like a devouring flame, that the hearts of men are steeped in natural wickedness. It is a reality, Ryan's thoughts spun as a newly acquired sore pained his brain. Evil was a reality, like a holocaust, like a storm, like a tidal wave. Who can explain the dark deviousness and hatred of the evil human heart? The world was a comedy for those who think and a tragedy for those who feel, he remembered reading somewhere. Was that true? But after what he had just witnessed, what about those who both thought and felt?

Mankind could not rid himself of hatred, Ryan thought. Now he knew as the vision of the exploding Peugeot flashed in front of him, that all men lived in hatred for all other men. From the single root of hate blossomed the poisonous fruit of all vices. But how could a man destroy natural hatred in himself? He saw that man's great conquest, great crusade, great adventure, was in the destruction of the hatred which was born in his own heart. Men were too heavy with history; their memories were too long.

They could not forget, surrounded and choked with the past as they were. Tradition was a labyrinth in which the world was forever caught.

Hatred was a perpetual miasma. We must be done with it. We must leave it, if we are to truly live. The tides of liberation over time had always been forced once more into the dark and formless future. The helpless and the innocent, reason and enlightenment, had suffered yet another death. The sleeping ages still slept in the womb of time, awaiting the avenging hour, awaiting the foolish voices that forget the past, awaiting the form and substance of heroic men who knew that tyranny and hatred never slept, and watched only for the hour to arise again.

Ryan's senses whirled in confusion and chaos; as he awoke from a dream where he heard the spectral voices of unborn men and women singing, their heads raised in in hope and triumph, in victory and freedom, in everlasting conquest over the forces of darkness and evil, superstition, ignorance and fear and hatred.

The world rolled away from him like a raveling ball of mist in the gray afternoon skies, vanishing into eternal fogs. The aching pain in his head and heart extended so that it seemed to him that all the universe throbbed with it. It was necessary to believe in oneself, but sometimes it seemed impossible he thought, as the Swiss scenery passed, the aesthetics of nature providing him with much needed surcease. One was a series of spasms and flashes, without much consistency he was telling himself, protean and infantile, but that would have to do, perhaps it's just how it was. All he knew for sure was that the loneliness was too hard.

On returning to Geneva, at the Cornavin Train Station, he made his way on foot to his hotel that he had checked into the day before, stopping at a payphone to leave his coded message with the Nova Scotia answering service, punching the button impatiently.

"I'm sorry, your call cannot go through as dialed, please…" The metric monotone with which "Ma Bell" adolesced her impatient erring children. Terror and dread immediately overtook him, once again, as he forced himself to calmly breathe in a deep cleansing breath of chilly air. He punched in the number again in a slow perfunctory manner, nearly bursting with relief when the call went through. He punched in his coded message, using the series of numbers and letters he referenced from the code book he took from the breast pocket of his wool jackets, that they had designed, and punched the star button to verify and finish.

Turning away from the pay phone he walked watchfully for the next seven blocks down the Rue des Alpes, the stone streets oozing medieval charm and history, the Jet D'Eau gushing its misty fountain of spray in the distance on Lake Geneva. He smiled in relief when he turned the corner on the Rue de'Lausanne and saw his moderate single story motel, where he had registered under the name shown on his visa, as Peter Weld. He walked, keyed open the door, and went directly to the mini refrigerator and proceeded to make a gin and tonic with real Schweppes quinine, to ward off malaria, he mused, and real Boodles gin that would ward off reality.

He crashed onto the middle of the bed where the springs had given down with the weight of wayfaring humanity, looking up at the dirty plastered ceiling into nothing, thinking about the day's occurrences, and the cold-eyed reproach of the facts he now knew, feeling like a diver groping downward into black water feeling for something which he hoped would be there, something which would glitter if there were any light in the depth. But there wasn't any light. He made another gin and tonic and awaited a nervous night's sleep and the next steps in the increasing drama of his family duty dance.

Chapter 39

He dreamt a dream, an abiding dream, vaguely similar to those he had before, of an impregnable world, filled with tolerance, amity, unity and peace, culture and tranquility, yet all his life he had now questioned something in his heart, as to what sustained people in their eternal unrelieved anguish. They were helpless, like seaweed moved by dark and restless tides, thoughtless, incapable of questioning, of revulsion and revolt. Had the dawn been forced to fall back into the night? Was the shout of liberation silent? Was the dream lost? Man had been compelled again to wait for another day of liberation. Against the lust for power of the tyrants and its betrayal of the oppressed and the helpless, and against the rapacity, treachery, cynicism and political expediency of the rulers, we must equally, set the hearts and hands of man. Against these, we must rise with sternness and passion, otherwise the cause of man against his oppressors is lost forever.

Would they endure, because they had no hope of doing anything else? Was there in the people some vast unconscious faith, some profound movement, which comes partly from themselves and partly from some deep and mystic source? Was there some divine moon which raises the tide in human hearts, and sends it roaring over the shingles of the world, bringing with it treasures and epiphanies of a new life, that could educate mankind above their instincts? For when personal issues are involved, reason takes a holiday. Was the secret of endurance, the primordial unthinking faith of the humble people that in them is eternity, the arching tidal wave, the source of all life, the promise of the future, and the outline of new frontiers of man's desire and man's hope?

Who could resist, his dream seemed to instruct, the people when they feel this immensity in themselves? No one. Neither past Kings or priests, or arms, or fury, or death. Could this be a new age of enlightenment, of consciousness, of recognition of a new iteration of tyrants, of understanding the power of the people?

Ryan stirred. He was being passionately moved by this unconscious muse. He heard a dim tumult in his ears, and closed his eyes once more to return to the vivid remembrance of his dream. This was only the dawn, came the message, in a trembling voice. The full moon may not be seen in our lifetime, but it is coming. Who can obscure the sun, and cause it to hurtle down again, beyond the black horizon? No one! The sound of the day will soon be here, when there shall not be Americans or Frenchmen, or Englishmen, Germans or Spaniards, Russians or Italians, Saudis and Turks. There shall be only man, and all the plottings of evil men and tyrants can only darken the day, like little passing of the clouds. They cannot halt the sun in its course.

The rivers of the world flow through every man's door, all attached by an umbilical cord to the farthest star. This was a truth which wicked men had through thousands of years tried to deny, with lies and superstitions, with treachery and greed. It was a truth not always known, for the universality of all men was rarely taught, but had become nurtured in a faith taught by its servants that promoted superstition and ignorance, oppression and bigotry, that had always set its face against the thinker. For the thinker, arouses other men to a realization of their dignity, before both God and man, and had given vitality, full of strange and angry thoughts, full of indignation against the oppressor.

It is they we must combat, and destroy, if brotherhood and compassion are to finally come upon the world. No disproportionally great and arbitrary power, whether secular or religious, can exist in the world without endangering the liberty and lives of all men. Man must be the passionate enemy of any servant of faith that engages in the pursuit of power and the acquisition of temporal authority.

The dreamer's dreams are impossible, but without a dream, and a star, no man can chart his course over the black waters of despair, and through the darkness of an awareness of reality, which is the source of despair. A dream once dreamt is a dream remembered in the hearts of men. But the fulfillment may not come for many years. In the meantime, those who participate in the struggle are lost. It is either exile or death. Incredible words without meaning, thought Ryan, as began to wake. Yet he felt a movement in his heart below the incredulity of his mind. So must the pagans have felt, at the first words of Christ.

He finally rose from his mysterious dreams feeling restless in his squalid, squeezed, square, solo sanctuary, feeling like the fugitive that he now was. He hoisted his malty bones from the bed and got into his clothes. He looked in the mirror at the mortal remains of his nerve wrecked being.

He opened the door of his motel room at seven-thirty and padded toward the lobby to retrieve the local and regional papers. The hiss of a car driving by with a broken radiator made a strange counterpoint, to the chime of the Church bells drifting over the city. Jackhammers rattled in the distance at some undetermined compass point and cars honked plaintively, as though calling to their children. He made a surprisingly good pot of Parisienne coffee and scoured the papers for news of the previous day.

There it was; the story itself read: There was only one passenger in the Peugeot automobile that could be positively identified: Ryan Davies from Minnesota, USA, Vice President of McWilliams and Associates, deceased. The car had apparently slid on slick roads through a guard rail, on the edge of the Nufenen Pass, twenty-three miles east of Sion, Switzerland. The car had been tracked, the article in the Geneva Tribune reported, to have been rented by Davies three days prior at the Hertz terminal at the Geneva Aeroport.

After reading the story of his demise for the third time, Ryan looked at the passport that had the name of Peter Weld on it, and took a deep breath trying to steel his nerves. Overwhelmed, and exhausted, all thought and emotion was beaten out of him. He was lost in his sense of self, the heartbeat he heard was the heart of the world. He breathed with the mighty risings and declines of the earth, the evanescence seeming less frightening than exalting.

The agreed upon plan of traveling to Paris and a hoped for rendezvous with his compatriots would be changed. After all, he had the advantage now. He was dead!

Chapter 40

From one end of Venice to the other this week, after the Christmas Holiday and a recent visit by the Pope, left the city oddly quiet, the streets and canals deserted except for shopkeepers and workers beginning another day's routine, while scattered here and there were revelers who had fallen in love the night before, returned from their parties by gondola, water taxi or some even on foot. That was the trouble with passion and Venice, having been inoculated with the virus of Italy, it was necessary to go back through the door into real life. The hotels that only a few days before had lit up its windows like bejeweled minnows with the papal visit were now dark and mysteriously quiet, in the jaded and cynical Venice with all its centuries of weary experience. To the old timers, like this man walking through the city, it brought back odd displacing memories of wartime just a fortnight ago.

The man's pace quickened as he walked to the western edges of the city, marveling at the massive amounts of building and decorating sponsored by the state and the religious communities of Venice during the Renaissance. The private residences, small palaces really, and many public structures were required to have facades on at least two sides so they could be seen from the water around this city built on a lagoon, as well as from the land. It was as if all these multitudes of buildings with their beautiful outer appearance were the bricks which built a fortress within a fortress, an observable metaphor perhaps for a battlement in which he himself had walled up for his own psychic needs to protect him from the threatening world beyond. To the present day, Venice remained one of the most beautiful cities on earth because of the Renaissance building in the seventeenth century. Just as with Florence, Venice was a Republic during the Renaissance period, controlling land in modern day Italy and much of the sea coast of the Adriatic and its numerous islands. It enjoyed a stable political and a thriving trade and mercantile economy, both of which survived the outbreaks of the Black Death and the fall of their major partner, Constantinople. Venice had the economy to support art and artists in a big way and did just that, making it a major port of trade, ready markets for whatever paintings and decorative arts Venetian craftsmen could produce, all this giving birth to the distinct school of Impressionistic painting, in the nineteenth century.

A work of art, the man's inner muse suggested as he walked through the veritable art gallery of the city, wasn't really just one thing, it was everything. It was not this or that, it was all, as he peered with haste into a provincial art gallery in one of the small modestly priced cafes along his route. There was no single path to its meaning and significance or the pleasure it gave. What was valued most in early Renaissance painting was the tender feeling of a countryside and an emotive calm in the heart, a certain irresistible naiveté in what must have been the stormiest of ages. It was of its maker's time and its beholder's time, and it held, woven into itself, what Botticelli heard in the piazza on his way to his workshop, what Rembrandt thought walking beside the Prinsengracht on a misty afternoon, and it could incorporate the morning light on the façade of Santa Croce or a letter from Rubens about the English Court, or Cezanne's view of the corner house through the woods, or a program for the decoration of a palace ceiling handed to Tiepolo by a Prince's astrologer.

There was no legislation, the walker thought, governing or limiting the meanings that might be found in art, no limiting of a future of the predictable passions that arts, poetry and grace could deliver. They were works of art that were forever fresh and constant again and again, giving back the bloom of first meeting.

Having ended his air journey from Rome to Venice, Harold Hennessy continued his walk finally reaching the modest motel on the fringes of the Schwabing district of the city, and knocked on the door of a room two doors down from his and was quickly summoned inside the room of Martha Connelly. They had both traveled to this location using different passports, three complete sets of tickets for the journey, the airline computers showing three different names traveling in four classes of service on various legs of the trip, switching between these as they traveled, pulling and discarding unused flight coupons along the way. The next morning they would leave by train from Venice to Innsbruck, Austria, where Timothy Vail and Patricia Childers had rented rooms at the hotel Ibis on the western outskirts of the city.

The early morning weather was wet and dreary with an uncomfortable frosty breeze making its way upon the city off the Adriatic. Harold

Hennessy stopped at a pay phone and placed a toll free call to Halifax. The call went through directly and he punched in a series of numbers and letters as instructed and waited for the coded message to be sent back to him. He waited, looking across the Grand Canal toward the Cathedral of St. Marks, where his partner stood pretending to read the morning papers. His heart raced with anxiety and dread as he filled his lungs with the damp Venetian air. The coded message came over the line and he diligently wrote down the cryptic numbers and letters on a small note pad he had pulled from the breast pocket of his coat. He replayed the message again making certain he had written it correctly.

He took another deep breath and walked toward Martha Connelly and slipped the piece from his notepad casually between the folds of her newspaper. She quickly sat down at the little café next to the Hotel Rialto and pulled the encryption code from her purse as she made a mock effort at putting on a new layer of lipstick. She said a silent eight-word prayer of "Oh God," ending with "help us." She made her effort to decipher the message just as a V-shaped flock of seagulls made their way above her to the canals next to the Cathedral. Suddenly she looked up at the traffic on the Rialto Bridge arched in front of her, her look void of any expression or emotion. Finally, she rose after what seemed like an interminable period of time and walked steadily down Canal Avenue, her orbiting mind repeating the words, "Now I know, now I know for certain!"

She casually strolled into a convenience shop along the avenue and moved to the book racks, looking at the newspapers and magazines, when she noticed the familiar figure not more than three feet away on the other side of the wooden book stand. She didn't look in his direction but whispered just loud enough to be heard; "Car exploded on Nufenen Pass, our compatriot well and safe under new ID at Geneva motel!" She thought she could see a mist of exasperated relief float over the top of the bookshelf as she moved away down along the aisle. Martha feigned shopping for a few moments and bought a guidebook of the Alps, paying the clerk in Lira. She caught herself from nearly breaking out into a skip as she walked along Canal Avenue, her partner more than a block ahead now, as they made their way toward the Venezia Santa Lucia train station.

Harold Hennessy settled into his seat on the 11:02 train, his partner two cars in front of him for the two-and a half hour trip to Innsbruck. He made a personal prayer to God as he had ever made, giving thanks for the news

Martha had provided him. He opted for the left side of the passenger car which would provide him the best views of the southern range of the Alps that would come into view in about two hours, he estimated. The car was nearly half full, dominated mostly by excited skiers making their way to the resorts of the Alps for days of skiing glory. He and his family had skied the Alps a few times and he knew that for skiers today the Swiss Alps were synonymous with thrilling runs and a chance to experience the glorious intensity of winter's sting. Reflecting on the Alps, he remembered what Percy Shelly wrote, "Dangers which sport upon the brink of precipices have been my playmate." Skiing here, Harold thought, is a modern example of an acceptable kind of horror. You can get as close to the edge as you dare. The grand and terrible and luminescent themes of life and death that the Alps engender were part of the area's worldwide mysterious appeal.

He and his family had loved skiing the mountains and the power they had to release one from everyday life. St. Moritz had become their favorite, although they had only vacationed there twice. It was a corrective to the ills of the big city and its multiculturalism, being close to the borders of France, Austria, Germany and Italy, was enchanting. St. Moritz seemed to offer the best source of the simulated sublime, a sense of surrendering to forces outside of one's control.

Instinctively, Harold looked around, checking the scenery inside the precision fast train. No one seemed to be in his wake. Had this gone too smoothly he thought? No hitches yet, nobody lurking behind in the shadows, to imperil their objective. They were a long way from the goal. Don't get overconfident, he told himself, as he watched the young tourists bobbing their heads up and down listening to their headphones.

He was no tourist on this trip to be sure, he thought. He was the traveler, the difference to the tourist being partly one of time, he thought. Whereas the tourist generally hurries back home at the end of a few weeks or months, the traveler belonging to no more one place than the next, moves slowly over periods of years, from one part of the earth to another. The tourist accepts his own civilization without question, while the traveler tends to compare the mechanized world with other cultures and rejects those elements he finds to his disliking. The traveler remembered the train trip all those years ago now he had taken through Paris and on to Switzerland two weeks after the war had ended, and how it was WAR, the one facet of the mechanized world he wanted to forget.

Tomorrow was the day, he thought, a modern day D-Day, newly created, mechanized world conflict awaited, and the thought shamefully frightened him to his core of his being. He knew now what war did to a man, pumping him full of inverted pride, making destruction so easy for him, so easy, indoctrinating with the sacred importance of the group, the squadron, platoon, and later the company, agency, corporation over the individual, turning a man vindictive and brutal far more cruelly than exile might ever do.

He no longer had the nerves of a soldier that he possessed some forty years ago. He was ignorant and blissful back then to the horror of war that he was about to experience and the thought of being a paratrooper when he entered the military was an easy decision, as it paid him fifty dollars more each month, than the regular G.I. How insanely lucky he had been to survive, he thought once again, his thoughts now on all his friends that had died, and the sublime price they had paid, with the cost of our freedoms buried in the grounds of the Normandy Memorial.

It was the quality of the conflict, he realized, that changes as it shifts from level to level but the quantity of conflict in life remains constant. The volume of the conflict never changes, the war and his business having schooled him in the lesson, like squeezing a balloon that just bulges in another direction.

He rode alone in silence as the train moved smoothly, taking him across the verdant meadows of the Alpine plains that slumbered in the winter, as the train's rails narrowed behind him as if traveling in a journey into nothing, the early morning clicking by, track section by track section, as he busied himself by naming the trees as they passed, their soft names somehow bringing comfort to his lonely skull: elm, oak, ash, hazel, larch, birch and maple, their leaves gone, living amongst the glorious heights of the alpine firs, the snows of winter upon their boughs. He too would fall like the leaves when it came his time, like the unseen leaf, the bud that was the glory of his birth forgotten before remembered. He named the trees softly aloud now, the aspen, the beech, the willow, and the locust, when he saw it leafless like a battlefield, reminding him again of war and the revitalization of death; that death does indeed live.

The whole world had been one cauldron of misery then and you walked through it grimly, setting your teeth, hardening your heart. But now that war again was just something defined in textbooks, the violence and killing, the moments of stress and fear bound in a neat sum of historical endeavor. It was something attempted, accomplished and ended. But that wasn't true. We were never over it. There was no immunity. It was like malaria without atabrine, the recurrences come and go, and come again, a month, a year, a lifetime later, and the shivers and sweats are every bit as intense as they were the first times. A soldier just got used to it, had to get used to it, and adapt.

His face embraced the vast expanse of the foothills as the snow-capped spine of the Alps grew rapidly on the eastern horizon, seeming to seek him and woo him, a man afloat who challenges yet fears the reef but seeks the harbor, now that his last mask may squeamishly die there, tender and open, willing no more resistance than a fruit's fresh spoiling in the winter air.

This hunt, this search, this reclamation of the past, the traveler mused now trying to brace his confidence, was like an effort to find mislaid keys, or tickets, or even a lost weekend, since such searches end willy-nilly when Sunday arrives and the curtain falls or the locksmith is called. It aims at the recovery of a life of an entire society even, not in the ruins like an ancient city hidden by sand, but one realized in its interiors as well as in its trappings, fully fledged freshly painted, something impossible in every sense of the can't be done, a fictive aim only perhaps to bring everything that life has touched, from the shady side of the tree where it snoozes in winter, depending upon the tree's endurance and solidity, to then fully realize the bounty of its spring leaves that breathe the sweet oxygen of life into the air.

He reminded himself how we are constantly, sadly, guiltily reminded of the paucity of our own recollections; life went on around us and we seemed to miss it, pretending to ponder our place but not really doing it, imagining that we had discerned connections, yet we failed to follow, being indulged by other obsessions, too distracted by the trivial, not retaining a fond touch or a glimmer of insight, a bit of wit, where we might have, in the distance between what happens and what we have understood, the habitual victim of our body's incapacities. The Basilisk, he remembered, dies from the look in his own eye when he peers for the first time into a mirror, the mirror being that from behind the bar, or the reflective windows of the train or the glassy surface of a still and silent sea.

As the Alps began to rise solitarily out of the rich countryside, the morning smell of a January thaw blew with the wind through the open window of the train with church bells ringing far in the distance.

Hennessy's thoughts were adrift as the aesthete who now values the intrinsic and the solemn worth of things in themselves, the doer and the viewer, one always going somewhere, the other already there. He thought that for anyone who had reached his age only the past had much duration, looking back at him, the unpleasant consequence of every such blotch is that his life registers itself as if looking back from a dirty mirror, ambition and regret having eaten the present, which it seems at best is a sliver of cake too small for its plate, while the future, it seems, will cease before having been.

Through the click and clack of the train he could hear the future on its run to get there, its labored push now up the mountain ridge of the Alps, sounding like the strained breathing of an old man on the stairs. In a spirit of disobedience to the current cause he looked back again on what he might have done, on the messes made and the few fragile triumphs, those successes found in some solitary achievement, its fruit kept seedless and dry and secret, by a closing cultural fist, rather than toward all that remains to be encountered, coped with and perhaps yet accomplished, in constant search for the leading man within his heart's play, praying that guilt or fear would have no harbor in a hero's heart.

What is the data that determines any person's life, he asked himself, as the train began to make its steady mount to the rarefied atmosphere of the Alps, of the things we desire to do, to think and feel? What ones should be discarded like the ashes of wood and what is it that should be retained, and how should the residue be measured and weighed? How should these elements be joined to one another, and why should we bother attempting to put the puzzle together at all, at so much expense of time and cogitation? It must be because our own aims, our worship and our animus, surely direct the construction of the gathering and the sorting of even the last scraps of information. For no one knows the truth either about himself or about anyone else, and all recorded acts and words are open testimony to our endless efforts to know each other, and our never ending failure to do so.

Was he playing the devil to his own Faust? he wondered, understanding that we often persuade ourselves of things to be true, things we feel clear to our feet that are false, in a world where the irony was inescapable, a father and son, friendly supplicants in search of their collective souls. Was he constantly inventing additional versions of himself, by making surprising responses to familiar situations or to meet changes in circumstances with an equally changed self and sometimes to prepare ourselves for surprising eventualities, as we often do in day-dreams? We populate our lives with the lives we need to live, his mind suggested, nervously writhing, dreaming ourselves into the selves we fear we are, or desperately want to be, and if we retell our little fictions often enough they pass from wishing to seeming as such and then to being so, reiteration being the prominent feature of reality.

Think only of the ambition of men and you will wonder at the senselessness of their ways, unless you consider how they are stirred by love of an immortality of fame, he remembered some philosopher had said. They are ready to run risks far greater than they would have run for their children, and to spend the money and undergo any sort of toil, and even die for the sake of leaving behind them a name which shall be eternal. Would Alcestis, the traveler wondered, his internal grief case spilling in mental angst, have died to save Admetus, or Achilles to avenge Patroclus, or Codrus in order to preserve the kingdom for his sons, if they had not imagined the memory of their virtues, which still remains among us, would they be immortal? All men do things, and the better they are the more they do them. In the hope of the glorious fame of immortal virtue, they desire to be immortal.

As the snowy Austrian Alps rose faster now before him and the Brenner Pass, the lowest of the Alps' passed could be seen in the distance north, he thinks now that one must make some reference to the religious heart to make any sense of it all. But even so, we must show the worm of doubt stirring within the heart of religion itself. It is the dialectic of religious trust and distrust. The matter, the traveler silently opines, can be approached differently by what broadly termed is the realist and the idealist. The realist claims not to flinch before the brute resistance of things, whereas the idealist takes pride in not being arrested by the same resistance. The idealist wistfully yearns, perhaps, perhaps. It is not yet, but it ought to be! I dream, I dream. The realist rudely retorts, this is not so, wake up you wistful innocent, I told you so. The idealist points us beyond to a hidden heaven, the realist reminds us with sweet glee, that life on earth is hell.

The world, he rightly muses, is not black and white, but a vast zone of gray consciences that stands between the ignorant men of evil and the pure victims. We all inhabit this gray zone, we all can be induced to become part of the apparatus of death for trivial reasons and paltry rewards. This was the terrifying truth of the war of his generation and the horror of the Holocaust and the Zionism that cravenly embedded it.

As he rode, every moment seemed to be a window on all of time. He thought of how he had set out to get order and position for himself and of the undenying confusion of his life, the blot and blur of his years. He stared out and saw the rich unworked land, the rich Eden of farm and pasture that lay at the base of the great raw lift of the Alps.

He imagined the farmer of his youth long ago, the lean industrious farmer walking above his reins behind the oxen plow. The sky was full of windy white shags of clouds. A thick blade of snowy mist washed slowly around the rampart of a mountain peak. He thought of his fifty or sixty years, his vanished youth, his diminishing strength, the frustration and struggle of much of it. He had the quiet despair of a man who knows the forged chain may not be unlinked, the threaded design unwound, the finished unfinished, the done undone.

The traveler looked out upon the satiny sheeted snow tiered farm fields and the red roofed buildings in the quaint Alpine valley towns, thinking how we seem to spread our wings for a new fight, daring to pride ourselves, like the modern Prometheans, with being the absolute original, but in turning away from the originating experience of the holy, we risk the dying of light though we call this death enlightenment. Is postmodernity now waking up to this death? The traveler reconceived that man's condition is dual, that man infinitely transcends man and that without the aid of faith he would remain inconceivable to himself, for who cannot see that unless we realize the duality of human nature, we remain invincibly ignorant of the truth about ourselves, our own crooked timber, unable to perceive? For, tragedy is an imitation not of men, but of action and of life, and life consists of action, its end is a mode of action, not a quality. Now it is character that must determine man's qualities, but it is by their actions that they are happy or the reverse.

Hennessy's muse was relentless now as the train made its steady climb to the Brenner Pass, where in 1940 Hitler had met Mussolini in conference as prelude to World War II, that perhaps their current cause was as of the American patriots in the eighteenth century, to fight off their British subjects, who understood, that it was not in numbers but in unity that our great strength lays. The proceedings at first appear strange and difficult, but, like all other steps which we have already passed over, will in time become familiar and agreeable, and until the accomplishment has come to fruition perhaps the American Continent felt as he did now, having put off some unpleasant business from day to day, week to week and over many years, knowing it needs to be done, yet hating to set about it, wishing it was over, continually haunted with the thoughts of its necessity.

He knew that in order to discover our duty rightly, he had to take his children in hand and fix his station a few years farther into life, that eminence will present a prospect which a few present fears and prejudices conceal from sight. Yet he knew deep within him that the blood of his children would curse his cowardice if he shrunk back at a time when a little inner resolve might save the whole of the operation and make everyone happy. From the extremes of danger to safety from the tumult of war, to the tranquility of peace, could be engraved a name with the point of a pin on the tender bark of a young oak, the wound enlarging with the tree, until posterity would read it in full grown characters.

Chapter 41

The train pulled into Sta. Innsbruck HBF at three p.m. and the two travelers walked three blocks in the center of the city, checking into their respective rooms at the hotel Ibis on Sterzinger Strasse with new passports, to prepare for their three and one half hour early morning train trip to Basel Switzerland over the Arlberg Pass through Zurich.

The gothic four story stone building that was the national Bank of Basel, stood on the corner of 4th street and Vincennes and looked like a Roman fortress as Harold Hennessy casually strode toward it the following day just after noon. They had done their surveillance of the bank and studied all the emergency exits on the first floor and in the lower level where the safety deposit boxes were located. As he entered the double door glass entryway an elderly woman turned the corner two blocks east of the bank walking aimlessly, window shopping along the way. It was a wide eyed, crisp blue sky, high noon day, as the stooped over elderly woman continued to walk and window shop, now directly across the avenue from the bank. If there was thought to be any problem that loomed, the code to her partner in the bank would be given and she would proceed inside the bank to take action.

Looking in the reflection that the windows provided she surveyed the area around the bank for anything, anybody, that seemed out of place. Instinctively she slipped her right hand into her navy wool blazer pocket and gently wrapped her fingers around the tiny beeper. All things seemed smooth so far. They had figured it would take only ten minutes at most, to finish with the business that needed to be transacted. A single beeper tone would let her know when he had the documents in his possession.

Inside the bank, he presented his real passport and IDs to a bank vice president. "Good morning, Dr. Duffield here," he said resolutely with congenial eye contact. So, in Switzerland, he thought, men who were entrusted with money were doctors. Why not, he thought, after all money wasn't both a disease and a cure? Walter Davies proceeded down the polished marble circular stairway to the vaults of deposit boxes. There was a hygienic, almost religious quiet there that made him hesitate to speak above a whisper, among all the wealth that was lying in the hush of the vaults. He placed his key in the lock of deposit box 384, slid the heavy silver rectangular box that was at his eye level toward him and breathed with relief as he removed the familiar lease documents and ownership conveyances and placed them securely inside his rollaway suitcase.

Just seconds earlier the elderly woman saw something she thought might portend danger. Two men in dark long jackets had mysteriously appeared, one standing on each corner of 4th and Vincennes. Instinctively as per planned she crossed the street and entered the bank, nodding warmly at a customer leaving the bank's glass double doors. She quickly saw what she hoped she would see, as her architectural scan of the bank had indicated. Casually as if it were an everyday practice she activated the fire alarm with her left hand just as she felt the pulsation of the beeper she held with her right hand in her jacket. She quickly exited the bank and walked down Vincennes noticing the two men she saw earlier now standing together at the end of the block, as the emergency sirens sounded off throughout the bank's interior and exterior. She turned the corner at 3rd street and Vincennes, walking more crisply now and not in the drama of her previous stooped condition.

Walter, on hearing the alarm go off just after beeping Sophie, took immediate plan B action and darted out the emergency exit that they had scouted months ago just behind a series of credenzas on the first floor on the south side of the bank. He walked quickly down the alley in back of the bank as they had diagrammed in their planning, taking a left on 3rd street proceeding toward St. Alban Rheinweg that ran along the southern edge of the Rhine. As he proceeded to cross Weidengrasse off 3rd, a black limo quickly stopped in front of him and a back door opened and a soft reassuring voice summoned him inside. "Good to see you Mr. Davies," said a man with a black and white collar. The driver was then instructed to take a sharp turn off Vincennes and two blocks down, at the direction of his fare, stopped quickly at the corner to pick up another fare, an old lady.

"We lost him." It was Borgen's director of operations calling from Paris. "It was at the national Bank of Basel,"

"What happened goddammit," Borgen raged from across the Atlantic. "There was a fire alarm, sir, and we figure he exited through one of the rear emergency doors. Our men think he must have had help, there was no fire anywhere in the building."

"Get me the surveillance camera films," the head of the agency bellowed.

"Yes sir right away…" As Borgen madly fisted the phone into its cradle. He looked and saw that his hands were trembling, he did not like surprises, nothing not directly at the tip of his spear, and he could feel the rages of anger beginning to well up inside of him.

"The tape from the bank, sir, shows very little, sir, just a businessman with a briefcase and then an elderly woman entering, from the front entrance."

"Replay that surveillance tape again," Borgen barked, Matt standing behind him in his office watching the screen mounted on the wall. "Re-wind it, hurry dammit," he growled, his face beginning to turn more ashen and gray than he had ever seen it before, Matt noticed. "Run it in slow motion. Stop it right there," he screeched at the speaker on his phone. "Stop it right there on the old lady."

She seemed to be hiding her face, Borgen sensed, as she was exiting the bank. "Okay roll it again," he bellowed with a violent fury that quickly filled the room like a dark ominous thunder cloud, making Matt take a reflexive step backward. The tape ran forward once more and a sense of horror and dread suddenly blackened the mental ligaments of the agency head's brain.

It was the walk, as he watched the old hunched over woman walk out of the bank, that unique confident stride he was certain he recognized. He could pick it out anywhere, any place. Now he knew it, it had to be, he thought, hoping desperately he could somehow be mistaken. He sat in silence behind his massive desk transfixed, frozen with fear, looking at the image he saw on the screen.

"Sophie," he mouthed just loud enough to be faintly audible, as his jowled chin dropped to his chest. Matt turned away, enjoying a wry grin, giving Sophie a psychic high five as he left the office.

Borgen stomped around his desk now and barked out orders into the speaker phone. A half-dozen lieutenants on the other end of the line scribbled as he ranted. "Cover the airport, check every airline, notify Paris and London and check with customs."

"Sir," Borgen's secretary spoke over the intercom. "NSA operations are standing down on the Davies operation. They received a call from Rome. All operatives and sleeper cells have been ordered to stand down. Delta clearances have been terminated."

Borgen gasped in disgust as the screen on the wall went black.

Chapter 42

The Archdiocese of Basel, the home of the Bishop Otto Wust, was located in Solothurn forty minutes southwest of Basel, set in the pristine forests of the Alpine Valley. The good Vatican Cardinal Castilla had sent one of the auxiliary Bishops and a driver from the Solothurn Archdiocese at the precise time Walter Davies had informed him that he and his partner would be at the bank that day.

Relief and release of tension, neither of the two riders in the limo had ever quite felt crossed their nerve ends. It was an ecclesiastical ecstatic energy release they felt. They both thanked Bishop Denis Theurillat profusely as they traveled southwest along the Rhine, as Sophie removed her costumed image of an old lady. The Bishop seated in front of them blessed them for their bravery and the strength of their courage.

The following day after a one-night layover at the Archdiocese, they would travel to Berne under diplomatic immunity with the Bishop and fly to Paris along with the Bishop, where they would meet Timothy Vail, aka Ryan Davies at a predetermined location near Charles De Gaulle Airport, then the four of them would fly on to Washington DC, to the Vatican Embassy.

A copy of the original lease documents for the mining operation that Walter had taken from his safety deposit box was made with a Vatican seal of the sovereign state of the Holy See, and sent directly to Cardinal Castilla in Rome, the originals carried by Walter Davies in the official diplomatic pouch of the Vatican.

Arthur Borgen and his demonic agency having been outwitted and beaten.

Chapter 43

Winnie, now the new senator from Minnesota, had spotted a chink in the OFAC contract, the use of selective enforcement of breaking laws and thinking they had infinite impunity. The government was being transformed from public service, into a device for privatizing profit and she was about to drive a political truck through it. She had excited the scrutiny of the head of the SEC's transaction section, the self-appointed Gauletier of American business morality. He was a quarrelsome ambitious bureaucrat who used the weight of the law to feed a Freudian, poor-boy need to push important men around, damn the expense and the consequences. His noisy pursuit of some corporate transgressor, Winnie, though, perfectly illustrated Oscar Wilde's description of fox hunting: the unspeakable chasing the unbeatable.

Many in Washington, especially the fellow senators she worked with, had discovered there was, in Winnie McMillan, a mysterious and indefinable element of greatness, which had nothing to do with fame or her handmaiden acclaim, or false buffoon notoriety. She spoke so simply, yet gently and had a smile of singular sweetness. When she laughed with her colleagues, she laughed with her eyes as well as her lips, and a glow, clear and translucent, would light in them. Her manner was soft and deprecating, as if she felt a deep humility. If her opinions were vehement, they were nevertheless not dogmatic or arrogant. She was generous, sympathetic, subtle and sensitive and was a devoted friend and felt no enmity for any one. There was no bitterness or hatred in her. Above all, those she worked with quickly gleaned that she was compassionate and merciful, loathing nothing but injustice, cruelty and oppression.

Perhaps it was the sum of all things that made her great. She seemed to possess them all, whereas others might possess one or a few. Perhaps she lacked reserve in her virtue, for she had no reticences in mercy, love, tenderness and honor. There was no moderation in her goodness; her heart to her fellow senators seemed as wide as infinity. She was like a spring that gushed inexhaustibly, not confined by the politics of caution, not made brackish by constant consideration of her own good, not restrained or thickened by the fog of judiciousness or self-restraint. She did not at all exhibit the common trait of most of the delegation of representatives and senators in Washington who chose, not to stand out but rather, to fit in.

She gave all of her heart and did not ask if by doing so she displayed wisdom, prudence or moderation.

She personified the greatness of great men that is in the complete abandon and openness of their souls. Winnie's greatness was in her infinite passion, the boundless horizon of her spirit. Some of her greatness resided in her lack of artifice, and in her noble disregard of the disapproval, incredulity or contempt of others. She had a lofty and fervid innocence, which, however, was not unconscious of evil. For all this, she was adored by many, and violently hated as well by those who saw her as a threat to the ongoing stasis in the halls of a growing conservative congress. It was a sad fact that throughout the testimony of history, that greatness in a man is the unpardonable sin.

It was with zeal that she came to learn that it was as if Borgen's OFAC agency business plan was to get their world wide ranging paw into every decent sized cookie jar they could find and clip off a share, if not all, of the national grocery money. The sin of unchecked over weaning pride was often a very useful petard with which to hoist overconfidence. She knew that in Washington, sharp ears could pick up the squish of the legal putty being forced into the cracks and crevices of these dubious government alphabet agencies. Winnie would make them feel, the Davies family and Sophie were sure, that it was not much fun to be rich, making them feel like they had cheated at cards, because a country that dispenses its welfare to its privileged and not to its helpless and undefended is headed for trouble.

Winnie could see, after the perspective that Sophie had provided her, that Borgen had a sort of native slyness you often find in men of small intellect. He was most probably part of a cult of rabid supply siders who had a framed copy of Andrew Carnegie's *Gospel of Wealth*, adorning the walls of his office. He was an image with no more substance than smoke, for who striving knew no bounds. You had only to look at Washington to know that the age of the cheap intellect and rich had arrived. Winnie hoped to throw every one of them out and bust their meters.

They would fall like a heavy statue in the desert toppled by the uncontrollably shifting sands. They would become the casualty of an inferior age, in an age now changing its wings for the better. Winnie would reveal Borgen's agency and the other current heroes of business, for the puffed up public related human fabrications that they were, while being presented as leaders and statesmen, feeling themselves secure on the pedestals of prominence and success, carpeted by society's manipulated skills, that would reveal not inspiration and vision in the highest councils, but short sightedness and narcissism.

Americans had become notorious for their self-defeating shortness of perspective. They treated history like an unwelcome old relative to be pensioned off if someone else could be found to bear, or at least share, the expense. We were witnessing, she was certain, the secession of the successful, where they had abandoned our public services and were losing important advocates. The uphill climb of the rich accelerated the downward spiral of a society as a whole, leading to widening inequality, heightened estrangement and the moral amnesia that estrangement required.

Winnie recalled the words of the great sociologist of the modern state, Max Weber, as she waited in the large caucus room of the Russell Senate Office Building. "Every bureaucracy seeks to increase the superiority of the professionally informed, by keeping their knowledge and intentions secret. Bureaucratic administration and its agencies always tend to be an administration of 'secret sessions' insofar as it can. It hides its knowledge and action from criticism… The concept of 'official secret' is the special invention of the bureaucracy, and nothing is so fanatically defended by the bureaucracy as this attitude… In facing a parliament the bureaucracy, out of a sure power instinct, fights every one of the parliament to gain knowledge by means of its own experts or interest groups… Bureaucracy naturally welcomes a poorly informed and hence a powerless parliament, at least insofar as ignorance agrees with bureaucracy's interests."

Winnie grinned inwardly now as she saw the broken titan Arthur Borgen sitting in front of her in the congressional hearing room, his face ashen as a hunger striker's, wishing somehow he could maintain the stewardship of his own political neck. He had long ago committed to the dark storm, releasing the mad devil's hunger all men have in them, which lusts for darkness and evil profit.

Sophie, sitting with Walter and Ryan, thought Borgen looked to have the weariness of a failed salesman, defeat and despair that inhabited his veins, his nerves, his bones, having finally taken him over, darkening his conscience, his skin looking as tired as his clothing, as he sat amid the wreckage of his furniture, like a Roman senator undisturbed by his city's tumbling marble all around him. He had a face now as severe as Dante's, she thought, his eyes fiercely defensive, mouth bitter, his upper jaw seeming much grander and higher ridged than ever before, his entire profile looking like a wounded bird of prey of some sort. Like the Roman senate in the last days of the republic, could he and his agency and others like it be brought back to life and cleansed of its endemic corruption? Failing such a reform, Nemesis, the goddess of retribution and vengeance, the punisher of pride and hubris, waited impatiently for her meeting with him.

Such men as Borgen, Sophie thought, did not realize that their own vision of human nature was distorted. They prided themselves on their "toughness" and fortitude and intelligence, which had enabled them to accept so black a picture of the planet with such easy tolerance. They looked about them and saw everywhere nothing but the myriad shapes of privilege, dishonesty, and self-interest and were convinced that this was inevitably the way things were. These men were all the victims of an occupational disease; a kind of mass hypnosis that denied them the evidence of their senses. It was not until the real substance of their "toughness" and intelligence was demonstrated to them in terms which they could grasp, that the bubble of their unreal world suddenly exploded before their eyes.

Many of them were so incapable of facing the harsh reality and the truth that they blew their brains out or threw themselves from the high windows of their offices to the streets below. Those who faced it and saw it through like the man who sat before them, who had once been plump and self-assured, now shrank and withered into premature and palsied senility. If Sophie had her way, Borgen would be buried stoneless in solitary under a gnarled tree.

Sophie had long observed, that in the whole temper of the times, as was now plain to her, the dangers that lurk in those latent atavistic urges which man has inherited from his dark past.

As he listened to the committee chair sitting before him, a chain of recall ground against his memory and every insult and humiliation he had ever been forced to bear flashed before him, as wickedly bright and hurtful as though he was enduring each all over again.

Winnie smiled to herself and threw a glance toward Walter, Ryan and Sophie sitting in the hearing room, as she sat on the committee that was confronting him as he responded to the questions of his agency's activities.

It was the first discernible rise out of the agency head. No more than a slight wrinkling of the surface, but to the experienced fisherman it was evidence enough of the presence of a very large creature of evil, lurking below the surface. Walter had been measuring men and exploiting their weaknesses for forty years. His instincts were honed as were Senator McWilliams'. They both sensed conclusively that the agency head testifying in front of them knew what the district attorney was talking about, but bringing the fish to fry might be another matter altogether.

Eventually the full weight of public outrage would make itself felt and the press, anxious to redeem itself for its somnolence it had taken for so long, would lead the way, seeing to the dismantling of the agency and the eventual imprisonment of its director.

Chapter 44

One month later in March, the Minneapolis *Star Tribune* announced the successful completion of the acquisition by the Davies Investment Group of Everest Minnesota, of the iron ore rich multi precious-metal mining operations of the Oliver Mines previously owned by United States Steel.

The Oliver Mines operation newly named the Everest Find comprises approximately eight thousand hectares in five different mining concessions located six miles southeast of Everest, Minnesota. The mineral deposit that would start to be mined in July, was the G-7 deposit which had achieved commercial production in May of 1932 and comprised high grade iron ore, with newly discovered high grade lodes of gold, silver, copper, palladium, coltan, zinc and hard rock lithium.

A draft study estimated that the operation could ultimately produce five point eight billion pounds of copper, one point two billion pounds of nickel, one point two billion pounds of zinc, one point six billion pounds of coltan, and four million ounces of palladium. It should also deliver three thousand, two hundred tons of iron ore concentrate, one million ounces of gold and twenty-five million ounces of silver, along with substantial yields of titanium, lead and hard rock lithium. The project has a "net present value" of $2.7 billion after taxes and the minerals are anticipated to be marketable to customers across the world.

The Everest Find is structured as an ESOP, an employee owned company, a cooperative community trust. The Davies family and their partners felt that the planet's riches, soil, water, air, minerals, the genome, were created by no man and therefore should be the property of none, but held in common stewardship for all beings, as opposed to being a piece of property.

The Davies partners understood that companies change from being property to being communities when employees own a majority of shares and thus control the business. This is when management becomes responsible, not to outside shareholders with little interest in the company beyond returns on capital, but to the body of employees. Control of the machinery of The Find would be local, held by the people who work at it, where all who were affected by the production, the consumer and other producers, have effective ways of expressing their desires. To establish cooperative control of production, combining the advantages of centralized efficiency with local controls in a complex, technologically advanced society, would be an art demanding thought and experimentation.

The company meetings would become occasions when management reports back to employees, and has to deal with questions and discussions among the people who have an intimate knowledge of what has gone right and what has gone wrong in the preceding period, and what the remedies might be. As a way of creating a more egalitarian society, employee ownership and control would have many advantages.

It would enable a process of social emancipation as employees of The Find become members of a team. It would also put the scale of earnings differential under democratic control: if the body of employees want big income differentials they could choose to keep them. Most importantly it involves a very substantial redistribution of wealth from external shareholders to employees and a simultaneous redistribution of the income from that wealth. Research on such firms has shown they generally have high productivity rates and often earn superior returns for workers.

The company would not publicly report its earnings, though its independently evaluated share price and other plan financial information would be reported to the U.S. Department of Labor. Each year The Find would add to its employees' ESOP accounts based on a share of their compensation. All employees also would get cash bonuses based on profitability. The stock of The Find would be held in trust until the employee retired or left the operation, when it would be bought back by the plan. It was hoped that long serving employees could retire with more than $1 million in stock proceeds, which could then be rolled into a retirement account. The Find's goal was to reach more than $2 billion in sales within the next two years.

The Find worked diligently with the pollution control agency and the mining agencies in Minnesota, to earn regulatory approval to conduct its operations, meeting the highest standards of the EPA's environmental impact study.

Spokesman and trustee for the Everest Find, William McMillan, stated that they believe there is significant exploration potential at The Find and they are thrilled to be a major employer in the area where the six hundred and seventy initially employed will have direct ownership in the operations. The majority of the activities when operations begin the second week of July, will be the shoring up of the old mine shafts and annexes, with a focus on an accelerated in-fill drilling program to extend known mineral deposits.

In the end, McMillan explained further, as a socially owned and directed enterprise, it will display that life not money, a life that creates circles of empowerment, will remain the ESOP's enduring measure of value. The power of The Find's employees, and the surrounding community's citizens, many of whose antecedents had made a living in one way or another on what was drawn out of the earth, would not be wasted, like the mined earth they labored to bring to the endless demands of mankind.

Chapter 45

The Davies family and friends and all those gathered on July 4 in Everest and Bearskin Lake had never been so happy, no man ever had, Ryan guessed. The Davies family happily stood in the large crowd in a communal drink. The skirmishing was finally over, it had been dangerous and luckily the death of any family member had been avoided and the cannons had been dragged back rumbling away from the front. Thank God for Sophie, Ryan had told Nan on his return from Europe. Sophie and her researchers at the *Progressive* Magazine had been invaluable in putting their intricate plan to retrieve the ownership conveyances together, with the duplicity and craftiness, false forwards and the false leads that were necessary.

The possession of real power and the ability by their actions and ideas to cause great changes like this, gave a man a fulfillment beyond the ecstasies of love or the laughter of children. At this moment, today, with the establishment and the final opening of The Everest Find, they possessed that power and possessed that happiness. They could no nothing more now than watch the operations unfold and let the local managers and miners hired do what generations of their ancestors had so successfully done before.

Ryan and Nan, Walt and Mary and Colleen and Dan, took leave of some of their many local guests along the terraced steps and walked down the lawn toward the lake shore and the series of party deck floats that spread across the water directly in front of the Davies' series of shoreline docks. Halfway down, in front of a wide blue sky, the glittering lights sparkled off the lake and draped the party decks and the guests enjoying the celebratory music.

Ryan took Nan softly in his arms, his Nan, his other half of the sky and kissed her gently. Her lower lip tasted like a ripe little fig. She was holding their precious new-born two-month old daughter, nestling snugly in her arms. She had brought life once more, like apples gathered in her skirt, as she liked to say; as simply and purely as that. Their new baby Christina Nichols Davies was born May 2 and she had immediately stripped the scales from their hearts. Looking into those baby blue eyes was like looking at the face of God.

She had no mask or pretense. Her defenselessness was overwhelming. This intricate little creature, frail as a fallen snowflake, this exquisite crafting of blood and bones and skin lying so calmly in Nan's arms, was truly a humbling moment for Ryan. She had the same nose and azure eyes of their boys.

Ryan extended a finger toward her that the baby ignored and instead gazed into his eyes, mesmerized by the movement of his lips and the deep resonance of his voice. She cooed a high-pitched half-hiccup. Christina then flung an arm above her pink blanket and wrapped her hand around his finger. A bubble of saliva glistened on the baby's lips and they watched the tiny rainbow the afternoon sunlight made there. "Oh little love bug," Nan crooned, as Christina nuzzled her face toward her breast.

They were so in love, a love that was unwilled, because true love cannot be willed. Their love had always been real and true, that plunging sense-darkened inebriation of love, that fierce, sight-clouding need for each other. Most people didn't live, Ryan mused, as he looked out upon the blue calm of the bay. They did time, liked drugged prisoners with the illusion but not the reality of freedom and love. Love withheld could age people too quickly, cripple people, just as praise withheld could turn ones entrails to stone. Love was like the southwest wind now softly drifting toward them, fretting the lake. It lifts out of the world's sweet edges and breathes against our eyelids, it falls like spring rain and rises like honeydew, drenching the farthest reaches of the heart.

Mary beamed a radiant smile at them, as if she could read Ryan's thoughts, while she and Walt walked arm in arm down to the lakeshore, happy, knowing now that the sacred trust confided to her by her father would not be betrayed. Your family is really never in your past, she mused, you carry it around with you everywhere. The eternal smile of her father and mother from beyond the grave would be a most welcome reward.

Walter planned on decanting a dozen bottles of Lafite-Rothschild '67 for the celebration of the opening of The Find. It would be a public benefaction beyond recall. They would at last come to feel free, to become smug in their memories, smug and at last snug and secure beyond the reach of others in their one ultimate impregnable un-purchasable redoubt. It had always been Walter and Mary's hope to personalize those feelings and give them an effigy poignant and grand like carved tombs in the old vast Cathedrals, perpetuities that the afflicted citizenry and the neocons that conned them would suddenly come upon and know, to be awed, for they had taken the best way, a new solution, a new way, that would let all the flowers fully bloom in glory.

There would at last be a return to a world that for too long had seemed imaginary, a world of middle class decency, of backyard clotheslines, first haircuts and firehouse parades; the full weight of human possibility. This was not just a noble gesture or a vacuous emblem of moral amplitude. It was real, decent, livable jobs again for a community that had suffered so much and deserved so much more.

To Mary and Walt, and the rest of the Davies family, and friends, it was joy, triumph and infinite relief and vindication, all within the bubbly atmosphere of wine, Champagne and laurel wreaths. They hoped they had made the best and happiest ending that they could, in this world, made it happen out of the flax and netting and the leftover trim of someone else's evil life. They all wished this to be the truth, they had done it to keep the innocent safe and the guilty punished, and make it, as the world should be, and not as they found it. There had been a vast conspiracy of hope out there within the family and among all their close friends, and in the end and at last, finally, even though the laborers were few, a great harvest was attained and hope had triumphed.

The July sun was beaming amber, a radiantly comfortable, seventy-five degree glow over the lakefront festivities as Sophie and Jim, Winnie and Will, Dave and Jenny Duncan, Lois and Bud Anderson, and a surprisingly trim and fit looking Billy Jenkins arrayed in a fresh new outfit, and his fiancée, and Matt, freed recently from the psychic atrocities of his self-possessed, now ex-wife, approached the Davies through the growing press of party attendees, the lake reflecting their grand celebratory images as they moved toward them, shimmering through the screens of their white wine contentment.

Mary stole away just a few feet from the crowd of their friends and turned toward them, with the shimmering azure blue, crystal clear waters providing her backdrop.

"We want to thank all so very much for your wonderful wise participation in bringing this family drama to a successful end. From all that has happened, the family had always realized that when we help others, even in small ways, such as by sharing smiles or unnoticed acts of kindness, we come closer to our own enlightenment and our own salvation. Winnie, thank you, sincerely, for bringing that rogue agency to justice in your duties as our good senator, from Minnesota. We love you and your family so much."

Now Mary paused for a moment as the music on the party docks drifted over their heads, and taking Nan's hand in hers stepped forward in the direction of Sophie and Jim standing above on the crest of the sloping lawn. "We were all so distraught back here at home not knowing how matters were playing out when the three of you were in Europe. It was an everyday torture, until we finally got that call from Walter and Sophie at the Basel Archdiocese. Sophie, my dear girl, we are all so thankful to you, it is beyond the reach of my words to describe the depth of our gratitude for what you have done to see this mission through to its successful fruition. I, we, would be honored, Sophie, if you consider yourself to be part of our family."

"The honor is mine," Sophie quickly responded, her eyes glistening with un-spilled tears, as were Mary's and Nan's and the others, as they all embraced her.

Mary stood tall trying to dry her tears and took a manila envelope from Walter. "As you know we have received many letters of congratulations from people in this state, and throughout the country, even the President sent a note of recognition. Thanks for that, Winnie." The new senator nodded, giving an arched eyebrow, along with a wink of recognition. "However, I think none is more special than the message included in the memo of congratulations from Cardinal Castilla at the Vatican, who as you know, Walt met with in Rome." Mary looked up, her eyes filled with a kind of misty wonder, as she searched the eyes of the others. Mary took the embossed papers from the envelope, took a deep breath and read the letter aloud.

"Dear Davies family and friends. When Cardinal Castilla told me the story of your family's plight and the brave spirit you displayed, it reminded me of the story of little Zacchaeus, in Jericho. He went up the sycamore tree to see the Savior come by because there was such a big crowd. He was a tax collector hated by his own people for working for the Romans and, besides, Roman money made you unclean. He was an Israelite, but he gave up absolutely everything in his pursuit of money. He gave up his community. He gave up his reputation. He gave up his honor. He gave up his integrity. He gave up his friendships, all in the pursuit of wealth. Then one day he meets Jesus, and how does Jesus treat him? He honors him. Grace beyond measure. He honors him, and so overwhelmed by God's grace was Zacchaeus, that he said, 'I will pay back everybody that I ever cheated four times what I took from them, and then I am going to give half my money to the poor.' What do you think he is going to have left after that? Not much, and yet his heart was so enraptured with Jesus that he was willing to go all the way and give back everything that was his idol. What enabled him to turn from his idol? Grace beyond measure. It was a love he experienced that was beyond understanding. He fell in love with the Savior. So, instead of money, Jesus became his overwhelming positive passion in life.

"Time and the long topography of history shift, but man, and the eternal verities, which are the nature of man, remain forever the same. Man is the most undying potential in the mix of chaotic flux. Even in the most despairing moments, I have remembered this. Even when I have seen the wallowing of men, and the ruin they have created about them, I believe. I must believe that in them are all potentialities of angels and that these potentialities, through the ages, must finally emerge. One must always have faith, not in humanity, but in what humanity may or can become.

"The Christian spirit is one of compassion, of responsibility and of commitment. It cannot be indifferent to suffering, to injustice, error and untruth.

"It is in our deep silence, that wisdom begins to sing her unending, sunlit, inexpressible song: the private song she speaks to the solitary soul. It is his song and hers. It is the unique irreplaceable song that each soul sings for himself, with the unknown Spirit, as he sits on the doorstep of his own being, the place where his existence opens out into the abyss of God's nameless, limitless freedom. It is the song each one of us must sing, the song of grace that God has composed Himself, the song He may sing within us. It is the song of His mercy for us, which if we do not listen to it, will never be sung. If we do not join with God, in singing this song, we will never be fully real, for it is the song of our own life welling up like a stream out of the very heart of God's creative and redemptive love.

"Jesus said, with His life, death, and resurrection, that the Way, when followed in a hostile world, meant love and faith to the point of revolution. Jesus' life said, redeem the times, not with your own strength, for you have none and will be destroyed if you rely on it, but redeem the times by joining with others in a community of faith and resistance to death because the Way of Resurrection demands it. The human family demands it. Truth and love demand it. And if you meet the demand, the Way of the beautiful Boundary Waters will sing its deepest silence, its sharpest beauty, into your being, in the Life giving form of the cross.

"I congratulate the entire Davies family and friends that have endured successfully to make The Everest Find become a reality through your bravery and determination, your capacity to care, to love, beyond the point of suffering, to perform such a good deed. You have met the demand! It is the song of your own life welling up like a stream out of the very heart of God. God's love doesn't seek value, it creates it. You have become the responsible stewards upon the earth, upon the citizens of Everest, upon the Iron Range of Northeast Minnesota. Justice can only flow from changed hearts. I urge you to take this harvest of men's hearts with rejoicing.

"You have become the unhidden instrument of His Divine action, the ministers of His redemption, the channel of His mercy, and the messengers of His infinite Love. Just as Zacchaeus experienced in Jericho, it is truly an act of GRACE BEYOND MEASURE."

Mary looked up from her reading, her eyes glistening with tears unshed and looked at her dear friends standing attentively before her. "The letter," she continued, "is signed by Pope John Paul II." She handed the two sheets of official Vatican stationary to Sophie and the others to read. "I suggest that we frame this letter and the memo from Cardinal Castilla and place it in a prominent place on the walls of our administrative offices in town, if you are all in agreement."

Affirmation was given by all.

The moon rose that evening with a singular agent beauty, frosting the pines with a quivering light, liquid and cool, its shadow magically reflected in the calm mirror of the lake, under the clear sky that was swept with stars.

Just life for now, Sophie thinks later that evening as she walked toward the four huge floating party docks, slung above with nets, black gauze like festoons, and lights fitted in glass net floats bathed the celebrants in soft ruby, amber and indigo hues. The entire scene seemed to be floating on the still inky water of the bay. The band on the long front deck of the Davies' home was a rambunctious bunch of local sixties rockers called the Electras. They played with modest skill and great enthusiasm, but everyone was having fun dancing to rock roll beats.

The family members gathered for the celebration and the upcoming display of ambition and hope they had designed for the opening of The FIND and the fourth of July fireworks. The Northern sky was swimming in moonlight, and was alight with fireworks displays, and a dazzling array of stars; so low to the horizon that it seemed you could reach up and stir them, as family and friends sipped their Lafite-Rothschild.

"Wow," Jim Theno exclaimed as they all watched from the party dock, while the current sun-burst certainty of fireworks blossomed into beams of wondrous color and collapsed in a drizzle of tiny sparkling lights. Then, it was dark except for the stars, silent except for the lapping of the reflected starlit waters on the shores of Bearskin Lake, as the great moon blazed in the cloudless bowl of a depthless sky. Jim stepped beside Sophie next to Ryan and Nan but seemed to have nothing to say. For a few seconds everything seemed to stop. Even the crowds gathered along the lake shore had fallen quiet. The noise that carried over the crystalline water was the busy clamor of Everest's revelers, awaiting the next display.

"Well," Jim said. "That's the end of it."

"Do you really think so? I have a feeling that my father and his agency, even now disposed of, may have just been the beginning, especially if the world keeps on developing the way it has. Imagine if what we have accomplished over the last year might only ensure the world will continue its selfish downward spiral."

"I meant the fireworks, Sophie," he said softly looking at her, his azure eyes sparkling like the stars, gleaming against the glittering sky. Without thinking Sophie reached out and took his hand and they walked in silence along the water, sipping wine as they moved gracefully hand in hand, while the warmth of their hands radiated directly up their arms to the love in their hearts.

Perhaps someday, Sophie thought, they all might be allowed to return here together, to see the mistakes of their successors and perhaps then, for the first time since man began his education among the carnivores, they would find a new wisdom that had fought and won against old prejudice, a new world that sensitive and timid natures could regard without a shudder.

The entire world seemed mute and even the sounds of the party had faded away. Then suddenly there was a final up-reaching rush of spark and flames far above the stately white pines and firs that surrounded the lake, as a last rocket chugged into the sky. It climbed in a stately manner for a few seconds before its tail of fire disappeared into the stars.

An instant of silence, an instant of darkness, and then all at once, a huge, sparkling glorious blossom appeared in the starlit sky. It was The Find's new community approved logo, the image of Diogenes, in constant search of the honest man, an incandescent, scintillant chrysanthemum of flame and color that seemed to fill the entire dome of the night with countless petals of white and scarlet, gold and violet and green.

It's true Ryan silently told himself, as he and Nan gazed up into the brilliance of the color that played in her eyes like jewels, backlit by the summer night stars. All life does run toward one moment, emerald clear, one moment your whole aching life builds to. That moment, now, is a pure raining glory, a true communion, forever and ever, world without end amen.

"It's a miracle," Nan heard herself exclaim.

"Some say there are no such things as miracles," Walter whispered, standing next to them with Mary. "There are only commitments or defections of men. But I disagree." His eyes bright blue and glistening at the glorious light show. "It is a miracle, it truly is!"

The crowd started to cheer, but the sheer beauty of the moment caused them quiet. The great flaming flower image of the Greek God hung in the starlight, having no boundaries but the broad compass of the heavens, for about seven seconds, held together as if by prayer and magic, by the will and hope of the good people of the Iron Range, reigning above Bearskin Lake, like the biblical Galilee, in a theatre meet for great events, a cathedral under the stars, to proclaim its high decrees, before it finally broke up into brilliant points of light floating earthward, going out one by one as the festive noise of the city and lakeside faded away, until all at once there was nothing left but night, silence… and above, across the roof of the world, the quiet orderliness of the stars displayed their brilliance, emitting a sense of freedom. It was like two skies on top of one another. You couldn't tell where heaven ended and the earth began.

And then, the full moon, like hope above them, edged its way high into the western sky, suddenly illuminating the sign of love, an amazing piercing point of light, forever steadfast upon The North Star.

The Christmas Star!

Just then the Everest High School Marching Band, as if on cue, belted out its rousing rendition of "Sweet Caroline".

There would still be more days to travel in this life, and the man that makes the journey would be shaped by every day and every person along the way. That glorious day would always be part of their journey. Soon enough the days would close over their lives, the grass would grow over their graves, until their story was just an unvisited headstone.

But this experience would remain alone: a fleeting glimpse of the utmost possibilities life may hold for man.

And now, the people were singing "Sweet Caroline". They were all pierced with an ecstasy, an ecstasy that was proud, exultant, joyous and glorious. There had never been so many people along the lake, on the light sparkled floating docks, on boats floating in the bay. Never, had there been so much joy to break the silence, with singing and laughter, which rose sweetly up over the pine-lined shores.

And the gleeful crowd sang, "So good, so good!"

Then suddenly all fell silent. The life circles of all the people gathered touched each there in the silence of the night. The stars were out, strewn thick and close in the deep blue of the sky, the milky-way glowing like a silver veil. Ursa Major wheeled gigantic in the north, the great nebula in Orion was a whirl of shimmering star dust. Venus flamed, a lambent disc of pale saffron, low over the horizon of the lake. From edge to edge of the world the constellations paraded like progress, a mysterious sheen of diaphanous light engaged itself, expanding over all the earth, serene, infinite and majestic.

Out of nowhere, a lone cellist appeared in front of the crowd along the lakeshore, and then a young girl came and stood in front of the cellist with a small flute and played the beginning notes to the "Anthem of Europe". Another cellist appeared and then another both with young girls standing in front of them playing the introductory notes to the glorious piece.

As the cellists joined the girls in playing in unison, the violins appeared, then the oboes, the bassoons, the flutes, the French horns, the clarinets, the trumpets, the tubas, and the timpani. The Iron Range symphony orchestra had arrived, to everyone's delightful surprise. Then the forty members of the Iron Range chorale joined the eighty piece orchestra to perform Beethoven's Ninth Symphony fourth movement of "Ode to Joy".

For nearly ten minutes the orchestra was conducted and played in a crescendo of beautiful symphony unsurpassed, and then the chorale burst into song, joined by the huge throng of revelers, to sing the final stanzas.

"You millions be embraced, the kiss for all the world! Brothers, above the starry canopy, there must dwell a loving Father. The Joy of Man's Desiring!"

The voices of the choristers were the voices of unborn men, raised in hope and triumph, in victory and freedom, in everlasting conquest, over the forces of darkness and evil, superstition, ignorance and fear and hatred. The Find!

The End